T0283764

Praise for DARK RISE

"A propulsive new fantasy. I simply couldn't put it down."

—V. E. SCHWAB,
New York Times bestselling author of *The Invisible Life of Addie LaRue*

"A story rendered with devastatingly brilliant detail. You won't be able to look away."

—CHLOE GONG,
New York Times bestselling author of *These Violent Delights*

"Intricate and immersive."

—RAINBOW ROWELL,
bestselling author of the Simon Snow Trilogy

"Beautiful, classical, and deliciously dark."

—JAY KRISTOFF,
New York Times bestselling author of *Empire of the Vampire*

"Abundant action and a profusion of plot twists fuel an adrenalized pace."

—*PUBLISHERS WEEKLY*

"Classic. Pacat's writing is atmospheric and full of intriguing, complex characters."

—*KIRKUS REVIEWS*

"A taut, captivating fantasy worth every ounce of the hype."

—POPSUGAR

"Pacat is a master at character design, and you'll instantly fall in love."

—TOR.COM

"Lush, dark, and dangerous. A YA fantasy that begins breathlessly and rarely lets up."

—BOOKS + PUBLISHING

"Will hook readers until the last page. Characters could entice you on one page, and then stick a knife through your heart on the next."

—THE NERD DAILY

ALSO BY C. S. PACAT

Dark Rise

Fence Volume #1

Fence Volume #2

Fence Volume #3

Fence Volume #4

Fence Volume #5

Fence Volume #6

Captive Prince

Prince's Gambit

Kings Rising

The Summer Palace and Other Stories

C. S. PACAT

DARK HEIR

Quill Tree Books
An Imprint of HarperCollinsPublishers

Quill Tree Books is an imprint of HarperCollins Publishers.

Dark Heir

www.epicreads.com

Library of Congress Control Number: 2023940810
ISBN 978-0-06-294617-1

Typography by Laura Mock
23 24 25 26 27 LBC 8 7 6 5 4
First Edition

For Johnny Boy

You nosed your way in
and changed my life
I'll miss you

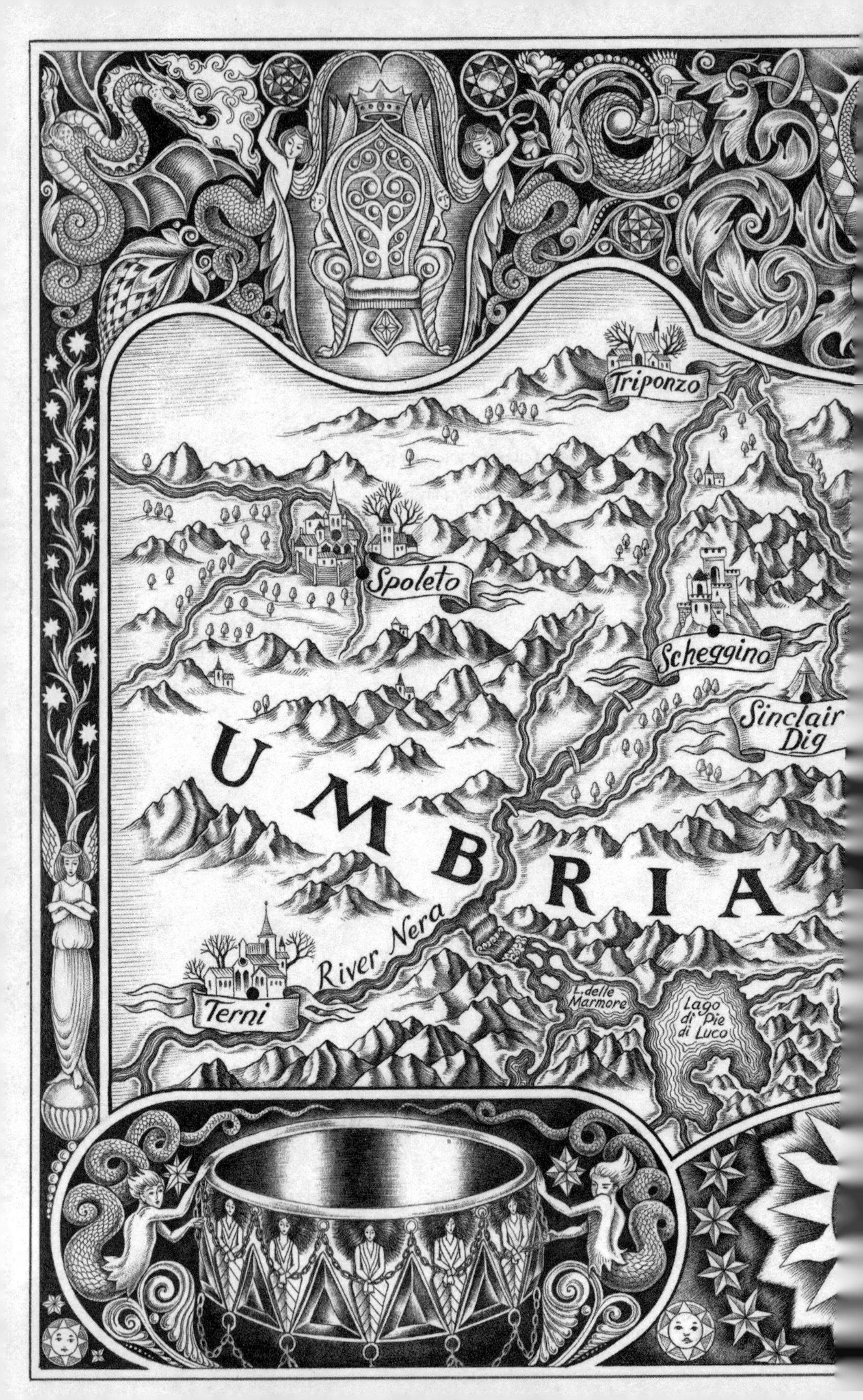
Triponzo
Spoleto
Scheggino
Sinclair Dig
UMBRIA
River Nera
Terni
L. delle Marmore
Lago di Pie di Luco

Mount Coscerno
The Leap of Faith
Sinclair's Dig
Undahar
A MAP OF THE
Valnerina, Umbria,
1821
ALSO CALLED THE BLACK VALLEY
Scheggino & The River Nera
Mount Coscerno & The Sinclair Dig
faithfully reproduced

DRAMATIS PERSONAE

—*In London*—

THE REBORN

WILL KEMPEN: The Dark King reborn.

JAMES ST. CLAIR: Raised believing he was a Steward, James's true identity was discovered at age eleven: he was the Dark King's deadliest general, Anharion, reborn. James escaped the Hall of the Stewards to serve Sinclair in his quest to return the Dark King to life. There James learned Anharion had been a warrior of the Light, enslaved to the Dark King by a magical collar. After Will killed Simon and returned the Collar to James, James swore to follow Will.

DESCENDANTS

The Blood of Lions

VIOLET BALLARD: The daughter of John Ballard and his Indian mistress, Violet was brought to London by her father. Escaping Sinclair with Will, Violet learned that she possessed the Blood of Lions, and that her father had raised her so her half brother, Tom, could ritually kill her to gain his "true power" by killing another Lion. Violet has sworn she will not serve the Dark King like her Lion ancestors.

TOM BALLARD: Violet's older half brother, and a mentor and protector to Violet during her childhood. Tom serves Sinclair and took the *S* brand to prove his loyalty. He has a close relationship with another of Sinclair's pseudo-court, Devon, the last unicorn.

JOHN BALLARD: Violet and Tom's father, John Ballard works for Sinclair.

The Blood of Stewards

CYPRIAN: Cyprian was a sheltered novitiate weeks from taking his test to become a Steward when his brother Marcus, in shadow form, attacked the Hall, massacring its inhabitants. Cyprian is now the last of the Stewards, but has never drunk from the Cup.

MARCUS: Cyprian's brother, Marcus was on a mission with his shieldmate, Justice, when he was captured by Sinclair. Kept alive in a cage until his shadow overwhelmed him, Marcus was unleashed by Sinclair on the Hall of the Stewards.

JUSTICE: The Stewards' greatest fighter and champion, Justice rescued Violet and Will from Simon's ship the *Sealgair* and brought them both to the Hall. When Justice's shieldmate, Marcus, became a shadow and attacked the Hall, Justice died fighting him.

EUPHEMIA, THE ELDER STEWARD: The Elder Steward tried to train Will to follow the Light, but died before the training was complete. She defeated Marcus during his attack on the Hall, then asked Cyprian to kill her before her shadow could take over.

JANNICK, THE HIGH JANISSARY: James's father and adoptive father of Cyprian and Marcus. As the head of the jannisaries—the non-military side of the Stewards—Jannick was a man of great knowledge but also exacting standards. Jannick was killed by Marcus in the massacre at the Hall.

GRACE: Grace was one of only two survivors of Marcus's attack. Grace's role as janissary to the Elder Steward gives her unique knowledge and insight into the secrets of the Hall.

SARAH: Sarah was the second survivor of Marcus's attack. A janissary whose role was to tend the plants in the Hall.

The Blood of the Lady

KATHERINE KENT: Pressured by her family to make an advantageous marriage, Katherine was engaged to Simon Creen, son of the Earl of Sinclair. Discovering Simon was killing women, Katherine fled to the Hall of the Stewards with her sister, Elizabeth. Katherine died at Bowhill after learning Will was the Dark King and drawing Ekthalion to challenge him.

ELIZABETH KENT: Brought by her sister, Katherine, to the Hall of the Stewards, ten-year-old Elizabeth learned that she possessed the Blood of the Lady when she touched the Tree Stone during the attack on the Hall by the Shadow King.

ELEANOR KEMPEN: The mother of Katherine and Elizabeth, who gave them up to hide them from Sinclair. She raised Will as her son knowing he was the Dark King, but tried to kill him before her death.

The Blood of the Dark King

EDMUND CREEN, THE EARL OF SINCLAIR: One of the richest men in England with a trading empire that spans the globe. Sinclair is the head of a pseudo-court of descendants with powers from the old world.

SIMON CREEN, LORD CRENSHAW: The son and heir of the Earl of Sinclair, Simon planned to raise the Dark King from the dead by killing all the descendants of the Lady, including Will's mother. Simon was killed by Will at Bowhill.

PHILLIP CREEN, LORD CRENSHAW: The second son of the Earl of Sinclair, Phillip inherited the title of Lord Crenshaw after his brother Simon's death.

—In the old world—

SARCEAN, THE DARK KING: The Dark King and leader of the shadow armies, Sarcean swore to return to the world after his death and ordered his followers killed in order to be reborn with him.

ANHARION, THE BETRAYER: Light's greatest fighter, Anharion swung the course of the war when he changed sides to fight for the Dark King. He was known as the Betrayer, but had been ensorcelled by a magic collar.

THE LADY: Legends say she loved the Dark King and then killed him. When the Dark King died and swore to return, she had a child so that her line would survive to fight him on his rebirth.

DEVON: The last unicorn. When humans hunted unicorns almost to extinction, Devon was captured and his tail and horn cut off. In order to survive, Devon transformed into a boy. Thousands of years later, he is a member of Sinclair's pseudo-court.

VISANDER: A champion of the old world.

PROLOGUE

VISANDER WOKE CHOKING. His chest was constricted. There was no air. He coughed and tried to heave in breath. Where was he?

His eyes opened. Blind, he saw nothing. There was no difference between his eyes being open or closed. Panic lifted his arms and he tried to push up, only to hit wood a handspan above his face. He couldn't sit up. He couldn't breathe, his nose clogged with the cold, heavy smell of earth.

Instinctively he groped for his sword, Ekthalion, but he couldn't find it. *Ekthalion. Where is Ekthalion?* His numb, cramping fingers found wood on all four sides. His shallow breathing shallowed further. He was lying trapped in a small wooden box. A casket.

A coffin.

Cold fear at that idea. "Release me!" The words were absorbed by the box as if swallowed. The sick, terrible thought came: This was not just a coffin. It was a grave. He was buried, his sounds smothered by earth above and around him.

"Release me!"

Panic crested. Was this it? His awakening? In a sightless, soundless cavity, while no one above knew he lived? He tried to remember the moments before this, disjointed fragments: riding his bonded steed Indeviel; the Queen's cool blue eyes on him as he spoke his vow; the sharp pain as she ran the sword through his chest. *You will return, Visander.*

Had she done this to him? It couldn't be, could it? He couldn't have returned into a grave, awakening buried deep beneath the earth?

Think. If he was buried, there would be wood above him, and then earth. He had to break the wood, and then dig. And he had to do it now, while he still had air and strength. He didn't know how much air he had left.

He kicked at the roof of his prison, a jarring pain in his foot. The second kick was part panic. A sharp cracking sound meant he had splintered the wood. He could hear his own gasps of breath, dragging in what was left of the thin air.

Crack! Again. *Crack!* Earth spilled in like water breaking through a leak. For a moment he felt a burst of success. Then the leak became a collapse, a cave-in, cold earth rushing in to fill up the coffin. A desperate panic exploded in him, his hands flying up to cover his head at the thought he would be smothered. He coughed, the dust particles so thick that they choked him. When the dust settled, the cave-in had reduced his space in the coffin by half.

He lay in the small, lightless pocket that was left to him. His heart was pounding painfully. He remembered the moment when he had gone to his knees and sworn. *I will be your Returner.* The Queen had touched his head as he knelt. *You will Return, Visander. But first you must die.* Had it gone wrong? Had he been buried by mistake, those around him believing him truly dead? Or had he been discovered by the Dark King? Buried as punishment, knowing he would return, only to awaken trapped?

He imagined the Dark King's pleasure at his suffocating panic. It would delight that twisted mind to think of Visander buried alive, his terror unseen, his shouts unheard. The spark of hatred in Visander ignited, the burn bright in the dark. It drove him, stronger than the need to live, his need to kill the Dark King. He had to get out.

He reached down to the front of his garments and tore at what felt like silk. He tied the silk around his face, to protect his mouth and nostrils from the earth that would rush in to cover him. Then he drew in a breath, all the air he could gather, and this time punched with every bit of his remaining strength at the splintered wood above him.

Earth collapsed down onto him, filling the last of the space. He forced himself to push upward into it, trying to claw up through the dirt. It didn't work. He didn't break the surface, and now there was earth all around him, and no air, just the stifling press of the soil, a putrid petrichor that threatened to force its way down his throat.

Up. He had to go up, but felt total disorientation: surrounded by pitch-black earth, he lost all sense of down or up, digging, but in which direction? Horror overwhelmed him. Would he die, a blind worm traveling the wrong way in the dark? Pain stabbed his lungs, his head dizzy, as though he'd inhaled fumes.

Dig. Dig or die, think of his purpose, the only thing that drove him, past the panic, past the dimming of his thoughts like the closing of a tunnel—

And then his grasping, reaching hand broke out into space. His lungs screamed as he pushed desperately toward it, breaching the muddy ground in a grotesque rebirth, pushing out his face, his torso, dragging himself from the earth.

He heaved in air—air!—great, gasping heaves that coughed and retched out a black substance, the dirt that had found its way into his mouth and down his throat. It took a long time for the retching to stop, convulsing tremors in his body. Vaguely, he was aware that it was night, that there was turf under his fingers, the empty branches of trees over his head. He lay sprawled on the ground that had just entrapped him, reassured that it was beneath him, a joy he had never appreciated before. He lifted his forearm to wipe at his mouth, saw the tattered silks that clothed him, and felt a strange wave of wrongness.

When he looked down at his hands, they were not only torn and bloodied but—they were not—his hands—

Everything spun around him dizzily. He was dressed in strange garments, thick skirts that dragged down from his body heavily. He could see himself in the moonlight—these torn, muddy hands were not his own, these breasts, these tendrils of long blond hair. This was not his body; this was a young woman whose limbs he could not easily control, an attempt to stand sending him stumbling to the ground.

Light flared, and at first he flung his arm up to shield himself from it, his eyes unused to anything brighter than the dim moonlight.

Then he looked up into the light.

There was a gray-haired older man standing in front of him holding a lamp aloft. He was staring as though he had seen a phantom. As though he had seen someone die and then met them again after they had clawed their way back up from out of the earth.

"*Katherine?*" said the man.

CHAPTER ONE

WILL CRESTED THE bank of the River Lea and felt his stomach drop with dread.

All he could see on the marsh was desolation. The scented wet green of the moss, the undulating grasses were gone, replaced by a crater of ruined earth with the broken arch at its center, like a gateway to the dead.

Was he too late? Were his friends all dead?

James reined in beside him on the snowy-white Steward horse Katherine had abandoned. Will couldn't help glancing sideways to see James's reaction. With his blond head hidden by the hood of a white cloak, James might have looked like a Steward of old, riding through ancient lands. Except that he was young, and dressed in the height of London fashion under the cloak. His face gave nothing away, even as his eyes fixed on the destruction that had been the Hall.

Will couldn't let himself think about what he was doing here with James beside him. He shouldn't have come back. He shouldn't have brought James with him. He knew that. He had done it anyway. The wrongness of that decision rose with every step. He forced his eyes forward, and kept his mind on his friends.

At the edge of the ruined earth, the horses balked, Will's black gelding Valdithar jerking his head up and down, nostrils flared wide, sensing twisted magic. Beside him James was trying to force his white Steward mount onward, while his London horse reared and plunged on its lead behind him, trying to break. The spooked, resisting horses were the only living things to walk the charred ground lit by sullen embers, a deep silence enshrouding them because there were no birds or insects alive.

But the worst sight of all was the gate.

The Hall of the Stewards was meant to be hidden by magic from the world. A passerby would see only a lonely old stone arch crumbling on the wet earth. They could walk past it, even walk through it, and never leave the marsh. Only those of Steward blood would pass through the arch and find themselves in the ancient lofty corridors of the Hall.

But now the stone arch was a gash in the world. On either side of it was the empty marsh, but through it . . . Through it, Will could see the Hall, plain as daylight.

It looked wrong; a laceration; a rent.

Like sticking fingers thoughtlessly into a wound: he imagined a wanderer on the marsh sticking his head in, bringing men from London to poke around inside.

"The wards are down," James said.

Under the hood of his white cloak, James's face still showed nothing, but the tension in his body was transmitting itself to his horse.

Will tightened his hands on the reins. The wards weren't just down; they had been ripped apart by the same pulverizing force that had torn open the marsh.

There was only one thing that could have done this.

Had the Shadow King released at Bowhill torn down the wards? Had it taken the Hall? Had it killed everyone he knew?

The darker thought, the deeper fear worming and twisting:

Was it sitting now in dark malevolence on its throne, waiting to welcome him?

"Shall we?" said James.

It was skin-crawlingly wrong to be able to just ride inside. The Hall should not be so open, exposed to the outside world. Will wanted a Steward to come striding out of the gloom, saying, "Stop! Back!"

But none came.

"The only place the Dark King couldn't conquer," said James, "and now he could walk right in."

Will was unable to stop another sideways look at James. But James had his blue eyes on the courtyard, utterly unknowing. Will's own thoughts, a tangle of fears and suspicions that he kept hidden, were more aware. Riding in without resistance, was he fulfilling his own dream? His dark desire to take the Light's last refuge?

It was an eerie form of conquest—not with the armies of the Dark at his back, the citadel smoking rubble, its citizens ground into submission. Instead he and James rode in alone through open gates, the battles of the past empty silence as their horses' hooves rang jarringly loud.

He saw the remains of the vast, abandoned courtyard, the immense walled citadel the Stewards had called their Hall no longer patrolled by guards in shining white on the ramparts, or softly sounding with sweet chants and bells, but hollowed out, dark and empty.

The Hall is yours now—ruined and destroyed. He flung the thought almost angrily at the Dark King—his past self. *Is that what you wanted?*

Beside him, James's face was expressionless. James had grown up here, then spent years trying to tear its ramparts down. Was he moved? Indifferent? Pleased? Afraid?

You can't really mean to take me back there. James had said it while sprawled on the inn's narrow bed. He looked like an expensive possession, and he talked like one too. But he'd played at being a possession for Simon, while working against him the whole time. And for all the insouciant lounging, the invitation only extended so far: look but don't touch. When Will had said, *You said you'd follow me, didn't you?* James had smiled with invidious amusement. *Your little friends aren't going to like it.*

His friends might all be dead. He and James might be the only ones left, and that was the darkest thought of all. His friends who knew him as Will, who kept him as Will, because they didn't know what he had learned at Bowhill as the ground rotted around him: that he was the Dark King.

A sudden bell clanging, shattering the silence. James jerked toward the wall.

"Someone's still here," said Will, swinging off his horse as the sound of the bell faded. But it felt like a ghost warning to a dead city, so silent and unlived-in was the Hall. Silence sank into his bones, a cold, skeletal dread.

"Will!" He turned as the huge double doors split open, and saw her running down the stairs.

Relief. She looked just as he remembered, with her short curling hair and her scattering of freckles, dressed in her London boy's clothes.

"Violet!" he said as she cleared the last of the main steps, taking them two at a time.

They embraced, his grip on her hard. *Alive, you're alive.* It was not like Bowhill; his failure on the Dark Peak hadn't killed her as it had killed Katherine.

It was more than that. In her warm arms he felt tethered to this world, to *Will*, after days riding through the ghosts of the past with James. It was an illusion that he wanted so badly to believe that he held on longer than he should.

He made himself let go, because she wouldn't be hugging him if she knew who he was. Behind her, he saw Cyprian looking relieved and pleased as he came down the steps. Dressed in his novitiate's tunic, Cyprian was an exemplar of his Order, his long brown hair loose down his back in the traditional Steward style, his face handsome in the untouchable manner of a statue.

He looked so much like a warrior of the Light that for a moment Will thought—surely Cyprian would see through him, would just look at him and know, declare to the others, *Will is the Dark King.* But Cyprian's green eyes were warm.

"Will!" Violet punched his shoulder in her characteristic way, snapping Will to attention. She was strong enough that it hurt a great deal, and his gladness of it felt like a painful homesickness. "Why did you run off? Idiot."

"I'll explain everything—" Will began.

"And you," said Violet to James, with friendly, exasperated familiarity. "Your sister's been so worried, she'll be so glad to have you back, we all are—"

"I think," said James, pushing back the hood of his cloak, "you've mistaken me for someone else."

And the white horse, and graceful body, and blond hair resolved into the deadly, exquisite boy they had last fought to a standstill, his lip slightly curling in a patrician face as he swung down from the saddle to confront them.

Cyprian's sword came singing from its sheath. His eyes were deadly. "You."

Will had been prepared for James to face a hostile reception. Of course, he had known the others wouldn't like it. James had caused the death of every Steward in the Hall. Will had planned for resistance, prepared to tell half-truths about himself, and speak calmly for James, who was here to help them stop Sinclair.

But in the hectic muddle of the last few days, Will hadn't thought about what seeing James would do to Cyprian.

Now Cyprian faced his brother's killer, his features bloodless, his hands steady only because Stewards trained for hours every day not to ever let their sword hand tremble.

"Cyprian—" Will said.

Cyprian's eyes stayed flat on James. "How dare you come back here."

"No warm welcome?" said James.

"You want a welcome?"

Cyprian's sword was already moving, a killing arc meant to slice James in half. "*No*," said Will as James's power flared, slamming Cyprian backward.

Cyprian hit the wall, his face contorted, his sword clattering to the ground. The air was sharp with static, Cyprian struggling hard against the invisible force of James's power, holding him in place.

"Now, now," said James, his eyes glittering, "That's hardly hospitable, little brother."

"Take your filthy magic off me, freak," said Cyprian.

"Stop it." Stepping between them was like stepping into a whirlwind, power lashing in the air around him. "*I said stop.*" Will forced himself forward, getting one hand on James's chest, the other clasping the back of James's neck. He was taller than James; barely, perhaps an inch. Just enough to make James look up at him.

"Stop your magic," said Will.

"Call off your pet Steward," said James, keeping his eyes fixed on Will's.

He didn't hesitate, his grip hard on James, his gaze locked on James's magic-blown pupils. "Violet, keep him back."

Behind him, Will heard Cyprian swear, and knew Violet was doing just that. A second later, the static in the air vanished. Will didn't let go of his hold on James, even as he heard Violet's voice behind him.

She sounded grim. "Will, what is he doing here?"

He forced back his memory of James at the inn, swearing to follow him. "He's here to help us."

"That *thing* is not going to help us," said Cyprian.

"Help us do what?" said Violet.

Will finally loosed his hold of James, and turned to see that Violet was still holding Cyprian against the stone wall by the base of the steps.

"Stay alive," said James. "When Sinclair gets here."

"Sinclair?" Violet's words were suspicious, confused. "Not Simon?"

There was so much he needed to tell her. He could still smell the acrid burned stench of the earth, could see the black blade sliding from its sheath any time he closed his eyes.

"Simon's dead." Will didn't say more than that. "His father is the one we're fighting." Sinclair, who had planned it all. Sinclair, who had taken James in as a boy and raised him to kill Stewards. Sinclair, who had given the order to kill Will's mother.

"Dead?" Violet said. As if the Stewards hadn't trained Will to do just that. As if his meeting with Simon could have ended any other way. As if he'd be here alive if it had. "Then—"

"I killed him."

The words were flat. They didn't describe what had happened on that mountainside. The birds falling out of the sky, the blood bubbling up from Simon's chest. The moment when Will had looked up and met Simon's eyes and known—

"I killed the three Remnants, then I killed him."

He knew he sounded different. He couldn't be the same—not after driving the sword through Simon's chest, on the blasted earth where his mother had bled out years earlier. The Shadow Kings had hung in the sky like witnesses.

"But . . . how?" said Violet.

What could he tell her? That Simon had drawn Ekthalion, and Will had survived the blast because he was its master?

Or that Simon had looked surprised at the end, his eyes wide as he died, not understanding even as his life bled out who it was that had killed him?

You're him. Katherine's last words. *You're the Dark King*.

"He's Blood of the Lady." James's drawl cut through the silence. "That's what you've trained him to do, isn't it? Kill people."

James didn't know either. James believed he was a hero, when the real Blood of the Lady was Katherine, lying dead with her face marbled like white stone.

"I'll tell you everything," said Will. "Once we're inside."

Except that he wouldn't. He had learned from Katherine that he couldn't. She had died at Bowhill because she had found out what he was, and drawn a sword to kill him.

Beneath that, a more primal memory: his mother's hands around his throat; his scrabbling need for air; his vision dimming.

Mother, it's me! Mother, please! Mother—

"He's not stepping foot into the Hall." Cyprian's eyes were on James.

"We need him." Will kept his voice steady.

"He *killed us*." Cyprian's eyes were on James. "He killed all of us, he's the reason that the Hall is wide open—"

"We need him to stop Sinclair."

It was what he'd always planned to say. Because he knew it would work on Cyprian, who always did his duty.

But it was different with Cyprian's eyes in a tumult and Violet staring at him, trying to understand.

"He's Sinclair's assassin," said Cyprian. "A traitor, without emotions or remorse, he killed my father, his own father, ripped him to shreds and used my brother to do it—"

"Look around you," said Will. "You think Sinclair isn't coming for the Hall now that it's wide open? The Final Flame? The Undying Star? Anyone can walk in here." He was hurting them by bringing James here. He knew that. His own presence was worse. It spat in the face of the Hall. "You want to stop Sinclair? James is how you can."

Cyprian's green eyes flashed with furious impotence. Faultless in novitiate silver, he looked like the embodiment of a Steward.

But the time of the Stewards was done. Without James, they could not stand against Sinclair. That was what Will had to keep in the forefront of his mind.

"You really believe in him?" Violet said to him.

"I do."

After a long moment, Violet drew a breath and turned to Cyprian. "James was Sinclair's closest ally. If he's turned on his master, we should use him. Will's right. Sinclair's coming for the Hall; it's just a matter of time before he gets here. We need every advantage we can get."

"So that's it?" said Cyprian. "You just trust him?"

"No," said Violet. "I don't trust him at all. And if he tries to hurt any of us, I'll kill him."

"Lovely," said James.

"She is just giving you fair warning," said a voice from the top of the stairs. "Which is more than you ever gave to us."

Grace stood in the doorway in her blue janissary robes. She was one of two janissaries who had survived the first attack on the Hall. The other janissary, Sarah, must have been the one who had rung the bell, thought Will. Unlike the others, Grace didn't welcome Will back, or even greet him by name.

"If you're finished squabbling," Grace said, "there's something you need to see."

"Scared to face what you've done?" said Cyprian.

They stood at the gaping mouth of the main entry, where the first of the crumbling high towers beetled. Once an endless warren of giant arches, vaulted chambers, and edifices of stone, the citadel was now a dark, macabre maze. Will and the others had avoided going into any of its buildings since the massacre, staying in the gatekeep by the outer wall to avoid the gut-churning interior passageways. Having seen it after the slaughter, no one wanted to re-walk those paths.

James's gaze surveyed the entrance. He looked more like part of this ancient place than anyone, his beauty like one of its lost wonders. But his lips curled unpleasantly.

"I told them when they ran me out of the Hall that I'd come back to walk on their graves."

"Then you will get your wish," said Grace, and disappeared into the gloom beyond the doors.

No more than a step inside and Will gagged, raising his arm to cover his mouth and nose. They had cleared the bodies, but it still smelled of decaying blood and rot; the gore that they hadn't had the time or stomach to remove.

Grace waited for him, a grim pragmatism in her eyes. It was worse for her, he thought. This had been her home; her whole life. All it had been to him was—

A person he could never be; a home he could never have.

Even James stopped when they reached the great hall. The bodies were gone, but the devastation remained: the torn banners, the shattered furniture, the hastily assembled barricade that had not protected the Stewards. Cyprian's expression twisted, looking at him.

"Admiring your handiwork?" Cyprian said.

"You mean Marcus's handiwork."

James lifted his eyes to Cyprian calmly, and Will had to step between them again, feeling as he held them apart that he was shielding James, even as James was a kind of shield to him. As the Dark King's lieutenant, James was the one bearing their hatred of the Dark King.

"This way." Grace had taken a torch from one of the wall sconces. She held it aloft as she spoke, making her way deeper through the forest of white pillars into the great hall.

At the far end the thrones of the four kings loomed. Each carved with the symbol of its kingdom, the empty thrones stared down in lost majesty, made for figures greater than any human king or queen. The sun, the rose, the serpent, and the tower.

They walked toward them, an uneasy procession.

"The Dark King wanted those four thrones more than anything," said James.

"No," said Will, and when the others turned to him in surprise, he heard himself say, "In his world there wouldn't be four thrones. There would only be one."

A pale throne that rose to blot out the world. He saw it in his mind's eye, part of the vision the Shadow Kings had shown him, and the swirling of his own half-remembered dreams.

They stopped at the edge of a great chasm, a depthless hole in the floor. Only when Grace held the torch over it did Will see that it was not an abyss; it was the remnant of a Shadow King, its horrifying form burned into the marble, like a pit into which they might all fall. The Shadow King's hand stretched out as if it was reaching for its throne.

Will looked at Violet. She had a grip on the shield in her hand so tight her knuckles were white. Then she looked up at him, her eyes full of shadows.

For a moment they shared a wordless understanding. As he had fought the Shadow Kings on the Peak, she had fought a Shadow King in the heart of the Hall. He felt the same connection to her he'd felt when she saved his life, dragging him from a drowning ship.

He wanted to tell her again how glad he was to see her, that she was his star in the night.

That he'd never really had friends growing up, and he was so glad she was his first. That he hadn't meant to turn that friendship into a betrayal. That he was sorry the boy she'd been friends with wasn't real.

"When it came, the sky turned black," said Grace. "It was so dark you couldn't see your hand in front of your face. We lit lamps so we could saddle the horses, but even the lamps could barely pierce the dark. We could hear it, shrieks and cries, coming from the great hall. Violet came here to fight it and buy us time."

Of course Violet had done that. Violet would have fought, even knowing the fight was hopeless. Will remembered the terrifying power of the Shadow Kings, and tried to imagine facing one with only a sword.

"We were mounting when a scream came so loud it shattered all the Hall's windows. The dark was dispelled, like a sudden dawn. We stopped our flight and came here, to the great hall. We saw what you see, the Shadow King fallen, his body burned into the floor."

"You stopped a *Shadow King*?" For all his power, this had truly shocked James. "How?"

"The same way I'll stop you if you step out of line."

Violet stared back at him, unblinking. James opened his mouth, but Grace spoke first.

"This is not our destination, only a waypoint," said Grace. "Come."

Will quickly realized where Grace was taking them.

It felt like a sick parody of his first morning here, when Grace had brought him along these very paths to see the Elder Steward. The architecture in the Hall got older, the stone thicker. He didn't want to return there now, to the dead heart of a dead hall. The black, dead branches of the Tree Stone had always disturbed him, a reminder of his failure, spreading out like—

—like the black veins spreading across Katherine's body, her chalk-white face, the staring stone-black of her eyes—

And then they turned the corner, and he saw the Tree of Light.

Rebirthed, remade; as if the air itself glowed with life. Branches bright, with drifting filaments like starlight, and a wondrous profusion of light.

The Tree was the Lady's symbol; life in the dark; a declaration of her power.

He couldn't help it; he was drawn forward. It was like seeing the first green shoots in a desolate wasteland, and more than that, a promise of hope and renewal.

"You lit the Tree," said James in an awed voice.

"No," said Will. "It wasn't me."

He thought of all the times he'd tried to light it. *The light wasn't in the stone, it was in her,* the Elder Steward had said.

It had never been in him.

It was so beautiful. He reached out, unable to stop himself, and put his hand on the trunk. As darkness blots out the sun, he half expected it to dim—or to hurt him, to burn his flesh from his bones. Instead he felt its warmth pulse through him. It felt like a dream, like some long-forgotten comfort. He closed his eyes as he let it flow into him. The soft joy of peace, affection, and acceptance, and he yearned for it, as a lost boy yearns for home.

A girl's voice said, "What did you do to my sister?"

CHAPTER TWO

WILL JERKED AWAY from the Tree, guiltily.

Elizabeth's legs were planted and her hands were fists. She was staring at him furiously.

She had never resembled her sister. Katherine had been beautiful, with the gold ringlets and wide blue eyes of a porcelain doll. Elizabeth had flat dun hair. Her eyebrows were dark, pulled down into a terrible frown. Underneath her furious gaze was a tense dread, as if she was halfway to guessing what had happened.

He needed to tell her that her sister was dead. He couldn't stop remembering Katherine's chalk-white face spidered with black veins, the feel of her cold stone body under his hands, and the overwhelming peaty smell of the gouged earth, like the land's blood. *Will, I'm frightened.*

He tried to think of what he would want to hear, if their positions were reversed. He didn't know. He didn't have much experience of comfort. He knew Elizabeth valued the truth. So he gave it to her.

"She's dead," said Will. "She died fighting the Dark King."

The Tree still glowed with light as he spoke. It felt as though surely it should flicker. Katherine would have delighted in this place. She had loved beautiful things. But she had never had the chance to see it. The Hall he had brought her to had been dark and dead.

"You're lying."

But he wasn't. He had told the truth, if not his part in it. He was conscious of the others in the room watching, hearing the story for the first time. *Careful, careful.*

"She guessed where I was going," said Will, "and she followed me out of the Hall. She found me at Bowhill."

She'd found him in the cratered earth, with Simon's blood on his hands. He hadn't been thinking clearly. Maybe if he had—

"She was brave. She was trying to do what was right. She drew the Blade to fight the Dark King. It was the Blade that killed her." He said, "Nothing can survive once the Blade is drawn."

There was so much he couldn't tell her. He couldn't tell her that her sister had drawn the Blade on him. *You are him. The Dark King.* He couldn't tell her that her sister had died in pain and afraid.

I tried to stop her and I couldn't. She didn't believe me when I begged her not to pick up the sword.

"I laid her body in my mother's farmhouse and sent for your uncle. He came with your aunt to bury her."

He had waited with James at the inn in Castleton until Katherine's family had come, her uncle and two men Will didn't recognize stepping out of a hired carriage. He'd watched them from a distance, making certain they couldn't see him. They had gone into his mother's cottage and borne Katherine out under the gray sky, a funereal procession.

It had felt like the end of another life. From his first sight of her, standing on Bond Street looking for a carriage, she had been part of the dream of what might have been—of warmth and hope and family. And on that ruined peak he had thought, that is a dream I will never have again.

"Why did you live?" said Elizabeth. Her eyes were red, and her fists were tight.

The hair rose on his arms. "What?"

"Why did you live? If nothing can survive when the Blade is drawn."

Her relentless child logic cut right into him. Her face was set in stubborn lines. He remembered that she'd seen through him that night too. *I knew you'd sneak out. You're a sneak.* He spoke carefully.

"I can touch it," said Will. "I'd touched it once before. On a ship." He couldn't say why. The others were in the room listening.

She said, "You're lying. You did something."

"Elizabeth," said Violet gently, stepping forward. "Will told you what happened. He would have stopped it if he could. Any of us would have."

"You went after her in London." Elizabeth's fisted hands clenched tighter. "You tracked her down."

"It's not his fault," said Violet.

"It is his fault," Elizabeth said to him, her whole body trembling. "It is his fault, if it weren't for him, she wouldn't have come here. He didn't care about her, he was sneaking about, trying to get at Simon! He made her come here. He made her follow him!" Her face twisted, and she flung the words at him. "She wouldn't be dead if she'd never met you!"

Hands in her skirts, she ran out of the room.

"Elizabeth—" said Will, and he made to go after her, but Grace held him back, even as Sarah quickly followed Elizabeth out.

"Let her go," Grace said. "There is nothing you can say to her. She has lost her sister."

Katherine had been his sister too, or as close to a sister as he had. But those were words he couldn't say. He closed his eyes briefly.

"I just—" He'd been so alone in those days after his mother's death, with no idea what to do. He remembered that first night, curled in the hollow of a tree stump, clutching his bleeding hand. "She shouldn't be on her own."

"Sarah will be with her," said Grace. Unspoken were the words *she shouldn't be with the one she thinks killed her sister.*

He knew that. He knew he shouldn't be the one to go after her. He could feel the wrongness of it. But the Kent sisters were his mother's daughters . . . her real daughters. He felt the painful wedge where family should be as he looked up at the Tree's light.

"Elizabeth lit the Tree, didn't she?"

Violet nodded. "It happened when we fled here, almost by accident. She tripped and put her hand on it, and it started to shine."

"The *girl* did this?" said James.

A look passed between Cyprian and Violet: discomfort that James was here, learning their secrets. Will ignored it. He told James the truth, deliberately.

"She's Blood of the Lady," said Will. "Like Katherine."

Grace said, "Like you."

She still didn't understand. None of them did. Maybe it was too terrible for them to imagine that Will might be the cuckoo in the nest.

He could feel his mother's hands around his throat. *Don't you hurt my girls.*

"If Elizabeth is Blood of the Lady, she might be your family, a cousin, a sister," said Grace. "Did your mother ever talk about another child?"

It was cutting too close to the truth. "She never told me anything."

Not until the end. Will forced himself to turn away from the Tree, curling his fist around the scar on his palm and turning his back on its light. "We've seen what you wanted me to see."

He took a step toward the door, only to find himself stopped, a hand on his shoulder.

"No," said Grace, holding him back again. "The Tree of Light is not why I brought you here. There is something else."

Something else?

Grace nodded. Beside her, Violet and Cyprian looked as surprised as Will felt. But Grace didn't enlighten them; she simply waited, looking at him expectantly. Finally, after a long silence:

"Will," she said. "What I have to show you is one of the most private matters of the Hall."

Grace didn't elaborate. She didn't look at James, but he was undeniably the reason she was holding back. The Dark King's paramour, lounging by the door.

"You mean, 'Get out'?" inquired James politely, his lips drawing back.

"No. We're in this together," Will said, as James's eyes flashed in surprise. "All of us."

Cyprian and Violet exchanged looks. Will stared down his friends.

"Very well," was all Grace said.

Moving to the far wall, she lifted her hands and placed them on the stone. They fitted into smooth imprints, as though many hands before her had touched precisely these points, wearing the stone away.

"This is what I brought you to see," said Grace. "Not the Tree. But what lies beneath."

"Beneath?" said Will.

Grace pressed against the wall, and with the grinding sound of old machinery, the stones beneath her feet split open, until she stood at the top of narrow stone steps that led down endlessly.

"I've never heard of a room under this one." Cyprian had taken a step back.

"It is known only to the Elder Steward and her janissaries," Grace said, and gestured for Will to descend. "One of the Light's last secrets. A reminder that what we see is only a small part of what is there."

Will went down the steps first, his heart beating strangely. Halfway down, he stopped in awe at what he saw.

A translucent light infused the walls, the vaulted ceiling, even the air, as the softly glowing roots of the Tree twined down, a thousand glimmering strands encasing the room in light. A gentle, warm peace suffused the air, as if the wondrous light could nurture and restore, healing all it touched.

"I thought I knew everything about the Hall," said Cyprian in shocked reverence behind him.

"Did you?" said Grace. "But the Light still has its marvels, even after all this time."

There was a simple plinth in the center of the room, carved with words in the ancient language. Above it, Tree roots hung suspended, like glowing stalactites. Will came forward, running his fingertips over the words.

"The past cries out," he read softly, *"but the present cannot hear,"* and felt a chill pass over him.

There was a small stone casket on the plinth. All his attention fixed on it. The stone casket was so unassuming, and the Tree above so monumental.

He said, "What's inside?"

"The Elder Stone," said Grace.

He was barely aware of the others descending the steps behind him. He could feel the sanctity of this place, a place of great power, and yet he couldn't drag his eyes from the casket.

He took a step toward it. "What does it do?"

"I don't know. I've never seen it." Grace said it simply.

Shocked, his eyes flew to her face. "You've never seen it?"

"It is the Hall's greatest relic, passed down from one Elder Steward to the next," said Grace. "None but an Elder Steward has ever opened the casket."

The air around had its own taste, its own flavor, noticeable even with the humming surround of light from the Tree's roots. Violet and Cyprian didn't seem to notice. Even Grace looked unaware. *Can't you feel it?* he almost said. Only James was reacting to the stone casket the way he was, his eyes fixed on it, his breathing shallow.

"It's magic," James said, and Will wondered if this was how magic always felt, a shivery sensation under his skin, jittery and exhilarating.

Grace gestured to the casket. "She asked that it be given to you."

"To *me*?" said Will.

"When the Tree of Light began to shine."

Of course. The Elder Steward had believed he was Blood of the Lady. She had left the Elder Stone for the one who had lit the Tree, and he would take it under false pretenses, as he had taken everything else.

He could see the others waiting for him. Violet stood closest to the stairs with Cyprian beside her, and James a step farther inside. They were all looking at him with different levels of trust and expectation.

He reached out, and pushed open the lid of the casket.

The Elder Stone sat inside, a piece of dull white quartz about the size of a ha'penny coin. There was nothing special about it. But then the stone began to shine.

Particles of light seemed to float upward from the stone's surface, and Will felt aching wonder as they coalesced, forming a shape he knew. White robes and long white hair, translucent but visible, streaming with light.

Beside him, Grace gasped, and Cyprian let out a sound, both of them faced with the head of their Order, who they had believed dead, her body burned on the pyre, sparks rising into the night.

The Elder Steward.

She smiled the kindly smile that he knew so well, and the feeling in him swelled until it was painful.

"Will," she said. "If Grace has brought you to the Elder Stone, it means the Tree of Light has begun to shine."

She didn't know. He fought the desire to tell her, to beg her forgiveness, to kneel in front of her and bow his head, so that she could rest her hand on his hair and tell him . . .

What? That she accepted what he was? That she forgave him? Stupid, stupid. He knew how dangerous it was to want acceptance from a mother.

The girl lit the Tree. He knew he should say it. His heart was pounding.

"Elder Steward," he said, forcing down the painful yearning he felt. "Is it really you?"

She shook her head gently. "It is only what of me remains in the Elder Stone," she said. "Just as you speak now with me, so too have I spoken with Stewards of old . . . their voices guiding my hand."

"You've talked with the Stewards of the old world?" said Will.

"In times of great need," said the Elder Steward, "the Elder Stone is a source of great wisdom . . . but like many magical objects, it diminishes with use and age. It was once a monolith as tall as this room. Now that small piece before you is the only part left."

Will looked down and saw to his horror that each particle of light floating upward to form her image took a piece of the stone with it. The Elder Stone was disappearing by the second. Soon it would be gone altogether—

"Yes," she acknowledged with a sad smile. "We don't have much time."

He pushed down all the words that he wanted to say, the need for her guidance, the fear that he didn't know what he'd become without her, the ache rising in his throat.

"I did what you asked." He kept inside himself how it felt to push a sword through someone's chest. "Sinclair can't raise the Dark King. I'm . . . I made sure of that."

But the Elder Steward shook her head, her expression grave. "Sinclair is a greater threat than you know."

"I don't understand," said Will.

The Elder Steward was so bright, the light streaming through and around her. But her eyes on him were grave.

"You must go to the Valnerina," said the Elder Steward. "The Black Valley in the Umbrian mountains. In a town called Scheggino, you will find a man named Ettore Fasciale. Only with Ettore can you stop what is to come."

"What could be a greater threat than Sinclair returning the Dark King?" said Will.

The Elder Steward shook her head, her eyes troubled. For the first time since Will had known her, frustration entered her voice as if she struggled against constraint.

"I have sworn never to speak of what lies in the Black Valley. But this I can tell you. You must find Ettore. If you do not, all you have faced will seem but a skirmish in the great battle that lies ahead."

Valnerina. The Black Valley. The name made him shiver. He imagined the Dark King unleashing raw terror and destruction. Himself standing atop a pile of the dead—or was it Sinclair, surmounting a throne, looking out at the ruins of a once-green land?

"Already Sinclair's forces move toward you," said the Elder Steward. "And with the wards down, there is no way to hold him out. You must not be here when he arrives."

"You mean—leave the Hall?"

"Sinclair cannot be allowed to capture any of you. For you each have a part you must play, and the stakes are too great for any one of you to fail."

She seemed to smile down on him.

"The Tree of Light shines for you, Will. Do not be afraid."

That was too much, even for him. "I'm not the one who—"

Grace's hands closed over his own, shutting the casket.

"No—!" said Will as the Elder Steward vanished, his pounding heart the only sign she had been there at all.

He felt as if she had been snatched from him. He turned on Grace, then saw her face was streaming with tears, though she looked back at him with that unbending pragmatism.

"Do not waste the last remnants of the Stone," said Grace. "She has told you what you must do."

Cyprian's expression mirrored Grace's, wide-eyed and trembling as if he had received a religious visitation. Violet looked hollowed out, her hand on her sword hilt. Even James looked rattled, his usually insouciant expression ribboned with shock.

"Wait for us in the gatekeep," Grace said to the others.

She turned to Will as the others ascended the stairs. He was still looking down at the closed stone casket that held the last fragment of the Elder Stone. The Elder Steward had looked so real, yet she had been an illusion. She always had been—he had to keep reminding himself of that. She had never really been his mentor; she had trained him by mistake, just another Steward tricked by the Dark King.

Grace looked at him calmly. "Do you waver in your duty?"

"You know I'm not the one who lit the Tree."

"You're the one who stopped Simon."

"Who killed Simon," said Will. The words sounded flat, even to his own ears.

"She entrusted that task to you," said Grace. "Not to the girl."

"The girl lights the Tree while I kill people." It just came out. He was too shaken by what had happened. He wasn't being careful.

"The Dark must be fought," said Grace. "That takes killing as well as light."

"Does it?"

All those hours of practice, the Elder Steward guiding him patiently, attempting to help him bring the Tree back to life. Her faith in him had never wavered, even as doubt had gnawed at his insides.

"We each have our role to play," said Grace.

And what is mine? he didn't say.

He knew what he'd see when he climbed the stairs to the Tree Chamber, the familiar words carved over the door, now filled with new meaning.

He is coming.

CHAPTER THREE

"YOU HEARD HER. We wait for Will in the gatekeep," said Violet. She turned to James, still unnerved by the vision of the Elder Steward. "It's this w—"

"I know the way," said James, and simply strolled past her.

It was galling. He showed no humility or remorse. He ought to be behaving like a penitent, thought Violet. He ought to be in chains, the kind that dragged and clanked. Or better yet, the obsidian manacles that would block his power. He hadn't liked that at all, last time.

Instead he looked as if *he* was the one barely tolerating *her*. What was Will doing, bringing him back here? If Sinclair really was on his way to the Hall, then Will had brought in a Trojan horse with enough magic to kill them all.

Violet set her teeth. "You don't get to just *wander off*." She took hold of James's upper arm. "This way."

She could snap his bone. He could throw her off with magic. He looked down at her grip like it soiled his jacket.

"Are you offering your arm like a gentleman caller?"

Cyprian was following them. His gaze never left James. Earlier, James had called Cyprian *little brother*, but they weren't related by blood. James's father Jannick had adopted Cyprian after he'd thrown James out of the Hall.

James had killed Jannick, too. Violet had brought Jannick's body to the courtyard in a wheelbarrow and put it on a pyre.

She increased the pressure of her pincer grip on James's arm. "When will Sinclair get here?"

"How should I know? I haven't seen him since I stole the Collar."

"Of course you haven't," said Cyprian. "You were waiting to see who won before you chose sides."

"Won?" James laughed, soft as breath. "You haven't won."

Violet frowned. "What is that supposed to mean?"

"It means you don't know Sinclair. You heard the ghost lady. Simon was never the head of the snake. That was his father. Sinclair's coming to take your Hall."

James's unlikable blue eyes gleamed. She felt suddenly chilled by all he might know. He had been part of the inner circle. There were even whispers that he had been Simon's lover, though James had always denied it. To have been so close to Simon and then to have betrayed him . . .

"Your surrogate father," said Cyprian, bitterly.

"That's right," James said evenly.

"Then you should have no problem helping us," said Cyprian. "That's what you do, isn't it? Kill fathers?"

"And brothers." James gave an intentionally cold smile.

This time she had to take Cyprian by the front of his tunic and hold him hard against the corridor wall while the heat in his green eyes calmed to a simmer. James's voice was rich with amusement.

"You just throw him about? No wonder he's following you around like a puppy. I wonder if he'll give himself fifty lashes for having impure thoughts. About a Lion, no less."

She flushed and deliberately didn't look at Cyprian when she let him go.

"Walk it off," she told Cyprian. "I'll take him back to the gatekeep."

She might as well have said, *Steward, hold to your training.* He gave a single, stilted nod, and turned, striding away so quickly that his long hair flared out behind him.

"My hero," said James dryly, as she took him by the arm again and propelled him down the hall.

"In here," she said, leading James into one of the gatekeep's smaller rooms and letting the door shut behind them.

"A prison?" he said.

"Just a room," she told him.

The wall was curved, echoing the shape of the tower outside. A single worn rug that might have once been red was the only covering on the stone floor. A stool with three legs was the only other furnishing, by a window like a thin slit in the outer wall.

She had left Cyprian outside. She was alone with James. The room was empty.

"And, what? You brought me here to ask me more questions? To find out all I know about Sinclair?"

"No."

She swung, the impact a satisfying crunch. James went sprawling into the opposite wall. There was blood on his mouth when he lifted his head. The retaliatory lash of magic never came, though she could see the impulse flare in his eyes.

"That was for a friend of mine," said Violet. "His name was Justice."

Unnervingly, as she watched, the cut began to mend, and the bruise that had begun to spread receded. It would soon be as if she'd never hit him: violence without evidence. It made her want to hit him again, made her want him to show some consequence for what he had done. She curled her hand into a fist instead.

James pressed his tongue into the vanishing cut in his lip. "I thought daddy's little favorite would be the first one to rough me up."

"He still might." She looked again at James's impossibly beautiful face. The smear of blood on his lips was all that remained of her strike. It declared with carmine arrogance that he was untouchable.

Violet said, "Why did you really follow Will here?"

"To the victor go the spoils?" James was deliberately provocative.

Violet flushed. "Will isn't—"

"Isn't?" said James.

"Will thinks you're here to help us. He likes to believe the best of people." She drew in a breath. "Maybe he's right about you. Maybe he isn't. But if you betray his trust, you answer to me."

"You think you could take me if I really wanted to fight?" His voice stayed pleasant.

"You might be more powerful than I am," Violet forced herself to say, "but I've fought you before. I know how your power works. All it takes is one slip in your concentration."

He just looked back at her with that galling arrogance. She wanted to crack it.

"Simon only kept you around because he liked having power over people from the old world," she said. "Will isn't like that. If you want a place here, you'll need to earn it."

A muscle tightened in James's jaw. But he only shrugged a single shoulder as if in jaded agreement. "Simon liked playing at being the Dark King." She found her cheeks heating as the meaning of those words sank in. "Did you expect me to deny it? But his father is different. You don't have to play at power when you have it. Sinclair's empire spans the globe. He has hundreds of followers bearing his brand. If they attack the

Hall, you'll need me to fight."

A network spreading out like cracks in ice, so that nowhere was safe to stand. She thought of Sinclair's operations, of which her family's business had been only a tiny part: the ships, and men, and money, and powerful friends. She drew in a breath.

"Sinclair's a recluse," said Violet. "He's never seen."

"But killing his son will have gotten his attention," said James. "Don't you think?"

Cyprian was in the gatekeep when she returned. Depositing James in the circular room below, she ascended the stairs to where Cyprian waited, a fire burning low beneath the large stone mantel. His handsome face was still with concentration. He sat with his legs folded up underneath him, one of the Steward stress positions used in their meditations. He did this regularly, just as he performed the Steward sword forms every morning and evening, the ghostly rituals of a Hall that didn't exist anymore.

You don't have to, she wanted to say to him. Even if the Stewards were still alive, these were meditations and exercises designed to control his shadow. But Cyprian had no shadow inside him, and never would. Those days were done.

Yet there was a part of her that liked it—that had always wished she could do it too.

He must have seen something of her thoughts in her expression, because he stopped and smiled ruefully.

"Is it strange that I still practice the forms, and walk my morning rounds in an empty Hall? I know it is time to move on, but to what? This is all I know." Cyprian's voice was wistful.

"It's not strange," said Violet. "I still do the exercises Justice taught me."

"Did you know I was jealous when Justice began training you?" admitted Cyprian, and she looked at him in surprise. Sarah and even Grace talked more about the days before the massacre than Cyprian, who kept his feelings to himself. "People had started saying that if Marcus didn't come back, Justice would take me as his shieldmate. I knew I could never replace my brother. But to be a shieldmate . . . that was a bond I always wanted. Until I found out what it was."

A suicide pact, each sworn to kill the other before the shadow inside them took over. Cyprian's voice was only a little brittle. She looked at his too-handsome face, like the carving of a paragon, made to inspire others to great deeds.

"I used to be jealous of you too," she told him. "I used to sneak in to watch you practice. You weren't like the others. You were perfect. I wanted to be just like you."

She flushed as Cyprian looked at her with startled eyes. But:

"If you seek a training partner," said Cyprian, into the quiet, "I would be honored to train with you."

The thought was oddly exhilarating, like being accepted into a club she never thought would have her. Cyprian had always been the best of the novitiates, setting the standard for excellence. The feeling she used to have watching him practice redoubled.

"I do," she said, too quickly. "I mean, I'd like to." She drew in a breath. "We can keep the forms alive together."

He gave her a strange smile.

"What is it?"

"The time of the Stewards is ending, and the only person I have to say that to is a Lion."

"I forgot, you hate those." She frowned.

"No, I just meant—"

Ten nights ago, she had come out of the great hall, the dead Shadow King burned into its flagstones, to see Cyprian approaching with the others behind him.

He'd dropped to his knee, his fist over his heart. With his green eyes cast down to the ground and his long hair falling about his face, he'd said, *You have saved the Hall.*

She had dragged him up and hugged him, feeling so fond of his silly formal ways and his awkward, stiff reciprocity, like he didn't know what to do. She had even felt fond of the way he had flushed for no reason, even as she had found herself flushing a little too.

"I just meant thank you," said Cyprian, quietly.

What had Cyprian and James's relationship been like before James had betrayed the Hall? She knew what it had been like after. When James had run away with Simon, Cyprian had stayed to be the perfect Steward in his place, following every rule, forging himself into the embodiment of their father's rigid Steward ideals. The good son, the best of the Hall, the pride of his father.

If James had killed her brother Tom she wouldn't have been able to stand it. It was a testament to Cyprian's training that he was stomaching James's presence at all, sitting in place with his jaw set and that roil of discomfort in his green eyes.

"You're right to worry about James," she said. "I'm strong enough to break iron chains, and even I couldn't stop him if he really wanted to hurt me."

Or to hurt Cyprian. Or Will. Or the others. She was almost realizing it as she spoke: of course, James's magic was deadly. But Will had always been so confident that he could beat James, she had simply believed that she could too.

Now she saw that James had a peculiar vulnerability to Will, a connection to him, which they had exploited each time they had fought him. Without that . . .

"What's he really doing here?" said Cyprian.

It was the question she hadn't been able to answer. "Will has a way of drawing people to him." James. Katherine. Even, in a way, herself. All of them had been pulled into this world by Will, stepping out of their lives to follow a boy they barely knew. "He thinks people aren't defined by their past lives or their blood. Maybe James—"

"James killed Stewards," said Cyprian. "Not his past self. Him. Why would Will bring someone like that into the Hall?"

The truth was that the presence of the blond boy in the room below disturbed her. Cyprian was right: James was a killer, and whether or not he'd been coerced in his past life, he'd killed by choice in this one.

"Will must have his reasons," said Violet, frowning.

She found Will in the great hall.

Her footsteps slowed as she walked through the doors. She didn't like coming back here. Instinctively, she shied away from the thicker pockets of darkness under eaves or outflung statuary. She avoided shadows now, a part of her expecting the face of the Shadow King to coalesce out of them.

She finally understood why the Stewards had always kept a light burning, a single spark to ward off the dangers of the night. It was because they had each known shadows, and the slow, creeping onset of the dark.

Will stood in front of the dais, looking up at the thrones. Standing alone in this ancient place, he was a dark, otherworldly figure. His black hair was a tumble over his night-pale skin, the sharpened planes of his face, and the flash of his intense dark eyes. He had always been striking, but it was as if the events at Bowhill had carved away everything in him that was soft or boyish, leaving only a hard core behind.

"I'm sorry," he said. "I should have been here."

She said, "You faced them too."

He didn't have to answer. It was there in the new silence around his words, the new look in his eyes. He had fought Shadow Kings at Bowhill as she had fought them here in the Hall.

She said, "The others don't understand. They've never really . . . they've never really faced the dark."

He said, "No."

I wanted you here. She didn't say it. She wouldn't have wished that on anyone.

"We need to talk about Sinclair. About Italy. About the Elder Steward—"

"I know. We'll gather the others in the morning." Will nodded once.

"If Sinclair doesn't attack tonight," she said.

She could imagine it too easily, torches in the night converging on the Hall. The Hall had always felt so safe. Now it felt frighteningly vulnerable. She didn't know why Sinclair wasn't here already. And then she thought, *He's burying his son.*

She remembered the day they'd met, Will bruised and chained in the hold of a ship, with water swirling inside. He was changed since then. She could see it. It echoed the change she felt in herself.

"Do you remember when we first came here?" It seemed so long ago; they were both so different.

"You were scared the Stewards wouldn't accept you," said Will, "because of what you are."

She nodded, and then pulled out the shield. "I saw this that first day . . . and I picked it up during the fight."

The shield was really a fragment: a piece of metal about the length of her arm, with a jagged edge where it had been broken. It retained some of its shape, convex with a grip that she could use to hold the shield on her arm.

Here in the great hall she couldn't help remember the moment her hands had closed on it. Scrabbling in the refuse for any weapon, she had been so sure that she was going to die. But when she'd lifted the shield, the hall had rung with the sound of metal, as the shield deflected the Shadow King's sword.

Will said, "The Shield of Rassalon."

"It protected me from the Shadow King," she said. "It's how I defeated him."

Will looked up at her in startled recognition as he quoted the words of the Elder Steward. "'The time will come when you must take up the Shield of Rassalon.'"

On the outer curve, the face of a lion gazed out at her from the shield as if it knew her. A powerful, ancient recognition, it had felt like having a friend of great strength and warmth. A lion, fighting by her side.

She spoke in a rush. "There's so much I don't know about him. About any of it. Why did Rassalon fight for the Dark? Who was he?"

The Stewards had talked about Rassalon like he was their most hated enemy, a cold-blooded lieutenant of the Dark King.

What she felt from the shield wasn't darkness; it was a steady warmth, a wise, noble presence that offered her its strength. The shield seemed to radiate goodness and power in equal measure.

Will said, "You want to know who you are."

"Is that so strange?"

"You don't need a shield to tell you," said Will.

He'd always had that kind of faith in her. But with the shield in her hand, that sense of the vastness of the old world came over her again. She felt as if she had touched the edge of something immense that she had barely begun to understand.

"Don't you think if we knew what had happened in the past, that we'd have a better chance of fighting it?" Violet said. "Think about it—how much do we really know about the Dark King?"

Will's dark eyes gazed back at her. "We know he destroyed the old world."

"But how? What happened? Don't you want to know?"

All they had were fragments, old legends, imperfect accounts. It didn't tell them what had really happened. It wasn't just Rassalon who was a mystery. Will was Blood of the Lady, but who was the Lady, really? They didn't even know her name. Even James didn't know the name he had used in the past. He knew himself only by what the forces of Light had called him: Anharion, the Betrayer.

Will didn't answer. His eyes were on the thrones. Was he thinking of the Shadow Kings they had both faced? Will said, "You think that's what we'll find in Italy? The truth about the Dark King?"

There was something in his voice. She said, "Will . . . what really happened at Bowhill?"

He turned to her, and for a moment there was a look of such yearning in his eyes that she was sure that he would speak. But in the next moment the look shuttered, and all he said was, "It doesn't matter. You protected one sister. I couldn't protect the other."

"Will—"

He shook his head. "One day, when we're finished with Sinclair, when we're safe and comfortable together, I'll tell you."

"All right," she said.

She thought they were done, but after a step toward the doors he turned back to her.

"Violet, can I ask you something?"

"Of course."

His tone was casual. His posture was relaxed, his limbs arranged in an easy pose.

"The Dark King." His voice was easy. "What would you do if he did return?"

"I'd kill him." She said it fiercely, instantly. "Before he could hurt our world. All of us would."

Will didn't speak at once. She found herself searching his face, but in the shadowy hall, she couldn't really glean anything.

She said, "What is it?"

"Nothing. That's good," said Will. "I'll see you back in the keep."

CHAPTER FOUR

THE MOMENT HE was alone, Will picked up the knapsack that he had been hiding from Violet, struck tinder to a wall torch, and continued through the great hall into the corridors, until he was in the old forbidden section of the citadel.

The architecture here was different, older and more monumental, like that of the rooms surrounding the Tree Chamber. Its strange, simpler shapes loomed up on either side. He passed the huge shattered stone column that lay across the center of a room with no ceiling like a landmark pointing his way. Retracing his steps from memory, he found the door that was now wedged open, and descended into the room of relics that had once housed the Shadow Stone.

The last time he had been here had been with Violet. She had opened the heavy doors, they had descended into the underchamber, and he had walked through the rooms to the Shadow Stone.

Thinking back, he had been drawn to it.

How else could he explain finding his way through the corridors to the door, and through it, down to the prison of the kings beneath? Violet hadn't wanted to enter the final chamber. She had been repelled, while he had been entranced, reaching out for its black surface.

Had the Stone been calling to him? Or he to it?

He didn't know. He only knew that the Shadow Stone had welcomed him, one of a series of Dark artifacts that responded to him, trumpeting his identity to any who would listen.

His grip on his knapsack tightened. Last time he'd come here had been before. Before he'd known for certain what he was.

The Dark King. Sarcean the conqueror. The Destroyer, reborn into this time.

Now he looked with different eyes at the artifacts around him, that appeared to be put together haphazardly. They weren't just scraps of old lives, they were scraps of *his* life: pieces of a world he had lived in, then destroyed.

The bone-like shelves of white-spined books—did they hold stories of his rise? The vessels of agate, gold, and crystal—had he used them, held them in his hands? The twisted claw that gleamed like glass, the scatterings of scale, the strange-looking teeth—were they creatures he had commanded?

He had stayed alert, making sure he wasn't followed. He was far from the gatekeep where the others were sleeping. But he still stopped and waited.

Because no one could witness. No one could know.

He let the silence of this underground chamber sink into his bones, until there was no sight or sound of a single soul in here with him and he was certain he was utterly alone.

Then he drew from his pack the three Dark armor pieces he had taken from Simon's Remnants—the shoulder piece, the half helm, and the gauntlet—and tossed them to the ground.

Even touching them was evidence of who he was. If any of the others saw him do it . . . he knew what would happen. He'd seen Katherine draw the sword. He'd felt his mother's hands around his neck.

He'd heard Violet say it, with no hesitation.

They'd kill him. Or die trying. There was no acceptance waiting for him on the other side of that revelation. The others could never know. He was the Dark King. But he could refuse his fate.

He stared down at the black pieces of metal, like a stain on the floor. Like a brand marking his identity. And he swore to his past self, *Sarcean, I'm going to defeat you. Whatever your plans are in the Valnerina, I'm going to stop them. Like I stopped Simon. Like I'm going to stop Sinclair. I will give you no foothold in this world, or in me. No one will ever even know you came back. Your attempt to rule ends here.*

He moved out into the room and began to systematically pick up each of the Dark artifacts collected there and heap them on the ground with the armor. He forced himself not to pause or study any of them, no matter how intriguing they were: a sphere of obsidian with a hollow center, a black knife carved with dark flowers, the belt the Stewards had used to test novitiates before they drank from the Cup.

He stared down at the pile when he was done. This was it, every Dark artifact, every temptation to learn more, every piece of evidence incriminating him, every dark particle of himself. He would raze it to the ground.

He threw his torch down on the pile. The fire caught with abnormal speed, the flames rancid black and green when they touched the objects. It burned unnaturally, hotter than red fire, as if responding to his presence. He watched the belt curl, and the metal start to turn red. It was painfully hot. He didn't move. He stayed there until the metal melted down into a sludge.

Until there was nothing left of that life but ash and blackened stone.

Only when it was done did he rise and ascend the stairs.

A light glowed, like a single campfire in the night. *No one should be here.* Will came forward, drawn as if by a phantasm to a half-open door, where he stopped.

There was light coming from Jannick's study. In the halls of the dead, it was like the glistening of a ghost. This place was deserted, but for that eerie, flickering light. Will drew in a breath, put his hand on the door, and pushed it open.

What he saw wasn't the ghost of a lost Steward, except that perhaps it was, another inhabitant wrenched out of his time.

James was sprawled in his father's chair. His jacket was flung over the desk, his shirt loose on his body. He sat with his boots up on the lip of the desk's open bottom drawer, ankles crossed. Dangling from his fingers was a silver flask that he appeared to have stolen from his father's desk, the drawer still open. Lifting the flask to his lips, he looked up at Will.

"Here to drag me back to the gatekeep?" said James.

"I thought Stewards didn't drink," said Will.

He couldn't imagine a Steward using alcohol, except perhaps to sterilize a wound. Stewards imbibed the Hall's clear revitalizing waters, or a delicate green tea with refreshing herbs, avoiding anything that might release their shadow.

James lifted his father's silver flask in a little salute. "The Stewards don't. Deny the flesh and preserve the sanctity of the body. For janissaries like my father, it's something of a gray area."

He held out the flask to Will.

He should say no. He looked at James, with his shirt loosened, his glinting lashes at half mast, and the candlelight turning all his edges golden. He should keep James at arm's length, as he had on the ride here. Adopt the professionalism of a leader, deploying James's powers where they were needed. Be there for him as a friend, a trustworthy companion. He should say no.

On the docks, the men had sat around swilling gin after work. He had learned to drink to seem like one of them. He'd been nervous: his mother had never let him drink even a sip of country wine. Had she been scared he might lose control? And then—what? His first coughing splutter of dock gin had burned his throat. The men had laughed, slapping him on the back. He'd been terrified that he had drawn attention to himself, that his reaction had given him away, and maybe it had. *That mama's boy can't hold his liquor.* He wondered not for the first time which of the men had sold the boat boy's life for a bag of coin.

This felt the same, drinking with someone who couldn't be allowed to know who he was, his heart beating, *Careful, careful.*

With his cravat untied and his ankles crossed, James watched him as if he knew it, a dissolute indulging in the last luxuries of a lost world.

Will took the flask and lifted it.

He ought to have known Steward liquor would be nothing like the harsh spirits the men guzzled on the docks. The flask held ambrosia, its scent transporting him to an orchard tumbled with sweet blossom. A single sip and he was swept away by wonder, the aching beauty of a lost kingdom. He had never tasted its like. He likely never would again; the artisanal methods of the Stewards had died with them.

Will passed the flask back. James took another swig.

"He'd hate this," James said. "I was never allowed in here." He was talking about his father. "If you were summoned to the study, it meant you were in trouble. The novitiates were all terrified of him." His smile had an edge.

Will had been afraid of him too, though his had been the fear of discovery. Jannick had been suspicious of Will from the start, because Jannick had known the enemy could come in any form. Six years earlier, it had come in the form of his own son.

Now Jannick was dead, and if anyone knew the real identities of the boys who sat drinking in his study, they would recoil in horror. *I shouldn't be here.*

"Let me guess, you were always in trouble," said Will.

"No, I was a goody two-shoes," said James, who looked like a golden temptation to sin. "Does that surprise you? My livery spotless and my armor shined. All set to be the youngest Steward in a generation."

A new understanding fell into place: James's adopted brother Cyprian, striving to be the best, pushing himself to exhaustion in drill after drill. The Hall's prodigy, chasing a ghost.

"Until they found out what you were," said Will.

A tilt of the flask in acknowledgment. James took another drink, and then passed the flask. Will lifted it, that wild, sweet Steward ambrosia. He still had that pure taste in his mouth as he spoke casually.

"Did they try to kill you right away?"

"They're Stewards," said James. "They kill themselves, you think they'd be lenient with anyone else?"

No. They wouldn't. He knew that. Kill it before it becomes a threat, that was the Steward creed. They had intended to kill Violet. They would have brought the sword down on her neck. But James had been eleven years old, manifesting powers for the first time. A child, not understanding why his family was trying to kill him. Will could imagine the scene too well.

He heard himself say, "You only learned what you were when they tried to kill you."

Mother, it's me. Mother, stop, I can't breathe. Mother—

Instead of answering, James said, "You know, I always wondered what it would be like to see this place brought to its knees."

"And how is it?"

It had been long enough since the attack that a thin film of dust covered everything. The last moments of the High Janissary, preserved like stone strata. Soon even that would be gone, along with all memory of the Stewards.

"Everything I dreamed," said James, showing his teeth. He raised the flask. "Let's toast. To ending the Stewards once and—"

Will's hand was on James's wrist before he knew what he was doing, stopping the flask from reaching his lips. "I'm not going to toast to that," said Will, "and neither are you."

Time seemed to slow, thick and molten like metal in heat. "You know, there aren't a lot of people I let put hands on me." James didn't even glance at the place where Will held his wrist, holding his gaze instead, blue eyes glittering.

"I know," said Will.

"So this is how it's going to be? You hold my hand and pretend that you have power over me?"

Will didn't back down, his thumb hard on the thin skin of the inside of James's wrist.

"The Stewards meant something to me," said Will. "And they meant something to you too."

As if in a little climax of distaste for the words, James pulled his arm free, stood, and strode over to the other side of the room, where he leaned his palms against the mantel. Will could see the line of tension across his shoulders under the fine fabric of his jacket.

Will knew better than to speak, though there was so much that he wanted to say. That he'd been on the run for months before the Stewards had found him. That they'd given him a bed and a safe place to sleep. That the Elder Steward had believed in him, and that he didn't blame James for his allegiance to Simon because he knew how much you owed to the person who took you in.

He wondered how drunk James was, how much he'd downed before Will entered. James was surrounded by his own ghosts: the life he might have led if he had taken his whites. If James had passed the Steward tests, Cyprian would be his brother in arms, maybe even his shieldmate.

Will had brought James to the Hall, and James had come displaying a bravura confidence belied by a night drinking in the study of the father he'd killed. Will wanted to say he knew how much that meant.

He wanted to say that he knew how it felt to be responsible for the death of the Stewards.

"I didn't think Marcus would kill the horses."

James spoke with his back to Will.

The light in the room came from six candles: three on the desk, and three on the mantel. James must have lit them when he entered. There was just enough light to see the words in the pages of the open book. *Omnes una manet nox.* When James turned back, his eyes were dark.

"We used to go to the stables together. Marcus loved horses. Well, in that repressed way Stewards love anything. He'd bring his horse an apple, spend extra time brushing her coat. That's absolutely *outré* for a Steward. Father approved of Marcus, so I could traipse around after him. Otherwise it was all chants and practice. 'Your training is everything, Jamie.' That's what Father used to say." A humorless smile.

"And then you got yourself a new father," said Will.

"And now he's trying to kill me too."

James still had the flask in his long fingers, and now he lifted it, the salute ironic. "Don't give your loyalty to a killer."

"No," said Will.

CHAPTER FIVE

"THE VALNERINA," SAID Will, spreading out the yellowed map the next morning. "It follows the River Nera from these mountains"—he pointed—"all the way down to the Tiber. We need to get there before Sinclair."

Violet leaned in with Grace and Cyprian to look at the map.

They had gathered in the gatekeep. James, in his exquisitely tailored jacket and trousers, was leaning against the stonework by the mantel. The veiled lids and the languid pose was much as it had been last night, but his manner was that of a courtier deciding whether the room's entertainments were worth his time.

The others were on edge, aware that the Hall was wide open, Sarah's watch on the ramparts their only warning if Sinclair's attack came. Because the Valnerina was not Sinclair's only target. Sinclair was coming for this Hall even as he stretched his network out toward Italy. Sinclair's reach was so large it seemed impossible to outpace or fight.

Violet said, "How?"

Will didn't answer. The map stirred something uneasy in him. Even the names seemed to whisper to him. *The Black Valley. The Blind Leap. The*

Black River. He knew very little about Umbria beyond the old books he'd read on his travels with his mother. It loomed in his mind as a place with its own history of Roman antiquity, the bones of a great past always present.

"We pack and ride out." Cyprian's shoulders were squared, ready to do his duty and leave, though the Hall was his life, the only home he had ever known. "Sinclair's coming. We need to move fast, and stay ahead of him."

"There might be another way," said Grace.

Everyone turned to face her.

She shared Cyprian's immaculate posture, but unlike Cyprian she often kept her own counsel. Now she spoke.

"We don't have to travel by ship," said Grace. "We don't even need to leave the Hall."

Will stepped forward, not understanding. "What do you mean?"

"We can use one of the other gates."

Will looked instinctively at the door. Outside, the immense gate to the Hall of the Stewards arced above them. He remembered riding through it for the first time, watching a line of Stewards vanish as they passed through a broken arch on the moors.

"The *other* gates?" Will said.

"There are four gates." Grace pointed to the gate where they now camped. "North." And then she pointed to each direction. "South. East. And west."

"And?" said Violet.

"The Stewards only use one of them," said Grace.

The gate above them was carved with the image of a single tower. The idea that there were other gates was new. Grace's words seemed to unlock a disturbing set of possibilities.

Cyprian was shaking his head. "There *is* only one gate. It opens onto the Abbey Marsh. The other gates lead to nowhere, to a kind of limbo, part of the magic that shrouds the Hall."

"Because they're not open," said Grace.

Those disquieting words swirled in him. *A door,* he'd once said to the Elder Steward. *A door that I can't open.* "I don't understand."

"Did you think the Hall was in England?" said Grace. "It isn't. The Hall of Kings was a meeting place. Each of the kings came here from their own lands, to gather and converse. There are four gates. Four gates for each of the four kings. Each one opens in a different place."

"You mean . . . the northern gate opens in England . . . but the others—" The idea was so impossible it was difficult to absorb.

"Open somewhere else," said Grace.

A gate that led to another country. It couldn't be true, could it? A form of travel bypassing mountains and sea? Will's mind raced with questions. Was this how the ancients had journeyed? Stepping from one part of the world to another?

Could they travel the same way? If so, could they reach Ettore in Umbria before Sinclair even knew they were gone?

"How do you know this?" said Cyprian.

Grace didn't answer. Cyprian looked disturbed. It was likely unsettling to realize she knew things about the Hall that he didn't. Only Grace had known of the chamber under the Tree of Light. Only Grace had known of the Elder Stone. Will wondered what other secrets Grace kept, details known only to the Elder Steward and her janissary.

"Over the years, many artifacts have been unearthed in Italy," said Grace. "It's a good bet that one of the gates opens there—or near there—"

"We just need to find the right gate."

Will said it as if it decided things. Perhaps this unconventional shortcut would give them the advantage they needed against Sinclair.

Yet there was something disturbing about opening a gate. Bringing power like that back was like waking a great beast that slumbered beneath the earth. *Three great beasts,* he thought. There was no way to know what would lie behind the three gates when they opened. They would be flaring a part of the old world into life.

"If the gates are closed, how do they open?" Cyprian said.

"With magic," said Grace.

"Stewards can't use magic," said Cyprian.

It was inevitable, the drawling voice from behind them, the insouciant pose, one knee drawn up, shoulders leaned against the wall.

"But I can," said James.

"No," said Cyprian.

James's mouth twisted. "Wouldn't want to pollute your pristine Hall with magic."

"It's Dark magic."

"It's not Dark magic," said Will. "It's just magic."

"He's killed Stewards with it."

Cyprian's green eyes stormed with a clear desire to cast James out. Or perhaps, like Elizabeth, to simply leave.

Will made himself say, "And now we're using it to stop Sinclair."

They gathered in the courtyard with packs and their horses.

With the threat of an attack from Sinclair looming, they had decided to split into two parties. At Will's suggestion, Grace and Sarah would stay to find objects to barter for a ship's passage to Italy, in case the gates didn't work and regular travel became necessary. Violet and Cyprian would accompany Will with James to the gate.

Elizabeth was conspicuously absent.

Will tightened Valdithar's girth and tried not to think about her avoidance of him. She was the only person here who had known Katherine. He wanted . . . he wasn't sure what he wanted. His feelings for

Katherine were raw-edged now that she was gone. He had viewed her as a means to strike at Simon, but everything had changed when she had kissed him and he had realized, wrenching away in shock, who she was.

He knew he didn't deserve to mourn, and that Elizabeth was not his family. He bit down on the part of himself that wanted to find her, to check on how she was.

Grace and Sarah had come to see them off. James strolled up, and Violet handed him the reins to his black London Thoroughbred. Cyprian was riding James's white Steward horse, and Will watched James take this fact in with a little curl of his lips. But he said nothing, just took the reins Violet held out to him.

"Your shield's broken," said James.

"You're in yesterday's clothes," said Violet.

The horses were laden with packs, sustenance for a day's journey, with enough to spare in case the expedition ran long. Will had brought a wrapped parcel of his own.

"There's something I need to give you," he told Violet.

He went to Valdithar's saddle pack. Unwrapping the cloth-swaddled bundle, he took out a sheathed sword. For a moment he just held it, feeling its weight.

"Ekthalion," said Violet.

The sword that had been forged to kill him. In the ancient world, someone had wanted to do that badly enough that they had fashioned a magic sword for that single purpose . . . in those long-ago wars, it had been the only thing able to harm the Dark King. And now here it was, waiting.

Quiescent in its sheath, only its carved hilt could be seen. Etched into its blade beneath were the words of the prophecy. Will could read the old language, its true wording. *He who wields the blade will become the Champion.*

Violet looked nervous. The last time she had seen Ekthalion

unsheathed, it had spewed black flame that had killed men and destroyed Simon's ship, the *Sealgair*, its blade corrupted by the Dark King's blood.

"I took it from Simon," Will said. And with a single smooth motion, Will pulled it from the sheath.

Violet threw herself backward, shouting, "*Will, no!*"

It was a moment before she realized that nothing had happened. No explosion, no rain of death or coruscating black fire. She uncurled herself slowly, looking back at the sword.

The blade Will had drawn was pure silver. It winked in the daylight. There was no sign of the corrupting black flame.

"You cleansed the blade," said Violet, in awe.

"No," said Will. "Katherine did."

Violet had come forward, drawn to the sword. "What about the prophecy? I thought whoever cleansed Ekthalion was destined to be some sort of champion."

"She was a champion," said Will, running his fingers along the writing on the sword's sheath. "She was Blood of the Lady. But she came to the Hall too late."

Too late for her, and too late for the Stewards.

He hadn't known when he had followed the instructions of his mother's old servant Matthew that he was stealing another child's destiny. Even without the guidance of the Stewards, Katherine had found her way to the Hall. She had found her way to the sword. And she had drawn it against the Dark King.

Violet looked along the silver length of Ekthalion. Then she looked up at Will. "You should at least learn to use it." Her lips quirked.

She was doubtless remembering the few disastrous attempts he'd made to practice sword work with her. The missteps in footwork. The thunk of the blade into the bedpost.

He remembered it too, remembered her on the bed laughing,

remembered the warm, good feeling of companionship that had been utterly new to him.

Then he remembered driving his sword into Simon's flesh.

He had sworn to defeat the Dark King. He had sworn to stop the plans of his past self. And that meant that if anything . . . went wrong, he had to make sure there was someone who would kill him if it was necessary.

He looked down at the sword forged to kill the Dark King.

Then he looked back up at his best friend. Violet was a force for good. Violet wouldn't falter.

He said, "I think . . . it should go to you."

"Me?" Violet gave him a strange look, like she didn't quite understand.

"You're the one I trust to do what's right."

He held it out.

Violet stared at it in a moment of decision.

On the ship, Ekthalion had burned out the bodies of any who had tried to touch it. It was cleansed now, but the memory of its destructive power lingered. Even reaching out for it was an act of courage. He remembered squeezing his eyes shut against battering fear as he held out his hand for it, anticipating his own death on the ship.

Squaring her shoulders, Violet took it, her hand wrapping around the hilt. She stood with sword and shield, and it looked right, Rassalon's Lion on her left arm, in her right hand the sword of the Champion. She unbuckled her own sword, replacing it with Ekthalion.

They rode out.

It was unsettling to think they were following the path of the old kings, or that they might be about to open a gateway to the Valnerina, where Ettore held the key to stopping Sinclair. *All you have faced will seem but a skirmish.* He couldn't guess what lay beyond the gate.

They rode deep into the citadel, where buildings gave way to untraveled ruins, the place so large the Stewards had inhabited and maintained only a small fraction of it. They reached sections of the Hall that Will had never visited, past cracked pillars, through rooms where shafts of light shone down from scraps of missing ceiling. Three times, they had to dismount and lead the horses over giant pieces of broken stone.

No one had come to this part of the citadel for years. It was ruined and deserted, as if it had been left to founder. It made him wonder why the gates had been abandoned, and what lay beyond them. Will imagined women and men of the old world streaming through the gates, fleeing to the Hall as the armies of the Dark closed in, the gates clanging shut for the last time. Which had been the final gate to shut? The last kingdom to fall? Serpent? Rose? Sun? Will buried the thought: his past self hadn't fled with the refugees. He had been the one pursuing them.

They had been trekking through ruins for perhaps an hour, when they came upon the gate.

"We're here," said Will, looking up.

The courtyard was an uncanny, distorted mirror of the northern courtyard. Its size was the same, but most of the flagstones were rubble, the ground blanketed in weeds and grass that had spilled out of the cracks, clumps of dandelion, and scatterings of white clover.

The east gate itself rose to an apogee like steepled hands. Set in the outer wall, it was a different shape than the round arch of the northern gate. But like the courtyard, it was the same size, as if each of the four kings had entered the Hall with arrangements of scrupulous equality.

"If Grace is right, one of the four kings lived beyond those doors," said James, his eyes on the gate.

"You think it was the king I killed?" said Violet, slinging her sword on her shoulder. "Or one of the others?"

The gate doors were barred with a thick metal crossbeam, rust-fused to the door iron. Where the northern gate was carved with the symbol of a tower, these doors bore a stylized rose. It matched the rose emblazoned on the throne in the great hall. *Tower, rose, serpent, sun*. Carved into the stone on either side of the doors, it seemed to confirm everything Grace had said.

Now that they were looking at it, the enormity of what they were doing bore down on him. Opening a hole in the world, with magic that had not been used in thousands of years. Will drew in a breath.

"Before we can try any magic, we need to open the physical doors," said Will.

"I'll do it," said Violet.

They dismounted and tied up the horses on the far side of the courtyard. Violet approached the archway warily.

She looked small in front of the towering doors, a speck in front of a mountain. After assessing them, she put her shoulder under the metal crossbeam. The rusted bar screamed with the grating dissonance of tearing metal as her young body braced and flexed.

With a great metallic booming, a seam appeared, the doors opening on unnerving, empty limbo, from which came a peaty smell, as though the marsh lay beyond even if it could not be seen.

"It's as you said," Violet said to Cyprian, who was staring at her. "The doors open on nothing."

The four of them looked out at the view, as Violet stepped back, panting.

"My turn," said James.

He stepped forward, but there was no ancient script that he could read, or clear sign telling him what to do. Will walked forward with him, drawn by the leftmost carving of the rose. It was smooth, as if many hands had touched it, reminding him of the wall stone Grace had used to open the Tree's underchamber.

"This emblem . . ." He put his hand on it.

James said, "I feel it too."

He had mirrored Will, standing before the emblem on the right. The past felt very close. A ritual just out of memory.

James said, in a strange, slow voice, "Two symbols . . . it takes two people to open a gate . . ."

Lesser talents, Will almost said, and bit down on the words, which seemed to come from a deep place. He could almost see it, two robed figures, standing on either side of the gate, raising their arms to touch the carved emblems.

"You're strong enough to do it alone," said Will. He knew that, deep in his bones. And alongside that, a new quality to his pulse. A proprietary thrum. *Prove it. Prove yourself. Show me.*

"The question is, what do I do?" said James, coming forward.

"Face the emblem," said Will.

James moved so that he stood right in front of the carved rose.

"Can you try to—push magic into it?" said Violet.

"Push magic into it?" James's amused voice was dry.

Violet flushed. "I don't know how it works."

"Clearly."

"Put your hand on it," said Will.

James reached out and placed his hand right over the rose. Nothing happened, but the sense of ritual intensified.

"Fill it," said Will. "Fill it up with your power."

James's lips parted, and Will felt the sharp tang he felt every time James started to gather his power. The emblem under James's hand started to shimmer. Will felt a throb, as if the air itself was pulsing. Then the arch itself began to shine, spreading up and out from James's hand.

"Tell it to open."

"I— Open," said James.

"Say the true word," said Will.

"*Aragas,*" said James.

The air under the gate rippled. Scattered glimpses of something else began to appear and disappear, like fragments of a dream. The light was changing, the view growing darker. Will held his breath at the huge, impossible vision rising thirty feet from paving to arch top.

"It's working," said Cyprian, and the words sounded shaken.

"Get the horses," said Will. "We cross as soon as it's open."

"Why is it so dark?" Violet's voice, also shaken. "Is it night on the other side?"

It looked like night. The coalescing view was pitch-black in places, dark blue in others, with shafts of light filtering down from hazy patches of light above. Will could barely make out the ruin that swirled dimly into sight, wavering columns and huge broken steps. Tendriled plants swayed back and forward in the un-light.

And then Will saw a shape undulating across the sky, its motion languid, unnaturally slow for flight. Like a bird—but—

—it wasn't a bird—

The horror of realization, too late.

The gate wasn't opening at night. It was opening underwater.

"*Close it! Close—*"

His words were obliterated by the roar as, with the violence of a geyser, dark sea exploded into the Hall.

Will inhaled and choked, his lungs filling. He was thrown backward, water drowning him, wet salt in his nose and mouth. He struck out desperately for a hold, and found nothing, just the violent bursting swirl of the sea. In a jumbled panic, he thought the whole ocean would empty itself here, filling the citadel, until it too was submerged, like the ruin he had glimpsed beyond the gate.

And then, as suddenly as it had erupted, it ended.

The spume of water dropped to the ground, leaving them all gasping like fish thrown onto the planking of a boat.

The gate was closed, its magic source cut off.

James. Coughing out salt water, Will pushed himself up to his knees, his clothes soaked, dripping and heavy. To his left he saw Violet expelling water violently. One of the Steward horses had pulled free from its rope and reached dry land. The other looked drenched and aggrieved. Cyprian had been standing to one side of the gate, with the result that much of the ocean had missed him. He was sloshing across the remaining water, and offering a hand to Violet.

But he couldn't see—

"James!" Will was racing over as James collapsed, his face dead white. "James!" Will splashed to his knees in the water, pulling James up and against him. Ocean cold, James was barely breathing and his eyes were unfocused. It was more than just shock: he looked utterly drained, as if the gate had pulled out all his strength, Will the only thing holding him up. "James, can you hear me? *James.*"

"Let's not try that again in a hurry." James's usual drawl was blurred.

The rush of relief was palpable, clutching James in his arms. Will let out a shaky breath.

"What happened?" Cyprian was staring at the gate.

The empty limbo was once again visible through the arch, making the underwater world they'd glimpsed seem surreal, as if it had never been.

"That was the ocean," said Violet, in a soft, stunned voice.

"An underwater kingdom?" said Cyprian.

"No," Will heard himself say. "It was a citadel, just like this one." A painful sense of loss sliced at him. "It's been so long, it was covered by the sea."

The thought of the other gates was suddenly awful. Who knew what might lie beyond their doors? Will forced himself to put aside the image of that watery ruin.

"Whatever we saw, this wasn't the right gate."

"Then we try again," said Cyprian. "There are two gates left."

"Oh, certainly," said James. "Just point me at them." Blond tendrils streamed water. He could barely lift his head, but his lip curled effectively.

"He's too weak," said Will. "He needs time to recover."

He looked back up at the gate. He could feel James's wet skin against him, beneath the layers of his sodden clothes. James was cold, too cold even to shiver, having poured all of himself into the gate.

"And we need time to regroup. Whatever's on the other side of the gate," Will said, "we need to be ready."

CHAPTER SIX

"IT'S A GIFT she's been brought back."

"It's unnatural. It's the Devil's work."

"It's the Lord's mercy. You saw her, Mrs. Kent. The way her body was petrified like stone. It was an illness, some kind of malady we mistook for death. And God's grace has restored her—"

Visander's eyes opened.

Voices. There were voices coming from beyond the room where they had brought him, weak and barely able to stand. His captors huddled together outside the door and whispered about him in tones of apprehension and fear.

He remembered his arrival here in snippets. The gray-haired man who had found him had shouted for help, calling himself uncle to this body. They had fed him some kind of drink, coaxing it down his throat. He had coughed it up, and it had come up grainy with mud and dirt from out of his gullet and stomach.

In a tiled room two women had washed him, scrubbing him down, his mind revolting at the body that was not his, while the dirt sloughed away from his skin and hair. The room was foreign, full of strange furnishings and objects he didn't recognize. Even the white robe they had dressed him in was a style he had never seen before.

Waking now, he saw he was on a bed stuffed with the feathers of dead birds, still wearing the white robe. Above him, fabric hung in a draped canopy of light green. His head felt dizzy, his thoughts thick and his limbs wrong. But his eyes fell upon the muddy garments that had been stripped from him. It was not a dream. He had returned, to a place he did not know, into a body that was not his own

"Where is the Queen?" he had demanded as they had first manhandled him. "You must take me to her." His voice had come out harsh with disuse. It had not been his voice, girlish and thin, dizzying him.

"What language is that? What is she saying?"

"I don't know—she looks sick, like she's—"

He had been able to understand them. But they had not been able to understand him. How? How did he know their language when he had never heard it before? *Her language*, he thought, with a shuddering, revolted feeling toward the flesh that he wore and could not operate. He had the sudden urge to tear it off and find himself underneath. Why had he come back in this woman's—*Katherine's*—body? Where was his own body?

Where was his sword, Ekthalion, and his steed, Indeviel? He was a champion without a blade and a rider without a mount. He thought, *Indeviel, I swore I would return and I will. I will find you and fulfill the oath we swore on the Long Ride. And with you at my side and Ekthalion in my hand, I will strike down the Dark King.*

"Mr. Prescott," he heard now, the words coming from outside his room. *"I'm so glad you came. We didn't know what else to do."*

"Sinclair was happy to send me, Mrs. Kent. He thinks of your daughter as family. Had her wedding to his son taken place, it would have been so."

"She's not herself. She speaks in tongues, it's as if she doesn't know us—"

"May I see her? Where is she?"

"Through here—"

Visander pushed himself up on the bed just as the door swung open.

The man who entered was an older human, dressed in a black jacket that gave him the shape of an elongated triangle, wide shoulders tapering to a thin waist and long legs. His hair was gray, cut short with long sideburns. He had an air of authority, peeling dark gloves from his fingers as he entered.

"Who are you?" said Visander, and then felt a wave of dizziness, unsure if the words had come out in Katherine's language or his own.

But the human appeared to understand him, his expression changing the moment Visander spoke. He halted for an instant, and then he came forward more slowly. He didn't stop until he reached the edge of the bed, where he sat, disturbingly close, the mattress dipping at his weight.

"You don't know me?" said the human.

Should I? Visander wanted to spit at him. He felt vulnerable in this bed, barely clothed while the human wore heavy fabrics. He wanted to reach for his sword, and had to remind himself that Ekthalion was missing. It made him feel naked, more so than the thin white robe: no weapon.

"I am Mr. Prescott, a solicitor to the Earl of Sinclair," said the human, when Visander didn't answer. "His eldest son, Simon, was engaged to the daughter of this family. Her name was Katherine." The human—Prescott—kept his eyes on Visander and his question mild. "Who are you?"

I am Katherine, Visander knew was what he was supposed to say, to preserve his secret. He did not know who here was enemy and who was friend. Yet something about the way this human looked at him made him speak the truth.

"I am Visander, the Queen's Champion, returned to this world to kill the Dark King."

Prescott smiled.

The expression filled his eyes with gratification. He looked at

Visander the way a man might look at a bounty that has fallen into his lap when he expected nothing.

But before Visander could speak, Prescott rose from the bed and moved back to the doorway. There he spoke to the woman in the hall.

"I have excellent news, Mrs. Kent. Sinclair's younger son, Phillip, will honor Simon's engagement with your niece."

"Mr. Prescott—!" the woman said.

"Let them be married at once. She will recover better at Ruthern. We'll move her there for her convalescence. Sinclair has an exceptional physician, and the country air is greatly restoring."

"But the strangeness of her words," said the woman, "the manner of her return; are you not concerned that she—"

"Not at all," said Prescott, looking back at the bed and meeting Visander's eyes. "To return from the dead—is that not a blessing?"

The bedroom was crowded with humans. The older man and woman who called themselves Katherine's aunt and uncle were present. The aunt's eyes were wide with concern, the uncle's face stern. And there was a priest, a seamy, unsavory man who behaved obsequiously toward Mr. Prescott. A younger man with a shock of dark hair arrived last, looking harried and on edge. Prescott greeted him with the name Phillip. There were a great many humans, more than Visander had ever stood among before.

Katherine's uncle supported Visander's weight as he rose out of bed, still wearing the white bed robe. Visander's head swam, his mind barely present. There was a hushed, hurried atmosphere, as if these were subterranean dealings.

Phillip came to stand next to him nervously. A man of average height with dark hair falling into his eyes and a white-cheeked, pinched expression on a fine-boned face, he kept looking toward Prescott as if for approval. "But are you sure?"

"She is a bride worthy of you," Mr. Prescott said. "A bride worthy of Him. I believe He would approve heartily of all we are about to do."

Bride?

The walls of the room seemed to close in, the gathering suddenly sinister. He tried to get free, but his body was still weak and would not obey him. His limbs were not under his control, his hold on this body faltering at hazy intervals. He couldn't move, held up by Katherine's uncle. This room was not his prison; this flesh was. His grip on the human language flickered in and out, and his head was foggy.

The priest spoke quickly, as if nervous and hurried, glancing at Mr. Prescott often. When he was done, Phillip cleared his throat, lifted a ring, and spoke. "With this ring I thee wed, with my body I thee worship, and with all my worldly goods I thee endow."

He stepped forward, sliding the ring onto Visander's finger, and then put his hand on Visander's cheek and leaned in as if he was about to—

Visander took him by the throat. *"Do not touch me, human."*

Phillip choked, and the room became chaotic; the people crowded in it tried to prize Visander's hand away from Phillip, shouting words Visander didn't bother to listen to. They finally succeeded, and Phillip staggered back, clutching his throat.

"Do not presume that because this body is weak I will not kill you if you touch me again," said Visander.

"I don't understand what she's saying," said Phillip.

"I'm sure she'll warm up to you," said Mr. Prescott.

"To those whom God hath joined together let no man put asunder," said the priest, quickly.

He came to at night, in a moving carriage with black rectangles for windows. It jolted and bumped, and a jerk on his arm made him realize he was tied by the wrist to an interior rail. His clothes had changed, heavy skirts and a vise around his waist that constricted his breathing. He jerked on the restraint, looking up to the two humans in the carriage with him.

Phillip sat across from him with a sulky expression, his arms folded, his head turned moodily to one side. He had the look of one who was greatly put upon, although he was not the one tied up, nor was he wearing a waist bind, as far as Visander could see. A memory of the priest conjoining him to this human in a bonding ceremony made something dark and risible claw up in him.

"Don't be afraid," said Mr. Prescott carefully. "We are taking you to a friend."

"I am not *afraid*." Visander's head for the first time felt clear. "If you and this trifling wish to live, you will release me from these bonds and take me to my Queen."

"You must know that isn't possible," said Mr. Prescott gently. "You were—dormant—for a long time. A lot has changed."

Something uneasy stirred in him then, a thought he did not want to face. The terrible satiny enclosure of the carriage was jumbling together with the padded satin of the coffin, as if dirt would soon start pouring in—

"Let me out," said Visander.

Mr. Prescott shook his head. "I told you, that isn't possible."

"Let me out!" Visander jerked at the railing with his bound wrist. "Human worm, you dare make me your prisoner?"

"You are not a prisoner," Prescott said. "But there are certain—"

"I don't understand you when you speak that language." Phillip's sullen voice cut into their exchange.

Prescott answered mildly. "Then you should have learned it, as your father asked of you."

A derisive breath. "Learn a dead language? What's the point?"

"For one, you could speak to your lady wife."

"She's not a lady. She's some sort of lunatic soldier from a dead world."

Phillip turned to regard Visander with an irritated expression. "Besides, she came here, didn't she? Oughtn't she to learn English?"

A dead language? A dead world? The satin walls of the carriage were closing in, and it was hard to breathe, Visander's head swimming.

"You're the heir now. In a few weeks, you'll be sailing for Italy. Your duty there is to—"

"*Simon's* duty," said Phillip in a bored voice, reciting it like a litany: "Simon's duty, Simon's ship, Simon's bride—"

"Let me out."

"Your brother took his role seriously—"

"*Let me out*—"

"She's talking again," said Phillip.

Another wave of dizziness. His comprehension of their human words was unsettling in its own right, like a last gift spat out from the mind of this dead girl.

"If you hold me here," Visander made himself say, "my people will not rest until they have hunted you down and killed you both."

A long pause followed, and Prescott was looking at him oddly. Then:

"Very well," said Prescott. "Stop the carriage!" He gave a sharp rap to the roof of the carriage. Outside, a faint "*Whoa there*" from the driver as Prescott moved forward toward Visander.

"What are you doing?" Phillip sat up in an alarmed posture.

"Letting her out."

"Are you mad!"

"No," said Prescott. "She needs to understand."

And he cut the ties that restrained Visander with a small blade he drew from his coat.

Visander was already half stumbling, half falling out of the carriage, legs tangled in his heavy skirts. At first, he just gulped in air, released from the confined inner space. *Free. Free.* Collapsed, his fingers curled into the dirt, grateful for its steadying presence. He finally pushed himself up, sitting back on his heels and feeling the fresh air on his face.

Then he looked out at the world around him.

His carriage was one of a train of four carriages riding in a small convoy at night. Men atop each of the carriages were pointing long tubes of metal at him, while Prescott disembarked holding up a hand, as if to ward them off.

They had stopped on a muddy cobblestone road clustered with unfamiliar structures, dark and stifling, reeking of smog and refuse. Thickly crowded, they were houses, hundreds of houses, a suffocating mass stretching endlessly from his vantage on the sloping hill, spewing burned tree smoke out into the air, loud with grubbing, grimy misery. He was looking out at a world filled with humans, living their short lives with no fear of the shadow, neither fleeing toward a mage, nor looking up with nervous dread for the death that came when the sky turned black.

The realization was rising in him like bile. He hadn't seen a single mage since he woke here, hadn't felt a single spark of magic, and that was its own stifling darkness, a terrible thought clawing its way up his throat.

"How long?" he demanded.

He hadn't seen anything he knew, not the soldiers on the long march into battle, not the winged creatures in the air, not the spires of the towers still not taken, nor the glories still remaining, defiant and unbroken, the strength of their last defenders blazing out into the night.

"How long?"

Galloping with his Indeviel, wind whipping his face, exhilarating in his bond with his steed. *You will have to leave everything here behind,* the Queen had said. He had made that sacrifice, with no time to say goodbye. He had not even had the chance to throw his arms around Indeviel's white neck and embrace him for the last time.

His Queen's hand on his face had made him shiver. He had sunk to his knees. *You will Return, Visander. But first you have to die.* A sharp pain in his abdomen, and he had looked down to see her sword in his guts, closing his eyes and opening them in—

—a coffin—

He had fallen to his knees in the dirt of the road, his skirts flaring out around him. "*How long since the war?*"

He was aware of Prescott coming up behind him as his flesh shivered uncontrollably, his hands splayed in the dirt.

"I told you," said Mr. Prescott, looking down at him. "We are taking you to a friend."

CHAPTER SEVEN

"DRINK."

The moment they had James safe back in the gatekeep, Will lifted a flask containing the waters of Oridhes, remembering how much it had helped him after he had been beaten in Simon's hold. It had been his first experience of the Stewards, Justice beside him in the dark, grimy inn room, and a taste of magic on his lips.

"If you don't mind, I've had enough water," said James.

He'd had to half carry James inside. Laid out by the fire on Will's sleeping pallet, James gazed up at him through wet golden lashes he barely seemed able to lift. He wasn't warming under the blankets, as if even the last scrap of energy his body used to make heat was gone.

"It's restorative."

"Compassion for the Steward killer?" said James. "Or are you just making sure I can open the next gate?"

Will hadn't known magic could drain someone to this extent. He hadn't known how magic worked at all. A part of his mind carefully collected the information: the magic came from within James, and he could use it up. He could use up everything he had.

He could have died fueling that gate. Will couldn't let that fact go. He'd asked James to do this, and James had stepped up and done it, opening a gate that in the old world had taken two to power, even though he wasn't trained and hadn't yet reached his full strength.

"I'm making sure you don't fall unconscious."

"A warrior who takes care of his weapon." James's words were brittle, armor hinting at a crack. "Polishes and oils it before he puts it away."

That felt too close to the secret part of him that had felt pleased to see James do as he ordered. That felt pleased that James was here, in a place he didn't want to be, only for Will's sake. It made Will want to keep him safe, give him warmth and approval, tell him he'd done well.

"You drained yourself." *For me.* "For us. I'm grateful."

James was gazing up at him, his hair still damp, his face pale against the cushions. His eyes were searching.

"You knew what to do," said James. "At the gate."

"And I know what to do after," said Will. "Drink."

He lifted the flask urgently. The truth was, Will had no idea if it would work. But as Will tilted the flask to James's lips, the waters had an effect, bringing a hint of color back into his skin.

"Now rest," said Will.

He pushed James's damp hair back from his forehead to make him more comfortable. Then as James closed his eyes and gave himself to sleep, Will rose from where he knelt.

He saw the others staring at him. It was Violet who took a grip of his upper arm and pulled him to one side.

"Will, what are you doing with him?"

She spoke in a low voice, glancing back at James sprawled out by the fire.

"He can help us," said Will. "He *has* helped us. He opened that gate."

"I know why he's here. I meant why are you fluffing his pillow?"

"I'm," said Will, "not *fluffing his*—"

"He's the Betrayer. You don't need to give him a hot drink and a blanket."

It was Will's turn to flush. James lay like a sleeping Ganymede, his enervated beauty belying the cruelty and destruction he had rained down on the Stewards. Will hadn't fluffed James's pillow, but he had brought him a drink and a blanket. And hung his jacket to dry on the mantel. And his shirt.

Violet said, as if she couldn't help it, "You were like this with Katherine too."

"Like what?"

Violet didn't answer, just stared at him flatly. "Did he at least say when he could open the next gate?"

"A day or two," said Will. "We can use the time to plan our approach better."

She had brought him to the far side of the room, out of earshot of the others. Grace and Cyprian were having their own murmured conversation closer to the door.

"I don't like it." Violet was frowning. "With the wards down, we're wide open."

He didn't like it either. "We make the best of it."

"I'll watch James." There was something challenging in her eyes, as though she was daring him to argue.

But he only nodded. The truth was, he trusted her to keep James safe.

And there was something else he needed to do.

He went out onto the battlements and looked out at the limitless space, the wide night sky and rolling marsh stretched before him.

Up here, the fallen wards made the Hall feel shockingly exposed. He couldn't help but wonder: If the other gates could be opened, could this one be closed? Perhaps it could, as the other three gates had once been closed. He imagined walking out of the London gate, then closing it from the outside, shutting up the Hall forever.

Sarah was on watch, ready to sound the warning bell, a peal of sound splitting the black ice of the sky if there was trouble. She stood like a custodian in blue on the wall lip. As Will drew closer, he saw that there was a small lumpen figure next to her.

"Can you give us a moment alone together?" he asked Sarah, and thought from her expression she was going to refuse, but after a moment she grudgingly stepped aside, moving away down the battlements closer to the bell.

The small figure didn't move, just stayed there, hunching even more. A gargoyle. A piece of stone.

"I don't want to talk to you," said Elizabeth.

"I know," said Will.

"I don't care what they're saying. You're not my brother."

"I know," said Will.

He sat down next to her. Their legs dangled down over the edge.

"When I find out what you did to my sister, I'm going to kill you."

"I know," said Will.

She looked like she'd been crying. Her eyes were red and puffy under the dark eyebrows. She stared out at the marsh in silence. After a long moment, as if curiosity had built and built until it overrode her determination to ignore him, she said:

"Why are your clothes wet?"

He let out a strange breath, and looked down at his sodden sleeves. He supposed it did look odd. The sky was clear, with no sign of rain, and he looked like he'd just emerged from a pond.

"We opened the east gate. It led to a kingdom so old it had sunk into the sea." That eerie dark vista swimming into view. "When the gate opened, all the water burst into the Hall."

"Fish too?" Her eyes were wide.

"I didn't see any fish."

"I like fish," said Elizabeth.

He looked down at his hand. Were these the kind of small conversations that families had? He'd never done this kind of thing with his mother. He felt the cold night air in his lungs.

"I never had siblings," said Will. "Just my mother. She raised me as best she could, but there weren't a lot of . . . I suppose it was difficult for her. I don't have any mementos. Except for—" He lifted his scarred hand to the medallion that he wore around his neck.

He felt like he stood on the edge of a precipice. Like it was the last part of himself that could be the hero the Stewards had wanted. A talisman of the Light, meant to fight the Dark King. He took it off and held it out to her.

"It's not much," said Will. "But maybe it will help you someday."

"It's old and broken," said Elizabeth.

She was clutching the medallion tightly in her small hand. Her words seemed to hang like the white thread of her breath.

"She would have wanted you to have it," said Will.

His neck felt bare; it was the first time he'd been without the medallion since Matthew had died.

There was a silence. In a voice that sounded like it had pushed itself out of her against her will, Elizabeth said, "What was she like?"

Will said, "She was like your sister."

"You mean she was beautiful," said Elizabeth. Under the frozen crust of the stars, she said, "Mrs. Elliott said Katherine was a gem of the first water, that means of the highest degree."

It had been Katherine's defining quality: beauty. Her family had pinned all their hopes on it. Simon, a connoisseur of beauty, had bought her with jewels and a title. No one but Will had seen her on the Dark Peak with Ekthalion in her hand.

Will supposed his mother had been beautiful too, but it was not his main impression of her. He remembered . . . He remembered most of all how much he had wanted to make her happy.

"Do you think she gave us up because we were too much trouble?" said Elizabeth.

"You're not too much trouble," Will said. "You're smart and brave. She gave you up to protect you."

"She didn't give you up," said Elizabeth.

"No," said Will. "She kept me right to the end."

"Why?" said Elizabeth.

Two different childhoods: Will had grown up with her, and Elizabeth had grown up without her. Now they were both here alone.

"I—"

CLANG, CLANG, CLANG!

Will's head jerked toward the sound as Elizabeth leapt up. *The warning bell.* Scrambling up, he saw Sarah shouting as she pulled on the bell rope. He couldn't hear her so close to the bell. He followed the arm she had thrust out to point into the dark.

Dozens of torches, accompanying hundreds of riders, all of them converging, like a wave of black water rising up to swallow the Hall.

Sinclair's men were here.

CHAPTER EIGHT

"HOW MANY?"

Violet saw Will and Sarah descending the steps, the sound of the bell still echoing. Sarah was babbling about, *Hundreds, there's hundreds.* Sinclair's men, here sooner and in greater number than they had hoped. The single lit torch flickered in the cold night air beneath the battlements.

"Can we fight our way out?"

Violet had her hand on her sword, ready to do whatever was needed to protect her friends. Because what Sarah was describing wasn't a scouting party. It was an army. The kind that was sent to take a castle. Sinclair's men were here to take the Hall.

"God, you Lions are all the same."

The familiar drawl from the gatekeep's door. Pale and holding himself up with a hand braced on the doorjamb, James looked like a consumptive heroine from a painting, the kind that dies beautifully.

"You can't fight them. This isn't an ancient battle. They'll have guns," said James, "and they will shoot you with them."

He was, frustratingly, right. But she'd once asked Justice why Stewards fought with swords instead of guns, and he'd said, *A magic user like the*

Betrayer can stop a bullet. Do you really want to face him unarmed after you've fired your only shot?

"You can stop bullets," said Violet to James. "Can't you?"

"Can I? Maybe when I'm not falling over."

"What a pity your magic gave out right when we needed it," muttered Cyprian.

"What a pity you have two saviors and they're both useless." James gave a thin smile as he gestured to Will and Elizabeth.

Sarah spoke up loyally. "Elizabeth has conjured light."

It was Elizabeth who answered with glum child pragmatism, "It's just light. It doesn't do anything."

"How much time do we have?" said Violet.

Baying floated across the courtyard, a distant herald of a phantasmal night hunt.

To her surprise, James paled. "Dogs?"

"Hundreds of them," said Will. "We saw them from the battlements, running ahead of the horses."

James pushed himself away from the door, then swayed. Will was immediately at his shoulder, catching his collapse. James said, "We have to go. Now."

"What is it?" Violet stepped forward.

He ignored her, speaking only to Will. "You need to get Violet out of here. Unless you want to be killed by your own Lion."

"*What are you talking about?*" said Violet, and James looked like he wanted to get as far away from her as possible.

"It's Mrs. Duval." James dropped his insouciant manner, his words serious. "If she sees you, she will turn you. We need to run."

"Turn—me—?" James wasn't even looking at her, his eyes fixed on Will.

"Mrs. Duval has her own power. I've seen her make Tom kneel. All it takes is a glance. You can't let her lay eyes on your Lion."

Violet felt fixed to the spot. Mrs. Duval had power over Lions? She wanted to say it wasn't true, but what if it was?

"There's nowhere to run," she heard herself say. "There's only one way in and out of the Hall."

Even as she spoke, she knew what came next, as if a dark torrent of fate was leading them all to a single destination.

"We can leave through a gate," said Will.

That unnatural wall of water rising in front of her and then exploding out into the courtyard was all she could think of.

"The east gate's underwater," said Cyprian, almost reading her thoughts.

Will said, "There are two gates left."

South, and west. South meant cutting directly across the Hall, a long path choked with buildings, hard to navigate, with uncertain footing. West meant following the wall as they had done that morning, but in the opposite direction.

"The west gate is closest," she said.

"You need to get me there now. We all die unless I get that gate open." James ignored her, speaking to Will in that private way they had.

"You're too weak," said Will.

"We don't have a choice."

The barks and cries of the dogs were now distinct, and accompanied by the occasional shouts of men. James looked afraid at the sound, throwing another tense look at her. She wasn't used to seeing him look like that. He was scared of her. She looked around at her friends with a cold, sinking sensation. With James gate-weakened, there was no one strong enough to stop her if James was right and she could be turned. If James was right, she could kill them.

Her strength was her greatest asset. Now it made her feel like a threat.

It should have been a battle, she thought. That was what felt right. Sinclair's men attacking and the warriors of the Hall holding them back.

Violet imagined the Stewards in white and silver manning the walls, a bright force ready to fight the armies massing in the black night below. That was how it was meant to have happened, not the six of them alone, with a child, unable to protect the Hall.

Will made the decision for all of them. "Grace and I will get the horses. Violet, you get everyone else to the gate." Grace gave her own short nod. Will said, "We'll rendezvous with you there."

"But the Hall—" said Sarah.

"The Hall fell when the wards came down." Cyprian was the one who said it. "The Elder Steward has given us our mission." He drew a breath and took a last look around the courtyard.

"Elizabeth!" shouted Will, and Violet saw that the girl was running back into the gatekeep.

Violet swore and followed her at a sprint, only to find that Elizabeth had grabbed a sheaf of papers, and was stuffing them into the front of her pinafore.

"It's my homework," said Elizabeth, defiantly. "Katherine told me when we ran to take what was important. I took this." She was white-faced, as though daring Violet to disagree. "I brought it from Aunt's house." Violet opened her mouth, then thought better of it.

"Oh, come on!" said Violet, grabbing the girl's arm and dragging her back out to the others.

She emerged just as James lifted his head, as if in response to some silent signal. "They're here," James said.

They had dropped the portcullis and barred the doors. Violet knew very little about castle warfare, and had imagined a frontal assault, Sinclair's men battering the doors until they broke through.

Instead she heard the whistling sound of ropes being thrown. In a flash, she realized the obvious: They weren't going to break down the doors. They were going to come over the walls. Then they'd open the gate from the inside, and let in the dogs and that woman—

"Get to cover!" Will said.

The first shot rang out from the battlements, exploding the masonry near her feet. She took James from Will, half expecting to have to carry him bodily. Then with the others she ran for the Hall door.

In fact, James kept up, a single arm slung around her shoulder, though he didn't look like he could continue his stumbling pace for long. The real limit was Elizabeth's child legs. Violet ushered the girl inside, then slammed and barred the door, trying not to think of James's warning that she was the real threat.

She could already hear shouts from the courtyard. She looked at James's pale face and Elizabeth's small body. Then she turned to Cyprian.

"We need to slow the men down, or these two won't make it."

"This corridor is a bottleneck," said Cyprian.

He had understood her perfectly, coming to stand beside her. The two of them would fight here, buying as much time as they could.

"The rest of you keep running." She gave the order as she pulled the Shield of Rassalon from her back. "We'll hold Sinclair's men here, then catch up."

Cyprian was already drawing his sword beside her.

The men came through the door, a dark burst of deadly intention, guns aimed right at them.

She had seen Cyprian practice in the training yard, watching from the sidelines sick with jealousy at his perfect form. She knew he was brave. After all, here he was facing down a charge, and doing it standing beside her, with no care that she could be turned into a weapon by the woman who was coming.

But she had never seen him fight up close.

The gunshots missed him: he'd moved based on the direction of the muzzles; he seemed superhuman in his speed, as if he was dodging the bullets themselves. He was already cutting down the first of the men as she flung up her shield and heard three bullets careen off, the impact jarring her arm. Their bullets expended, she knew not to give the men time to reload. She charged as Cyprian whirled and knocked a man down.

She fought beside him. His sword blocked the cuts she couldn't; her shield swung to knock back threats to his side and back. The Steward style was made for pair fighting, hers based on power, his on precision. Different, yet they fit, an exhilarating match. He flowed like water, into spaces and gaps. She blocked a hit, then took the man by the collar and heaved him bodily at his companions, who tumbled, broke, and ran.

In the pause, their eyes locked, a moment of startled recognition. The first wave was defeated.

And then the second wave arrived.

Outside in the courtyard, the portcullis must have been winched open, because this time there was a flood of terrifying dogs, followed by horses that Sinclair's men simply rode into the Hall. They could fight men, but not hundreds of crushing pounds of horseflesh. There was nowhere to run. In a last instinctive movement, Violet pushed in front of Cyprian, her body braced for what she couldn't stop, hoping that somehow her strength would be enough to withstand a cavalry charge.

Sudden as a cave-in, the roof above descended. Huge chunks of masonry extinguished the view in front of her.

She stared, stunned, at the fallen stone. Turning, she saw James in the passage behind her, one hand outstretched, the other clutching the wall, his face whiter than a Steward tunic.

"You're welcome," James said.

He saved my life, she thought in shock. Cyprian looked as if James had grown two heads. For a moment they both just stared at him.

Then Violet closed her mouth. "Stop showing off and go." She shoved James back down the corridor, with Cyprian following. She could hear the baying of dogs and the faint orders from the other side of the cave-in. *"Get to them! Break through, or find a way around. Now!"* She ran on.

A night hunt through ancient ruins. They covered ground as quickly as they could, but the dogs were never more than moments behind. She imagined Sinclair's men spreading through the Hall like poison through veins. It was the end of the Hall, she thought. She remembered Cyprian's last look around the courtyard, and wished she had given the place a farewell too.

Even Cyprian was panting and exhausted when they reached the rendezvous point, Will waiting by the gate on Valdithar. Grace was on one of the two surviving Steward horses, with the second on a lead alongside James's black Thoroughbred and Katherine's and Elizabeth's horses, Ladybird and Nell. Enough horses for everyone, if she and Cyprian rode double.

It was unsettling at night, a towering arch crowned with a sun symbol. The sun took on a strange quality in the dark. *Night sun,* she thought suddenly, and shivered. She remembered that horrifying wall of water. They had no idea what lay on the other side of that gate.

Growing closer, the sound of dogs, baying for blood.

She came forward quickly, forcing her nerves down. Before any flare of magic, she had to do the heavy physical work of opening the rusting doors. James was approaching beside her. His shirt and jacket still trailing open, he looked like he could barely stand. Was he strong enough to open the gate?

She couldn't worry about that. Remembering the shriek of protesting metal when she had forced open the ocean gate, she said to James, "Be ready to work fast. The second I force the doors, they'll hear where we are."

James stepped forward, nodding once. She waited until he was in position, with his hand on the sun symbol carved at eye level beside the arch. Then she pushed against the doors.

The scream from the gate was frighteningly loud in the cold night. She paused, panting, and in the silence, a chilling returning cry drifted back to them, the dogs alert to their location. Her mind flickered with the uneasy thought *Some doors aren't meant to be opened.* She ignored it, muscles cording with effort, and pushed harder.

The first give, a gust of air, a widening gap. Above her the carved sun hung over a void. The huge doors stood open. She looked out into the black nothing.

"They're coming," said Cyprian in warning.

"Hold the horses," said James. "They spook around magic."

Instinctively, she and Cyprian ranged out to guard him. It reminded her uneasily of the three Remnants surrounding James on the London docks while he gathered his power. She knew James's need for concentration left him vulnerable. She felt uncannily connected to an ancient practice of warriors fighting to keep mages alive, because only magic could defend against shadows. It made James a high-value target. She could imagine a long-ago battle and the cry going up: *Protect the mage!*

"Stay close to the gate," Will warned. "We don't know how long James will be able to hold it open."

Or if he can open it at all. Nothing was happening. There was no flare of light or change in the view under the arch. *He's too weak.* James looked exhausted, eyes shut and jaw clenched with effort. If James couldn't open the gate, they would all be trapped here.

"There they are!" The first of Sinclair's men appeared in the courtyard, one of them shouting, *"It's Simon's Prize! Don't let him use magic!"* Another lifted his pistol, pointing it right at James.

She was running before she knew it, running hard.

"Violet!" shouted Cyprian as she threw her arm up into the path of the bullet, feeling it hit her shield with a silent apology to Rassalon. *Protect the mage!* She only just evaded the slashing blade of a knife and saw another man lifting a pistol. And then she was in the thick of it, fighting.

The jaws of a dog were opening for her throat; she swept at it with her shield before she came up and knocked out the man with the pistol, slashing the arm of the second. She barely glimpsed Cyprian urging his horse hard into a tangled clump of Sinclair's men as she swung her head toward the gate.

James was visibly shaking, his hair damp with sweat. Will was between James and the attackers as if he could act as a human shield. But there was no way she and Cyprian could hold Sinclair's men back, there was no natural chokepoint here, and men and dogs were already spilling into the courtyard, a buckling, overwhelming force—

She screamed, "James, open the goddamned gate!"

Elizabeth was shouting at him, "Do it! Do it now, stupid!"

James redoubled his effort, chanting something under his breath to no effect. Will wheeled his huge black horse, like a dark avenging angel, and shouted, "James, *aragas!*"

James let out a wrenching cry, as if something inside him was tearing, and a visible surge of power arced from him into the carved sun.

Balefire shooting skyward, then a hole in reality. It towered over them, Sinclair's men dropping their weapons to stare dumbfounded or cower back from it like supplicants hiding their eyes from God. The gate blazed open, and Violet saw the impossible. A dark vista; not England, a foreign land opening up before her eyes. A wave of disorientation, because the moon was above her, but she could see a second moon through the gate, as two distant parts of the world were brought together by unnatural magic.

"I can't hold it!" James's voice was thick with effort.

"Go!" screamed Violet. "Go!"

Grace brought her hand down hard on the rump of Cyprian's horse so that it bolted across. Elizabeth was forcing Nell the pony after them. Will drove his huge black horse forward, grabbing James by the collar of his jacket and physically dragging him across the gate's threshold. Violet brought up the rear on foot, grabbing Sarah's bridle and hauling the spooked Ladybird toward the gate. She was almost through—

Everything stopped.

She couldn't move. She couldn't speak. She couldn't breathe.

A woman was walking out across the courtyard.

She had large somnolent eyes and a severe nose, with shiny black hair pulled back from her face. She wore trousers as Violet did, with a high-necked jacket and boots that rose above the knee. She had the confident grace of a predator walking among easy prey.

And Violet knew, as Ladybird's bridle tore from her hands, that she was frozen because of this woman, and that her body was no longer under her own control.

Mrs. Duval.

James had said she would be turned. James had said she would kill everyone. She hadn't been scared enough of that, but the cold fear flooded her now, at the loss of any control over her limbs. She couldn't move. She couldn't fight.

She could see the gate, and beyond it her friends. She was close enough to smell the scent of cedars and the crisp green of a forest at night.

"Violet!"

Will, wheeling back toward her, was too far away. James, half-collapsed in Will's grip, was too weak. And Grace was holding Cyprian and his horse.

But Elizabeth had dug her heels into Nell and was driving straight for her.

As Violet watched, Elizabeth raced her pony back over the collapsing threshold of the gate. She was screaming silently, *No, Elizabeth! Go back!*

The gate flared, then shut. Unable to move, Violet saw the faces of the others—Will's horror, Grace's shock, Cyprian's desperation—a second before they vanished, leaving her, Elizabeth, and Sarah behind in the courtyard.

CHAPTER NINE

WILL'S STOMACH TWISTED with dizzying disorientation as the ground under his horse's hooves changed from paving stones to soft grassy earth. Turning his horse desperately, he saw a single glimpse of the courtyard silhouetted through the arch, Violet frozen in place, Sarah trying to control Ladybird, and Elizabeth riding furiously back into the Hall.

And then the courtyard was gone, vanished; under the arch a wide night sky pricked with stars.

It was cold and quiet. Dark shapes of beech, ilex, and ancient oak stretched out for hundreds of miles.

He stared. The air smelled different. The moon was in a different place; the sight caused a second wave of dizziness, as if the whole world had shifted around him. His thoughts still pounded with the chaos of the courtyard battle, but there was no battle here, just the silent slope of a mountain scattered with forest. Through gaps in the trees, he could see moonlit glimpses of a dark, tree-thick valley and distant rising hills.

"*Violet!*" screamed Cyprian, throwing himself down from his horse and running for the gate.

Will was moving before he realized it, down off his own horse, grabbing Cyprian desperately back before he threw himself through the stone archway.

"Take your hands off me!" Cyprian was struggling. "We can't leave her! We can't leave her there!"

"Look at where you are!" said Will.

For this lone stone arch stood high on the edge of a mountain cliff, and to pass through it was to hurtle over.

Cyprian gasped and seemed to see it for the first time. Stones from their feet dropped away into the dark as Will teetered, then flung Cyprian back to stagger three paces, collapsing unbalanced to his hands and knees, the two of them panting.

Will clutched the stone of the arch and its invitation to death: a leap out into the darkness to hover, then plummet. Nausea rose, as though the ground tilted. The sense of displacement was immense, the countryside around him taking on an unreality.

He had been spat out of a courtyard that had now disappeared. Only Cyprian, James, and Grace were here with him. The others were still trapped in the Hall—

Violet. He had made a terrible mistake. No one was meant to have been left behind. The chaotic chase in the Hall and the gate's hemorrhagic pull on James had wrecked them. He'd had his world ripped away from him, and it had happened with frightening ease. He felt as he had when Katherine had picked up the sword at Bowhill, as if he was stumbling through a world that he didn't yet know or understand, fighting a past self who knew it only too well.

Elizabeth—he'd made a promise to protect her, and instead—

They were alone on a mountainside, hundreds of miles from home.

He needed to get back to them. He looked up, seeking to reassure himself of the others' presence. Cyprian was on his hands and knees, pushing himself up and heading toward James, collapsed on the stone-strewn earth.

"Cyprian—" said Will as Cyprian reached James and dragged him up, pushing him against the stone of the arch with the terrifying drop behind him.

"Open it! Open it back up!" Cyprian said.

"He can't," said Will.

"I said *open it,*" said Cyprian.

"He can't, look at him!" said Will.

James was lolling in Cyprian's grip, his eyes barely opening, his face smeared with blood from his nose. He was too exhausted even to snark back.

"We need to get back to her!" said Cyprian, his grip tightening.

"*Stop it!*" said Will. He pulled Cyprian away from James, who was immediately sent sprawling to his hands and knees, a stumbling collapse, too close to the beetling edge. "Stop—it won't get us back there!"

Cyprian made a guttural sound of frustration. "She's trapped there," he said. "And Sarah. And Elizabeth!"

"And James is the only person who can open the gate!" said Will, standing between Cyprian and James. "Are you going to kill him? Throw him off the cliff?"

He could see the full truth hit Cyprian. He seemed to take in his surroundings, the utter isolation of the mountainside. James, sprawled right near a cliff edge. And Grace, still on horseback, several feet to the left. The high crisp night air made the snap of a twig under her horse's hooves too loud.

"Then we wait," said Cyprian. "We wait right here, and as soon as James can open the gate, we go back."

"We don't even know where 'here' is," said Will. "We might be—"

They were cut off from their strongest fighter. They didn't know what they had arrived into. Had the gate flared when they had crossed over? Were there legends here that something might come through? The landscape suddenly seemed sinister, full of the unknown.

"Look at the gate," Grace said.

She was gazing up at the colossal structure of the arch, so different from the one on the Abbey Marsh.

A sun emblem was carved at its crest, a circle with curling rays. The arch itself was intact where the arch on the marsh had been broken. It was monumental, wide enough that two horses could ride through abreast. That thought was disturbing: a procession into thin air; the other side of the gate was a sheer drop.

"The Leap of Faith," said Grace, in a reverent voice. "That's what the Sun Gate is called in the old writings. I never understood why, until now."

The Blind Leap had been the words written on the map. Will shivered at the new name. Faith indeed: if the gate closed as you stepped across, you would plunge.

"This is the Sun Kingdom," said Grace. "We're really here. We're really—"

"What's that sound?" said Cyprian.

A rumbling, muted and dull, but familiar from the battlements when he'd first seen Sinclair's men riding across the marsh.

"Horses!" said Will. All the old instincts came flaring back into life. *Stay off the roads. Stay out of sight. No thoroughfare is safe.* "Move! We need to get to cover—!"

"Get me up," said James, his voice barely a whisper.

No time for niceties. He slung James's arm over his shoulder and dragged him up. Was it his imagination, or was James lighter than he had been yesterday? James felt barely there, as if the gate had hollowed him out. Will thought with a shiver of the Elder Stone, vanishing into air with every use.

Will passed the tree line while Cyprian and Grace took the horses, racing under the shadowed canopy and out of sight of the road. He could already see points of light flickering through the thick foliage and moving along the curves of the road, torches held aloft by riders—

"Get back!" said Will, leading Valdithar in front of Grace and Cyprian to block any pale glimpse of their white horses from view.

A mounted squadron was trotting with military precision on the road below, right where they had been. Flaming pitch torches lit the two front riders, who held banners aloft. Those farther back were harder to make out. At least two dozen men, wearing black livery, with leather straps across their chests and long muskets at their backs. But it was the undulating banners that Will fixed his eyes on. They bore a symbol he had grown to hate.

"The three black hounds," said Will, his stomach twisting. "Sinclair's men."

"How can they be here already?" said Cyprian.

Will mounted and pulled James bodily up with him. "They didn't follow us through." As they rattled past, he saw that the soldiers were accompanying two covered wagons. "They were already here." Was Sinclair one step ahead? Had he already found what he sought in the Black Valley? "We need to go, now."

As gaps in the trees opened, Will heard faint sounds. In the night silence, distant clangs, metallic and arrhythmic, but constant. It sounded like the clamor of the docks, where the industry of a thousand men combined in a hammering, banging cacophony.

"What is that?" said Cyprian.

"It's coming from that cliff," said Will.

There was a faint light there too, limning the edge like an unnatural sunset. The sounds grew louder as they drew closer.

Will went cold at the sight that stretched out beneath him.

Half the mountain was missing. In its place was a huge earthworks, lit with the red flame of torches that gleamed like embers in a fire grate. It stretched out into the night, an unearthing; a yawning pit, and from it the gates and towers of a black citadel were half-revealed, emerging from the mountain like a dark Stymphalian bird from the egg.

And the sounds—the sounds they had heard—

They weren't the sounds of dock work. They were the sounds of digging.

Picks and shovels, ceaseless, hundreds of men working through the night. It was a single vast excavation, the mountain reverberating with the clangor of metal hitting rock.

"Sinclair's digging up half the mountain," said Will.

He had known that Sinclair had digs: the gentleman archaeologist plucking morsels from across the globe, displaying his prizes in England. He had known archaeology was the basis of Sinclair's disturbing magical collection.

He had never imagined an excavation on this scale, a black hole in the earth, consuming the mountain.

"Why? What's Sinclair looking for?" said Cyprian.

It was as if the answer was on the tip of his tongue. He couldn't drag his eyes from the hole. If he stayed here, what would he see unearthed? A shape that he recognized, spires and cupolas pulled up out of the dirt like a terrible memory that surfaced when all had thought it forgotten.

"That's far enough," said a man's voice, and Will turned to see five of Sinclair's men with pistols, pointed right at them.

CHAPTER TEN

"*LET ME GO!*" Elizabeth tried to breathe, but had a man's heavy palm over her mouth, stifling with the smell of dirt and flesh. Panicked, she tried to kick and get free, but her captor held her with frightening ease.

Across the courtyard, Sarah was being dragged from her horse by the hair. "*They're not here!*" Elizabeth heard the men around her saying. "*They vanished!*" There were shouts and chaotic movement by the gate.

She saw Violet kneeling next to the woman called Duval, and that was all wrong. Violet wouldn't kneel. Violet would fight.

"No!" Elizabeth said, or tried to say, the sound muffled. As she had charged back through the gate, all Elizabeth had been thinking was that Sarah was being stupid and didn't know how to ride Ladybird. You couldn't tense up or yank on the reins when Ladybird was spooked, you had to relax and stay as calm as possible. She had been going to tell Sarah that. But then the men had closed in, pulling her off Nell, and the gate had winked shut, and the awful feeling came that they were cut off here.

Get up, Violet. Get up. But Violet didn't get up. Something about Mrs. Duval was stopping her.

"They haven't vanished into thin air," said Mrs. Duval. "They went somewhere." A few of the men had reached the gate and passed harmlessly through it, out beyond the outer wall and onto the empty marsh, where they looked around with confusion. Without taking her eyes off Violet, she said, "Brother, find out where they went."

Brother?

A man stepped out in front of Sarah. He had the same dark hair, but in his case the strong features were caved in by three claw marks, scars running diagonally across his face. He carried a cane and leaned on it when he walked, which he did with a pronounced limp. "Your friends. Where are they?"

When Sarah didn't answer, he hit her across the face with the cane. "I said, where are they?"

Sarah didn't speak, just curled in on herself. Elizabeth's hands became small fists. *Get up, Violet. Get up, get up—*

"Are you protecting them? They left you here." He hit her again.

Sarah made a sound of pain but didn't speak.

"Tell me, or I promise you—" The cane lifted.

"*Leave her alone!*" Elizabeth sank her teeth into the hand covering her mouth and stomped down on her captor's foot. "Ow!" said the man. His grip loosened, enough for a small girl to slip.

"Stop it!" Elizabeth flew at Mrs. Duval's brother, pummeling him with her fists. "Stop hitting her!"

He didn't react beyond a single swear word, so she snatched the knife that she saw under his black coat and stabbed it into his thigh, and he swore again and grabbed at his leg. "You little—"

Elizabeth kept swinging the knife as Mrs. Duval's brother made a garter out of his fingers, blood welling up from between them. "*Somebody deal with her,*" he ordered, and Elizabeth didn't have a plan after that, but maybe Violet would get up, maybe the others would come back, maybe Sarah would—

A pistol shot, like the sound of a branch cracking.

Everything stopped.

In the silence that opened up, Elizabeth found herself panting, slippery knife in hand. The men had fallen back from her, but it took her a long moment to see why.

A mousy-haired man on the edge of the skirmish was holding a pistol pointed right at her. It was smoking. He had fired it. *Deal with her*, Mrs. Duval's brother had said.

But she wasn't hit.

Sarah, Elizabeth realized as her hands began to shake. Sarah had torn herself free to throw herself in front of the shot. She was collapsed on the ground in front of Elizabeth, hands on her abdomen.

"Hold your fire!" said Mrs. Duval, and only then did Elizabeth see that there were many men holding pistols at the ready.

Elizabeth found herself standing next to Sarah in a little cleared circle, the knife clutched in both her hands so tightly it was shaking. She could see Sarah's blood spreading out on the ground. The man had been aiming low, for Elizabeth. The bullet had hit Sarah in the stomach.

"Put the knife down, or I kill the Lion," said Mrs. Duval.

Elizabeth looked up to see Mrs. Duval holding a pistol of her own right at Violet's temple. *Please get up, Violet.* Sarah looked hurt. Badly hurt. And there were pistols pointing at Elizabeth too, men ready to shoot her from all points of the yard.

"It's all right, please," Sarah said, though she didn't look all right, she was bleeding, there was so much blood. "Please, Elizabeth, put down the knife."

Elizabeth let the knife drop from her fingers.

"I'm sorry. I'm sorry, I didn't mean—"

Immediately, she was grabbed again and pulled away from Sarah, who was also taken in the grip of one of the men and hauled to her feet, with no care for her red-stained tunic.

"Throw the girls into the wagon," Mrs. Duval said. "The Lion comes with me."

Elizabeth hit the wall of the wagon with a jarring burst of pain in her shoulder.

The wagon was stuffed full of as many bits of the Hall as the men had been able to grab at short notice, and Elizabeth pushed up from where she found herself sprawled over bags full of lumps, with her hands tied in front of her. And Sarah—

Sarah was already inside, lying in the far corner.

"She's hurt," said Elizabeth, but the man ignored her and just slammed the door closed. "She needs a doctor. She needs a doctor!"

Silence answered her. A second later the wagon jerked into motion.

"I'm sorry." Sarah's voice was barely there, as if she was using all her strength just to whisper. "If I hadn't lost control of my horse—"

Sarah wasn't getting up from where she lay. She was pale and breathing shallowly and there was so much blood on her blue tunic.

Simon kills women, Katherine had said, but those words hadn't been real to Elizabeth.

The morning after the Shadow King's attack, Sarah had taken Elizabeth's hand and shown her courtyards and gardens with strange and beautiful flowers, a pond with carp in it, a tiled mosaic of a lady. She had told Elizabeth about a time when the Hall had been a place of knowledge and learning, drifting chants, and the simple, ordered life of the Stewards.

The men had thrown Sarah in here like a sack into a warehouse. Elizabeth didn't know what to do. There was so much blood. Elizabeth took Sarah's hand and held it.

"We're going to Ruthern. They'll have a physician. And they'll have—" She thought about what Katherine would like. "Cream meringues. And jellies. And apricot ices."

"That sounds nice," Sarah said softly. "We don't have those in the Hall."

Sarah was like Katherine. She liked nice things, and making things nice. Sarah had tended the Hall's flowers. She had liked the simple pleasures of planting them, and watering them, and sketching them. *We have flowers that grow here that don't exist anywhere else in the world,* she had told Elizabeth. Then the look in her eyes had turned sad. *Had.*

Katherine had never done well when bad things happened, like when the goat Mr. Billy had gotten into the laundry, and Katherine had cried about her dress and not seen the funny part. Katherine didn't like blood. Katherine didn't like guns. She would have been very frightened, in a wagon in the dark.

"Don't frown," said Sarah, softly.

"I'm not frowning."

"I know I'm not very brave. But I won't tell them what you are. I'll die first." She was so hurt the words were a whisper.

"Shut up. You always think you're going to die. You're not going to die. Shut up." She was holding Sarah's hand tightly.

"All right," said Sarah, with a small smile.

He was shooting at me, she didn't say, in the dark. *He was shooting at me. You didn't have to.*

"I'll make it so that things are nice," said Elizabeth in a rush. "I won't frown. I won't mess things up. I'll find you a—a dress of the first water. And I'll, I'll let you ride Nell, she goes nicer than Ladybird."

"Did you know," said Sarah softly, "I was a janissary because I failed my test, but I always wanted to be a Steward."

"Sarah," said Elizabeth.

"Look up," whispered Sarah. "Do you see? Even in the darkest night . . ."

Her fingers in Elizabeth's went slack, and the light in her eyes went out. There were no stars above, just the wooden covered wagon. Elizabeth held her hand until it went cold.

She cried for a long time. Then the feelings inside her became a kind of tempest. "Hey, help us! Help us!" She kicked the door, but it didn't do anything. They just rode on with Sarah in the corner. They rode for long enough that Sarah stopped being a person and just started to be a body, a thing that would have to be carried out when the wagon stopped.

She pressed herself against the wood of the wagon. She thought of the Tree lighting up, and tried to will something to happen. *Light up!* She tried with all her might. But nothing changed in the dark, enclosed space of the wagon. Sarah had died protecting the Blood of the Lady, when that didn't matter. Light didn't matter. The Lady was useless.

Finally, the carriage stopped.

They had traveled for hours. They might be in London, or farther.

She wiped her eyes on her sleeve. What would Violet do? She fixed the idea of Violet in her mind. Her short dark hair and strong profile. The way she had drawn a sword from its back strap in one smooth motion. Violet was strong. Violet did things.

Violet would get out.

Elizabeth drew in a breath. The men outside were shouting, and probably unloading the other wagon. It was still dark. And it was raining. She thought that was good. By the time they were finished unloading, the men would be wet and tired, and she would be fresh and rested.

First she had to free her hands.

Violet would simply snap her bonds, but Elizabeth couldn't do that, so she shifted around and tried to wiggle her fingers into one of the sacks.

Groping, she felt something round and flat and made of porcelain, which she smashed, wedging the edge and using it to saw open the rope tying her wrists.

Now she had to get past the men outside. How would Violet get past them? She remembered Violet swinging her shield in the courtyard. Elizabeth groped around more deeply in the sack until she found something heavy. It was a firedog.

She crouched in the dark with it, while the men moved around outside. After a while, the activity and the voices faded along with the clinks of harness and the sounds of horses. Then the door opened.

Elizabeth swung the firedog.

She used two arms and threw her whole body into it, half expecting it to hit knees or a stomach, but the height of the wagon meant that it hit the man in the head. He made a sound, staggered, and collapsed, a slow, almost comical keeling over. He didn't get up.

She ran, ducking to avoid the grabbing of hands that never came, unseen as she ran through the stable's double doors and into a courtyard. Without breaking her stride, she saw the way out.

The courtyard was wide and dark, and she was running through the wheels and undercarriages and legs walking around near the inn door. There was a set of gates leading out, guarded by a watchman dressed in a shabby long tailcoat, his matted hair hanging in hanks about his face. If she kept running fast, she could get past him, because he wasn't very good at his job. He was talking to a kitchen maid and not looking at the gate.

As she ran, a door opened toward the rear of the inn. Men were rushing out with lamps and gesturing to move quickly, greeting a newly arrived carriage, shiny and black with three black hounds painted on the doors.

Elizabeth stopped running.

A young lady's shoes were stepping down from the carriage. She knew those shoes. They came from Martin's, white silk with a pink embroidered rose. She'd had every detail of them pointed out to her: the quality of the silk, and how the rose even had tiny green embroidered leaves, and how extremely they were *à la mode*, which meant *in fashion*.

Elizabeth's eyes grew wider and wider.

It was like a scene out of memory. That was Mr. Prescott offering his hand to help the young lady disembark, just as he had done at the inns on their journey from Hertfordshire to London. Those were the pearls and gloves Simon had sent on their engagement, sending the whole house into an uproar. That was the hairstyle Annabel had taken five weeks to learn, singeing her fingers on hot irons as she curled wet hair around strips of paper.

And the young lady, wearing a primrose dress and a new bonnet from which golden curls spilled, framing an oval face and wide blue eyes that Elizabeth would know anywhere.

Elizabeth said, "*Katherine?*"

CHAPTER ELEVEN

"WELCOME TO THE Bull's Head, Lady Crenshaw."

Visander looked around at the dirty inn, crowded and stifling, reeking of the barbaric human practice of searing animal flesh and consuming it. The floors were boarded and encrusted with grease. Bile rose in Visander's throat. The flue of a chimney stood out from the bare wall, black all the way up with soot from burned trees. Men were grouped around the fire, throwing their heads back and laughing raucously. At the tables closer to the door, he saw beards shiny with splashed beer, of which the room also smelled strongly.

"*You expect me to believe a friend of mine waits in this stench and filth?*" He lifted his arm to cover his mouth and nose.

"Be patient," said Prescott, beside him.

The obliviousness of these humans was surreal. Like lambs born in clover, they did not fear a threat. There was no lookout, no nearby shelter. They had no concerns beyond sating themselves, laughing, and shouting trivialities. It set his nerves on edge.

He realized he was braced for war, for the sound of the black horn, and the winged death from above, the shadow attack that always came.

He remembered the fields of Garayan, corpses rotting in their armor, the sky black with carrion birds as far as the eye could see.

And Sarcean, always Sarcean, whose dark whispers haunted his dreams.

A wave of uneasiness rolled over him. This world was thick with humans who seemed to know nothing of the war—who had never fled with the constant stream to the nearest mage because magic was the only thing that could hold back shadows, even as the mages themselves fell, one by one.

He had to believe that his Queen's plan had worked, that he had awakened in a time and place to stop Sarcean, that there had not instead been some terrible misfire that had stranded him in a human world in a frail human form. Yet with every grimy human sight, his choking, claustrophobic panic grew, stifling dirt filling up the small, cramped space in his coffin.

"I believe a friend of ours is waiting?" said Prescott.

"That is my cue to drink," muttered Phillip, peeling off toward the beer, as the innkeeper directed them to the third door at the end of the hall.

The room was small and dark, as if humans were a race that cleaved to dim caves. It was meant to be slept in: there was a bed, a small desk, a fireplace. The fire was consuming the last of its single log, its glowing embers provided the room's only light, along with a small lamp.

Inside he saw a human boy with a cap pulled low on his forehead, sitting on a padded chair in front of the fireplace, reading a book with a blue cover that he closed, turning and rising when he heard the door open.

He was young, perhaps fifteen, thin-limbed, with sharp features. His hair was white despite his youth. His skin was very pale.

He was no friend. He was no one Visander knew. Visander opened his mouth to say that.

Their eyes met. He watched the pale boy frown at him as at a stranger, then stop, his eyes widening in shock as he seemed to look past Visander's body to see the essence of him.

And it was something in his eyes—those colorless eyes with their hint of blue—that Visander recognized in turn, though he'd only ever seen them with a horizontal pupil.

It was him. Visander would know him anywhere. In any place. In any form.

Visander was striding across the room before the door even closed, his arms around the boy in a hard embrace.

"Indeviel."

He was here. Warm, flesh and blood, real and here. The relief was extraordinary; it crashed over him like a wave. He was speaking words of happiness, of gratitude; they spilled from his lips without thought. "You're alive. You're alive." He could feel his world restored in the warmth of Indeviel's body against his own. "I found you, and we are whole again."

The boy made a stifled sound, and with a violent spasm of movement flung him off.

Shocked, Visander just stared at him, as the boy stared back at him with pupil-dark eyes.

"Indeviel—"

The boy's chest was rising and falling rapidly, his body tensed for flight. He was staring at Visander with an expression Visander had never seen on him before.

"Don't call me that," said the boy. "That's not my name."

"Not your name?"

"My name is Devon. And you—you're not—"

The boy—Devon—was standing off from Visander as though he might bolt.

"Indeviel, it's me, Visander," he said. "Your rider."

Devon's pale eyes stared out of his face, his white skin blanched to a shocking shade, pale as a ghost.

"I know I must look strange to you, as you do to me, but—"

It was true Devon's form was strange, standing on two legs and speaking human words, but there was some essence of him that was the same, like wrapping arms around a curved white neck.

"You died," said Devon.

It was the first acknowledgment that Devon recognized him, and he ought to have felt a burst of relief.

"And returned, as I promised," said Visander. "This place—it was terrible to awaken here and think myself alone. So it must have been for you here without me for dozens of years—"

Instead of speaking, the boy started to laugh, an awful sound. He said, in a voice of utter disbelief, "Dozens of years?"

"Devon." Visander said the unfamiliar name, and it felt so wrong, like the physical distance between them. Slowly, carefully, he said, "What is it? What's wrong?"

"What's *wrong*?" The sound of that terrible laugh rang in Visander's ears. "Years? You think that's all it was? You think you were gone like a man who steps out for a moment and is greeted as a long-lost friend on his return?"

"How long?" He remembered with a hollow, empty feeling the human world he had seen stretching out endlessly around him when he had stepped from the carriage. "How long have I been gone?"

"You died," said Devon. "And then everyone died. And a great silence fell; the silence of rot and emptiness and decay. And in the long march of endless time, sands covered the great cities, seas swallowed the buildings, and humans choked every part of this world."

The room felt too small suddenly, the walls seeming to press in on him, the lingering earthen taste of the grave filling his mouth.

He knew—he knew that he'd died and awoken. Yet the way Devon was looking at him . . . The crowding of time passing pressed at Visander. A world full of humans, oblivious to the dangers of the war. A world with no sights or sounds he knew, and no single spark of magic.

"Then who is left?"

"I'm left," said Devon. "I'm all that's left."

Visander remembered—kneeling by a sun-dappled stream, scooping up the refreshing water, sensing something behind him. Looking up, he had seen the shy creature watching, a young colt. Their eyes had met; startled, a flash of silver, and it was gone.

"It can't be."

A pale boy in a small, dirty room, dressed in crude human garments, wearing animal hide on his feet. Devon had drawn back, pressing himself into the opposite wall as if by instinct.

Visander reached out to touch him. "My steed, I—"

"Don't," said Devon. "I am not that young colt I was. I will not bend my head for your bridle, or take your bit between my teeth."

Devon's white face was cold as snow, his eyes like pale chips of ice. Visander felt dizzy.

"But you work with these humans. Why?"

"Because they're going to bring the old world back."

"Bring it back? How?"

"By raising the only one who can."

"No," said Visander.

It was as if the dark pit of the oubliette opened at his feet, a great abyss with no bottom. He remembered the shadows sweeping over the field at Garayan, the lights going out one by one. But he had always had Indeviel beside him. Now—there was a terrible new look in Devon's eyes that had never been there before.

"Who else has the power to remake the world in his image? To restore it to the way it should have been?"

"No," said Visander. "I don't believe it."

Devon said, "He will rise, and drive every human from this land."

As he spoke, he dragged his cap from his head, and Visander saw the misshapen stump in the middle of his forehead. He felt sick, a violent nausea, at a desecration even Sarcean had not dreamed to inflict. He imagined Indeviel downed, alone and afraid as they held his head in place and sawed off the horn.

"You saw the Sun Palace fall," said Devon. "I saw the world go dark, until only the Final Flame was burning. You think the war was the hard part? The war was nothing; it was the long dark that came after, the baying of the dogs and the hunt, our world turned to dust, until there was nothing left but humans, and I swore if I had my time again I would fight on the opposite side."

A unicorn, fighting for Sarcean. Visceral horror climbing in his throat—was the room getting smaller? Smaller and darker, like the inside of a wooden box.

As if for the first time, he saw the boy in front of him, two legs instead of four, human clothes buttoned up to his chin where there had once been the pure white curve of neck, colorless hair instead of that long waterfall mane, and a ruined stump in the middle of his forehead where the long, pearlescent spear of his horn should be.

The sight was so wrong that Visander felt the room starting to fade.

"Has it been so long that you've forgotten? What he was? What he did?" He stared at Devon as at a pale stranger.

Instead of answering, Devon said, "You can't fight him. You're too late."

"Indeviel, *what have you done?*"

He strode forward and gripped Devon by his two slim shoulders. He found himself looking down into a beatifically passive face, pale eyes gazing back up at him with utter assurance.

Visander could think of only one thing that could have caused this: Sarcean's cold, beautiful face, his eyes filled with terrible amusement.

He made a desperate plea. "You don't have to fight for the Dark. You can come with me. You're a *unicorn*."

He saw his words have no impact. How could Indeviel be so far out of reach, an untouchable white-haired boy, who seemed a thousand years away?

"There's nowhere to go," said Devon. "It's just humans, as far as the eye can see."

Visander's gorge rose, and suddenly the room was a small wooden casket, and he was choking, with the taste of the earth in his mouth.

"Don't you remember our vow to each other? The pledge we made before the Long Ride?"

Devon stared back at him, his eyes widening, as if the answer surprised him, when very little ever surprised him anymore.

"No," said Devon. "I don't."

CHAPTER TWELVE

"KILL THEM! THAT one is a Steward!"

"A Steward? Simon will pay, handsomely."

"What is your order, Capitano Howell?"

"Bring them here." The captain of Sinclair's soldiers spoke a schoolboy's Italian. He was young to be a captain, an Englishman of perhaps twenty-eight years, with a rigidly upright posture, straw-blond hair, and pale eyes. He dressed in the uniform coat of an officer, with its double row of brass buttons. But the coat was black instead of red, as if Sinclair kept his own army. A man drawn from the upper classes, Will thought.

The men with him were mostly locals, by their looks and their way of talking. The little Italian Will spoke he'd picked up in snippets of dialect from Neapolitan sailors carousing the banks of the Thames, or the few Piedmontese washed up in London reminiscing about their long-lost glories in battles against Napoleon.

But he understood the musket muzzle in his face and the words, *"Move and we shoot."* Will counted at least fifty men, all armed. Too many to think of resisting, even as he was taken by one of the men in a hard grip.

Last time he had been captured by Simon's men, Violet had rescued him.

It was hard not to think about that. He could imagine her saying, *I went to all that trouble to get you through the gate only for you to get captured on the other side?* He had to find a way to get back to her. Even as he tried to think, he felt the painful reality that this capture was taking them farther away from the gate.

Cyprian was dragged forward. "We know what to do with Stewards." This was in heavily accented English. The local who spoke took hold of Cyprian's chin roughly.

"Let go of him."

Near to collapse, James was holding himself up only with a hand on the trunk of a birch tree. His demand caused an outbreak of derisive laughter from the man holding Cyprian. He didn't let go but instead gave Cyprian's face an infuriating series of little open-handed taps, not quite slaps. With an amused look, Captain Howell looked down at James from his horse.

"And who are you?"

"I'm James St. Clair." James could summon an astonishing amount of arrogance for someone who was about to fall over. "And if you don't let them go, you'll answer to Lord Crenshaw."

A scornful sound from Captain Howell. "Lord Crenshaw?"

But one or two of the other men exchanged looks. *Il premio di Simon,* Will heard, alongside a few flickers of fear.

They didn't know Simon was dead. The news hadn't had time to reach them. Will and the others had arrived in an instant, but any messages sent from London were still traveling slowly across the Alps. Another wave of disorientation. Stepping through the gate was almost like stepping back in time, to a place where Simon was still alive and in power.

Captain Howell was neither cowed nor impressed. "Show your brand."

"If you know who I am, you know I don't have one," said James.

"How convenient," said Captain Howell. He was already gesturing to the man who'd held Cyprian. "Take him, Rosati."

An older man with the dark hair and olive skin of the region, Rosati was hesitating. "If he really is Simon's Prize—" Rosati spoke in accented English.

"He isn't," Captain Howell said.

Rosati took James by the arm with a great deal of trepidation. When he didn't immediately burst into flames, turn into a toad, or succumb to any magical malady whatsoever, Rosati seemed to swell in confidence, getting rougher in his treatment. "Move it!"

"*Hai ragione. È solo un ragazzo*," Will heard behind him. The other locals seemed to grow in confidence too.

"You'll regret this," said James.

"Will I?" Howell seemed amused. "Ride ahead to the dig, and alert the overseer Sloane that we have prisoners." He spoke to Rosati, who pushed the enervated James into the wagon.

The dig. It sent its shiver down into Will as his hands were tied behind his back roughly. He felt it, that dark shape they had seen rising out of the mountain. *There's something in these hills.*

"I want a dozen men out to search the area. If you see anyone, if you see so much as a single bandit sniffing for treasure, I want to hear about it."

Howell's eyes scanned the dark as Will was thrown after James and Grace into the first of four supply wagons. He found himself sprawled among blocks of black marble.

"Stewards! Where did they come from? We heard nothing from the scouts." Captain Howell's crisp, upper-class accent outside.

Rosati's uneasy voice answered. "You don't—you don't think they found a way to open the gate? Sloane says—"

"The gate is a myth," said Captain Howell. "Stewards are flesh and blood. They can't appear out of thin air. Can you."

There was an awful flesh sound of impact. Then another. Cyprian was thrown into the wagon a few minutes later, landing awkwardly, his hands tied behind his back. Even in the dim light inside the wagon, there was visible bruising on his face, which was wet from blood and spit. The fabric of his tunic was stained with blood, which had turned the star red. When he pushed up, his green eyes were fixed on James, full of anger, with something painful underneath.

"Is this how you treated Marcus?" said Cyprian.

James's own eyes were hazy, but his lips parted, and Will immediately kicked him with his leg. "Whatever you're about to say, don't." And then: "Here. Wipe it off on my jacket." Cyprian looked humiliated but wiped the spittle off his face, an ungainly process when he couldn't use his hands.

"We need to get back to the gate and find Violet." Cyprian said it through a bruised jaw and split lip.

"The overseer."

James's head rested against the black marble behind him; his words were little more than breath.

"He's a man called John Sloane. He'll verify who I am. He knows me." He said it with his eyes closed. "I'll get us out of this."

Cyprian's split lip curled as the wagon jerked and began to move. "Yes, selling yourself to Simon has proven so useful."

James's eyes opened, two lash-shaded slits. "You think you're so—"

"That's enough, both of you," said Will. "Arguing won't get us out of here."

The wagon was moving downhill along that old mountain path, a bumpy ride full of shouts and the sound of horses' hooves outside.

"You know something about it." He turned his eyes to Grace, who had spoken of it at the Leap of Faith. "About where we are."

"The Sun Kingdom," said Grace. "It was the first of the four great kingdoms to fall." She spoke as the wagon rattled onward. "There are records in the Hall in Latin, transcriptions of oral histories from the region taken in Roman times when the Dark King was thousands of years dead. *Finem Solis.* Sun's End. When the Sun Palace fell, a great darkness covered the land. They called that day—"

Undahar.

"—the Eclipse."

The words sank into him, and with them blossomed a terrible awareness of Sinclair's dig, all those men delving deep into the dirt, seeking in the mountain for something that should not be found.

"The seat of his power," said Grace. "He ruled from there, sending out his shadow armies to attack the other kingdoms. With the Sun King gone, it was given a new name—"

Undahar.

"The Dark Palace," said Will.

Or thought he said it. He felt a strange shaking, as if the ground swelled and throbbed.

"The Dark Palace?" That was James.

Cyprian said, "What is it?"

Breathless laughter, edged with bitter irony and exhaustion. "Oh God," James said. "I died here. That was what Gauthier said. Don't you remember?"

"Will," he heard.

"'Rathorn killed the Betrayer on the steps of the Dark Palace.' If that's really what Sinclair's digging up, we—"

"Will!"

Grace's hand was on his shoulder, shaking him. No, that wasn't the source of the shaking. The ground wasn't steady. He said, "There's—something—"

A lurch to the left threw everyone sideways. Another. Screaming—it was the horses, with men shouting at them and at each other. "*Stay where you are!*" Another careening jerk from the wagon.

"What's happening?" he heard Grace say.

"I don't know," said Cyprian.

Were hailstones hitting the wagon? No, it was rocks, as if someone had tossed a handful of pebbles from above, dislodged because the mountain shook. Will could feel it, an unearthly percussion; deep, deep down in the dark. Something under them was cracking open—

"Will?" he heard distantly. "What's wrong?"

"Stop," he said, or tried to say.

The earth rippled like a sheet, throwing the wagon upward, only to crash down again. And then explosions on either side of them, like the burst of cannons. Stone impacting on stone, all around them. The men were screaming, "*Rockfall!*"

A cascade; the air shook and rocks fell like celestial bodies, pulverizing themselves as inside the wagon they were thrown back and forth across the blocks of black marble. "*Stop.*" No one heard him over the screams and crashes from outside. "*Stop!*" The whole mountain was shaking. A jolt sent him sprawling forward. A moment later a slab of granite sheared through the corner of the wagon, and he glimpsed the outside. He saw horses rearing, torches dropped and burning, men's faces in a rictus as rocks fell like comets, like falling stars.

"*STOP!*" Silence followed the ringing command. He was curled over, gripping the ropes that bound his hands, panting.

The ground was still. The ground was still, but the power that had caused this . . . it waited, more sinister in its silence. *You're here,* it seemed to say. *And I am waiting for you.* Will looked up just in time to see Howell flinging canvas over the splintered wagon top, blotting out his view.

Will turned immediately to the others. Fear clutched at him. Had they heard him? Had they heard—?

Clambering upright, the others seemed busy with their own confusion, the rockfall too loud to let his call be heard. "What was that?" said Grace. "What was—?"

He could hear snatches of Italian from outside the wagon, calls to take up position and get things back on the road. It was terrible not to be able to see outside.

"I can hear them outside. They don't know what's happening," said Grace.

"It was an earthquake," said Will.

The surety in his voice was a mistake. He should sound as uncertain as the others. He wasn't thinking straight, his head whirling. He curled his hands into fists, remembering his time on the docks hiding the scar on his hand. *Don't. Don't let them see anything.* But they didn't seem to notice his slip, continuing to talk among themselves.

"They may be common in this region," said Cyprian. "We should stay alert for aftershocks."

There won't be any. He didn't say it aloud this time. The innate knowledge felt dangerous and wrong.

"Hya!" came the call from outside, the wagon jerked into life.

It was slow progress down the mountain. They stopped and started multiple times, the road littered with rocks and branches that must be cleared. The underground thunderstorm had ended, but the sense that he was approaching something terrible grew stronger. *I'm waiting for you,* it seemed to whisper. And the sounds of digging that had first been a distant echo grew steadily louder, as metal tools hit rock over and over again. By the time the wagon stopped, it was a cacophony, surrounding them on all sides.

The doors were flung open. Will half expected to see a towering palace, dark and beautiful, singing its siren welcome. He was shocked to find himself instead in a claustrophobic, canvas-pinned tunnel. The sounds of digging added to it, as if they were entombed in stone underground, trying to mine their way out with picks that made little impact. The lamps that hung overhead were modern, and there were patches of scattered dirt and stone on the ground where the earthquake had shaken it down from the roof of the tunnel.

"The men are frightened. No one wants to let them inside," Rosati was saying to Captain Howell, speaking in a low voice under one of the lamps. "They blame the newcomers for what happened. They're saying the earthquake is the work of the Stewards—"

"Get Sloane. Tell him I have prisoners." Captain Howell peeled off his riding gloves.

A man of perhaps forty years arrived just as Will was pulled out of the wagon. *John Sloane,* thought Will. *The overseer.* In a stiff waistcoat, a dark blue, long-tailed jacket, a brushed-forward hairstyle, Sloane looked like an inhabitant of an officious English clerk's office, not a torchlit tent encampment.

"I don't have time to deal with captured bandits, Captain," Sloane was saying with a wave of his hand as though his mind was elsewhere. "There are collapses and cave-ins all over the dig."

"These aren't bandits," said Howell. "They're Stewards. With a boy claiming to be James St. Clair."

"St. Clair! Have you had one of your turns? You think a wagon could hold that creature?" Sloane made an expression of distaste. "I met him in London. He might have the face of a mistress, but he has the heart of a monster, he would tear your flesh off your bones if you so much as looked at him."

"Sloane," James said.

Emerging from the wagon, James looked every inch his usual self, except for his color, paler than usual, and his hands, tied at the wrists in front of him. John Sloane blanched white, a frozen statue with his mouth open. He looked like a man faced with a nightmare.

James said, "I recall meeting you in London, too."

"Untie his hands. Untie his hands! Quickly!" said Sloane.

"But Signore Sloane—"

"I said *untie his hands!*"

The soldier nearest the door was fumbling with a knife, using it to cut the rope binding James's wrists.

"Mr. St. Clair. I'm so sorry. We had no message. No word that you were coming." Sloane was half bowing, half wringing his hands.

"I can see that," said James, and he put his freed hand casually on the side of the wagon.

"And—and where is Lord Crenshaw?" Sloane's eyes darted to the wagon, as though Simon might appear at any moment. He looked haunted.

"Simon will be here in two weeks. To view your progress personally."

"We thought we were on schedule," said Sloane, babbling. "We sent word only last week; we're close, we've uncovered several significant—"

"Then you have nothing to fear," said James.

His single hand on the wagon was the only thing holding him up. Will's stomach clenched, but Sloane was too terrified to notice.

Only Captain Howell looked skeptical, his eyes narrowing as they tracked over James. "Why haven't we heard he's coming? Why doesn't he have luggage? Why is his companion dressed like a Steward?"

James's blue eyes lifted to him.

"Captain Howell, please! My apologies, Mr. St. Clair, my captain doesn't know what he's saying—"

"That's quite all right, Sloane," said James. "Your captain simply wants a demonstration."

Captain Howell's expression changed. His face turned red, then darkened. He opened his mouth, a rictus: nothing came out. His hands lifted to his neck. He choked, coughing, scrabbling at his neck, as if trying to prize away fingers that weren't there.

Will felt himself flush, the slow, hot spread he felt every time James used his power, mixing confusingly with the throbbing in his head. Captain Howell was on the tips of his toes, as if hoisted. His face was now a violent purple, and his chokes were desperate, guttural. Will flung out an arm to stop Cyprian, restraining him with a hand on his shoulder.

"He's *killing him*," said Cyprian.

"No," Will heard himself say. "It takes a long time to strangle someone."

Sloane had also taken an abortive step forward. But he didn't intervene, taking his cues from James, his eyes flitting from James to Howell and back again.

"We're tired from the road, and we've been inconvenienced by your men." James spoke to Sloane casually, his expression serene as behind him Howell choked to death. "I expect you can show us to a room?"

"O-of course," said Sloane, laughing nervously. "We sleep in tents, but we have restored several of the rooms of the citadel. . . . If that suits you, of course?"

"It suits me."

James followed Sloane, Will and the others bringing up after him. Only when they had passed him was Howell finally released, dropping to his knees behind them, gasping in air desperately.

The dig in torchlight was a mess of tents, earthworks, and planked walkways over trenches. Half-excavated stone structures rose out of the dark, bristling with scaffolding. In the trenches, pickaxes rose and fell in continuous rhythm.

Sloane escorted them across several of the walkways to a tent, one of many pitched in the easternmost part of the dig, part of a barracks where laborers slept on hard ground. Sloane waved his hand at them. "These are workers' tents, for the menial class. Your men can sleep here."

Will felt James's hand come to rest on the back of his neck, fingers curling into his hair, a possessive gesture unmistakable in its meaning. "This one stays with me."

Will flushed, blood hot in his cheeks. He had not shared a room with James before. There had been two rooms at the inn at Castleton. Staying with James was a terrible idea.

Sloane looked nervously from one to the other. "Yes, of course, *Anharion.*"

He took Will and James to one of the stone structures, where he stopped at a set of doors, pushing them open while servants entered to light lamps and put torches into the two upright sconces inside the doors.

"These will be your—shared rooms."

It was disturbing to see that their rooms had once been part of a building of the ancient citadel. Three steps down, a set of arches held by six pillars curling in unusual shapes, adorned with carvings he couldn't quite make out. As servants set out clothing, blankets, water, and cups, Will saw the room was kept warm by a fire of birch logs cut from the surrounding hills. Set along the far wall, the bed at least was reassuringly modern, an English four-poster with draped hangings and a headboard.

"A conceit, but"—Sloane smiled—"perhaps *He* slept here."

Will felt James stiffen, but all he did was say, "Leave us."

"Of course." Sloane bowed and left.

The instant the door closed, James collapsed. Will, ready for it, caught his weight and maneuvered him over to the bed. James's condition was worse, far worse than it had been in the Hall.

Will pushed back the covers and laid James down on the mattress, quickly taking out the flask containing the waters of Oridhes. James's lips parted and his throat worked when Will tilted the flask, and after long seconds, James's eyes opened slightly, a glimmer of blue under gold lashes. He was breathing easier, looking back at Will with hazy attention.

"I told you I'd get us inside," said James.

"And you did," said Will.

Sitting on the bed alongside him, Will gazed down at James, his shirt and cravat in disarray, his perfect hair tumbling out of its shape in strands that seemed to invite the brush of a finger.

His relief that James would recover almost spilled out into words. *You did it,* he wanted to say to him. *For me. I'm grateful.* There was a deeper part of him that was pleased in ways that he shouldn't be at how far James had pushed himself. *For me,* it also whispered. *You drained yourself. You gave me everything you had.*

"Your Lion is alive," said James. "Sinclair wouldn't have sent Mrs. Duval if he just meant to kill her."

James was trying to reassure him—half-dead, and still trying to prove himself. Had the Dark King ever seen him like this? Did James even know he was doing it?

But Violet was gone and no reassurance could bridge that aching distance. He couldn't forget that the gate had vomited him out here with James, locking him off from both Violet and Elizabeth, as if separating him from those most likely to keep him in the light.

"Just rest," said Will. "We'll talk tomorrow."

He stood up, picking up a cushion and a blanket and tossing them onto the long seat nearby, planning to sleep on it. When he turned back, James was watching him from the room's only bed.

"Shy?" said James.

Will put a hand on the back of the long seat. "I'll sleep here."

"He won't kill you just for lying down next to me," said James.

"Who won't?"

"You know who," said James. "My jealous master."

He wasn't talking about Sinclair. He was talking about another figure whose shadow extended out from the distant past.

"I think he might very well kill someone for that." The words just came out.

"Then stay where you are."

Mordant blue beneath his lashes. Will stopped, a breath in and out. Then he deliberately stripped off his jacket and waistcoat, so that he was down to shirt and breeches.

He came to the opposite side of the bed. An expanse larger than his room in the lodging house in London: there was no danger that they would touch each other.

"He never slept here," said Will. And again he heard himself: too certain. He wasn't being careful.

"I know," said James.

Hard to breathe around those words. If James had been Cyprian or Violet, he would have helped him out of his jacket and boots. He didn't, wondering if that gave him away. Or perhaps no one was casual with James, who likely didn't faint into men's arms often. Or invite them into his bed.

"This wasn't the Dark Palace. They're digging in the wrong place," James said.

Will toed off his own boots. He didn't say that he knew it too, that he could feel it. James's words had taken on the tongue-loosened quality of one in a fever dream, or on the edge of sleep. Will drew in a breath. Then, because James had made it a challenge, Will laid himself down next to James on the bed.

He felt James shift, heard his sharp intake of air.

Will said, "Don't make me move back to the long seat, I'm comfortable."

James's voice was breathless with shocked wonderment. "Even when I see it, I don't believe it."

"What?" Will turned his head to find James's blue eyes on him.

"You're the only one who's not afraid of him."

Quietly. As though James didn't understand it. As though he didn't understand Will. It was the last thing James murmured as his lashes lowered and his breathing evened out. His sleep was one of utter exhaustion.

Will rolled onto his back, forearm thrown across his temple, staring up at the old stone ceiling. And because there was no one left awake to hear, Will allowed himself to say it.

"You're wrong."

The soft admission went unheard in the dark. His head throbbed; the mountain lay with its warren of empty undiscovered rooms and corridors silent and unwalked.

"I'm terrified."

CHAPTER THIRTEEN

VIOLET WOKE TO the creak of wood and the slapping of waves, and to the distinctive ridges of planking under her limbs and head. When she tried to move, she realized that her hands were manacled with the same strength-sapping metal that the Stewards had used to restrain her.

A wave of panic crested over her. She could smell the sea. It must be the sea, because it lacked the nauseating fumes of the Thames, and there was a briny salt smell, fresh and clear. And she had never felt a ship move like this on the river. There was deep water on all sides, lifting the ship up, then smacking it back down.

With each second that passed, she was sailing farther and farther away from Will.

She had to get out. Forcing herself past the dizziness that the Steward manacles always produced, she pushed herself up only to find herself in a large metal cage with bars. She swung her manacles at the cage bars. The *clang* rattled her bones, but the bars did not budge and the manacles did not spring open. Letting out a furious sound, she rammed the bars with her shoulder as hard as she could.

It did nothing. Bruised and breathing hard, she looked out at the hold. It was smaller than the *Sealgair*, but she could see the crates and tied stacks that were the ship's main cargo, herself merely an afterthought. Closer to her, she saw bins full of armor, several of them emblazoned with a star. She realized that she was looking at crates full of items from the Hall of the Stewards, and that she was part of a shipment of looted cargo sailing toward an unknown destination.

The hatch swung open.

Striding confidently in her long boots, Mrs. Duval came into the hold. She wore a different cloak, as if at least a day had passed since Violet's capture. At her side was the man from the courtyard, the one with his face carved out by three claw marks. He still carried a cane, his limp even more pronounced than it had been before Elizabeth had stabbed him.

Violet's eyes fixed on the metal object Mrs. Duval held in her hands.

In the next moment, she flung herself up and over to the bars. "You give that back!"

"Now, now," said Mrs. Duval. Their eyes met, and Violet's limbs seized up. Just as she had been in the Hall, she was being held in place. Her hands were on the cage bars, but she couldn't move them.

"You care about this quite a lot." Mrs. Duval held up the Shield of Rassalon, turning it over speculatively. "It's broken."

"You don't deserve to touch it!" spat Violet.

"I'll confess, I don't care about an old shield," said Mrs. Duval. "But a Lion is big game." She kept her eyes on Violet, with the hypnotizing power of the snake, as Violet was unable to look away. "The biggest game I've ever brought down."

Violet felt a violent hatred of everything that was happening. She hated the cage. She hated being frozen, unable to move. She did not want her shield in the hands of that lady.

"Where are you taking me?" said Violet.

She wanted out of the cramped hold of this ship. She couldn't be here, so far from the courtyard in the Hall of the Stewards. To have been ripped from the others, to know she was being carried farther and farther away with every passing breath—

"Step back from the bars," said Mrs. Duval.

"Where are you taking me!"

"I said step back," said Mrs. Duval, and to her horror, Violet found herself taking a step back. She stared in shock at her captors through the bars. Oh God, James was right: Mrs. Duval could make her do things. Not just freeze, but move, do her bidding. She had to force herself to think, to reason, though her heart was racing.

"You can't control me all the time," she said slowly, "or you wouldn't have to use these manacles."

"Smart, aren't you," said Mrs. Duval. "But I expected Gauhar's girl to be smart."

The name seemed to drop into her like a stone into deep water. "Who?"

"You don't know your own mother's name?" said Mrs. Duval.

Violet couldn't move, yet she felt something inside her open that made her feel very young and small. *Gauhar.* She'd never heard that name. She'd never heard any name like it. Was it her mother's first name? Surname? Was that even how they did things in India? She didn't know, had never been told.

That woman, Louisa Ballard had only ever called her. *Don't you talk about that woman.* A memory worked its way free from that deep place inside her. A woman's voice, a wide river, steps leading down to the water where people were bathing, kindness and laughter. *Gauhar.* She clamped down on it, as if it threatened her safety.

"Do you not know what you are?" said Mrs. Duval. "Or do you only know what the Stewards have told you?"

"Keep your mouth off the Stewards," said Violet.

"Then tell me, in your own words."

She stayed stubbornly silent. She half expected Mrs. Duval's power to drag the words up out of her throat. When that didn't happen, she said defiantly: "You can't make me talk! Your power's not strong enough!"

"I can make you do this," said Mrs. Duval. "Leclerc, open the gunport."

Violet found her body made marionette, a horrendous feeling, walking forward against her will to stand at the bars in front of Mrs. Duval. With a short, sharp gesture, Mrs. Duval tore the star from the front of Violet's tunic. Then she gave an unpleasant smile and opened the front of the cage.

"Fetch," she said, and tossed the fabric out the gunport.

Violet tried to stop herself moving. She tried with every bit of strength and will she had. She was at the open gunport, and then she was climbing out of it like a hatch, staring down at the churning ocean water beneath where the ship's wood sliced it.

She threw herself over—almost. Suspended, her limbs wouldn't move as she teetered over the drop. She wanted to scream, knowing she hadn't saved herself. It was Mrs. Duval who had stopped her, frozen, on the edge of leaping.

"Shall I make you jump overboard?" said Mrs. Duval. "Lions aren't good swimmers."

Held rigid, she could make no gesture of defiance, her heart pounding. The ship rocked with the sway of the ocean, whose wet depths had so recently sprayed into the Hall through the gate. She remembered its ghostly underwater tower.

It was true that Violet couldn't swim, having never learned. She had grown up on the London docks, but no one swam in the thick molasses of the river. She imagined throwing herself over, not even struggling, just blindly jumping off. The water would close over her head, leaving only a foaming swirl, and even that would be swallowed up by the next wave.

"You won't. You need me alive." She made herself say it. "After you're done with me, you're going to give me to my father."

Mrs. Duval only smiled, a gleam of teeth. "Little Lion. You really do have no idea what you're caught up in."

"Then tell me."

"You think your destiny is to fight. But it's not." Mrs. Duval's eyes stayed on her, the unblinking stare of a reptile. "It's to be eaten."

Her blood drained while she couldn't move. She thought of her father saying he planned for Tom to kill her. Her father had built a cage in his house to hold her, and she had only just escaped in time.

"What is that supposed to mean?"

"You'll find out soon enough," said Mrs. Duval.

A stringless puppet, she was marched back into the cage, and behind her the cage door was relocked. She stared impotently under Mrs. Duval's cold eyes, until Mrs. Duval turned to the door. A release; the compulsion vanished.

Instantly, Violet was throwing herself at the immovable bars. But she found herself shaking, her legs barely able to hold her. Violet realized with a shock that she was exhausted: her muscles had been stiffened in a spasm the whole time Mrs. Duval had been controlling her.

"You won't get anywhere if you make my sister angry," said a man's voice.

She scrabbled around. With a shock, she saw that the man with the scarred face was still in the hold, standing back in the shadows, watching her. She had forgotten he was there.

"I'm Jean Leclerc," he offered. "You'll be in my charge until, well. Until our work is complete."

"What happened to your face?" said Violet. "Get too close to a cage?"

He flushed and the scars reddened. "You should count yourself lucky that you're not being taken to your friends."

"What do you mean?" she said with a cold stab of apprehension. "What do you know about them?"

"You should count yourself lucky," Leclerc said, "that you're—" Leclerc broke off, blinked, and his face almost rippled. "Violet?" She stared at him. He took a step closer. "Violet—!"

She stepped back instinctively, cleaving deeper into the cage. Leclerc blinked again and shook his head. He said, with a little confusion, "You should count yourself lucky." He shook his head again.

Then he turned and limped his way out of the hold.

CHAPTER FOURTEEN

SARCEAN WAS STRETCHED out luxuriously, on a sun-warm marble bench under a spray of orange blossom. The fresh scent sweetened the sun-dappled air, on which white petals drifted. He felt blissful contentment, limbs drowsy in the sun, shifting lazily from his back to his side, when he heard footsteps.

A golden figure was approaching up the path. Dressed in gold armor, pulling off his gold helm, loosing his gold hair to spill down his back. Breathtaking in the sunlight. And familiar, a beloved presence that brought welcome with it.

The king's champion, the Sun General. One day, he would be called Anharion. But that was in the far future. For now, he was—

He was beautiful, so much so that to look at him was to ache. But the real ache was the warm look in his eyes.

"I had not expected to find you here," Anharion said.

"But you came anyway," said Sarcean.

"I hoped to see you," said Anharion, and sat beside him, looking down at him.

His throat was bare, exposed skin, vulnerable as an unplucked flower stem. He wasn't Anharion yet. He wasn't wearing the Collar. The affection in his eyes was real.

"The king asks if you will join me for a demonstration fight at the games to celebrate his royal engagement."

"I must decline." Sarcean gazed up at him.

"I will go easy on you."

"Are you not the king's champion?"

A glint in those blue eyes. "I did not say I would not win."

Sarcean stretched, lithe as a fish, the silk of his own long hair spread out around him, night dark. He was aware of Anharion watching him. He knew that Anharion sometimes watched him like this, though he had taken vows, and it was forbidden.

"And if I were king?" said Sarcean.

"If you were king . . . ?"

He reached up and took a lock of that long gold hair, like sunlight spilling through his fingers.

The words were soft, too soft to be entirely playful. "If I were king, would you be my queen?"

"You dream." Anharion smiled, as if he indulged his friend's whimsy, though his cheeks burned.

"A pleasant dream," said Sarcean.

Anharion looked down at him and said, "Wake up."

Will woke with a start, staring up in confusion.

"Will, wake up."

"I—" he said, disoriented, unsure where or when he was. Anharion staring down at him resolved into a far more difficult person, whose eyes were a challenge or a provocation, and who held his lips always on the edge of a sneer.

"James?" said Will, dragging his mind into the present.

James relaxed and withdrew. Will saw all the other differences in a rush: Younger. The golden armor was now an elegantly fitted brocade coat. The way James moved showed a heightened awareness of his body, as if used to being looked at.

The absurd thought occurred to Will that if James had grown up a Steward, he would have kept the long hair.

God, they had been *friends*; they had served together at the same court, under the same king. That idea was so utterly new that he couldn't stop turning it over and over in his mind. There had been a time before the Collar, a time they had met in the sunlight, and in Anharion's warm words the sweetest hint of flirtation, an indulgence Anharion offered to no one else, though Sarcean knew well that Anharion would never—

"Strange dreams?"

Will closed his eyes to push away the past. He had to exert effort to keep his body relaxed and not curl his fingers into his palms.

"Something like that."

"It's this place," James said, frowning.

Will pushed up, leaving the bed. He made his way to the basin and pitcher, where fresh clothes had been laid out for him. He splashed water onto his face, the shock of cold intended to drive away the young man in his dreams.

No, what he'd seen—it hadn't been just a dream. It had been a memory, his feelings and reactions so strong he'd woken up with Anharion's name on his lips.

Careful. Oh, careful.

Casually, "Did I say anything?"

"'Run, run,'" said James, with a shrug. "You were tossing and turning."

The idea that he might talk in his sleep was not something he'd thought to guard himself against. But he should have. It wasn't the first time he'd dreamed of Sarcean, nights filled with flickers of that presence, that power blazing in his veins, shadows stretching out below him to the horizon.

But it was the first time he'd dreamed about the time before, when Sarcean had been a young man, when he felt like he was flesh and blood, full of hopes and feelings.

James said, "You can tell me."

He shouldn't. He shouldn't tell anyone. He knew what happened when he did. Katherine, his mother . . . James wasn't going to smile down at him as Will teased him about being his queen.

And yet . . . the temptation . . . to ask for acceptance and just once to find it . . .

"I dream about him," Will said, letting a single piece of the truth leak out.

His heart beating, he lifted his eyes to James. He didn't see immediate rejection. As the seconds stretched out, he thought—maybe—maybe. Pull like an undertow: he wanted to. He wanted to tell him, to find in him a harbor, where they could be two lost souls together.

James was Reborn. James knew how it felt to be judged for the actions of a past self. *I was Sarcean,* he imagined saying. *I'm trying to make up for it, to do good and help my friends.* For a moment the need was so great that his chest hurt. To have someone understand him, to have someone believe in him . . . He imagined James putting a hand on his shoulder, saying, *I don't care what you are.*

James's voice was eager. "Do you see how she kills him?"

"No," said Will, shuttering and turning away.

He made himself pick up a towel and casually wipe his wet face. Keep his motions simple. Keep any tension out of his limbs.

Just another conversation. Everyone wanted to kill the Dark King.

"And you?"

"Me?" said James.

"Do you dream about him too?"

James flushed. "You know what I was. You can guess what I dream."

Heat scalded Will's skin, the image of Anharion still half in his mind, the sweet look in his blue eyes as he gazed down at Sarcean, who had reached up to run fingers through his long, golden hair—

"No, I didn't mean—" James's flush deepened. "I don't remember my dreams. But sometimes when I wake up, I can't move. Trapped in sleep, but awake, and it's as if . . . there's a great power bending over me. And it's whispering—"

Find you.

"—I will always—"

Find you. Try to run.

The door to the room opened.

Will swung around, to see a young Mediterranean gentleman, followed by a young African lady in a green day dress.

"Well?" The young man said impatiently, "Can you open the gate?"

Who are you? Will opened his mouth to say, when the image in front of him resolved and he suddenly understood what he was looking at.

It was Cyprian and Grace, dressed in modern clothes.

Will stared at them. Cyprian wore a dark brown coat and very neat fawn trousers, his shirt somehow whiter and more crisply pressed than that of other gentlemen, as if displaying his overly proper personality. Grace was striking in a green dress that gleamed against her dark skin and set off her long, elegant neck.

"Well? Can you?"

James was still so pale he looked like a man dead, but he answered determinedly, "Of course I—"

"No," Will said. "He's not ready."

The others turned to look at him. He felt their surprise, and James's surprise. Will stared them down.

"We don't know that," said Cyprian. "Not until we try."

"He's too weak," said Will. "Look at him. Or can you tell me you wouldn't fall over if I gave you the slightest push?"

"I—" James began.

"I won't risk his life," said Will.

"You're risking Violet's life," Cyprian said. "She's worth a hundred of him."

"We don't have a hundred of him," said Will. "We only have one." He pushed Violet's absence aside. Solve each problem as it came.

"Then—"

"If James dies trying to open that gate," Will said, "it's two weeks over mountains, then a ship back to London before we reach Violet. This way, we—"

"Someone's coming," said Grace, before any of them could argue further.

A young local man in threadbare brown knee breeches and ankle jacks appeared in the doorway.

"Mr. Sloane and the other gentlemen are taking breakfast in the overseer's tent," said the young man, "if you would like to join them."

"Tell him I'll be there shortly," said James.

"Very well, Anharion."

And left at James's casual gesture. Will let out a breath he hadn't realized he was holding. Cyprian had a strange expression on his face.

"We play along. For now," said Will. "When we get back, we talk again about the gate."

Instead of answering, Cyprian kept staring at James. "They really call you that?"

James went toward the pile of clothes that had been left out for Will, perhaps part of Sinclair's cargo sent ahead.

"What?"

"Anharion."

"Why not? I'm betraying them, aren't I?" said James, with a thin smile.

And he tossed Will his clothes.

In daylight, the dig was immense, with an army camp's worth of canvas tents pitched amid ancient buildings half emerging from the mountain. They crossed plank bridges over huge trenches where laborers dug ceaselessly, others carrying stones and earth in baskets to dump in wagons pulled by long-suffering donkeys.

Even for a man like Sinclair, it surely represented a huge investment. Will looked around, cataloging each sight. It must have been active for years, off-the-books and hidden from the Stewards. The question was: What was Sinclair digging for?

"I look like Violet," said Cyprian, attempting to hide his legs with an ineffectual tug on his waistcoat, a chaste maiden forced into revealing garments.

"The dress is worse," said Grace. "You can't move in it at all."

"You two need to blend in," said Will. "Don't play with your clothes. Stay in the background. And keep away from anyone with a title or a posh voice."

"Don't talk to your betters," James elaborated unhelpfully.

"Who are our betters?" said Cyprian, dangerously.

"Everyone," said James, "but especially me."

"We're supposed to be his servants," Will hurried to say. "These people have a strict hierarchy, and we're on the bottom."

"I am not playing *his servant.*" Cyprian tugged again at his waistcoat.

"Nice legs," James remarked, making everything worse.

"*Blend in,*" Will said again, stepping in front of them.

Cyprian's green eyes flashed. "You mean act like an outsider."

"That's right," said Will.

"And how should we do that?" said Cyprian.

"Start by not calling them outsiders," said James as he passed them, stepping into the overseer's tent.

Inside, it was a picture of bizarre Englishness, a long table set up for breakfast, the silver trays heaped with bacon and halibut as if this were a London dining table. Plates were set with glasses and silver cutlery, and there were English teapots and sugar bowls in which the sugar in the humidity was slowly melting.

The seven men at the main table all stood up, hastily pushing their chairs back. They stood at rigid attention, their eyes fixed on James like the eyes of a rabbit as a wolf strolled into its burrow. *They're afraid of him.* Will recognized Captain Howell, with his blond hair brushed. He was dressed in yesterday's black captain's regalia, but wearing a new neck-cloth. The others were all in day clothes, Englishmen ranging in age from thirty to fifty.

"A breakthrough!" said Sloane, stepping forward to meet them. "Can you believe it? It was discovered this morning, thanks to the earthquake. After months, years of searching. The entrance to the Dark Palace is finally found. We'll make the first ingress after breakfast. Of course, you must lead the expedition."

"The expedition?" said James, while Sloane gestured frantically to give him the best seat.

"Your arrival is perfectly timed." The man to James's left was about Sloane's age, with neat brown sideburns and well-brushed hair. "We've been trying to locate the Dark Palace since we first began digging. Last night there was an earthquake that seems to have opened a path to the entrance. A superstitious man might say it was waiting for you."

The building tension of the earthquake, the rumbling growing stronger as he approached—

James gave him a long, deliberating look. "And you are?"

"This is Mr. Charles Kettering, our historian," said Sloane.

"Mr. St. Clair," said Kettering, with a short head bow of greeting. He spoke like a gentleman, and his brown jacket was of good quality, but he dressed in the slightly mismatched manner of someone who did not think often about clothes.

"A historian?" said James. "You study the old world?"

"Yes. You'll forgive me, it's quite an honor to meet you," said Kettering. "I've studied the ancient world in great depth, but to meet one who was actually a part of it . . . it's quite extraordinary."

He was looking at James like a dealer in antiquities inspecting a specimen of great interest. *He's not a curio,* Will wanted to snap. He curled his fingers around the wood of the table edge so as not to react. *Blend in,* he'd told Cyprian. He hadn't realized how hard that would be.

"And do I meet your expectations?" James said.

"It really is *quite* extraordinary," said Kettering again. "You look just like the descriptions. I wonder, if it's not too forward, whether I might ask you for a demonstration of your magic?"

"Just ask Howell to loosen his neckcloth," said James.

There was a scrape as Howell pushed his chair back and stood, glaring from the far end of the table.

"Have I said something wrong?" said James mildly, as Howell took a step forward, only for Sloane to hold him back, hurrying to say, "Ah, it seems as if breakfast has arrived."

Servants were lifting the lids from silver trays to reveal breakfast meats. After a long, deliberating moment, Grace took a sliver of potato onto her plate determinedly. Cyprian poured a single glass of water. Partly to cover for them, and partly because he was starving, Will heaped his own plate with sausages and preserves.

"A good English breakfast," Sloane was saying. "The locals here just seem to dip biscuits into things. Coffee. Wine." Scornful.

"You never explained why you arrived with no belongings," said Howell loudly. His voice, cutting across the table, was hoarse.

"I'm afraid we ran into trouble on the road," James lied smoothly.

"Bandits," Sloane agreed, as if this was a problem long known to him. "They're all through these hills. There are raids, attacks on our supply wagons." He waved his fork, ornamenting a pet topic. "They've guessed we're close. They're like hyenas stealing kills from lions. They'd snatch our find from under our noses."

"Find?" said James.

"It's miles from where we've been sinking shafts," said Sloane. "An hour's ride from this camp. Without that earthquake, we might never have found it. When we break the door seal this morning, we'll be the first to enter the Dark Palace in centuries. That honor must go to you."

"Perhaps we'll even find some of your own relics," Kettering was saying to James.

"My relics?"

"There's so much of yours to find—your room's furnishings, your adornments, your armor—"

"Am I your area of study?" said James, in a conversational voice.

"Only by association," said Kettering.

Sloane spoke up, waving bacon on a fork. "Kettering here is Sinclair's foremost expert on the Dark King."

Will had to use every particle of willpower he had not to react. But no one was looking at him. Everyone was looking at James, who sat with his own reaction so utterly extinguished that nothing beyond mild interest showed on his face.

"Is that so," said James.

"Yes, in fact. I flatter myself that I know more about him than anyone. Well, anyone living," said Kettering, with a nod at James, as if to say to an esteemed colleague, *I exempt you, of course.* "I would be very pleased to talk to you about him. It would add so much to my notes."

James smiled tightly. "You must know from Sinclair that I don't remember that life."

"Then perhaps you have questions about your master."

The silence that followed the word *master* seemed to burn, a scorching heat that shriveled what it touched.

"My master," said James, tasting the words.

"You can tell so much from what he left behind. You, for example."

"Me," said James.

"His prize possession. It is fascinating to see his tastes in the flesh. May I?" He put his glasses on, and gestured toward James's face.

James is not a possession, Will wanted to say. He had to force himself to sit still, to allow the idea that someone was going to put hands on James. His head was pounding.

As if all of this was normal, James shrugged an elegant shoulder and said, "Very well."

Kettering tilted James's jaw up to regard him, as one might admire a valuable vase. "Extraordinary," he said. "To think He kissed these very lips . . ."

It was too much. Will swept his cup from the table, the sound as it shattered causing everyone to startle; Kettering releasing James and turning toward the sound. In the silence that opened up, his friends stared at him.

"A happy interruption," said Kettering, breaking the tension and holding his hands up in surrender. As if the accident with the cup was a charming, coincidental warning from the universe. He said, as if sharing an amusing inside joke with James, "Of course your master wouldn't like others touching his things."

Cyprian approached Will later, as they readied to ride out.

"This is a mistake," Cyprian said, looking over at James, who was pulling on riding gloves with Sloane fawning over him, and two servants leading his horse out, its saddle newly polished and its black coat brushed to a gleam. "We're in his world. He has us utterly in his power. He's weak now. But when he's back to his full strength? We can't even leave unless he opens the gate."

"He's loyal to us," said Will.

"Is he?" Cyprian's voice was hard. "Don't forget that he was reborn to serve the Dark King."

"I never forget that," said Will.

CHAPTER FIFTEEN

THE EXPEDITION WAS a convoy of locals with digging equipment and packhorses, accompanied by two dozen soldiers to protect against bandits. Without soldiers, they would be sitting ducks to an attack, Sloane said. Boys walked alongside, swishing branches and saying, "*Su! Forza!*" to the two large mules who carried the heaviest packs.

Will rode near the front, rock spurs thrusting upward from the gorge where the river could be glimpsed below. There were long stretches with no path, just thick clusters of holm oak and the occasional manna ash. On one of the slopes high above was the Leap of Faith, but they seemed to be making for a different part of the mountain.

The closer they got to the palace entrance, the more the landscape began changing. They passed trees toppled and torn, then rode by ground that was fissured and split. It seemed to confirm what Will had guessed: that the entrance was the source of the earthquake, and they were getting closer. Will could feel it, the pressure growing in his head.

An eerie excavated road of ancient stone lay ahead. More than the unearthed buildings of the outer citadel, it seemed to conjure up a ghostly world.

"Arresting, isn't it?" said Kettering, riding beside him. "Until yesterday it led into the blank face of the mountain. Now—wait till you see what lies beyond."

As they drew closer, an argument broke out among the locals. "*La morte bianca,*" he heard, and, "*Non voglio andarci.*" No one wanted to ride on. But it was not bandits they feared. Will saw one or two of the locals make a warding gesture, fist clenched but the index finger and small finger pointed down, as if guarding against something unnatural.

And then, like a crack in the world, he saw it.

In front of them, the mountain was cleaved open. The earthquake had split it like an egg. Will saw several of the locals cross themselves at the sight. Others made that same gesture, two fingers to ward off evil. As they got closer, the sheer size of the crack towered over them, offering a dark glimpse inside.

It's here, Will thought, not even knowing what "it" was.

There was a burst of sound behind him, local men talking furiously in dialect. It was a minor revolt: they didn't want to go any farther.

"What's wrong?" said Will.

"They're superstitious." Kettering shrugged.

"Superstitious?"

"Local legends, no need to worry," said Kettering.

Soldiers shouted, threatening workers with whippings, and still most refused, staying out on the mountain slope. By the time they began to move again, their party was even smaller.

Will felt the temperature drop as he entered the shadow of the mountain, the two sides of the fissure rising to block the sun. There was an unnatural silence of no birdsong. Even the few locals still riding with them had fallen silent in favor of this tense, slow journey into the earth.

They rode like a scouting party through enemy territory. The beetling crevasse was claustrophobic. There was only a scrap of sky visible above them. Even that was blotted out as the rock narrowed overhead.

Until it was swallowed altogether, and they faced an immense cavern with steps split by the earthquake, its cleaving force stopping at the twelfth step, seeming to point the way. This was where the mountain had brought them. Had brought *him*. He could feel it as he had when the earthquake had opened the path to the palace. *Here. Here.*

Will's gaze rose, following the steps to where they led.

"Undahar," said Kettering.

The doors towered like giants above him, their surface a still black pond. They had no carvings or ornaments, dominating by their sheer size. Before them, Sloane's troop of men were no more than a speck. Their pitch-black surface proclaimed an ancient and absolute power. What is Italy? Who is England?

Kettering was already calling to the locals, who had begun looping ropes, ready to pull the doors open.

"These doors are sealed," said Grace. "We'll be the first people to enter since the days of the old world."

Feeling unready, Will looked at the others. James kept his eyes on the twelve steps that led to the doors.

"It's understandable to feel nervous," Kettering said, coming to stand beside James. "How many of us get to walk in the place of our death?"

"I'm hardly nervous." James's matter-of-fact voice made Will's skin prickle. "This is Undahar. I assumed we'd stumble over my body somewhere."

"Oh, it's unlikely your bones will have survived," said Kettering. "The body decays over time. But there may be relics of yours left to find."

The thought that they might trip over James's corpse hadn't occurred to Will. It had clearly occurred to James, though he didn't show it beyond a single steady question.

"What kind of relics?"

"The Collar we know was taken," said Kettering blithely. "But the armor made for you by your master might remain. If you wore it at the moment of your death, we may indeed find it here. It will mark the place where you fell."

"Like a turnpike," James said.

Will thought of Anharion, smiling in the sunlight. In his dream, Anharion's armor had been gold. But a dark bloom of awful knowledge told him that later Sarcean had dressed him in red. *Red as the gashes that can never mar your skin.* Will forced his eyes away from James. In front of him, the closed doors were secrets meant to be kept in.

Sloane called out, "Pull!"

Horses and men heaved as he envisaged the ancient Egyptians must have heaved blocks to build their grand pyramids. Centuries old, the doors ought to have protested, but they opened in a slow, silent movement, as though oiled.

A gaping mouth, they led into the utter dark of a palace buried under the mountain. James had stopped again, and was staring at the entry.

"You know, you don't have to do this," said Will in a low voice.

"Why wouldn't I?"

Because you died here, Will didn't say. "Because we don't know what we'll find."

"I'm not afraid of the dark," said James, putting a foot on the first step.

Sloane raised an arm to hold him back.

"No, no," said Sloane. "We send the locals in first. It's a safety precaution."

Before Will could object, two of the local boys entered, holding lamps on sticks. They were roughly his own age, shepherd boys turned to different work. They disappeared into the black doorway, the silence so long Will jumped at the sudden crack of a pistol shot. Kettering reassured him.

"That is just to frighten away bats. But we do not need to fear pests. This chamber was completely sealed. You see?"

And indeed, there was no swarming eruption from the doors, and a moment later they heard the voices of the local boys calling, "*Vieni! Vieni!*" Sloane folded his arms and looked pleased, clearly intending to remain outside.

Kettering held up his lamp on its pole. "Shall we?"

It was dark, the lamps on sticks their only light. The two local boys with Kettering went first, with James and Will following, and Cyprian and Grace bringing up the rear. But they didn't spread out. They moved together, a small boat of illumination traveling out onto a vast dark sea.

Passing through the doors, Will could see very little, tall columns emerging like shapes in the gloom as they approached. But it felt familiar, frighteningly familiar, as if he could reach out his hand and touch the past.

A step inside, he instinctively brought his arm up to his nose and mouth. "The air . . . Is it safe to breathe?" The smell was unnervingly stale.

Kettering said, "It's simply old. When an ancient room is sealed, thousands of years pass with little air mixing with the world outside." He spoke without much thought. "You have nothing to fear. If the air gets too bad, the lamps will go out."

God, were they breathing the same air? Had Anharion exhaled here for the last time, only to have his breath sealed up? Was that what now filled his lungs?

He looked sideways at James, lit in the small circle of light from his lamp, but James looked only tight-lipped and determined, as if steeled to face what they might find.

They went forward.

The ground under their feet wasn't flat; it was full of crunching things and piles of dust that they scuffed through, as though they stepped on the dead. The lamp shone over strange sights, shattered and half-tortured statues, scattered pieces of armor.

"The rate of preservation is incredibly high," said Kettering. "There are more artifacts in this one room than we've found at any other dig, even Mdina."

One of the local boys reached to touch a chestplate, and Will's hand shot out. "*No, don't touch the armor,*" he said in bad Italian. "*Don't touch anything.*" His hand was tight on the boy's wrist, remembering the Remnants in London, the staring dead faces of the men, and the way the armor had changed them. Eyes wide, the boy nodded slowly.

"Look," said Kettering, raising his lamp pole. "A depiction of the night sky ten thousand years ago."

Above their heads, a carved sky full of stars, a falling comet, a radiant moon.

"And here." Kettering was moving all the way to the end of the entry chamber. "The inner doors—"

Will looked. And saw—

—a golden spectacle, the doors thrown open on a thronged passage, people here to see the procession, ecstatic at the cavalcade that passed them, six abreast.

First rode the Sun King, a Helios on a chariot, with a gold mask covering his face, in his hand the royal scepter with the sun's rays coruscating from it. Behind him rode his golden general, Anharion: from beneath his helm his long hair spilled brighter than the gold spear tips of the white-cloaked soldiers that followed. Their progress was a river of sunlight, all those riding with the king dressed in shimmering white and gold.

All but one. With his long black hair and garments, Sarcean was like a crow among birds of paradise. He could feel the shiver of discomfort at his presence, the whispers of those around him, his own difference from them, though none of them were aware of the deeds he did in secret for the king.

He didn't care what they thought of him. He rode his black steed Valdithar, whose hooves struck blue sparks from the stone.

Looking around at the pomp, he felt an amused awareness of the eyes of the king's newest Sun Guard on him. The young man shared Anharion's coloring, hair a few shades lighter, the color of golden sand. If Sarcean was feeling magnanimous, he might indulge the young guard with his attention later in the evening. A dalliance, to pass the time.

The second set of inner metal doors opened, and the procession began to disappear inside. It was not long now before the lady who was to be queen arrived. His own plans could then be set in motion. The true secret that lay deep in the heart of the palace, that he would take and use to—

"Are you all right?" said James.

"I—" Will looked instinctively for Sarcean, to follow him to the secret, to find what he had sought, his whole body beating with the words, *It's here.*

There was no ghostly procession. The chamber was a dark, dead ruin. The floors were cracked. The pillars were toppled and strewn like fallen trees in a sunless forest.

All he had seen in his vision was dust. The Sun King was gone, the blushing Sun Guard had fallen out of memory, and Anharion was dead and buried. The blond, blue-eyed young man now beside him—

He looked at James, whose eyes were dark with concern. *It's this place,* James had said to him earlier.

"I'm fine," Will said, pushing himself away from the wall, blinking the past out of his eyes.

Ahead of him, he saw that Kettering was illuminating with his lamp the very same inner doors that Sarcean had walked through.

A gaping maw, they beckoned and repelled at the same time. Will wanted to shout at Kettering to stay back from them. Oblivious, Kettering was lifting his lamp and looking up at the giant structure.

"Remarkable."

Warped into a crumpled shape, and half-torn from the walls, the inner doors were disturbingly open, though they were eighteen inches thick and made of iron, carved and plated with gold.

"What happened to them?" Will came to stand beside him.

Kettering held his lamp to the misshapen metal. "Warping in the metal. Burn marks on the very stone. It looks like these doors were blasted open by magic. And the damage here is all on the *inside.* Whatever it was, I'd say they were trying to get out, not in."

A relic of some desperate attempt at escape, the doors beaten open by a being of immense power. *It's here.*

Kettering said, "And of course you saw the outer doors. They were intact. Pristine. Whatever it was did not get out."

"You mean it's still in here somewhere?" said Will.

"Hardly. Look at the weathering," said Kettering. "It was thousands of years ago."

That was even more disturbing. "You're saying it died inside, trying to get out."

"That's right. We won't find remains after this long, as I said. But we might find a belt buckle, a scale, a jewel. Something to identify our escaping friend."

It wasn't a friend, thought Will as Kettering was drawn forward, lifting his lamp to the door and then to the wall, where a huge scar was scoured across the marble, part of the same attack that had twisted the doors.

But it was where he had to go. He could feel it. Whatever Sarcean had planned, it lay inside. And Sinclair's men were on the verge of finding it. *Because of me,* a voice whispered. *Because I came here.*

"Signore!" a voice interrupted. "Signore Kettering!"

There was a burst of Italian as one of the local men came running into the chamber. Will came blinking back to himself to find that several of the locals had entered with Sloane and were speaking of an attack.

He felt unsteady, still half-tangled in memory, forcing himself back into the present with difficulty.

In the rapid exchange of regional dialect, Will could only make out the Italian words *la Mano del Diavolo.*

The Devil's Hand? He could make little sense of it. From outside, distant shouts were audible.

"*Il Diavolo* is what they call the leader of the bandits in these hills," said Kettering. "He and his lieutenant, the Hand—they attack travelers, raid villages. A group of foreigners—thieves and cutthroats; we can't let them near the palace!"

"Bandits," said Sloane. "Hyenas. Worse than hyenas. I told you."

"Signore, you must help us." The local man was addressing James. He was one of the laborers, with thick arms and rolled-up sleeves. "They're attacking the entrance."

"They'll loot with no care for what they'll destroy or unleash," said Kettering. "We can't let them inside."

"*Signore, piacere,*" said the local. "They'll kill everyone."

"Then, point me at them," James said.

CHAPTER SIXTEEN

COMING OUT OF the palace was like breaching the surface of water after being held under, gasping in air and blinking at the world. The real world; not the swirling shades and ghosts of the underground. Everything seemed too bright, surreal, as if the rocks and the trees couldn't quite be believed. Will tried not to look as he felt: stupefied.

Arm up! Be ready! The shouts felt distant, as if he'd been wrenched from a dream too early, caught between disorienting wakefulness and the deep pull to go back under.

He had emerged into a slaughter. A dozen shots; a dozen of Sloane's lead riders fell. Horses screamed and reared up, clustering them like cattle in a pen. Instead of providing reinforcements, they found themselves exposed and outnumbered as bandits thundered down the crevasse toward them.

"The Devil's Hand!" he heard again from the locals. "*La Mano del Diavolo!*"

It didn't seem possible, their soldiers decimated, the few remaining having already emptied their pistols.

"Ready yourselves!" called Captain Howell to the last of his men, preparing for the charge. They were trying to reload their pistols, desperately, in the last tatters of a line.

James strolled forward calmly.

"You have one chance to leave," he said, with breathless audacity, to the armed bandits around him.

"You're on our mountain." The leader of the bandits was an African woman in men's riding breeches, white shirt, and torn brown waistcoat. Her voice was low in pitch, her Italian accented. "Whatever you've found belongs to us."

She lifted a horse pistol in her left hand and pointed it unerringly at James.

La Mano, Will thought. *The Hand.* It was a nickname with bite: her left hand, which held the pistol, was her only hand. Her right arm ended in a stump four inches below the elbow, and was tied off with leather.

The men with her—it was mostly men—wore the tattered clothing of the region, velveteen short jackets and breeches, and linen shirts open at the neck. Many of them had handkerchiefs fastened to their buttonholes or tucked into their pockets. Round their waists they wore ammunition belts, or leather sheaths for knives, muskets, or pistols.

But they weren't Italians: Kettering was right. Will saw a man with the straight black hair of the far east, another with the red hair and pale freckled skin of the far north, neither common in this region. A ragtag cavalcade, they had nothing in common but their bloodthirsty smiles at catching a rich prize.

"Stand aside," said the Hand, "or we shoot everyone."

Her easy horsemanship relied on seat and legs, her steady gaze under her short dark hair said that if she shot, it would send a bullet right between James's eyes.

"All right," said James, casually. "Shoot everyone."

There was enough time for Captain Howell to say, "St. Clair, you stupid son of a—" before the Hand, not one to make idle threats, simply shrugged at James and shot him.

The breeze in a long-ago garden, gold hair spilling through his fingers as he looked up and smiled—

No! Will was running forward desperately. His only thought was to get to James, to push him out of the way, or to put himself in front of the shot. But he was too far away, and there were soldiers that he had to shove past, not fast enough.

The blast was loud; a firework, followed by the smell of acrid smoke. A shot, perfectly aimed. *He can heal,* Will told himself frantically. Oh God, could James heal a shot to the head? It was impossible, but Will had to hope. *He can heal. He'll survive. He can heal.*

But as the smoke cleared, that didn't seem to be what had happened.

James just stood, his amused, challenging gaze still on the Hand. There was no smoking hole between his eyes. There was no red plume on his clothes. There was no sign that he'd been shot at all.

The Hand's expression flickered, a slight frown as if she was unused to missing.

"*Fire,*" she said, a little impatiently, and this time the entire band behind her fired, a series of bursting explosions.

Captain Howell flung himself low. All of the remaining soldiers curled in on themselves like armadillos. Except James, who stood straight-backed, gazing at the Hand with no sign of urgency.

And then, in the long space after, Captain Howell's men started to unfold themselves. Realizing they had not been hit, each man was looking up, confused, to see that none of his companions had been hit either.

The air was thick with flies. The flies weren't moving. Will saw with a chill that they were not flies, but round dark balls of tin and lead, frozen in midair, one of them less than a foot from Will's face.

"I believe I'm feeling better," said James.

Will felt a surge of satisfaction and pride. *Try to take me on the steps of my palace with James by my side.*

"You may be the hand of the Devil," said James, "but I am the hand of a Master more powerful than any you serve, and this mountain is His land."

And he gestured with his hand.

The lead spheres hanging in midair flew backward into the throats of the men who had fired them. The closest bandits fell, their bodies riddled with lead, their lives cut short by James's gesture. *Sorcery! Evil!* the shouts began, amid plunging horses.

"I'd run if I were you," said James to the Hand. "Just a suggestion."

"*Retreat!*" Will saw the Hand wheeling her horse, both reins in one fist, shouting to her men, "*Retreat!*" They turned and began stampeding, the Hand bringing up the rear.

"Sinclair's witch," she said to James, "your time will come to burn."

She put her heels into her horse.

The bandits fled into the trees, pushing horses hard over uncertain ground. It was closer to a terrified stampede than a retreat, fueled by a primal need to get away from a force that they could not fight. Captain Howell's men looked like they wanted to flee too. Amid scattered corpses and half a dozen riderless horses they were left staring at James in varying states of fear, stupefaction, and disbelief, too scared to break and run.

Your weapon, James had called himself in the gatekeep. Now Will looked around at a rout James had single-handedly caused. James's presence in the Hall of the Stewards might have been an insult, but he had just demonstrated unequivocally the full scope of the power Will had brought onto their side.

"Well done, well done," Sloane was babbling from the sidelines. "I don't think they'll trouble us again in a hurry." He looked terrified.

James swung up onto his black Thoroughbred, a cold icon ready to lead a force onward.

"You killed all those men," said Cyprian, in a hollow, shocked voice.

"You're welcome," said James.

"I want that entrance guarded day and night." Sloane gave the order. "No one in or out without my personal authorization."

Will found himself oddly shivering, as if entering the palace had been a plunge into cold water.

He wanted badly to talk to James, but James had mounted up and ridden past him without a single acknowledgment. Arriving at camp, James was whisked away by Sloane to a dining tent.

So Will drew Grace and Cyprian into his room.

There was reassurance in the stout English four-poster bed with its harrateen hangings, and the long seat that might have decorated any parlor. This was his world, not that underground palace of disturbing dreams. Not those flickering images of the past that seemed to haunt him.

But the shivering returned as Will thought of the mountain. "There's something in that palace." He made himself speak through it. "The danger under the mountain, the calamity the Elder Steward could not name—it's inside that palace, and Sinclair is close to finding it. We don't have much time."

"What are you saying?" said Cyprian.

"We need to find Ettore," Will said. "'Only with Ettore can you stop what is to come.' That's what the Elder Steward told us. We have to find Ettore, and fast."

"You mean abandon Violet." Cyprian's jaw was clenched.

"I mean do what the head of your Order sent you here to do," said

Will. "Nothing is more important than stopping Sinclair. Violet would agree with me."

Cyprian turned away, and Will could see the twin forces of duty and loyalty warring in him. His hair, loose despite his modern clothes, fell down his back, his spine sword-straight.

"And if it was James who was captured?" said Cyprian.

"What is that supposed to mean?" said Will.

Cyprian didn't answer. It was Grace who spoke.

"The Elder Steward warned us that we'd face our deadliest threat here. I believe her. I felt a great darkness under the mountain. Will's right. We must find the man Ettore. And—"

"And?" said Will.

"The men who rode with us today, they were scared," said Grace. "Not just of James's magic. Of the mountain. There is something here. Something that they fear."

Signs to ward off evil, a fear greater than that of reluctant explorers entering an unknown ruin. She had seen it too. Will remembered the doors, warped and bent.

Something inside trying to get out.

"So we play along," agreed Will. "James is our lord and master. As soon as it's light, you two ride out to find Ettore. I'll stay here with James, and find out what it is in that palace they're trying to dig up." He gave the order knowing that Cyprian would follow it. Cyprian was the good soldier. He would do as he was told.

Cyprian frowned, and then said, as if the idea truly distressed him, "I'm not good at *deception*."

"I know," said Will. "It's your best quality. Find the village and find Ettore. Leave the deception to me."

CHAPTER SEVENTEEN

"COME IN," WAS the absent-minded call at his knock. Will pushed the door open.

Kettering's office was the cluttered refuge of a historian, covered with books and artifacts. Three of its walls were excavated stone; the fourth was canvas, as was the ceiling. Kettering himself sat at a makeshift desk, a jeweler's loupe to his eye, through which he was studying a fragment of a white marble statue, an ear with a curl of hair carved alongside it, the piece singed as if it had been in a fire.

"I can come back," said Will, "if you're busy with—"

"Not at all, just a personal matter." He put the white marble down on the table, where it sat like a paperweight. "You're the boy here with James St. Clair, aren't you?"

"That's right," said Will.

Kettering was removing the loupe from his eye. He polished it briefly with a cloth before putting it down next to the marble. "Well then, how can I help you?"

"I want to ask about the Dark King," said Will.

"Ah," said Kettering, the single syllable spoken in a new voice. "Did St. Clair send you?"

"You're the expert," said Will. "You know more about him than anyone."

"What is it you want to know?"

Every part of the office was overbrimming. The floor was stacked with straining boxes. The stone walls were crammed with shelves spilling over with papers of all kinds. Chunks of white marble were piled on any remaining surfaces, an arm here, a head there. Kettering was Sinclair's scholar of the ancient world, and he seemed to have stuffed half of it into this one room.

Will thought of everything he wanted to ask, the questions that gnawed at him. Who was Sarcean, really? What had caused his descent into darkness? Why had he turned on his friends?

Will met Kettering's eyes.

"What were his powers? How did he use them?"

Kettering sat back, as though Will had surprised him.

He regarded Will in that posture for a moment. Then, with a strange quirk of his lips, he rose from his seat.

"Come," he said, and led Will to the shelves on the side of his room.

Rolls of paper, dozens of them, were stacked in cylinders. The paper was fine, almost transparent. Kettering searched with a finger. "Ah." He took a cylinder down and unrolled it on the table, opening his arms wide to spread it out.

It was a charcoal image with a blurred, ghostly quality. At its center, dark-edged and frighteningly familiar, was the *S*.

Will almost jerked back from it, its power radiating out to him even in effigy. Kettering mistook his expression.

"Don't fear. It's just a rubbing. You're looking at the inside of a helm piece."

Will could see its lenticular shape in the gray, grainy filament. It looked like a helmet he had seen once before.

"We found it eight years ago. Our first real find, a single Dark Guard buried under barren earth in Calabria. He was riding alone, carrying a box. I believe he was killed before he reached his destination, and the box's contents taken. All that was left was the box and a few pieces of his armor," said Kettering. "It was really just—"

"Remnants," said Will.

"That's right."

Three dark sentinels standing watch over Bowhill, their horses' breath white in the cold air on the Dark Peak. Will had killed the helm's wearer first, cutting him down as he quailed in recognition.

"Control was one of two types of magic that Sarcean excelled in. There are stories of vast shadow armies bound to him," said Kettering. "Of hordes loyal to him overrunning all the Light's strongholds."

Will looked down at the curves of the S. He had thrown the helm into a fire in the Hall of the Stewards, melting it down into a sludge. This rubbing was an eerie ghost: the only part of that helm now left.

But maybe the real find at that dig had not been the armor, but the S carved into the helm. Will could imagine Simon's excitement at finding it. Simon had loved playing at being the Dark King.

"Simon used the design to make his brand," said Will.

Kettering nodded. "A crude copy. But effective."

Casually. "You don't have one." Will glanced up from the rubbing at Kettering.

"Nor do you," said Kettering.

He was leaning back, watching Will. Was Will imagining the almost conspiratorial gleam in Kettering's eyes, as though they understood each other? *I'm hoping Sinclair will give me one,* Will could have said, and didn't.

"You said control was one of two types of magic Sarcean specialized in," said Will. "What was the other?"

"Death," said Kettering.

Will went cold. He saw Katherine's face, chalk white and spidered with black veins. He saw the Stewards, torn apart in their own hall. He saw the vision the Shadow Kings had shown him, the sky black and the ground littered with bodies, miles and miles of the dead.

"Death?" he said.

But he'd known that, hadn't he? He'd known the Dark King had killed anyone who stood in his way.

"To kill people and bring them back?" said Kettering. "No one else in the old world could do that. Even to make a shadow. . . is that not to triumph over death? To grant a kind of immortality?"

Will remembered the Shadow Kings, their ravening need to rend and kill, their sole driving force the need to conquer.

"He only gave a shadow life," Will said.

"But his favorites were Reborn," said Kettering, after a little nod to say, *You do know your history.* "I didn't believe it until I saw him, but there is no doubt that James is Anharion." He spoke like a jeweler authenticating a gemstone, as if he might pick up the loupe again at any moment and regard James with it. "You only have to look at him, to witness what he can do."

Reborn. Brought back to life by the Dark King. Sarcean had been more powerful in death than Will was in life, with abilities beyond Will's understanding. Controlling armies, controlling life, controlling . . .

"But if St. Clair sent you, surely you really came to learn about the Collar."

Everything stopped. Will felt all his attention focus the way it had the first time he had seen the Collar.

Kettering leaned back, watching him.

"It was lost, wasn't it?" Will heard himself say.

That was a lie. He'd held it. He could almost feel its weight in his hands.

"It was lost," agreed Kettering. "But if it wants to be found, it will be. These objects have their own agenda. Like blind things seeking in the dark."

Will remembered how it had felt when he had picked it up, his whole body almost swaying toward James as the Collar tried to get to his neck.

"He should take care. Once it goes on, it doesn't come off. Whoever puts that thing around his neck controls him forever."

Will had to hope it was safe. No one knew what James had done with it after Will had given it back to him. James had never said, and Will certainly hadn't asked him.

"Why did the Dark King make it for him?" Will asked why because he refused to ask how.

Kettering raised his brows. "I could guess. . . . For the power. For the pleasure of control. But I think the answer is probably far simpler."

"And what's that?"

"He wanted him," said Kettering. "So he made sure that he'd have him."

Will went hot, then cold, the glimpsed plans of his former self always dark, glittering, and implacable. "If the Dark King was so powerful, how was he defeated?"

"No one knows," said Kettering. "But of course . . ."

"Of course?"

"He wasn't really defeated," Kettering said. "Was he?"

Will felt something turn over in his stomach. "He was killed by the Lady."

It was the one thing he was sure of: that at least once, the Dark King had been beaten. He looked up at Kettering only to find the man's eyes speculative.

"But what is death," said Kettering, "to one who can return?"

"What did you find out?"

James spoke as he entered the room, already taking off his cravat, sliding it from around his neck and dropping it on the long seat, where it slithered, arm to floor.

It bared the long, pale stem of his neck. Even in a dusty dig in the middle of nowhere, James had the look of a hothouse orchid, grown to be plucked at the right time.

Will tried not to think of his missing crimson adornment, the choker taken from a dead throat. *What is death*, Kettering had said, *to one who can return?*

"Cyprian and Grace are leaving for Ettore's village," said Will determinedly. "Scheggino—the locals say it's not far, half a day on horseback. They'll ride out at first light."

"While you and I stay and play at lordling and servant." James tossed Will his jacket as he said it.

"We need to find out what's in that palace."

Having no experience as a valet, Will had no idea what to do with the jacket once he caught it, and just laid it over the back of the long seat. When he looked back over, James's mocking blue eyes were on him.

"This should be fun. I get to tell the boy hero what to do."

Didn't you feel what I felt in the palace? Will bit down on the words. Being here with James, so close to the past, felt dangerous. He feared what it would mean to stay here for too long. But walking away would mean abandoning the Dark Palace to Sinclair.

He told himself that he'd spent days on the road alone with James traveling back to the Hall. He could manage a few days alone with him now.

"I haven't learned much," said Will, keeping his tone casual. "The laborers are drawn from the scattered hill towns. They've been told they're digging up classical buildings for an English lord with an interest in history. None of them know what Sinclair's really digging for. But they know something." Grace had been right about that. "They fear the mountain."

And they wouldn't say why. Faces had shuttered, dark eyes turning hostile at mention of the mountain, followed by stubborn silence.

"And Kettering? I saw you leaving his tent."

Will didn't change the relaxed posture of his limbs. "He thinks you're here looking for the Collar."

James went still. Since the night in Gauthier's cottage, they hadn't really spoken of the Collar.

"You've been quite industrious, haven't you," said James.

Will didn't answer. After hauling crate with the stevedores on the docks for months, it had been almost too easy for Will to step back into that role: the unassuming boy just helping out, and if you found yourself talking to him about life on the dig, it was just because he was there, and not because he asked any obvious questions.

But the stakes now were higher. The boy who had entered Simon's warehouse on the docks seemed like another person. Naive, unknowing, still trying to fight Simon through ordinary means. Sabotage seemed like such a childlike attack, as if he could unravel Sinclair's empire rope by rope.

"That palace was the Dark King's stronghold," said Will. "What could it hold, that Sinclair wants it so badly? Badly enough to spend his whole fortune looking for it? Digging for years out here without any sign of success?"

James didn't answer, but after a moment he spoke in a troubled voice.

"They won't tell me anything," he admitted, as if this, more than anything else, bothered him. "I'm supposed to be Simon's delegate, but it's all prevarications, or sudden silences when I enter a tent. What is it they're keeping from *me*?" James was frowning. "I asked Sloane when he planned to send a team back inside the palace. He said he needed advice from Sinclair. I told him that would take weeks, and that I'd authorize any expedition. He waved me off. He said he took orders only from the Earl."

Will straightened, staring at him.

"Who sends it?" Then at James's quizzical look: "Sloane's request for advice?"

"Why does it matter?"

"We should intercept the letter."

He was already picking up James's cravat and tossing it back to him. He watched as James quickly wound the cravat around his neck, then began the tie, crossing the two ends of fabric over each other.

The truth was he had more than one reason for wanting to go back out. It wasn't just the letter. He didn't know how it would be to lie down next to James again and close his eyes for another nightful of dreams.

"Come on." He pushed James toward the door. "We need to learn as much as we can."

Outside, the sounds of the dig were louder, the site itself scattered with points of light and flame, fire torches illuminating the digging trenches and blotting out the night sky overhead.

But—

"No, signore," said the quartermaster when they approached him. "It is true Signore Sloane delivers me his post. But I do not believe there is anything scheduled tonight, or tomorrow, or for any day this week."

"That's odd," said James slowly, when they were back outside the quartermaster's tent. "Sloane said he was contacting Sinclair tonight."

"Is he lying? Putting you off?"

"Why would he?" said James. And then, "Where are you going?"

"To check his tent."

To steal the letter went unspoken. James gave him a newly interested look. "You're sort of a sneak, aren't you." James's voice sounded pleased, as though he'd discovered a secret. "Does my paragon little brother know that about you?"

The answer was no, and James certainly knew it. Cyprian with his straightforward way of doing things would hate skulking around in the night. Elizabeth hadn't liked it either. *Sneak* had been her word for him. She hadn't said it with James's unfolding delight.

It was dangerous to show this part of himself in front of others. Even if James seemed to like it. He wouldn't like it if he saw all of it.

"Sloane's still in his tent," said Will as they approached.

There were lamps still lit inside, despite the hour. Was John Sloane still working? They could hardly rummage through the man's things while he was sitting at his desk. Perhaps he was writing his letter at this very moment. They would need to wait him out, but an indefinite wait outside where they could be seen loitering wasn't wise.

Will said, "Maybe you can use your power to pull Sloane's letter out to us."

"I can't. I have to be looking at it." James stopped, realizing he had just given something away. "You really are a sneak."

That word again. "I spent my life on the run," said Will. "I'm used to getting things done without drawing attention."

"People just tell you things," said James.

"I'm not trying to trick you," said Will. "We're on the same side."

"Only because I've joined your—" Will put a finger to his lips.

James went quiet, and then he heard what Will had heard: voices. By silent mutual agreement, he and James shared a look, then moved to stand right beside the thin canvas.

". . . pleased to report that we have broken through into the main palace." The overseer John Sloane was speaking as if reporting to a superior. "A fortuitous earthquake. It happened the night St. Clair arrived."

"St. Clair?" answered a cultured voice in the rounded, upper-class tones of King George's court. James went utterly still, the color draining from his face. "Do you mean to say that James St. Clair is there in Umbria with you?"

"He arrived Thursday evening," Sloane was saying. "He was traveling with an English boy and two Stewards. Is that not as you planned, my lord?"

My lord, thought Will. He felt his stomach pitch. *It can't be.* But a single look at James's stark white face told him it was.

"How?" James's hand closed on his upper arm, gripping him tight. "How can he *be here*?"

He couldn't. He was in London. He was the general who never came out from behind enemy lines, protected and untouchable. He was the recluse, the Earl who dispensed his lackeys to do his work, rarely seen despite the power his empire allowed him to wield in the capitals of the world.

Will's heartbeat sped up. "Are you sure it's him?"

"Will," said James. "It's Sinclair."

"Are you *sure*?"

"It's Sinclair. I know his voice."

The Earl of Sinclair, right inside that tent.

Was he fresh from London, peeling off his gloves? Ready to take possession of whatever lay inside the palace?

In all his months working on the docks, Will had never seen Sinclair. But he had imagined confronting him. He had imagined walking into his office in some dock warehouse. *You killed my mother.* In the earliest days, it had been a boyish accusation that Will had simply hurled at him. Will had never thought about what he would say next. But then, slow, steady, implacable, he had started to work against Sinclair in earnest. He had something to say to him now. *You killed my mother? I killed your son.*

I'm here at your dig and I'm going to end your empire.

Sinclair said, "James has betrayed us. He now works against us. We captured his other accomplices in the Hall. The young girl escaped. The janissary is dead. The Lion remains our prisoner, and is on a ship to Calais."

Violet's alive, thought Will. *She's alive. She's on a ship.* The relief he felt at that was tempered by the stomach-twisting thought of Sarah. It made his veins burn with anger that Sinclair so casually spoke of the death of one of the last of the Stewards.

"My lord . . . James St. Clair is a traitor? He is working against us?" said Sloane.

"Little Jamie is making a bid for freedom, but that is not a state he's built for," Sinclair said. "He is a dog who has slipped the leash, but will soon return home." James stiffened, and Will put a hand on his arm instinctively. "It is the boy with him who is dangerous. Will Kempen. He can't learn what we seek. Tell him nothing. And above all, keep him away from the palace."

Did Sinclair know Will had killed Simon? At least hunting Will would keep him away from the Lady's true descendant: Elizabeth. *Sinclair gave the order,* James had told him in the cells of the Hall. *Sinclair killed your mother.*

Will found suddenly that he needed to see him. He needed to see the face of the man who had ordered his mother's death. But when he moved to a gap in the canvas, all he could see was the back of Sinclair's head, and it was oddly wrong, with thick blond hair and broad shoulders clothed in an officer's uniform, wearing a familiar new neckcloth—

"My lord, shall I simply have them killed?" said Sloane.

"No. Keep up pretenses. My ship arrives in two weeks. I will handle them personally."

As Sinclair spoke, he turned into the light. Will felt the same disorienting wrongness that he had experienced when the gate opened on water.

The man speaking was not Sinclair but Sloane's captain, Howell.

Sloane's hands were clutched obsequiously. "Yes, my lord," he said with a little bow.

He said it to Howell.

The wrongness grew. The sight in front of Will fought with plain facts and common sense. Howell couldn't be Sinclair. Howell was a young military captain of perhaps twenty-eight years. He couldn't be the fifty-nine-year-old Earl of Sinclair, even in disguise.

Howell said in Sinclair's voice, "And keep them out of the palace."

"Yes, my lord," said Sloane.

"We'll speak again," said Howell.

And Will knew, with sudden awful insight, what was happening.

He pushed James back out of sight as Captain Howell swayed and said hazily in his own voice, "Mr. Sloane? I think I've had one of my turns."

Will kept pushing James back and away, far from the tent, as Sloane tried to coax Captain Howell to sit down.

"I don't understand," said James. "That was Sinclair. The way he spoke. The things he said . . . How can Sinclair and Captain Howell be the same person?"

James was staring at him, a haunted, bewildered look on his face. He really didn't know.

"You've never seen him do that before?" said Will.

"Do what?" James looked at him. "What is it?"

Will forced himself to speak steadily. He was trying not to think of the dig around him, all the men in all the tunnels excavating the past in the endless dark.

He tried not to think of the eyes of those men, turning to stare at him.

"In the Hall, Leda told us that the Dark King could look out of the eyes of men branded with the *S*. Look out of their eyes, speak with their voice, even control them."

"You mean—"

"That was Sinclair, controlling Howell's body."

James's jaw set, then he turned away, clutching his own wrist.

Simon had tried to brand James, over and over. James's healing abilities had erased the brand each time. Will stepped in and gripped James hard by the shoulder, forcing James to meet his eyes as that possessiveness reared up inside him.

"It didn't take," said Will.

"He wanted it to," said James.

There was no answer to that except the one he couldn't say. *He doesn't have you.* Anger surged at Sinclair and his crude attempts at control. At whatever he was trying to wrench up out of the ground here. At his plans, always one step ahead of Will's own. *I have you.* He didn't say that either.

"He knows we're here," said Will. And then, "Half the men here have a brand."

"You mean Sinclair could be anywhere," said James.

"Or anyone," said Will.

CHAPTER EIGHTEEN

WILL WOKE CYPRIAN with a hand on his shoulder. A trained fighter but with experience only of peacetime, Cyprian blinked sleepily. He didn't wake the way Will did, silently and immediately. Will felt a flash of protectiveness. For all Cyprian's extraordinary abilities, there was something almost fragile about him out here in the mountains. He was a young man pushing himself up in the tangle of sheets on the barracks bed, long hair mussed and bed shirt rumpled.

"What is it? Has something happened?"

"Get up," said Will. "We don't have much time."

He looked hurriedly around the barracks to see if they were already being watched or followed. James waited a little way off, still immaculately dressed after his day of acting like this dig's little lordling. He'd been given his clothing by Sloane, and although it wasn't quite of the same quality as the garments he'd worn in London, it still oozed with Sinclair's style.

Now Sloane knew it was an act. They were flies in Sinclair's web; likely they had been all along.

He felt like a fool. He had believed himself to be deceiving Sinclair, had believed that he'd been one step ahead. But he hadn't even known the scope of Sinclair's powers. He still didn't know Sinclair's plans at this dig, only that they were years in the making.

"You two need to ride out of here and find Ettore's village," said Will. "Now. Tonight."

Cyprian and Grace had taken seats on the barracks bed facing him, looking serious and ready even in bed shirts. "What is it? What's happened?"

Will said steadily: "Sinclair."

"Sinclair!" said Cyprian.

Will in brief words related the disturbing scene he and James had witnessed. He told them about Sarah's death, Elizabeth's escape, and Violet's transport to Calais. And he told them about Captain Howell, speaking with Sinclair's voice.

"Leda always told us Sinclair could control people," said Will. "Now we've seen him do it."

Grace turned away, hiding open emotion. Cyprian put a hand on her shoulder, the two of them cleaving together instinctively. Sarah's death meant that, as Cyprian was the last Steward, Grace was now the last janissary. It made her the only knowledge-holder left. The Elder Steward had always insisted, *The true power of the Stewards is not our strength. It is that we remember.* As the last janissary, that burden now fell to Grace, with Cyprian her Steward protector.

"Sloane knows who we are. You two need to go. You need to find Ettore before the whole dig locks down."

Cyprian turned back to them. "You have to ride with us. It's not safe here for you now."

"No," said Will, who'd been thinking it through since he'd heard Sinclair in the tent. "We stay and play the game. Act as if we don't know that we're discovered. Sloane isn't going to throw us in a cell; he'll be keeping up his own pretenses. A double bluff . . . We'll be watched but might still find some advantage. If we run, we lose access to the dig."

Grace said, "That is a pantomime that could lead to your death."

"Sinclair arrives in two weeks," said Will. "We need to find out what's under that mountain."

Cyprian looked at James, who was lounging against the tent pole, then shook his head. "I'll get the horses," Cyprian said.

"I know what it's like, you know," said James, appearing in the makeshift stable.

Cyprian ignored him. Saddling his horse in the dead of night, Cyprian felt the same mix of anger and nausea that he always felt around James. *Why are you here?* he wanted to shout. James's presence was wrong. Beneath the question lurked the words: *Come to finish the job?* James had killed every Steward but Cyprian. Part of the sickening cocktail of feelings James provoked was an always-present sense of real danger.

"The 'outside world.'" James leaned his shoulder against one of the wooden supports and said it like the answer to a question Cyprian hadn't asked. Cyprian ignored him. Of course James didn't offer to help, though the mission to find Ettore was urgent, and he must leave with Grace before Sloane gave the order to lock down the camp.

"The water is dank. The food tastes like sawdust. The workmanship's shoddy. You think it's just here, and then you find out it's everywhere."

He ignored the jolt of acknowledgment, and forced himself not to look at James, refusing to have anything in common with him. *There's something wrong with the water,* he'd said to Will, who had drunk some, then replied, amused and confused, *That's what water tastes like.* Cyprian had flushed, embarrassed by his own naiveté, glad Violet wasn't there to rib him about it, though he could imagine it, maybe even wanted it, feeling the shape of her absence keenly.

"And you try to learn the new rules," said James, his voice oddly muted, not its usual mocking self, "but there are no rules, and there's no one to tell you your purpose, or acknowledge you for following your path."

Cyprian ignored him. He checked his weapon and his saddlery twice over. And then, just to make certain, a third time. You could never prepare too well. He was aware as he did this that no one else would check his work, that neither Leda nor Father would stroll past to cast an eye over his tack. But as he led his immaculately groomed horse through the mounting yard, its saddle and bridle just so, he felt good knowing that he had achieved an exacting standard, even if he was doing it for ghosts.

James followed him out as he led his horse, his voice sharpening, as if he deserved a reaction and was bitter Cyprian hadn't provided one.

"Sword clean, hair brushed, star shiny," said James. "You really are the perfect Steward."

Cyprian ignored him.

"I bet you never snuck out of your room, or skipped a day of practice, or ignored the bell. Too busy bending over backward to keep Daddy happy."

Cyprian ignored him.

"And now you're off on your first mission, just like a real Steward, riding out in his whites, fighting off the Dark."

Cyprian ignored him.

"Missed a spot on your saddle."

Cyprian hated that he turned to look, only to find that the saddle was perfectly polished. When he turned back, James's eyes looked like he'd won something.

"That's what Father would say, isn't it?"

"We'll never know what he'd say," said Cyprian. "You killed him."

He swung up into the saddle.

"Are you sure you don't want me to come along, baby brother? You'll have trouble with those hill bandits without me. Since I've saved your life now twice."

Cyprian didn't look at him, just put his heels into his horse. *Don't call me that.* Better to say nothing.

Hold to your training. That's what Father would have said.

He rode out to join Grace.

CHAPTER NINETEEN

"SLOANE'S INVITED ME to his tent," said James.

His voice was tense as he paced their bedroom, his short, sharp gestures showing his discomfort, even with the door closed.

"A late dinner. Just the 'inner circle.' He hopes I'll join them."

The messenger had caught them just as they'd reached their rooms, James's eyes passing quickly over the paper. Walking back there, it had been too easy to imagine that all the men watching them were Sinclair. All the Englishmen here had a brand.

"You have to go," said Will. "We have to keep up the facade."

"The *facade*," said James. In his hand he held the invitation card left by the messenger as though proposing an afternoon call.

"We play along until the others get back from the village," said Will. "Sinclair told Sloane to keep us occupied. We have to do the same."

Easy enough for Will to say it, when it was James who would have to playact in front of Sloane, knowing that the eyes of his surrogate father might be on him.

"And if he tests my loyalty?" The words were brittle, like James's defiant exterior. The way he was standing, the braced, expectant tension in his body—Will realized it suddenly.

"You don't like it." Will said it like the revelation that it was. Ironic, yet it made so much sense. "You don't like deceiving people."

Of course he didn't. Of course, this whole time, he didn't. James had been tense since they'd arrived, the edge on those cutting remarks growing sharper. And he'd swallowed it down, and let Kettering touch him, and even killed people, just as he once had for Sinclair.

"God, this is what it was like for you, isn't it? All those years working for Sinclair while you secretly looked for the Collar?"

It was clearly not what James had expected him to say, his eyes widening just for a moment, before his mouth twisted scornfully. "That isn't—"

"You shouldn't have had to kill those bandits," said Will.

Of course, James knew how to play the sadistic dilettante in front of Sloane. He'd played that role for years, all the while searching for the Collar.

"I don't care about a few bandits," said James.

It was easy to forget that James had been raised in the Hall. He would have been a rule follower and a true believer like Cyprian. Raised to be good.

"You shouldn't have had to kill the Stewards," said Will.

It was as if he'd struck a core of truth, James's eyes widening further. Then James seemed to realize that his reaction had betrayed him. He gathered himself to cover it. "I *really* don't care about—"

"You shouldn't have had to kill anyone." Will made himself say, "You're not going to kill for me. Especially not Sinclair. I know he was like a father to you."

"But fathers," said James, tense, "are my speciality."

"Was that Sinclair's test of loyalty?" said Will. "Be mine, kill your family?"

James was silent. Because of course it wouldn't have been a single test,

James proving his loyalty to Sinclair not once but over and over again, acquitting himself in ruthlessness just as he'd acquitted himself in devotional duties as a Steward. Both of them would have liked it. Sinclair enjoyed exercising power over others. James wanted to prove himself. He thought of James pouring everything he had into the gate.

"All the eyes will be on you at dinner," said Will. "Put on a show. It will buy me time to look around." In fact, it would be the first time Will would be alone since they'd overheard Sinclair in Sloane's tent. It was the opportunity he wanted, and he wasn't going to waste it.

"Look around for what?" James didn't understand, and Will didn't expect him to.

"I'm going to find out what's inside that palace," said Will, "and I'm going to stop Sinclair."

"How are you going to do that when the palace is guarded day and night, and you have every eye in the dig on you?" James's brows arched.

"Ingenuity," said Will.

"Sinclair raised me," said James. "He knows all my tricks. He taught me half of them. He knows what I can do."

"He doesn't know my tricks," said Will.

Will waited till James was gone, then picked up a stoppered bottle of wine that had been left in their rooms and made straight for the badly disguised man Sloane had posted on watch outside.

Innocently: "Can you direct me to Captain Howell's tent? James St. Clair told me to invite him to Sloane's dinner."

The man snorted. "The captain's not going to dine with St. Clair."

Will had guessed that much. But he made his eyes wide. "I hope you're wrong. I was told not to leave Howell's tent till I convinced him."

"Hope you've got all night, then," said the man. And that was how

Will got his watcher to take him to Howell's tent, and leave him there, with all the time in the world to do as he pleased inside.

Entering, he held up the wine bottle and told a new lie. "Captain Howell. Mr. Sloane sent you this. He says he hopes you're feeling recovered."

"St. Clair's boy," said Howell, as though the name tasted foul.

Close up, Will could see that the bruising around Howell's neck was fading. The new neckcloth he wore to hide it had slipped down slightly below his Adam's apple. His clothes didn't have the same quality as Sloane's, and were showing signs of wear out here in the mountains.

But he took the bottle. He pulled out the cork with a single tug and ignored the niceties of glasses, bringing the bottle to his lips for a swig, more akin to the habits of men on the docks than those of a regiment captain.

Will was looking for the lingering signs of possession, but he didn't see any, except for a slight nervous edge that if he thought about it had been there all along.

Howell was looking at him in turn, after he swallowed the wine down, holding the bottle by the neck. "You're the one who shares his room." His eyes held slow, open speculation.

Will felt the air change, as *St. Clair's boy* suddenly took on a spectacular new meaning. Deliberately, he loosened his limbs. It was not an approach Will had ever tried with a man before. But you could not share a lodging house for boys and remain innocent of the world.

"He's never offered me one of those." Will glanced down at Howell's wrist, then back up again through his lashes.

Howell said, "How far would you go to get one?"

"It depends," said Will. "Did it hurt?"

"A great deal," said Howell.

"Can I see it?" said Will.

Captain Howell looked amused, as if he knew the game they were playing. He came forward. Stopping in front of Will, he began rolling up his sleeve. The suspense of a curtain lifting: the brand revealed was a raised, terrible mark.

"Can I touch it?" said Will.

A slow, spreading smile on Howell's face. The first time Will had seen the *S*, it had felt like a gaping pit, enticing him to fall. The truth was it had always called to him. Will's thumb pushed over the scar ridge. Howell had let Simon burn it on him, with a crude brand fashioned from a symbol none of them understood.

"Now there, boyo, what are you up to?" A low, pleased question, Captain Howell's other hand splaying on Will's waist.

"I'm learning what I can do," said Will.

His voice sounded different. He had pushed up from the table, his eyes steady. His grip changed from exploratory to commanding. It wasn't Sinclair's symbol. It was the symbol of the Dark King, waiting for its claimant. Captain Howell's expression altered.

"No, don't fight it," said Will. "Just let me."

Captain Howell's breathing had changed, subtly matching his, his pale eyes darkening with pupil and taking on the glazed look of prey.

"That's it." Will kept his left hand on Howell's wrist and lifted his right to cup the nape of his neck, his thumb resting on the esophagus, where James had bruised him. Their eyes met. Howell swallowed under his fingers; he could feel the rough scrape of the beard that was growing on Howell's neck.

But more than that, he could feel the *S*. He had always been able to feel it. A darkness that called to him, drew him in. He'd resisted since the first moment he saw it. Now he stopped resisting, let its call beckon him.

"I thought it would be hard," said Will. "But it's not, is it?"

All those months staring at candles, while the light refused to respond to him. All he'd had to do was step into the dark.

"You're mine already," said Will.

"*Master*," said Captain Howell.

Yes, thought Will, and with a lurch, he was inside Captain Howell's body, staring out of his eyes at his own face.

He gasped, and felt the air swirl into an unfamiliar throat. He could feel a hand on his wrist. It was his own hand. He was looking at his own face. The disorienting view showed him a boy with skin pale as white marble, whose eyes had turned completely black, as though his pupils had engulfed both irises and whites. Those black eyes blazed down at him, burning just as he'd seen them in dreams.

That's me. That's what I look like. He was that boy out there. But he was also Howell. He could feel Howell's arms, a different length than his own. He reached out, and Howell's hand lifted, thick fingered, his arm covered in curling fair hair. Howell had hefty meat on his bones, the kind that a wastrel dock boy couldn't hope to accumulate.

He's taller than me too. He felt heavy, cumbersome, like he was wearing an overlarge suit. But he could learn to use these limbs, he thought. He could adjust to their different balance and weight. He could walk Captain Howell now into Sloane's dinner—or his tent, or a meeting later, where Sloane might spill secrets. Assuming Sloane didn't recognize the signs of possession. If he did, Will could pretend to be Sinclair.

Or he could possess the body of Sloane himself. It was easy to imagine inhabiting other bodies, and the moment he thought it, he felt them, like glowing points connected by their brands. Dozens of brands on this dig, marking every single Englishman, as if Sinclair had needed absolute loyalty on this mission. Will felt—

The man outside, watching the tent. Sloane, and a handful of branded officers at dinner. The quartermaster, finding sleep difficult amid the ceaseless sounds of digging. Then nothing, but if he stretched farther—

A man holding carriage reins, the leather thick in his gloved hands. An older woman ringing a dinner bell, the sound clanging in his ears. A boy running through a crowd with a message in his hands. There were dozens of them, hundreds, spanning half the globe—

Howell. Where was Howell? Panic spiked as Will realized he'd left Howell behind. He reached out but couldn't find him. What if he couldn't get back to Howell's body? What if he couldn't get back to his own?

He sought wildly for something, anything that he could hold on to. But there was nothing, just this spinning absence, falling away from himself. He struck out, desperately, for anything familiar, anything to ground him, to tie him to himself—

—and he found himself looking out of unfamiliar eyes at a freckled countenance and that warm, handsome face that he knew so well.

He said, "*Violet?*"

She was staring back at him, and he could hear the sound of water and smell salt spray, as if he were on a ship.

It was her, truly there, in flesh and blood, warm and real, close enough to reach out and touch.

"*Violet—*"

"Will!" said James, and with a wrench, he was back in his own body in Umbria, gasping like a fish pulled from a stream.

James stood like a malefic deity in the doorway, his power sparking around him. Captain Howell was slammed into the far wall and pinned there, ripped away from Will with invisible force. Will turned his own head away quickly, squeezing his eyes shut to hide their unnaturally ink-black surfaces.

Oh God, had James seen? Will was breathing in gasps, eyes shut tight to hide them, still reeling from being out of his body. He dug his fingernails into his palms, trying to recover himself. *Don't let them know. Don't let them see.*

He felt James's hands on his shoulders—James's real hands—and he was forced to look up and open his eyes. A flare of panic at being uncovered. But James was looking at him with urgent concern, which meant his own eyes must have cleared of their black ink. Relief shuddered through him, even as he forced down anything that might give him away.

"Will!" said James urgently.

I found Violet. He couldn't tell James. He couldn't tell anyone. No one could know what he could do. He bit down on his tongue to hold the words back. Violet was alive. Violet was on a ship, likely sailing for Calais, as Sinclair had said. He must have entered the body of one of her captors. God, he had been *right there* on the ship with her.

"Will, did he hurt you, did he—" Will had never seen James like this. He didn't understand why James was concerned for him, and then he realized that James had seen Will and Captain Howell clutched together, and mistaken who was predator and who was prey.

The desire to laugh at the irony of it crawled in his throat. How funny to be receiving comfort as he had always craved. Because of course, it was based on a lie. James wouldn't be helping him if he knew what Will had just done.

A memory of the past spat itself out: *I'm vulnerable while I'm scrying.* No one had been allowed near Sarcean when his mind left his body, except Anharion, who always stood guard, and whose loyalty was absolute, because he was bound by the Collar.

But James wasn't wearing the Collar. He was protecting Will because he wanted to. *Sarcean never had this,* Will thought with a kind of weak longing, undone by what James was giving him.

"James, I'm fine, I'm—"

"How dare you put hands on him."

James was turning on Captain Howell, who immediately began gasping and gurgling against the tent pole. It was Will's turn to grip James's shoulder, pulling him back.

"*James.* You're crushing him. James! *Let him go.*"

Captain Howell dropped to the ground, coughing. His hand on his throat, he stared up at them. "What happened? Did I have one of my turns?"

"Your turns!" said James. "Sinclair was here?" His power slammed Howell back into the tent pole. The whole canvas rigging was in danger of coming down.

"James, he doesn't know what happened!"

James made a frustrated sound but released his power's grip on Howell for a second time. He glared down as Howell scrambled backward.

"Get out," James said to him. "Now."

Howell pushed up and out, hand still clutched to his throat. Will almost lifted his hand to his own throat in sympathy, though he felt nothing of Howell's airlessness or bruising. He had no continuing link to Howell, even if an impression of the man's body lingered in his mind.

"You have to be more careful," James said the moment Howell was gone. "You can't be alone with men who wear the brand."

"I'm fine."

Will was unsteady, still readjusting to his own body but unable to show it. He hid the strange dislocation he felt, as he hid the vulnerability of having almost been found out.

"Sinclair could be anywhere. You said as much yourself. You're the one he's after. You aren't safe."

As if Will was the innocent; the hapless boy; someone James followed but thought of as inherently naive. As if Will didn't know what Sinclair was capable of, when Sinclair had killed Will's mother.

"James, I'm fine."

He had seen Violet. He knew what he had to do.

CHAPTER TWENTY

"*LIFT ON THREE!*" Violet heard. "*One, two*—" Blindfolded and held frozen in place by Mrs. Duval's power, she felt the whole cage heave upward, then tilt as if it was being carried up stairs. She slid, and hit the rear bars. Fresh air, and the cries of a major port, all in French.

Where was she? Calais? It was the only French port she knew, a place where Sinclair's ships traveled often, a first stop for his dealings in the rest of Europe. The view of Calais was famous. She couldn't see it through the blindfold. What was she doing here?

The cage was tilting again suddenly, this time in the opposite direction—a ramp—until finally it was placed on what she realized was a wagon only when it jerked and began to roll.

She stayed alert, ready to rip off her blindfold the instant she could move. But there was no break in Mrs. Duval's power. Violet imagined Mrs. Duval sitting behind her like a squat toad, never taking her eyes off her for the entirety of the ride.

A jolt—the wagon stopped. From the swaying, the cage was being carried. Then it hit the ground.

Violet felt a hand in her hair. Then, like a magician revealing a stage trick, her blindfold was pulled away. She expected to see her father and brother waiting for her, whatever Mrs. Duval had said.

Instead she was in the decaying ballroom of an old French chateau. It was dilapidated, with rotting floorboards and mold patches on the ceiling, a vine creeping in through one of the dirty French windows. Empty and huge, with its dancers and socialites long absent, it reminded her a little of the training arena in the Hall of the Stewards.

Mrs. Duval and her brother Leclerc were standing at the far end of the ballroom. The cage door was open, and she was no longer under compulsion. Violet came out slowly, cautiously, into the center of the space.

The first thing she saw was the animals. There were mounted taxidermies, animals in strange poses. Heads of deer on the walls, big cats stuffed to look like they were pouncing. Staring at one of the frozen ibex, she saw it blink, and realized with a shudder that many of the animals were alive: a cardinal parrot beside a black cat, a rabbit beside a python, the breeds disturbingly alongside each other when they shouldn't be. It was an upset of the natural order, a kind of chaos that unnerved her. What would happen if Mrs. Duval wasn't there? Would the predators strike? Would the prey be eaten?

Leclerc standing among the animals was part of the uneasy picture, the claw scars distinctly scouring his face. She half imagined a larger predator padding into the ballroom, and then she thought—*That's me*. She fixed her eyes on Duval.

"Why am I here?" said Violet.

Between her and Mrs. Duval, a sword lay on the rotting floorboards, with a knife next to it. Weapons laid out, which didn't make sense.

"I'm going to teach you how to kill a Lion," said Mrs. Duval.

Violet looked down at the sword and the knife, then back up at Mrs. Duval.

"I know how to kill," said Violet.

"You know how to fight. But you have never faced your own kind." Mrs. Duval noticed the direction of her gaze. "Go ahead. Pick up the sword."

Violet did so, gingerly, surprised that she was able to move forward without any repercussions. Her fingers closed on the sword hilt and the knife handle, one in each hand. Before she could think or second-guess herself, she leapt the two steps toward Mrs. Duval, swinging the sword hard at her body.

"Stop," said Mrs. Duval calmly.

Violet found herself frozen in midair, her body hitting the ground shoulder first with a shock of pain that jammed into her teeth and turned her vision black. She lay where she'd fallen with her body unnaturally paralyzed, and saw Mrs. Duval's shoes stroll into view.

"I want it to be clear that I will not let you harm me." Black button-hook tall boots with small heels.

"Don't blink," said Violet, the words an empty threat. She knew already that Mrs. Duval's power wasn't stopped by a blink. But what would happen if Mrs. Duval closed her eyelids for more than a fleeting second?

There was nothing on these ancient floorboards to throw. Maybe she could throw her sword, make Mrs. Duval turn her head just long enough—

"Now," said Mrs. Duval. "Let us see what you can do."

The compulsion was lifted again. Sensing that things would not be straightforward, Violet bit down on her desire to fling herself or her sword at Duval.

"Well? Attack," said Mrs. Duval.

A sequence that Justice had taught her—Violet was shocked to find it countered. "You've learned the techniques of the Stewards, I see," said Mrs. Duval. "That will not be enough to kill a Lion."

"The Stewards are the greatest warriors alive," Violet flung back at her.

"Is that what they taught you? Lions are stronger than Stewards, and faster. More resilient. They can take a hit and keep going."

A teeth-rattling blow to the side of her head accompanied the word *hit*. Violet shook it off, blinking. As if the hit had dislodged the memory, she recalled that she had seen Tom take a battering from Justice and survive. Then she remembered how many Stewards Tom had killed.

"Why do you stop? You react like a Steward, injured and knocked about. You are a Lion. A hit like that shouldn't even make you flinch."

That made Violet blink again, for a different reason. Was Mrs. Duval saying her Lion blood gave her resistance to attacks? It was true that she didn't bruise easily. She knew she could jump from an unusual height and land safely. Picking up heavy objects did not pulverize her.

"You know almost nothing about yourself," said Mrs. Duval. "The Stewards have not taught you to take advantage of what you are."

"They taught me how to fight."

"They didn't teach you the Lion way; they taught you their way."

Mrs. Duval hit her again, and Violet found herself staggering forward from a blow that had seemed to come out of nowhere. Then she wondered if she had really needed to stagger. What would have happened if she had just stood her ground?

"You don't know your strength," said Mrs. Duval. "The best Steward facing the best Lion would die. Every time. Even with all their potions, all their deals with the Dark. You have learned from those inferior to yourself."

"The Stewards are not *inferior*," said Violet. But Tom had cut down Justice on the *Sealgair*. She could see Justice lying facedown in the cold water, his black hair spread out around him.

"What do you think a Lion *is*? Or didn't they tell you that either?"

Violet stared back at her furiously. She hated that she didn't know. It sparked the same feeling of muteness that she felt when Tom told stories of Calcutta. She shoved those feelings down as she always did, and focused her hate on Mrs. Duval.

"There were many with powers in the old world. The Blood of the Phoenix, the Blood of the Manticore. Unlike the Blood of Lions, they have gone extinct. But the Lions endured. You have your part to play. . . . *The day will come when a Lion will take up the Shield of Rassalon.*"

"I thought my fate was to be eaten," Violet shot back, but she was unnerved. It sounded too much like the words said to her by the Elder Steward.

"To eat or to be eaten," said Mrs. Duval, instead of answering. "Lions are strong, but they can be killed. You will need more than strength to kill your own kind. You have been taught how to win, but not how to kill. I will teach you. You will learn how to strike fast, without mercy, where your opponent is most vulnerable. I will teach you the body's weaknesses. The eyes, the throat, the liver."

"Why would I ever want to kill a Lion?"

"Because your fight with your brother will be to the death," said Mrs. Duval, and Violet's mouth went dry.

She lowered her sword, and was almost surprised when Mrs. Duval didn't immediately take advantage. A moment later Violet dropped her sword to the floorboards.

"I'm not going to kill Tom," said Violet.

"And when he tries to kill you?" said Mrs. Duval.

"He'd never do that."

"Didn't your family tell you anything? Tom Ballard will come to kill you eventually. Either you're trained to fight him or you're not."

Violet didn't pick up her sword. "Why would I believe you?"

Mrs. Duval said, "I knew your mother." Violet stared at her. "I knew what she knew. The laws that govern all your kind. *The death of a Lion bestows the powers of a Lion.*"

It was like she was hearing the words from far away. They sounded in her like a bell, calling to something deep inside her. *The death of a Lion . . .*

A memory; hands in her hair and a woman's voice singing. A skirt that was not the structured crinoline of English skirts but made of a different fabric. Green and yellow and loose in its folds. She didn't remember the words of the song. Or the pattern at the hem of the skirt. Or—

"You said her name." Her own words were far away. She had to push them out, and even then they didn't seem like part of her. It felt almost frightening to talk about. *Gauhar.* Her mother's name. The forbidden topic. *How could you bring that woman's child into my house!* "Before. You said her name. You said—"

Mrs. Duval didn't answer. "The pretender Azar killed Rassalon to take his power. But something went wrong. Azar took the shield, but the powers were not transferred. Rassalon was the last true Lion."

"The last true Lion." The words lit a spark, a connection to something beyond herself. To the warmth of those hands, an encircling memory of warmth.

"That was your mother's hope for you," said Mrs. Duval. "To take up the mantle of Rassalon. To return your family to their rightful glory. To be a true Lion. But John Ballard had other plans."

"I don't understand," said Violet. But it was this feeling she didn't understand, this ghostly connection to something long forgotten.

"Your father made you." Violet's stomach twisted at the word *made.* "And then he killed your mother." She stared at Mrs. Duval in horror. "He wanted her power for himself, and for his son. But as with Azar, something went wrong. He did not become a true Lion. So he brought you with him back to England. He seeks to learn what went wrong, and when he has the answer, he will serve you up to his son."

Violet felt sick. "Why would you tell me any of this? Who are you?"

"I am the last of the Basilisks," said Mrs. Duval. "And I know only a true Lion can stand against what lies beneath Undahar."

They threw her into a cellar.

Back in her cage—there was enough give on the chain to let her move a few feet in either direction, but she couldn't reach beyond the cage bars, let alone the stairs to the cellar door, or any of the disused wine barrels that scattered the underground room. The Steward manacles on her wrists sapped the strength she might have used to break the chains or pull them out of the wall.

En route, she saw glimpses of the decaying chateau, windows boarded up, white sheets over furniture, rooms with plaster crumbling behind peeling wallpaper to reveal ancient planking. Above one huge stone mantel she saw the carved words *La fin de la misère.* She didn't understand the meaning, but the words made her shiver.

At the same time, she felt raw with feelings awakened by Mrs. Duval. Her life in India was a handful of hazy memories, blocked to her by her own mind's swerving away. Most of them featured the Ballards, as though she had been born the moment she had been plucked by her father like a souvenir to bring back with him. She didn't remember her mother. She didn't remember feeling any grief at departure. Too young to understand—that was what her father had always said.

She remembered the ship, where she had run happily wild. She remembered arriving in London. She remembered the face of her father's wife Louisa, like the impersonal stone facade of the London town house. She remembered her first understanding that she was not to be one of them: the argument over where she should sit at dinner.

But before that, she had had a mother who had wanted her, who had made plans for her, who had had hopes and dreams for her. A mother who had come from a place that she knew nothing about, because she had avoided even mentions of India, frowning when Tom or her father talked about it, as though it made her angry, when maybe the feeling hadn't been anger after all.

Leclerc watched her from the stairs.

She waited for Leclerc to get too close, but he was meticulously careful, as though he was used to dealing with creatures in large cages. She looked at the scars across his face: maybe the source of his care now was his carelessness in the past.

She ought to play along, get Leclerc on side. That's what Will would do, she thought. She'd come upon Will captured and chained exactly like this, and the first thing he'd done was try to talk her into unchaining him.

He *had* talked her into unchaining him, if she thought about it.

How had he done it? Dark eyes that looked all the way into you, and a feeling that he'd give his life while expecting no one to come to his aid.

She watched Leclerc call up the stairs, and then take a tray from the kitchen hand who appeared. Instead of coming in range of her chains, Leclerc placed the tray on the ground, then pushed it toward her with his cane.

"You see? We are not your enemies."

The wooden tray itself might be a weapon, she thought, as she pulled it toward herself. She tore off a chunk of the stale bread and ate it hungrily, and then thought Will probably wouldn't have eaten it, suspecting it was poisoned or something.

Well, hopefully it wasn't. She took another bite. It didn't taste of poison, it tasted of stale bread, which truthfully wasn't that much better.

"If your sister can control animals," said Violet, chewing, "why didn't she help you with your face?"

Leclerc flushed. "The power runs in our family. When we are children, we test who has it, and who does not."

She stopped chewing. "What, they just throw you in with a wild animal?"

"As you see," said Leclerc.

The scars ran across his face like crisscrossing, meandering paths gouged deep into a landscape, white and raised, with pink puckering around the edges. His left eye was gone. He leaned heavily on the cane that he gripped in his right hand.

Violet said, "What kind of animal?"

"A lion," he said, and she felt her skin prickle.

"You mean like me?"

"I mean a real lion. Have you ever seen one? They are more imposing than you can imagine. Golden as the grasses in which they lie, heavy limbed, as though they have little concern in the world. But when they stand, they command all. You can see how large their paws are from the span between my scars. Of course, I was just a boy then." Leclerc gave a thin smile. "It was my father's test. To see if I had his power to control animals. I didn't."

"So you're the runt," she said.

Leclerc just gazed back at her from out of his ruined face. "I don't have Father's powers."

"But your sister does. Are you jealous?"

She could not disturb his calm. "You're wrong to mistrust my sister. She is the one who stopped the beast, when my family would have let it tear me apart. She got me out. She broke my father's hold over us both. So don't think that you can drive a wedge between us. My sister helps the weak. If you let her, she'll help you get free of your father as well."

She flushed in the dark. His story was unnervingly similar to her own: the father serving his child up on the altar of power. She didn't want to have anything in common with Leclerc. In her deepest fantasies, Tom learned the truth about their father and helped her the way Mrs.

Duval had helped Leclerc. But Tom hadn't ever done that.

"I thought your sister worked for Sinclair."

"She does . . . when she wants to," said Leclerc. "Rest assured, she and your father are not friends."

"So she's training me in secret? Sinclair doesn't know?"

Leclerc regarded her with an impersonal, assessing look. "What is a shadow?" he said. "Did you ever wonder that? What exactly was the deal the Stewards made with the Dark?"

"I know I killed one," said Violet. "That's all that matters."

"Not alone," said Leclerc. "Only with the power of Rassalon."

It brought her up short. The only person she'd told about the Shield of Rassalon's power against shadows was Will. And she hadn't even told Will all that had happened in that dark, lonely fight. She stared at Leclerc, to find him watching her in turn.

"How do you know that?"

"'Only a true Lion can stand against what lies beneath Undahar.'"

Those were his sister's words. Coolly, he lifted his cane and pointed at her tray with it.

"So eat up," said Leclerc. "You'll need your strength to complete my sister's training."

CHAPTER TWENTY-ONE

"GOT YOU, YOU little wretch!" A man's hand closed on her arm, jerking her back, her body unresisting, staring in shock at the girl.

"Let me go! Let me *go*!" Elizabeth struggled like a cat in a bag. "Katherine!" she shouted. "Katherine!"

Katherine didn't hear her, stepping through the inn door with Prescott and some fancy man in a tall hat. *Will said she was dead.* Had he made a mistake? *He lied. He's a liar.*

Her fury at him flared white hot, and she struck out at the two men holding her, by proxy. *Liar.* Katherine was alive. She was here, close enough to catch if she could just get free—

"Ow! She's kicked me right in the—!" Followed by a limping step and a great deal of swearing. "Throw her back in the wagon, and make sure the goddamned door's locked this time!"

The first of two men spoke as he threw open the door to the wagon. All her attention swung back to it. A gaping black maw: horror made her struggle harder at the thought of having to go back in there. *Not there, not with—*

The man at the door pressed his forearm to his nose and said, "Christ, I think the other one's dead."

The other man holding Elizabeth swore again. "Goddamn it." He was the shorter of the two, a stocky man with brown hair under a threadbare cap. "Pull her out then, make sure she's not faking."

"Don't touch her. Don't *touch her,*" said Elizabeth, with a roil of nausea, as the taller man dragged Sarah to the lip of the wagon, then swung her body as dead weight over his shoulder. He dumped it in the corner near some tied-up sheaves of hay. She wasn't faking.

Katherine's alive, Elizabeth told herself, the image of Sarah's open eyes sticking in her mind. *Katherine's alive. Katherine's alive.* She was really struggling now. She was trying to jam her legs against the wagon door so that the man lifting her couldn't get her inside.

"Need a hand there, Georgie?" the taller man said dryly, as the short, stocky man he'd called Georgie swore again, the heel of Elizabeth's shoe striking his shin bone with great force. She felt a sharp tug at her neck and heard fabric tear, fighting him uncaring. "You let go of me!" She wasn't used to jewelry, and didn't think beyond the brief pain at her throat.

"What's that? A Steward necklace?"

The tall man was reaching down. The medallion had come off her neck! She opened her mouth to say *That's mine, give it back!* when Georgie said sharply, "Don't touch it, you idiot! You don't know what Steward magic it has."

The tall man snatched his hand back, then made the sign of the cross for good measure. "Steward magic!"

Georgie said, "I'll get her back inside. You go tell Mr. Prescott the older girl's dead. Tell him I'll deal with this one." He gave Elizabeth a shake.

She bit his arm and Georgie swore again, rough handling her to the mouth of the wagon. A second attempt: when she wouldn't be pushed inside, he clambered in there himself and dragged her.

She found herself back in the enclosed space of the wagon, dark and silent; the whickering horses and the smell of hay seemed distant, as if they were in a private locked-away space.

A meaty hand over her mouth and a knee in her stomach kept her down, as if waiting until the taller man was gone. He held up the medallion so that it dangled in front of her face, and demanded:

"Where did you get this?"

"That's none of your business!" Elizabeth flung at him the moment he released her mouth from his hand.

"Did you find it? Steal it?" Stubborn silence. "You little wretch. This is Eleanor's necklace. Where did you get it?"

Eleanor?

The name made her stop, feeling a little breathless. "Who cares where I got it?"

"Eleanor's dead. You little turd. Did you steal from the dead?" He shook her hard.

Unbothered by the shaking, she was aghast at the accusation. "I didn't *steal* it! Someone gave it to me!"

"Who?"

"A liar," said Elizabeth. "Why's it matter?"

The man stared at her. He was a sturdy, somewhat red-faced man in a waistcoat and shirtsleeves with corduroy trousers. He looked like a laborer, or a stableman. He held her down with one hand and shoved the medallion into his own shirt with the other. Seeing it disappear felt as if a light had winked out.

"You give it back! You give that back to me!"

Too short to reach where he'd stashed the medallion, she pummeled him with her fists. He swore again, this time with a succinct word she'd never heard before. She would have objected, remembering her aunt's reaction when Katherine had once said *deuced*, if not for the thing he was swearing at.

The medallion was in her hand, as if it had jumped there.

She was staring at it. The man was staring at it. She remembered Sarah whispering, *I won't tell them who you are*. Sarah had died protecting the Lady.

"You're Eleanor Kempen's daughter," he said. "Aren't you?"

All the hair stood up on her arms. A part of her thought, *Is that her name?* She had always denied it. *She's not my mother.* But her heart was beating strangely, and the medallion was warm in her hand. *So what if I am?* She didn't say it.

"What's your name?" he said.

"Elizabeth."

"A queen's name," he said. "Like your mother."

She didn't know why her eyes were wet. She had never thought of herself as someone who had a mother. Like part of a line, as if this small piece of metal connected her to a past that stretched out.

"Listen," said the man. "There's a village fifteen miles east of here called Stanton. I can get you a horse, and clear the way. You can get out tonight, and ride there. Ask for Ellie Lange. She will know what to do."

It didn't make sense. "Why would you let me go?"

"Because I made a promise to the woman who owned that necklace, that if her child was ever in danger, I'd help her."

She gripped the medallion tight in her hand. She thought of Will saying, *She would have wanted you to have it*.

He was a liar, and couldn't be trusted. But there was a small child's part of her that thought maybe her mother was helping her.

"There's a few of us that know the old ways," the man said. "Who serve the Lady."

Had her mother really spent time gathering allies to help her?

Elizabeth drew in a determined breath. "I won't go without my sister."

"Sister?"

"Katherine. She's inside. With Mr. Prescott."

The man looked shocked. "Lady Crenshaw is your *sister?*"

"*Lady Crenshaw?*" said Elizabeth.

In London, the title had been all Katherine had talked about. *We'll live at Ruthern, and I'll be Lady Crenshaw, and I'll host parties, and choose menus, and we can eat whatever we like.* Elizabeth had said, loyally, *I like Cook's dinners.* And Katherine had hugged her and said, *We can still eat Cook's dinners. We can just eat apricot ices after.*

But then one night Katherine had come to her room, her face drawn with fear. *Elizabeth, we have to go.*

That was the night Elizabeth had learned that nightmares were real.

"She's not Lady Crenshaw. She's Katherine Kent. She'd never marry Simon, he's—"

A killer. He'd killed the woman whose medallion she clutched in her hand. He'd killed lots of women. And he was dead. Will had said that. But then, Will was a liar. Will had said Katherine was dead.

"She's not married Simon," said the man. "She's married Phillip. The brother."

Phillip? "But she's never even met Phillip!"

The man shrugged. Elizabeth frowned. It didn't make sense. She screwed up her face and thought hard. How could she find out if this man's story was the truth?

"Was the wedding at St. George's Hanover Square?"

The man shook his head. "It was private and done at night, with no one that I ever heard attending."

"That proves it!" said Elizabeth. "Something's wrong. She'd never get married in private. You've got to help her."

The man was holding his hands up to ward off the idea. He had crinkles around his eyes, which were blue. "Oh no. She'll turn me in. She's Phillip's wife. She's in it with him."

Elizabeth said, "She's Eleanor's daughter just like I am."

The man said the same word he'd said twice before.

"Aunt says that's a bad word," Elizabeth said. "She says *being well spoken means being spoken well of*. She says *manners make the man*. She says—"

He said the word again. "You wait here." Grudging. "Your sister's up at the inn with Phillip. I'll make an excuse to go knocking."

"Georgie what?" said Elizabeth, suddenly.

"What?"

"That man called you Georgie. Georgie what?"

"Redlan George," he said. "So that's Mr. Georgie to you."

She didn't wait there. She followed him out as far as the stable doors, where Redlan paused, looking out to the inn across the courtyard.

"That's strange," said Redlan.

"What?" said Elizabeth.

"Those men. They weren't there before." He frowned.

She peeked out from behind him. There were five men stationed ostentatiously outside one of the first-floor rooms. They hadn't been there earlier. They looked like guards.

"That's Hugh Stanley," Redlan was saying. "And John Goddard. Amos Franken." The names didn't mean anything to her, but they seemed to mean something to him. "You wait here, and stay out of sight."

She didn't want to wait, but she thought he was right about staying out of sight, so she hid behind two rows of barrels while he strode across the courtyard. From between the staves, she had a clear view of the five men.

Goddard and Stanley were playing hazard at a makeshift table with bone dice in a wooden cup. Of the others, two were watching, sitting on wood stumps, and occasionally breaking into raucous laughter. The last was the man Redlan had called Amos Franken. He sat on a crate by the door, slicing a red apple with a knife and popping the pieces into his mouth.

Goddard looked up from the hazard table and greeted Redlan with the words, "If you've killed the other girl, Prescott's not going to be happy."

Redlan gave a snort. "Open up, I've got orders to take the lady wife back to Phillip."

"I didn't hear about that."

"You're hearing about it now." Redlan held out his hand imperiously.

Goddard tossed the keys to him with a shrug. "Better you than me."

"Why's that?"

"A nutter," said Goddard. "Speaking in tongues." His eyes were already back on the game.

Hugh Stanley said, "Chance!" rubbed his hands together, then spilled the hazard dice out onto the table. Then he said Mr. George's word. The others laughed so loudly that Amos Franken stopped eating his apple and was drawn over, only to laugh himself when he saw what was on the table.

Redlan disappeared through the door. Engrossed, the men paid his departure no attention, and nothing happened for long minutes except that Franken finished his apple, put his knife down, and sat, newly caught up in the dice game.

And then Redlan brought his prisoner out, and Elizabeth swallowed hard.

It was her. It was Katherine.

Relief washed over her. It hadn't been a dream, or some mad hallucination, or some other girl. It was Katherine, her corkscrew golden curls framing her face. She had lost her bonnet, and her primrose dress had a tear in it. She wouldn't like that. She hated when things messed up her clothes.

Elizabeth took a step toward her, her eyes pricking and her heart overflowing with gladness that threatened to spill.

Katherine picked up the apple knife from the table and jammed it into Redlan George's throat.

But he's our friend, Elizabeth thought with blank shock as Redlan fell on the ground, his neck pumping blood. *You're killing our friend.* She just stood, rooted to the spot. Blood sprayed all over Katherine's primrose dress, as she lifted the knife again and slashed open the jugular of Amos Franken, whose apple core rolled to the ground.

Stanley and Goddard leapt up from the hazard table, knocking the dice and cup asunder. Stanley began to pull and load a pistol, desperately tearing the paper of the cartridge open with his teeth. Goddard scrambled away and began running for the main inn door.

He's getting help, Elizabeth thought blankly as the last man charged, tackling Katherine, who hit the outer wall with a look of astonishment, as if she hadn't been expecting to be driven back by the man's weight. A moment later, the man collapsed to the ground, his stomach spilling open, gutted by her knife.

Katherine stepped over him. She didn't look disturbed. She had the practical manner of a butcher about his business. She used the knife to slice open the rope on her wrists, having killed five men two-handed, like a bell ringer. The rope dropped to the ground. She looked up at the red-rimmed eyes of Hugh Stanley.

"Stay back, or I'll shoot!"

Stanley had loaded the pistol and was pointing it at Katherine, muzzle shaking slightly. Katherine advanced on him with the knife, ignoring the pistol as if she didn't even see it.

He shot her.

Elizabeth saw her stagger, a blotch of red blossoming on her stomach. She looked astonished, and touched the wound as if she didn't believe it, her eyes and mouth wide circles of surprise.

"I said stay back!" said Stanley, as she looked up again. A second later he toppled backward, Katherine's knife sticking out of his eye, where she had thrown it with unerring accuracy. Then she bent down and wrenched the knife out of Stanley's eye socket.

Elizabeth was running forward, grabbing Katherine's wrist and tugging her.

"Katherine! This way. We'll take horses. Come on!"

Katherine didn't move or greet her; she just looked down her arm with no recognition in her eyes. After a moment: "There was another," Katherine said, looking up toward the inn. "A man who ran."

"He went to get help. We have to go!" said Elizabeth.

"It may be easier simply to kill him," said Katherine.

Prescott was stepping out of the inn, John Goddard following right after. Prescott took one look at Katherine and immediately sent Goddard back inside, as if to get reinforcements.

"We need horses," said Elizabeth, tugging harder on Katherine's arm. "The stable's this way. Come on. Come *on*."

A grudging step, as Katherine finally allowed herself to be dragged toward the stables. "We have to go west," Elizabeth was saying. "There's help at Stanton village. A woman named Ellie Lange."

In the dark, straw-scented interior of the stables, Elizabeth looked desperately around for mounts, and saw only feathery-hoofed cart horses, too slow for anything but plodding. Suddenly, running from stall to stall, she saw a familiar face, with its brown and white patches like splotches of paint.

"Nell!" she said, and hugged her pony's warm neck.

A returning nuzzle unlocked a chamber of Elizabeth's heart. With a burst of loyalty, she decided that Nell was the fastest mount in all of England. She threw a bridle on her pony, then turned back to help Katherine.

Katherine was pulling open the door to a stall holding the kind of horse that should have terrified her, a chestnut monster of eighteen hands with a thick neck and powerful hindquarters. In London, it had been Elizabeth who had explained how to saddle Ladybird, while Katherine had barely been able to lift the saddle. Now Katherine didn't even bother with tack, she just swung up onto the horse's bare back to sit shockingly astride. With a tug of her horse's mane, she said something that sounded like *Vala!*, and they burst out of the stable doors.

Elizabeth scrambled up onto Nell, said, "*Giddyup, Nell!*" and found herself in Katherine's wake in a courtyard full of men shouting, men grabbing weapons, men snatching up lamps and strapping muskets to their belts. "*There they are! Get them!*" Hands grabbed for her ankles.

"*Go, Nell, go!*" Nell stretched out bravely, her short legs working furiously. With no other riding horses in the stables, they might really get away. Galloping hard out of the inn gates, Elizabeth felt a rush of hope.

Then, in the distance, she heard the sound of dogs.

She remembered the sound from the Hall, black dogs swarming the halls faster than they could run.

"We need to go west! They can help us at Stanton!"

Katherine didn't answer, just kept riding hard. The truth was, Elizabeth didn't know which way was west, and Katherine would have no way to tell either. In the dark, Katherine's primrose dress was the only pale spot, and Elizabeth followed it doggedly, a ghostly will-o'-the-wisp leading her off the road and into a dense wood.

You weren't supposed to ride fast in the forest. Crossing the Abbey Marsh the night they'd fled London, they had traveled at a snail's pace, the horses picking their way with care over the swampy earth. But Katherine didn't slow her horse, despite the dangers of rabbit holes, logs, low-hanging branches, or sudden drops that could break a horse's leg. Elizabeth ignored the branches whipping her face and prayed for Nell's safety as her pony followed Katherine's horse gamely.

The sound of the dogs grew distant. The trees clustered thicker and the ground sloped down. Finally, Katherine stopped, and swung off her horse.

She had stopped at the bottom of a decline dotted with mossy wet stones, where a glimmer of moonlight showed a dark, fast-running stream. Her horse started to slurp up water. Elizabeth dismounted and stayed at a distance.

Katherine leaned her shoulder against the trunk of a birch tree. She was holding her stomach, her pale primrose dress streaked with dark ribbons. After a moment, she took the knife and, as if she were peeling an apple, cut a winding strip of fabric from her dress and pressed it to the wound on her stomach.

Elizabeth looked at her, at her blood-streaked dress, at the knife she wielded with ease, at her cold, matter-of-fact attention to her wound. She had ridden for miles with that wound. She had killed five men with that knife.

Elizabeth felt all of the swirling wrongness coalesce into something she hadn't wanted to see, out here alone in the forest.

"You're not Katherine," said Elizabeth.

Katherine finished tying the last bandage, and only then looked up, as if Elizabeth was of little importance.

"You're not Katherine," said Elizabeth. "Katherine doesn't know how to make a bandage, or ride a horse bareback, or fight. She doesn't k-kill people. And she'd never wear primrose, it's too yellow for her hair!"

Katherine's expression curdled. "'*Katherine*,'" she said. The name was unpleasant in her mouth, as if she was tasting it and didn't like the flavor. "Who was she to you?"

Was. The hairs on Elizabeth's arms stood up. "She's my sister."

"Sister?"

Elizabeth said, "You've done something with her. What?"

"Your sister's dead," said Katherine.

Elizabeth took a step back. "Dead?"

It was what Will had told her. But Will was a liar. Katherine was alive. Wasn't she? Elizabeth stared at the girl in front of her. It wasn't a twin. It wasn't an uncanny resemblance. It was *Katherine.* Every particle of her was just as Elizabeth remembered. Except that it wasn't.

"That's her body," said Elizabeth, with rising horror. "You're in her body."

At once Elizabeth saw it clearly: a different person behind Katherine's eyes. It might be Katherine's face, but she was not the one animating it.

"*Give it back.*"

The person in Katherine just looked back at her coldly. Elizabeth flew up to her, grabbing the front of her dress and shaking it.

"Give it back!" And then, trying to reach her, "Katherine! *Katherine!* It's me, Elizabeth!"

Katherine took hold of Elizabeth and prized her grip off. "No Katherine exists to hear you. She is dead."

"You're lying," said Elizabeth. "Bring her back!"

"We are not two spirits inhabiting the same vessel," said Katherine. "She is gone like the last light at day's closing. There is nothing to bring back."

Elizabeth didn't believe it, wouldn't believe it. And yet the thing in Katherine's body was so coldly different, and had nothing of Katherine in it. Elizabeth stared at the unfamiliar expression, and the unfamiliar posture, and the unfamiliar hand still holding a knife.

"Who are you?"

"I am Visander, the Queen's Champion," said the body that used to be Katherine. "And I have returned to this world to kill the Dark King."

And suddenly she could see what he was: a soldier. She could see it in his efficient killing, his cold-blooded tactics, and the way that he was ignoring the hole in his stomach. She wiped her forearm across her face, which was wet.

"Well, we don't need you," said Elizabeth. "We already stopped the Dark King. So you can go back to where you came from, and give back my sister—"

Visander was suddenly intent on her. "You know of him? You know of—"

He broke off, and jerked his head around.

A spectral sound rang out over the woods. *No,* thought Elizabeth, her blood curdling. *No, no, no.* A tumbled memory of running through halls smeared with gore, and falling against a tree full of light, while that shriek echoed through the rooms of empty stone. She had heard that sound before, as the sky over the Hall turned red, then black.

"*Vara kishtar.*" Visander let out a breath. "Indeviel, you would loose the *vara kishtar* on me?"

A shadow, thought Elizabeth. *A shadow, a shadow, a shadow.* "What's a *vara kishtar?*"

"Dogs that are not dogs, yet they hunt." He looked down at the sticky hand holding his stomach. "They are following the scent of my blood." He began tearing more strips off his skirt. It had the same economical feel of battle preparation as when he had brought out his horse from the stable.

"Shadows," said Elizabeth, feeling sick.

"They are not true shadows," said Visander. "They are shadow hounds bound to a master." He took the bloody strips of skirt and tied them to the branch above him. "This will distract them, for a time."

He pushed himself back up onto his horse, hand clutching his stomach. He was not moving as easily as before. He looked down at Elizabeth. "Do not follow me. You are only a nuisance."

It took a moment for her to realize that Visander was leaving her.

"*No.*" She threw herself in front of his horse, but he evaded her quickly, guiding the chestnut without reins.

And then he just rode off.

Elizabeth stared after him with her mouth open. By the time she was scrabbling up and putting her heels into Nell's sides, Visander was far in the distance. Elizabeth rode gamely to catch up. But whatever had propelled Nell last time was missing. Nell did not now float over the ground; she ran with pony solidity, crashing through the undergrowth.

She saw the four dark shapes first, converging on Visander from each side. And with the terrible grace of their breed, the *vara kishtar* attacked.

The first one rose in a panther's silent leap that crashed the horse to its knees, screaming. Three of the shadow hounds fell on the horse, ripping open its throat and belly. The fourth leapt for Visander.

Elizabeth was off her horse, shouting at Nell to drive her off. "Run, Nell! Run!" Then she picked up a rock and was running toward the hounds.

Visander rolled, dodged the first leap, and came up with the knife. But he was pale, and clutching his stomach, and a knife for peeling apples could not kill a *vara kishtar*. The shadow hound sank on its hindquarters, beginning to spring again, another only a few seconds behind.

"No!" said Elizabeth. "Stop! That's my sister!"

She flung herself over Visander's body, turning instinctively to see what was coming.

A hound in mid-leap, its open jaws so close she could feel its hot breath, and she threw up her arms to cover her face and squeezed her eyes shut as she shouted, her fear and protectiveness and fury and will to live exploding out of her in a single burning eruption.

Light.

Effulgent, a bursting sphere, turning the air white. Opening her eyes, she saw the shadow hound dissolve in midair, and the second hound dissolve, and the others feasting on the horse dissolve as what was inside her flung itself outward, illuminating the forest bright as lightning in the night.

Where there is fear, bring forth a beacon. For darkness cannot bear the light.

And then it was over and she had nothing left inside her. She saw the shocked face of Visander staring over at her in the second before dizziness rose up to take her, and the light winked out.

CHAPTER TWENTY-TWO

A NIGHT RIDE on two Steward horses: he could almost pretend it was a mission.

His first mission. He was keenly aware of that. Grace was not his shieldmate, and they had no Hall to return to; still, he could imagine it was something that Justice and his brother might have done, sent to find one man among many, here in the Italian hills.

Marcus had never told him how big the outside world felt, and how small a Steward felt in it.

James's words rattled around in his head. *No rules, and no one to tell you your purpose.* He wanted to ask Grace if she felt as overwhelmed as he did. But Grace seemed to have retained a facility for the world, having been born outside the Hall. She navigated the customs, and the clothes, and the cuisine without any of his disorientation. He didn't want to learn that James was the only one who shared his feeling of continual adjustment and loss. So he stayed silent, and just let his horse walk next to hers, through the Valnerina in the early light.

Scheggino was a cluster of medieval stone houses arrayed on the side of a mountain. On the highest point was an old stone tower: the remains of a fortification now in disrepair. A stream flowed beneath one of the rows of houses, an offshoot of the Nera that they had followed to get here, winding down through the hills as if following where the darkness flowed.

Several of the villagers watched them arrive, staring from doorways and windows. Their redonned Steward clothing meant that they stood out, and so did their Steward horses. But the suspicious black eyes in weathered faces said that this was a village where every outsider was stared at with hostile attention and an expression that said, *pass on.*

Cyprian dismounted under the birch tree near the small stone bridge.

An osteria with a few tables outside under an awning stood on what passed for the main street. It seemed to have patrons, so he and Grace tied up their horses and pushed open the wooden door.

Stepping inside was like stepping into the gloaming. Patrons at the long tables were drinking red wine from low glasses and long-necked carafes in the dim light. A handful of young men sat with their shirts open and sashes tied around their waists. In the back, a man with a scarred face was eating meat from some kind of coarse brown earthenware.

All of them stopped talking when Cyprian and Grace entered.

"Good afternoon." Mustering his best Italian: "We're looking for a man named Ettore Fasciale."

The owner spoke after a silence, a man with thick black hair, a strong nose, and a black beard. "A common name."

"He might have visited here recently. Perhaps you remember him."

An unyielding stare. "People come and go."

"I believe Ettore would be eager to find us, too."

That stare again. "People come. And go."

This was getting nowhere. Cyprian turned for the door.

"What's it worth to you?"

A voice in accented English made him turn back.

It was the scar-faced man at the back table. Swirling red wine around in a dirty glass, the man had adopted a casual sprawl with one scuffed boot up on a nearby stool. He was staring back at Cyprian brazenly.

His cheeks and chin were stubbled with half a week's growth. He wore leathers, stained and dirty like his shirt. His scar traveled from the corner of his eye into his thick black curly hair that he wore roughly cut. He'd plopped the meat down in the earthenware bowl to speak.

Cyprian didn't recognize him, or any of the dozen men sitting around him.

But he did recognize the woman, her dark skin, her cold eyes, and the arm she had casually flung out over her chair back, that ended in a stump wrapped in leather.

A sudden shift in perspective: the men sitting at the long tables were not workmen; they were bandits. This osteria was full of bandits—three or four tables full of them. And if this woman was the Hand, then the man next to her was the Devil.

"Must be worth something for you to come in here after you killed half of my men in the mountains," said the Devil.

Behind Cyprian, a woman threw the heavy wooden latch, barring the door. A handful of the banditti stepped in to stand between him and it. Cyprian instinctively put his hand on his sword.

"Now, now." The one they called *il Diavolo* was a man of about thirty-five, heavy with muscle under his rumpled clothes, with a kind of disreputable gleam in his eye. "We're all men of business. We can make a trade."

A deal with the Devil. "You've seen the man I'm looking for?" Cyprian didn't lift his hand from his hilt.

"I might have," said the Devil. "But when you put us off at the mountain pass, you cost us a pretty penny. Didn't he, Hand?"

"That's right," said the Hand.

Money. He knew that outsiders did things for crude personal gain. This was the venal world outside the Hall, where loyalties were bought and sold. It was not the Steward way, but finding Ettore was too important to stand on principle.

"What do you want?" said Cyprian.

"A pound of flesh!" called one of the men.

"A barrel of wine!" one cried from the back table.

"A kiss!" called another.

"You heard them," said il Diavolo.

Cyprian flushed.

"He's not going to—" began Grace, frowning.

Cyprian held her back. He could see from the slow, pleased smile on il Diavolo's face that the words were meant only to provoke. There was no offer here, nor would there be. It was just a petty play, cat with mouse.

"He doesn't know anything," said Cyprian. "Let's go."

He turned. There were four bandits between him and the door, but judging from the state of their weapons, he didn't think they were very well trained. He didn't think he'd have any trouble fighting his way out. His hand dropped back to his sword hilt.

"You know, you remind me of Ettore," the Devil remarked.

Cyprian ignored him, cataloging the bandits in front of him. They had cutlasses and knives that they hadn't drawn yet. Grace had her hand on her own cutlass hilt, but he didn't think she was going to need it.

"He wore the same little white dress," said the Devil. "He had the same arrogance, waltzing in here making demands. He threw his weight around. Just like you."

Cyprian swung back around, his eyes wide. "Ettore is a *Steward?*"

A Steward—a Steward here? He heard his own voice, overeager. A Steward, alive in the remote hills of Italy. His heart was pounding. *A Steward . . . a Steward survived the attack on the Hall.*

If Ettore had been outside the walls during the attack, he might not even know that the Hall had fallen. Cyprian's heart lurched toward the idea: a Steward, alive, carrying the Light of the Hall with him. He had to find him. He had to . . .

"Oh, has that got your interest?" said il Diavolo.

"Where is he? Tell me," said Cyprian. And then, more forcefully, "*Tell me where to find Ettore.*"

"Rethinking that kiss?"

He didn't think twice about it. He drew his sword, but held the blade below the cross guard, showing the hilt.

"This is a Steward star. It's pure gold. It's worth more than everything in this tavern."

"Cyprian," said Grace.

It was the last Steward star on the last Steward sword. He was already using his dagger to prize the gold star from the hilt. He held it out. "It's yours if you tell me what you know."

The Devil gave a long, low whistle. "That *is* a pretty penny. You must really want this Ettore fellow."

Cyprian held the Devil's gaze. He'd never cared about trappings more than he cared about duty. "He's the only one who can help us on our mission."

He kept his hand out. Somewhere out there was a Steward. It was more than the mission. It was the Order, proof that the light could not go out. Another Steward, true north on a compass.

"Very well." The Devil waved the Hand forward, and she came and took the star, testing it between her teeth with a bite.

"It's gold." She nodded the affirmation.

"Then we have a deal." Without taking his eyes off Cyprian, il Diavolo said, "Vitali, fetch me the cloth I use to grease my saddle."

A man at the table behind him opened up a satchel, took out a piece of grimy cloth, and brought it to il Diavolo, who tossed it to Cyprian.

Cyprian caught it, not understanding.

He felt the expectant eyes of the Devil on him as he looked down at the fabric bunched in his hand. It felt soft, softer than the scratchy, rough clothes Sinclair's men had dressed him in on his first day at the dig. A familiar texture. He drew it open with careful fingers, a dreadful fluttering in his chest.

Under the grime, it was white, with a silver star.

"You want to know what happened to Ettore?" said the Devil. "I killed him."

He met the Devil's heavy, pleased gaze. Cyprian thought, *Used to grease his saddle.*

"Smug. Self-righteous," the Devil was saying. "Swinging his weight around. But he didn't know how the world worked. The real world. With real weapons."

In one smooth motion, the Hand drew a pistol and aimed it an inch from Cyprian's temple. "I told you he was like you."

Fury; the ruined scrap of Steward whites was like an open wound, the hope of another Steward proffered, then snatched from him. The pounding of blood in his ears was a terrible drum that drowned out his awareness of anything but the fabric in his hand and the smirk of the Devil.

Under that, an awareness of the danger he was in: a pistol at his temple.

Under that, a ludicrous annoyance that James was right, and he was having trouble with the bandits.

Steward, hold to your training. Cyprian moved, fingers gripping the Hand's wrist, then shoulder. A twist, and he had her in a tight hold, her back to his chest, his arm cinched around her throat. These bandits might be fighters, but they were no match for the best trained novitiate in the Hall.

Cyprian had the pistol jammed under her chin.

"I know how to use real weapons," said Cyprian.

In fact, Cyprian had never used a pistol. A coward's weapon, it did not require the skill or training of a blade. You simply squeezed the trigger. He could do that, he thought. The Hand was breathing shallowly, high in her chest.

Every bandit put a hand on his weapon, but the Devil gestured for them to hold back. The Devil kept his voice casual, as one remarking on the weather.

"The moment you fire, it's ten to one."

"Nine to one," said Cyprian.

A long, tense moment full of danger. Then the Devil lifted his hands in a gesture of friendly surrender, as though all of this had been genial.

"It's just a bargain, sweeting. No need to make it personal."

"Open the doors," said Cyprian.

The Devil inclined his head. Behind him, one of the bandits lifted the wooden bar from the doors and pushed them open.

Cyprian moved backward with his pistol still on the Hand. But Grace strode forward and plucked the scrap of white Steward fabric that had fallen to the ground.

"A star for a star," she said.

Il Diavolo didn't seem to be bothered by this at all. He just stretched out his arm over the back of his chair and showed his teeth in a smile.

"That's the second time you've crossed me," said the Devil. "There won't be a third."

It was Grace who reined in her horse and dismounted near the edge of the Nera. They were still too close to the village. Cyprian wouldn't have stopped at all, but the horses did need to be watered, and when he paused and listened, there didn't seem to be a cavalcade of banditti galloping after them. Cyprian slid off his own horse.

"How can Ettore be dead, when the Elder Steward sent us here to find him?" Grace had taken the grimy fabric out and was looking down at it.

She sounded shaken in her faith, for the first time since he had known her. As he saw her expression, he realized that carrying out the wishes of the Elder Steward had kept the Hall alive for her. Now that path had abruptly terminated: Ettore was dead. They had no guide, the scrap of fabric that she held a sign that they were truly on their own.

"She said only Ettore could stop what was to come," Grace said.

She looked at him as one utterly lost. He felt their isolation, out here in the hills, cut off from all they knew. There was no Steward alive in the hills of Italy. There was no Steward alive anywhere in the world. Grief came to him suddenly, as if the loss of Ettore was the last point of light winking out.

"It is down to us now." He drew in a steadying breath.

"You mean we must make our own path," said Grace. Instead of tucking the white fabric away, Grace held it out to him. The star was frayed and greasy with saddle dirt. He took it like a sacred object.

She gave him an odd smile. "If Ettore is dead . . . does that make you the Elder Steward?"

His eyes widened at the shocking, dark humor of it. "I suppose if there are no older Stewards." It felt like sacrilege even to joke about it.

"I am janissary to the Elder Steward," remarked Grace.

He shook his head as the absurdity of it all sank in. "If I am the Elder Steward, that makes you the High Janissary."

It was her turn to look shocked. And then they were both laughing, a strange laughter that was made up of something like sobs.

"Signore! Signore Stella!" called a voice.

Cyprian turned. A woman was calling to them from the tree line.

Had she followed them from the village? He had been certain they were alone. He scanned the countryside for signs of an ambush, but saw nothing.

"Mariotto in the village says you have come from the dig. Is that true?"

In a peasant's blouse and full skirts, she was a woman of about twenty years, her brown hair tucked under a scarf.

Cyprian shared a look with Grace, who nodded cautiously. "That's right."

"My brother. Dominico. He works at the dig as a mason's apprentice. Have you seen him? He is twenty-one. His hair is dark. His shaving does not keep up with his beard. He wears a kerchief around his neck. Signore, we are very frightened. We have heard nothing for three weeks."

Her description matched half of the young laborers on the site. But her fear was real, and she made the gesture that he had seen the men on the site make, as though to ward off evil.

"Frightened? Why?" said Cyprian.

And turned cold at what she told him.

CHAPTER TWENTY-THREE

A GARDEN; BUT this time, Sarcean was waiting.

His long hair was loose down his back. The simple black silks he wore were an affectation, declaring the sheer power of his magic. Even Anharion wore armor.

He trailed his fingertips over the petals of white blossom that hung heavy from the orange tree, walking along the path where sprays of flowers winked beneath arches, a pond nearby with its glimpses of colorful fish.

Consciously, Sarcean affected the manners of one unawares in a private moment. A young man who just happened to be strolling the palace gardens.

And then she entered.

She was younger than he had expected his prospective queen to be. Her coloring was similar to Anharion's, her hair the same length, loosely plaited. She was from the kingdom of flowers, and she was beautiful, likely because the Sun King would have his queen no other way. He thought, an ornamental bloom chosen for the sweetness of its scent.

"My lady," he said, pretending startlement. "Forgive me, I thought the gardens would be empty." This was a lie, for he had been waiting for her, choosing carefully a time when the Sun King would be absent.

"No, it is I who have disturbed you," she replied quickly. "I was told not to wander the palace alone."

"Oh? Why not?"

"They're afraid I'll meet one of the army commanders," she said, "the one they call the Dark General."

Sarcean reacted, suppressed the reaction, and considered her anew, a sequence that he was too sophisticated to show on his face. The Sun King's intended was not the formidable sorceress that he had imagined. She was a young lady, stepping unawares into a darkly tangled web.

"Sarcean?" he said, tasting his own name on his lips. "What did they say about him?"

He knew most of it, of course. They called him *the king's blade in the shadows,* though none knew the deeds that he was tasked to perform, or guessed that while many of the king's victories were celebrated in the sun, they were won in the dark.

"That he's dangerous," she said. "A seducer, an assassin. They call him the King's Shadow; they say his gifts are unnatural. They say he's a Darkbinder, that I should avoid him." She let out a breath. "There was more. I'm not sure I believe it."

"Why not? It's all true." It amused him, a cat with a mouse. He already knew his gifts made people afraid of him.

"Simple stories are rarely true," she said. "And if I am to be queen, shouldn't I know my subjects as they are, rather than as they are rumored to be?"

Sarcean felt a little blink of surprise.

"You seem to have a good heart," said Sarcean. "I hope the Dark General doesn't eat you alive."

She turned to him with sunlight in her hair; and the light wasn't coming from the sun, it was coming from her, seeming to brighten all that it touched. Even him, infusing his skin with warmth. She said, "But I am a Lightbringer."

And Sarcean, watching in shock, had never felt anything like this sweet exhilaration—

"And what is your name?" she said.

"Will," said a voice.

A hand on his shoulder, shaking him. Will opened his eyes. He expected to see the light all around him. Instead, it was dark.

"Will," said James, and Will came fully awake.

"What is it? Are the others back?"

"Not yet," said James.

He pushed himself up, disoriented. He wasn't in a garden. He was on the long seat in their room, having fallen asleep avoiding the bed. Fear squirmed in him again that he might have said something while he was sleeping.

"You were right. This place is—"

"I feel it too," said James.

James was dressed for dinner, but it was late. He'd been with Sloane. Playacting. He had that lacquer on him, hard and shiny. But the way he looked at Will was real.

Will's heart was pounding. He had seen Sarcean's first meeting with the Lady. He was sure of it. *They loved each other,* Will thought. That was the story. He loved her. She loved him. Then she killed him.

He'd felt it, the exhilaration of her presence, his yearning for the light. He told himself these were Sarcean's feelings, not his own.

And he told himself that what he had seen had been . . . before. Before the deaths, before the war. She hadn't looked the way she had when he'd seen her in the mirror, staring back at him with the cold eyes of a killer. With the cold eyes of his mother.

"Can I ask you a question?" said James.

Confidences were dangerous. He knew that. If James had caught him at any other moment . . . but the rawness he'd woken up with linked him to James with strange intimacy. In the dim light, he nodded, once.

"Why don't you use your power?"

How could he breathe when the space was suddenly airless? He made himself speak as casually as he was able.

"I can't," said Will. "I've never been able to."

"Why not?"

Hours spent with the Elder Steward, trying to make a candle flicker. A door inside him that wouldn't open.

You're unnatural. You're not my son. I shouldn't have raised you. I should have killed you.

"I don't know," said Will. "Maybe I don't have any."

He had used the brand to possess Howell. He had commanded the Shadow Kings. He had touched the Corrupted Blade. But he knew these were Sarcean's tools. Using them took no talent beyond his identity. Sinclair could use the brand to possess people. Even Simon had been able to command the Shadow Kings, to lift the Corrupted Blade.

Will's own power, locked away inside him, he had never been able to access. He could guess why.

An easy posture, even when his heart was pounding. He was good at lying.

He had to be. He was the lie, even when he told the truth.

"You do," said James. "I can feel it."

James was closer on the seat than he expected, his voice lower in response to proximity.

"You can?"

Every alarm in Will was sounding. *Too close. No one can see. No one can know.* James's invisible touch was soft against his cheek. The same touch had dragged him to his knees and unlaced his shirt. Now it slid over his skin and came to rest tenderly on his neck. He'd seen James choke Howell, and he knew every violent specific of how Howell had felt, the collapsing windpipe, the blurring vision. It was the gentleness of this caress that was causing him spiraling panic.

"You can feel mine, can't you?" James's voice in his ear, soft as the touch.

"You know I can." He felt it when James walked into a room, felt it even when James was depleted, a guttering flame, and Will wanted to curl around him, and nurse that flame into blazing fire.

"What does it feel like?" said James.

"Like the sun. Or something brighter."

The truth, even as he was breathing shallowly. James had always had his complete, helpless attention.

"It's the same for me. You're powerful . . . more powerful than anything I've felt. I can't look away." James said, "I could close my eyes and know you."

You do know me, he couldn't say. *You were mine in a past we can't remember.* Feeling it was dangerous.

"If I have power, I can't use it," Will said.

"Maybe you've used it without knowing," said James. "They say that on the ship, you called the Corrupted Blade."

Not with magic. He couldn't tell James that the Corrupted Blade had jumped to his hand because blood called to blood.

"You want to use it, don't you?"

Months of running from Simon's men, running from a past he didn't remember, then finding the Stewards only to learn that he was powerless, that he couldn't stop the dark machinery of that past from bearing down on him.

His own early plays against Simon felt like another life. He had been naive then, believing that he could outmaneuver the Dark King, before he knew that the Dark King was more powerful and more subtle, his plans seeded patiently, and metastasizing in the dark, in ways that could not be fought.

The word came out, an involuntary truth.

"*Yes.*"

He should have lied. But the need was too strong: If he had been able to use his power, he could have saved the Stewards. He could have saved Katherine. He could have saved his mother.

James's eyes were dark and earnest as the invisible touch dropped away in favor of the offer of flesh and blood: James had risen from the seat and extended his hand.

"Then let me help you."

CHAPTER TWENTY-FOUR

JAMES'S REAL FINGERS brushed his skin, and Will jerked back, pushing up and out of the long seat.

Perfect lips curled unpleasantly. "Don't want to get Dark magic all over yourself?"

"That's not it."

"What, then?"

He couldn't answer, caught in a trap. His heart was pounding, the snared animal seeing the hunter approaching. The dark, glittering potential of magic was seductive. The idea that he might have it, might use it. And the touch, a way he wasn't used to being touched, and liked too much.

A dawning realization in James's eyes.

"You're afraid of it."

He wanted to laugh. He couldn't. Something inside him was trying to wake up.

"You shouldn't be," said James.

Mother, it's me. Mother, it's me. Mother—

"You weren't afraid of yours?"

Another of those unpleasant smiles. "I was eleven. I didn't know what was happening."

"You mean your power—"

"Just came out."

James didn't say more than that, but Will could see the loathing in the High Janissary's eyes as he looked at his son, because he had seen it in the eyes of his mother. *My mother thought I was too dangerous to live, too.* But he couldn't tell James that.

"'Strong emotion,'" quoted Will, softly.

James's nod was so slight it was almost imperceptible. "When I'm angry. Or when I'm afraid. Or when I . . ." He broke off. "I had to learn how to control it. So that I could command it, rather than letting it run through me, wild. You need to learn to use yours too."

Will remembered his early lessons with the Elder Steward. All her methods had been about control, perhaps because the only magic she'd seen had been James's, explosive and ungovernable.

No one alive knows how to do magic, she'd said. *It is a lost art that perhaps we can find together.*

But that hadn't been true. James could do magic, and the sisters could too, Katherine and Elizabeth.

And if they could, then shouldn't Will be able to as well?

With the feeling of a man taking a first step along a path from which there was no turning, Will closed his eyes and admitted, "Mine is the opposite. It isn't wild. It's trapped. It won't come out."

"How do you know?"

"The Elder Steward tried to train me."

"The *Elder Steward?*"

Will nodded, and saw James's expression contort briefly.

"Of course. That's just like the Stewards. Use magic when it suits them. Eradicate it when it doesn't."

Kill one boy, train the other. A fatal misstep that had led to the ruination of the Hall.

"So how does a *Steward* train someone to use magic?" James turned back to him, his mouth a sneer.

"We worked from old accounts. We used Steward chants to focus the mind." Control and concentration. "I spent hours trying to light a candle flame." His own mouth twisted. "I couldn't even make it flicker."

How hotly embarrassing to say that in front of James. Under the heat in his face ran the seam of true shame that he had felt during each of those sessions, unable to do what the Elder Steward asked him to do to save the Hall. She had poured time into him, thinking he was her savior. Her last days, spent watching him fail.

"Stewards. They read about power in dusty books. But they don't really know what it's like. Not the way I do."

He was circling Will as he spoke.

"James—"

"Here," said James again, this time from behind him, his voice at Will's ear. "Let me show you." His hand dropped to Will's hip, as if to hold him in place.

"Can you feel it?" James said, and Will was parting his lips to say no when power arced and sparked.

Will's mouth flooded with saliva as the tang of James's magic hit. It was wrong. It was so wrong, an exhilarating rush of power and potential. He had always known it, felt it. When James had used his magic on the docks, Will hadn't been able to take his eyes off him.

"*Yes,*" he said, or thought he said. *Yes, yes, yes.*

James slid his fingers into Will's and lifted both their hands, pointing them toward the outcrop of granite in front of the excavated wall.

"What do you feel?" said James.

You. Anharion in an amphitheater, performing a demonstration for the Sun King. Sarcean watching from behind the throne. Anharion had offered, *Sarcean. Shall we have a match?* Sarcean had only smiled and demurred. *No, my friend. This is your moment in the sun.*

Anharion's power had been a glorious, exhilarating display of wonder that had always called to him. James pressed against him was a youthful version, bringing him in, close, where he'd never been. *You, you, you.*

In front of them, a slab of granite lifted out of the ground, gigantic, the size of a cart. Even to drag it would have taken a team of oxen, ropes, whips, and a driver. Defying reality, it lifted slowly up into the air, rotating gently.

Against him, James was trembling.

"You're close to your limit." The revelation was a surprise. "You have to concentrate to lift something this heavy." Will had known that before, had even used it against James, breaking his concentration to disrupt his power on the docks, and again at Gauthier's house at Buckhurst Hill. But to feel it— "Gestures help you, but you don't rely on them." He could feel that too, from James's outflung hand. And—

"You can feel the rock." The words a breath of revelation. Just as Will had felt James's invisible touch, James was aware, in a ghostly way, of the rock, its rough surface, its weight, as if his magic was another skin, sensitive to what it rubbed against. It meant, when James had touched him—

"My power is a kind of touch," said James. "Elizabeth—she conjured light. I can't do that." James's words curling into him. "Maybe you can't either."

He couldn't. He knew that. James's body was warm behind him. James's voice low in his ear: "Maybe you can do something else."

Something stirred, deep in his gut, a shivering sensation.

"I can feel it inside you," said James. "It's there. Under the skin. Let me try to coax it out."

"Coax it out?" said Will.

Behind him, James seemed as caught up as Will felt, his power drawn to Will just as headily as Will felt drawn to him.

"It's responding to me," said James.

"I don't think—"

"Shh," said James, the hand that was not tangled with Will's sliding up across his chest. "Let me."

Will shuddered, something inside himself raising its head, a dangerous, newly awakened sense.

"James—"

Soft lips brushing his ear. "That's it."

James's magic was flowing over his whole body in warm, slow, rippling oscillations, the gentlest pulsing. It was causing a corresponding ripple in him, somewhere in a deep, closed-off place inside.

A door. A door inside that wouldn't open.

"I can feel where it's blocked," said James. "It's so deep inside."

His own voice had a hint of revelation. His questing power slid over the surface of it, a slow, rubbing touch, and Will bit back a sound.

"Can you feel it when I—"

"Yes," said Will.

"How do you open a closed door?" said James.

You can't, you mustn't. He knew what he should have said. *Stop this. We can't.* His mind flashed with the memory of James opening the gate, pouring all of himself into it until he was spent, and the gate itself flaring open.

The Leap of Faith.

"Push magic into it," Will said.

The hot, sweet feel of James blazed through him, and he cried out. His veins lit up with power; he lost hold of his surroundings. He was barely aware that they had stumbled together, Will hitting the nearby table, James panting behind him, forehead pressed to Will's back, hand still clutched to Will's.

"I can feel it," said James, "I can feel—"

Not enough. "Push harder," said Will.

He was pushed painfully into the edge of the table, and he felt the clutch of James's fist in his hair, James unconsciously pushing at him as his power pushed inside. It flooded every crack, raced along every slit, looking for a gap, a weakness, a way in.

"There—" He could feel it, an almost imperceptible point, smaller than a hairline fissure, where James's power was questing, sinking, drilling. "There—"

As if his core was responding, as if every closed part of him would let James in, no matter the danger. Except it wouldn't; some last defense held tightly closed, even if whatever lay beyond was stirring.

"*Aragas,*" commanded James.

Open. And James's magic connected to something inside him, like a thread of fire touching an endless underground pool of gas and setting it alight.

Everything exploded.

Pain tore through him and he cried out. A primal force unleashed to destroy, it blasted out of him with obliterating violence. It was raw, pure power and it hit with a shattering wave, annihilating everything in its path.

And then it stopped, as suddenly as it had begun. The blast had thrown James back. And without James as a conduit, the door inside him was closed again.

Will came to in the rubble, panting and bruised. Vision blurred, he levered himself up into a sitting position. *James.* He looked around for James desperately.

What he saw was destruction.

The granite was dust, the ground cratered and black, with sloughed rock like melted glass. If the blast had been directed toward the barracks, everyone would be dead. *Sarcean. Shall we have a match?* Anharion had offered, and Sarcean had smiled and waved him off.

He turned. James was sprawled a way off, his shirt half torn off, bruising and cuts on his face healing right before Will's eyes.

"I felt it," said James. "Inside you. I felt—"

"Felt what?" said Will.

He could hear the shock in James's voice. He could see the new way that James was looking at him. Like he'd never seen anything like it before.

"God, I see why Sinclair wanted you. Why everyone wanted you. You're—"

He was staring at Will, his eyes full of awe.

"With that much power," said James, "you really could kill the Dark King."

Will stifled the awful sound that might have been a laugh, except for the way it threatened to come up out of him, harshly.

"Yes, that's what I'm for," he said. "Killing people." He dragged his arm over his face, wiping off the blood.

"I didn't mean—"

The cratered rock smelled acrid, like the remnants of a fire.

"Does that excite you? Want me to lay waste to Sinclair's people? Hand you a palace filled up with the dead? We can look out over desolation and ruin together."

He bit down hard, forced himself to stop the words, to cut off what crowded thick into his mouth.

James was staring at him, eyes dark as if Will wasn't acting like himself.

"You're not just a weapon," said James.

"Is that what Sinclair used to say to you?"

James flushed and didn't answer, and maybe that wasn't fair, but it could have been worse, it could have been so much worse, with how much Will felt like breaking things.

"We can't do this again," said Will, pushing himself out and away from the rubble. "Not ever."

It was clear something unusual was underway as soon as he stepped outside.

The men who usually hung about outside their rooms doing a poor job of looking inconspicuous were gone. There was no sign of Sloane's watchers. Their rooms were completely unguarded.

Even stranger, there was no sound of digging. Work had stopped. Locals were congregating in groups on the other side of the dig. Huddled, they communicated in urgent whispers, glancing around to make sure they weren't overheard. Every now and again a digger hurried across the site in response to an urgent call. The men looked on edge, even frightened.

It explained why no one had come rushing in after the magical explosion. Only one man even seemed to notice, slowing and blinking at the cracked stone as he passed. "Lovers' spat," James said, emerging from the room behind Will. The man flushed and hurried on.

"What's happening?" Will asked another of the men passing, only to recognize Rosati, the local frequently employed by Captain Howell as a translator.

But Rosati said nothing, just gave a single wary look, and that same warding gesture that Will had seen the workers use on the mountain.

With unspoken agreement, Will and James began to move toward the source of the disturbance.

They hadn't gone far before they heard familiar voices coming from one of the tents.

"This is wrong," Kettering was saying. "You can't send anyone else in. Not after what just happened."

"We've broken through!" said Sloane. "What happened, it's a sign. We're right on the edge of discovery!"

Will drew in a breath sharply. His eyes flew to James's and they exchanged a look.

"It was twenty-six men!" said Kettering. "The locals are throwing down their picks and refusing to dig. They're saying the place is cursed."

Sloane had no sympathy at all in his voice. "If they won't work, then find me men who will."

Kettering's voice grew even more unhappy. "And what are you going to do with—"

"We burn them," said Sloane. "Just like all the others."

"You can't," said Kettering. "You can't keep—"

"It's Sinclair's orders," said Sloane, opening the tent flap and gesturing to a nearby soldier who came, musket in hand. As Sloane strode off to make arrangements, Kettering ran a hand through his hair. "This is wrong. This is—" Kettering set off purposefully toward the place where the locals were gathering.

"Follow him," said Will, pulling James along with him as he followed Kettering through the tents. In front of them was a red glow, and it was hard to see at night, but it seemed a thick black column of smoke rose from it. Will could smell it, acrid and familiar.

Kettering had stopped.

He was staring at a huge firepit, already burning. A wheelbarrow was being brought toward it by a group of Sloane's soldiers. The wheelbarrow's contents were dumped onto the fire. But there was another wheelbarrow behind it. And another. And another.

Kettering was staring at the fire with tears streaming down his face.

"Whatever's in those wheelbarrows, we need to get a look at it before they burn it." Before whatever Sloane was hiding went up in smoke.

Will was not naive. He could smell the fire. But if Sloane's men really had broken through to some discovery in the palace, he had to know what had been found.

How easy it would have been if he could have scried into one of Sloane's men—or Sloane himself—and simply walked up to a wheelbarrow in his host's body. But he couldn't, not while James was with him. Nor could he easily rid himself of James for the required time. And besides, the skill was frighteningly new, and he was aware how vulnerable the ability left him afterward.

Will looked around himself for a diversion. "If we can somehow distract them, maybe—"

A support beam near one of the dig trenches exploded outward, the scaffolding surrounding it collapsing in a ruckus of crashing supplies and shouting men.

"You mean like that?" James said, lowering his hand, his smile breathtaking in the chaos he'd created, the cries going up, *"Aiuto! Aiuto!"* And in English, "Oi! Come and help us!" Everyone running toward the collapse.

"You don't need to sneak around untying ropes," James murmured as he passed Will, that smile still on his face. "You have me now."

A flutter at the words *you have me*. Will ignored it. They needed to be fast. He slipped over to the abandoned wheelbarrow while the men surrounded the collapsed trench.

He felt rather than saw James arrive, then go still next to him. His own eyes were on the shape in the wheelbarrow.

"'*Twenty-six men*,'" quoted James.

Will had moved bodies in a wheelbarrow in the Hall. This was smaller than most of them. A boy of perhaps ten or eleven, the same age as the scouts who had accompanied them into the palace. The boy's jacket lay over his head like a shroud.

Rosati had made the warning gesture. Will had seen the fear in the eyes of the locals. He thought, *They send the boys in first.*

Will drew in a breath and pulled back the boy's jacket.

He didn't realize he had staggered back until he felt James's hands on his shoulders, heard James's voice. "Will. *Will.* Are you all right?"

Black veins traveling up her arms, her eyes wide and afraid. He'd begged her not to pick up the sword. *Will, I'm frightened.*

"Will, what's wrong? What is it?"

He looked back at the body in the wheelbarrow. It was like looking at a memory. The dead boy's face was unnaturally chalk white, his veins ink black, like cracks. His open eyes were two black marbles. And Will knew without touching him that his skin would be cold and hard as stone.

A thousand miles separated them, but they were the same: locked in a dead rictus, as if whatever lay under the mountain was connected to her, dying in his arms on the hillside.

"I've seen this before," said Will. "With Katherine."

CHAPTER TWENTY-FIVE

"THEY CALL IT the white death," said Cyprian.

At the name, Will felt a chill on his skin. The four of them were sitting in James's rooms, exchanging information in low voices. Grace and Cyprian had used the chaos to return, sneaking back onto the dig with laborers' cloaks over their Steward clothes. Will had told them about the corpse in the wheelbarrow, expecting them to feel fear and unease—not expecting them to have the answers. But as he had described the stone-white pallor of the corpse, Grace and Cyprian had shared a look of recognition.

"The locals have legends about it," said Cyprian. "They say that when the mountain opens, the white death will spread and a great evil will rise."

Will couldn't help thinking of the twisted doors in the palace. Something inside, trying to get out.

"What is it? A pestilence? A plague?" he said.

"They don't know. It happens to those who wander too far on the mountain," said Cyprian, explaining what a village girl had told him, in fear for her brother's life. "In the stories, they burn the bodies, just like you say Sloane has done."

The mountain seemed to grow in Will's mind, a dark presence full of secrets. If the locals had enshrined the white death in their legends, it was not new. It had been part of this place for years, perhaps centuries.

"Sloane said he'd broken through," said James. "Twenty-six bodies . . . he must be close to the source of the white death. Whatever's inside that palace, Sinclair's almost found it."

"We have to stop him," said Cyprian. "We can't let him release a plague. We know it's in the palace. All the cases happen here."

"Not all the cases," Will said.

Cyprian looked at him with pure confusion. "What do you mean?"

Will had to push the words out, not wanting to speak of those events ever again. "Katherine died of the white death."

He told them what he had told James, describing the way Katherine had died. The corpse in the wheelbarrow with its black veins and too-pale flesh had merged in his mind with her body. The stonelike quality of it, frozen in a horrifying pose, trailing long blond hair—it was the same, alike in every detail.

"The corruption on the blade—" Each word was dangerous, and could expose him. He forced them out anyway. "When she drew Ekthalion, the corruption seeped into her skin, and turned her to white stone." He didn't want to say more; he couldn't. "I hoped that she might be the Champion. But she wasn't."

Or maybe she was, and was simply dead. Warriors of the Light didn't have much luck fighting the Dark King. He remembered carrying her to the cottage, heavy as the stone she resembled, his arms aching as he held her up, not wanting to drag her along the ground like a sack.

"You think that's what's in the palace? Some kind of weapon?" said Cyprian.

James was shaking his head slowly. "That's not what happened when

Ekthalion got loose on Simon's ship," he said. "The men in the hold were rotted and burned. The corruption from the black flame dissolved their organs. It didn't turn them to white stone."

It was not what had happened to the birds and animals that had died at the Dark Peak either. Or the grass and the trees that simply withered and died, rotting like the men on the ship.

Will couldn't help feeling that there was a piece he was missing, some vital part that he didn't yet understand.

"We don't have time to waste," he said. "We need to find Ettore. The Elder Steward said only with him could we stop what was to come."

Grace and Cyprian didn't answer. After a long, wordless moment, Cyprian straightened his shoulders, then he pulled out a scrap of material from his tunic.

White, grimy, and torn; it was a moment before Will understood what he was looking at.

"Ettore is a *Steward*?" said Will.

"*Was* a Steward," said Cyprian. "He's dead."

Like the gate slamming closed, leaving them stranded. On the scrap in Cyprian's hand was the gleam of a star. No Steward would leave their star behind. He saw the truth of that in Cyprian's and Grace's expressions. The man the Elder Steward had sent them here to find was dead.

Will thought of the boy lying dead in that wheelbarrow, who had been thrown onto the pyre to burn. He thought of Katherine, dying at Bowhill.

They all seemed to realize it at the same moment. There was only one way left to find out what the mountain held. But it meant evading their captors here and running toward danger.

"We need to get back into the palace," said Will.

"The whole dig is under lockdown," said Grace, shaking her head.

"Cyprian and I barely made it back here."

"Patrols have doubled since those deaths at the palace," agreed Cyprian. "We saw dozens of guards on our ride back from the village."

"A dozen guards won't be any trouble," said James, flexing his fingers.

"No," said Will. "You're not going to kill guards."

"I don't have to *kill* them to—"

"Or maim guards."

"Then how exactly do you plan to get inside?" said James.

"I can take you," a voice said.

The four of them turned toward the door.

Kettering stood in the doorway, pushing his glasses up nervously. Will felt James's magic flare at the same time that Cyprian's sword drew from his sheath. He put himself in front of both of them.

Kettering wasn't armed. His face was pale, his eyes darting from Cyprian to James. He looked scared. But he was here nevertheless.

"Why would you do that?" said Will.

Kettering turned his eyes on Will. "Those men who died of the white death today . . . dozens of bodies thrown into the fire . . . it's wrong. I signed up to study the ancient magic of the past, to help restore its wonders, not to see people killed."

Kettering seemed to have drawn on all his courage to say this. Will remembered Kettering's eyes streaming with tears at the pyre. Kettering had argued with Sloane to protect the workers when he hadn't known anyone was listening. He had answered Will's questions without reporting him to Sloane when Will had first come to the dig.

Will said slowly, "What is the white death?"

"I don't know."

"What is it that Sinclair's digging for?"

"I don't know that either."

James made a scornful sound. "Will, he's not going to tell us anything." His magic sparked again, threateningly.

"I know where the deaths happened," said Kettering hurriedly. "The men all fell in the same location."

"Inside the palace," said Will, and Kettering nodded slowly. "You made some kind of breakthrough." Another nod.

"We opened an inner chamber. The moment we unsealed the doors, the men just died, as if a white wave rolled over them."

"You didn't care about the safety of those local boys before," said Will. Kettering had stood by while Sloane sent boys into the palace. "What's different now?"

"That was a normal risk, the same as any dig!" said Kettering. "It's different knowing that people will die, their lives wasted, thrown away into the fire. The white death . . . anyone might be next! And if it gets loose? A magical plague spilling out into the population? I thought Sinclair and I had the same goals, a respect for the past, for the ancient world. But he is meddling with forces he doesn't understand. I fear what he might unleash, blundering around in that palace."

Will searched Kettering's face. Kettering had followed Sinclair this far, and he had a consuming interest in the ancient world, having devoted his life to its study. But his feeling for the dead workers appeared genuine. "Unleash?"

"What lies beneath Undahar?" said Kettering. "That is the question, isn't it? Sinclair has been throwing men at the dig for years. He never found the palace. It opened when you arrived. As if it was waiting for you." Kettering said the words to James, but it was Will who felt them resonate. "The earthquakes, the accelerating deaths . . . whatever lies beneath the mountain, I believe its time will be soon at hand."

That was disturbing to everyone.

These objects have their own agenda, Kettering had said. They would be riding into the heart of danger. Will felt that old sensation of a pit inside himself, opening up.

Will made his decision. "If you know where Sinclair's men died, then that's where we need to go."

They began to disband and ready themselves, the others exiting to gather supplies, and to find laborers' clothes to disguise themselves for the journey.

But there was something Will needed to do first.

"Cyprian."

Will touched Cyprian on the arm, turning him back. Cyprian looked at him quizzically.

"Violet's going to escape," Will said.

Cyprian's green eyes widened, both uncertain and desperately hungry for reassurance. Will felt again that odd protectiveness toward him.

Will said, "She's going to escape, Cyprian."

"How do you know that?" Cyprian was searching for the answer to a question that churned in him.

Will couldn't tell him the truth. But he'd thought it through carefully. Violet had come back for him on the ship. He would do the same for her, no matter what it cost him.

"There's no point breaking out on a ship," said Will. He had thought that part of it through too. He'd needed to wait for her to make landfall. "There's nowhere to go. But on dry land? Violet will be free before we even set out for the palace."

Cyprian opened his green eyes fully on Will's. "You're sure of that?"

"Very sure," said Will.

CHAPTER TWENTY-SIX

THERE WOULD BE no returning to the dig once they left, which meant Will didn't have much time.

He told the others he was creating a distraction, scooped up a bundle of clothes as a pretext, and let Sloane's guards follow him, knowing they saw a harmless messenger boy with a parcel for Captain Howell.

The second he was inside Howell's tent, he strode right up to Howell, not bothering with a greeting, put a hand on Howell's wrist, and pushed inside.

He saw Howell's eyes widen and he heard him give a cry of surprise, but he didn't pause until he found himself inside Howell's body.

Work quickly. Will had less than an hour before he was meant to join the others. He pushed further, using Howell's *S* brand as a conduit, casting himself into the web he remembered, following along the now-familiar paths, seeking out the body he had inhabited on Violet's ship, until, with a gasp, he opened his eyes.

His leg ached; a thicker sense of his body in space; objects in the room at strange angles. He was shorter. He couldn't see the room properly.

He squinted, took a step, and fell, grabbing for the desk. Half catching its lip, his bad leg screamed its protest. He let out a cry and just hung on to the desk for a moment as his vision cleared. Slowly, he pulled himself up, making no assumptions this time about how to stay upright on his shorter legs.

This wasn't a ship. It was an office, in the grand style but run-down, dilapidated, in an old building. A heavy oak chair accompanied the desk, a man's jacket hanging over it. In the hours since Will had last peered through his eyes, the man he was inhabiting had docked and disembarked.

"Leclerc! *Apportez-moi ces papiers!*"

Bring the papers? Which papers? He looked down at the desk. He would need to find what was requested if he wasn't going to blow his cover.

Am I Leclerc? Everything was blurry. He thought at first that his eyes didn't work. But when he groped around on the desk, his hand closed on glasses. He put them on, hooking them over his ears.

Blinking owlishly at the sudden clarity, he looked back down at the desk.

It was covered in papers. He could hear footsteps in the corridor, approaching. He let go of the desk and swayed, immediately grabbing on to it again. He tried leaning his weight against it surreptitiously, the sort of insouciant posture James might adopt. There was no way to find the right paper. Needing an excuse, he quickly took off his glasses and slipped them into his pocket, then he reached out to pick up a sheaf of paper at random.

He missed, a disorienting sensation: his arms were too short. He had to force himself to reach unnaturally farther, clutching the paper just as the door swung open.

The woman James had called Mrs. Duval strode inside.

"Well? Do you have the inventory?"

She was even more imposing close-up, with strong, angular features and piercing dark eyes. Surely she could look at him with those eyes and in one glance see he wasn't Leclerc.

Heart pounding with fear of discovery, Will held out the paper in his hand and pretended to squint even more than he needed to. "Is this it? I've misplaced my glasses."

She snatched it from him, glanced at it briefly, then threw it down onto the desk, rifling over the strewn papers and picking up the top one. "No. It's right under your nose." His vision was too blurry to see what sort of look she was giving him, but her tone was brisk, as if she was in a hurry. "And your glasses are here. In your pocket." He felt her pat his pocket rather than saw it. "I hope you won't have this kind of absent-mindedness with the girl."

"No—" He didn't know what to call her. Mrs. Duval? Some other name?

"Well, brother?"

"—sister."

She took the papers and strode out of the room.

He was left staring after her, with his heart pounding.

Inventory, part of this mind was saying. *What are they storing here?* He ought to look through the papers. But Violet was more important. And there wasn't time. Back in Umbria, he had less than an hour, and besides that was alone in a room with Howell, his jet-black eyes screaming his identity to anyone who might stumble on him. What would happen if his own uninhabited body was touched, or moved, or taken? Worse, if the others saw his eyes? Sarcean had used Anharion to guard him, viewing scrying as too dangerous. He felt that danger keenly now.

He hooked his glasses back on, then looked around and saw a thick chain of keys hanging by the door. His first piece of luck: he recognized immediately the key to the Steward manacles. He'd used that key to unlock those manacles himself. It was the confirmation he needed: Violet was here, and this was the way to free her. The only trouble was, he didn't know where Violet was being held.

Well, he would find out.

The door was six steps from the desk. He drew in a breath, let go of the desk, and made himself take a step. His eyes were fixed on the keys. Trying to reach them required far greater skill and concentration than walking around in his own body. Six steps, and he was clutching the wall again. *Too slow.* He couldn't help Violet like this, arriving at her cell in three days with the speed of a tortoise. He had to speed up.

He saw the shiny black cane in the stand by the door. Reaching for it, he felt his stomach flip. The *S* on his wrist—visible as his sleeve pulled back along his arm—was alive. It was hot and red, activated, almost pulsing. He pushed his sleeve down over it quickly, and took the cane.

Then he took the keys, and hung them ostentatiously from his belt, where they dangled, very noticeably.

Walking was still a tricky business, even with the cane, and he found himself with his palm on the corridor wall quite frequently. Searching for Violet would draw attention, but his difficulty controlling Leclerc's body made it a hundred times worse. So instead of limping suspiciously this way and that about the house, he followed his nose to the kitchen.

It was a big kitchen with a huge hearth and meat turning on a spit over a fire. In the center was a long wooden table scattered with flour and bowls. There was a cook in a stained apron, and two kitchen hands, one of whom looked up in surprise to see him as she kneaded dough with floury arms.

"What can I do for you, Monsieur Leclerc?" she said in French.

Right. He was in France. His own French, learned from a drunk Jean Lastier on the docks, was not superb. He blinked at the question, realizing that if Leclerc was named Leclerc, likely he was French too.

Apporter? Apportez? He said, praying his verb conjugations were correct,

"Take lunch to the prisoner."

That won him a look, flipping the dough over. "She just ate," said the kitchen hand, "not a quarter of an hour ago."

He drew himself up to his full height and tried to make himself seem as French as possible.

"Lions eat a great deal, madame," he said.

The dough stopped flipping. There was some quick muttering he didn't understand, along with the words, "Two lunches!" But the kitchen hand wiped her floury hands on her apron, and turned to face him. "Very well."

Casting his eye around the kitchen, Will said, "Bread rolls, hard cheese, meats. Put some water in a flask. And give her that—" Oh God, what was it called? "Piece of cloth. Blanket. Napkin."

The kitchen hand's eyebrows went up into her hair, but she got to work gathering the repast. While her back was turned, he saw a knife on the counter, a slim blade with a sharp point. He took it quickly and slid it into his belt, where it stuck out very obviously next to the keys, making sure that both the handle and a section of the blade protruded visibly.

"After you," he said to the kitchen hand when she was ready with the tray, hearing the mutter behind him, "*I told you he was skimming food.*"

"*And drink too,*" came the second mutter.

She led him down the corridor, making two turns before she reached a door with stairs leading downward, as though into a supply cellar. Descending the stairs was a minor nightmare, and he leaned heavily on the wall, making a show of his limp to hide his lack of balance when his legs didn't end where he expected.

"You can put the tray down outside the door," he said.

She didn't. She just stood and stared at him. "Don't you think you've harassed that girl enough?"

He had to push down his reaction to that, the burst of protectiveness and anger. He couldn't ask this kitchen hand, *What do you mean? What has he done to her?* He had to stay calm. What would Leclerc say?

"Are you here to work or talk?" said Will.

That had been a favorite saying of Jean Lastier when dockmen around him complained. He didn't think Lastier's other favorite saying, *la vie est trop courte pour boire du mauvais vin,* would be useful.

She put the tray down, an angry clatter.

He found himself alone at the base of the stairs, staring at a locked door, with his heartbeat accelerating. He fished out the keys that he'd clipped to his belt. The door lock was new-looking, so he tried the newest-looking key. It slid in smoothly. *Violet.* Violet was on the other side of that door. He made sure to quickly return the keys to hang again noticeably from his belt, and then the door swung open.

The room itself was a cellar with arched ceilings. It was older than the house above, with medieval stonework and an uneven cobbled floor. There were a few barrels stacked in the corner that might once have held wine. There was a lamp burning in the sconce by the doorway so that the cellar was not plunged into darkness when the door was closed.

And Violet, in the Steward manacles and on a long chain attached to the far wall, scrabbling up to face him as he entered.

She looked thin, with dirt smudged on her cheek, still wearing the same clothes she'd been in during the attack on the Hall. But her eyes were defiant, her glare at him so welcome and familiar that a rush of gladness swept over him.

He wanted to stride across the cellar and throw his arms around her in a tight hug. He wanted to unlock her chains and set her free. He found himself remembering the moment he'd been chained to Simon's sinking ship, when she had appeared in the hold. For a moment he imagined himself kneeling by her side and unlocking her manacles. *You broke my chains once. Remember?*

But he couldn't. He leaned his cane against the door and picked up the tray, no easy feat.

"Fattening me for the slaughter?" she said.

"That's lambs," he said in English, and then wondered with the jolt of one who has missed a step if he was supposed to have a French accent.

"I'm not going to kill Tom," she said, "no matter how many more of these training sessions you make me do. And no matter what you say to threaten my friends."

Her words were a shock. He hid it, smoothing his face. Glaring at him, she didn't seem to notice any difference in his manner.

"Your friends are in Umbria," he said, putting the tray down on the floor, "at Sinclair's dig near the village of Scheggino. They are too far away for you to warn them, even if you tried."

He saw her take in the information, her eyes narrowed.

But all she said was, "Sinclair's the one who needs the warning. Will's going to stop him."

Her faith in him warmed him, even as it redoubled his feeling of responsibility. *I will stop him*, he promised her silently.

"And what are you going to do from inside that cage?" he made himself say.

He saw her eyes drop to the keys.

Jangling noticeably on his hip, the keys to her manacles hung where he'd clipped them. He stepped toward her as he spoke, pretending not to notice where she was looking. Just Leclerc strolling forward, bringing himself in range of her chain. He'd calculated it carefully.

Even so, he was surprised how fast she moved, knocking him onto his back, then planting a knee in his chest to hold him down while she snatched the keys and undid the manacles, casting them off to the side. That speed and the economy of her strike felt new.

"I'm going to get out," she said, her hand on his throat.

He'd had a woman's hand around his throat before. He ought to have been terrified. Instead, he felt a helpless loving feeling of knowing Violet wouldn't hurt him.

"You won't get anywhere without a weapon or supplies." He kept his expression very blank.

She immediately snatched his belt knife. Using it to cut a strip off his shirt and tie his hands behind his back, she leapt up and quickly bundled the meats, cheese, and bread he'd brought, and wrapped it in the cloth with the water flask, slinging it across her chest like a knapsack. Then she stood over him.

"Where's the shield?" she said.

"What shield?"

"*My* shield," said Violet.

The Shield of Rassalon? He bit down on his tongue before he said it.

"I don't know."

Violet let out a breath of disbelief. "Liar. You're coming with me."

"What?" said Will, and it came out like a squeak.

"You heard me." The knife was pointed right at his liver. He supposed that was another new technique that she had learned. "You're taking me to the shield."

"I don't know where it is!" yelped Will.

That won him another poke from what was really a very sharp knife. "You're lying."

"Violet, honestly, I'm not," said Will, feeling so purely himself at that moment that he was shocked Violet didn't recognize him. "I really think it would be easier for you to escape by yourself, don't you?"

"I'm not escaping," said Violet. "You're taking me to the shield."

"I'm what?" said Will. "But—"

"Move it!" said Violet, shoving him forward.

With the point of Violet's knife still quite near his liver, he fumbled his cane into his hand and did his best to climb the stairs. Leclerc's injuries hid his own unsteadiness in the body—luckily. More luck, Violet seemed to know the way. She strode there confidently, which let him stumble along, hiding his unfamiliarity with the house, and receiving only a few knife pricks for his limping pace.

But when they entered a hall with a huge mantel and crest, he saw the motto and the family name carved beneath the crest, and his entire understanding of where they were going changed. *La fin de la misère.* Misery's End.

The name under the crest was *Gauthier.*

The executioner.

This is Gauthier's home, Will thought, his mind racing. *Where he lived before Sinclair found him.* And then, even more unnervingly, *This is Gauthier's family vault.* He was staring at a huge, locked vault door. A descendant of Rathorn, the Dark King's executioner. Gauthier had owned the Collar before James had reclaimed it.

What else might lie inside that vault?

Violet had taken his keys out again and was fitting one to the lock. No luck on the first try, but the second key fit. With a clicking and a grinding, an entire portion of the wall swung open, revealing stairs leading down into the dark.

The gloomy vault was crammed with artifacts. Like a room stuffed with a houseful of furniture, there was no wall that wasn't covered by a piece of ancient masonry or frieze, no surface that wasn't forested with statues, urns, and carvings. To walk in meant to slide your body past tables, statues, and columns displaced from their original settings. Then to clamber over gemstones and jewelry, piles of it like a dragon's hoard. Then he looked closer, and saw—

Sun emblems, eclipses. Rayless black spheres. This was a collection, an obsession, generations of Gauthiers trying to find any artifact pertaining to the Dark Palace, as if they were trying to find their way back there. As if they were searching for something that lay inside. Will felt the disturbing sense of forces converging on the palace, all of them racing for its prize.

He stopped in the room's center, where a giant black axe was mounted like a centerpiece. Beside it hung a black cowl that had to be a reproduction—didn't it? The axe, Will knew in his bones, was real. It was as real as death; the executioner's axe, it had a finality that struck cold fear, the kind of dark that snuffed out light. Along its head, in the language of the old world, were the words from which the family had drawn its motto: *den fahor.* Misery's End. It was the name of the axe that had risen and fallen on James's neck.

As he moved forward, he saw that under Rathorn's axe there were drawings, careful diagrams, numerical notations, and then to his shock he saw writing in the old language that said:

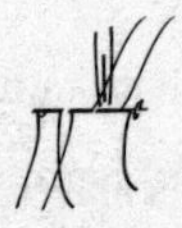

Undahar

He shifted the top sheaf of paper to reveal a drawing of the Dark Palace.

It crowned a world of utter darkness; a world so cold and rayless that forests were set on fire in a desperate hope for light. And from atop the spires of that darkly jeweled palace, he watched—he remembered watching—the coruscating domes of magic in the distance, the last defenses that soon would flicker and go out, assailed by ravenous shadows that did not tire or sleep.

In the shaky script of an aged, feeble hand, were the words in French, *None may enter Undahar and live, unless—*

The second page was missing. Or was one of the many pages scattering the desk. He reached out to snatch them up, to slip them into his jacket to read later, only to realize, rather foolishly, that he couldn't. This was not his body, and there was no use concealing the papers in the jacket of a man in Calais.

He needed time, then, to read them here. A sound made him turn.

Violet stood behind him, a familiar metal shield on her arm; Rassalon's lion eyes gazed out from its surface soulfully. She must have found it among the collected objects.

He had one opportunity for time alone to scan the papers. He had scant minutes left before his friends back in Italy came looking for him. He needed to use that time to learn all he could.

"Your shield," said Will with relief. "You can take it and go."

"I will, thank you," said Violet. And she swung the shield at his head.

Disoriented, he opened his eyes; he was Will, with a sore head. Pushing himself up, he saw that Howell had also been knocked flat. No way to reinhabit the unconscious Leclerc. No time left to find another host without real fear of discovery.

He had to get back to the others. He'd have to make up a story to explain his injured head. But when he lifted his hand to his temple, he realized there was no injury. The pain was a phantom, the bruises left behind in Calais, on someone else's body.

CHAPTER TWENTY-SEVEN

"SHE'S AWAKE," SAID a woman's voice, and Elizabeth pushed up hazily, blinking.

It was morning. She was in a lumpy bed, under a threadbare blanket. Across from her was the room's window and rough-hewn wooden door. In a small vase on a side table she saw a sprig of purple orchis that looked just-picked, lopsided with a bent petal.

The woman who had spoken was about thirty years of age, with brown hair, a plain dark dress, and blood on her hands and arms. *Blood?* Elizabeth came wide awake and jumped from the bed, throwing herself as far from the woman as she could, flattening her back to the opposite wall, her heart pounding.

She remembered the gaping jaws of the shadow hound, its hot breath, the glimpse of its red tongue. And something after that, some kind of flash—

"Don't be afraid," said the woman. "Your sister lost a lot of blood. But she's going to be all right."

Now she could see the whole room: there was an older man in here too, about fifty, dressed in country clothes with rolled-up white sleeves and a cap. And there was a second bed, where Katherine was lying unmoving.

It wasn't Katherine. It was that strange man from the old world. His dress was red all down the front from blood. There was a basin full of his blood on the side table next to him, and strips of bloody fabric. And a round piece of lead—a bullet that they had pulled out of his stomach.

He's not my sister. But that was harder to say now. Without Visander's animating consciousness, Katherine just looked like herself. As if she would open her eyes and be herself.

"My name's Polly," the woman was saying. "And this is my brother, Lawrence."

Maybe she would be herself, thought Elizabeth. Maybe the last few days had been a bad dream. Maybe in a second, Katherine would wake up.

"Ar ventas, ar ventas fermaran," Katherine started to murmur in the dead language. Elizabeth shivered.

"She's been speaking like that," said Polly. "In tongues."

"We won't stay long," said Elizabeth. "We'll just get better and go. Where is this?"

"This village is Stanton."

"Stanton!" said Elizabeth.

"Your sister brought you here before she passed out."

Stanton was the village Redlan George had told her to find. Katherine (Visander) must have tracked it down, even weak with loss of blood.

She looked like she had fainted. It was such a familiar sight that Elizabeth half expected her to peek an eye open and give Elizabeth a secret wink. Katherine had learned how to faint two years earlier, which she had done to get out of engagements. Katherine would faint, Aunt would rush in with smelling salts, and Katherine would rouse and smile weakly, insisting she was all right.

You shouldn't lie to Aunt, Elizabeth had said the first time, and Katherine had sprung out of bed and hugged her in that spontaneous way she had. *I know. Come on, let's go downstairs.* Elizabeth had resisted those hugs sometimes, not realizing that one day they would end.

Elizabeth could feel the expectant looks of Polly and Lawrence on her. They were already too conspicuous, one wounded girl dragging another into a village. But Redlan had helped her. Redlan had told her it was safe.

Right before Visander had killed him. Elizabeth drew in a breath.

"I heard there's a woman here called Ellie Lange," said Elizabeth carefully. "Do you know her?"

Polly shared a quick look with Lawrence.

"You were in a sleep like death," said Polly. "Perhaps you ought to rest."

"You do know her, don't you," said Elizabeth.

"She's my aunt," said Polly, after a reluctant pause.

"Then you can take us to her."

"She doesn't—see people."

"Why not?"

Silence. There was something they knew. Something they weren't telling. She felt its importance in the tense quality of the air. It seemed to fill up with a thousand unspoken words as the two shared another look. Elizabeth stepped forward urgently.

"A man named Redlan George sent us." *He said you would help us.* "He said Ellie Lange knew my mother."

In the thick silence, the man's face filled with disbelief. But Polly looked like she had half been expecting the question.

"It can't be," said the man. Polly held him back.

"What was your mother's name, child?" said Polly.

"Eleanor," said Elizabeth.

"I told you we shouldn't have taken them in!"

"Your sister is the spitting image," said Polly, as if with heavy knowledge. "When she turned up on our doorstep with her dress all blood, it was like history was repeating."

Elizabeth stared. Was this woman telling her that her *mother* had been here? That she had stood with a bloody dress at the same door?

"Aye, we knew her," said Lawrence, angrily. "She stayed here for a while. She's the reason Mrs. Lange can't—"

Polly hushed him. "Why don't you go downstairs and get some firewood, Laurie. We're running low." And when Lawrence seemed to object for a moment, she said, "I'm all right. I'll just settle the girl back to bed."

Lawrence didn't like it, giving them a look that seemed to say, *This room is full of trouble.* But he left them alone, and as he did so, Elizabeth ventured farther forward from the wall, toward the chair by her sister's bed, her eyes on Polly.

"You do know something!" said Elizabeth.

Polly didn't answer, just looked at her, troubled. "I know why you fell into that sleep."

It wasn't what Elizabeth had expected her to say. "I—was just—"

"It's the old power, isn't it? You used too much of it."

Elizabeth stared back at her. *Dark jaws opening to devour her, her eyes screwing shut, and a flash—* Her hands made two fists in the fabric of her skirts.

"What do you mean?"

"I was just a girl the first time your mother came to Stanton."

"*First* time?"

"She came here three times," said Polly, "to give birth."

"What?" said Elizabeth, and suddenly sat down.

Blinking at the inside of the room, she realized that she had been born here, in this village. Maybe in this very room, or close to it. Stanton was her birthplace, and it was maybe for this reason that Redlan had sent her here.

No, not Redlan, the Lady. He was the Lady's envoy. *She sent me here.* She felt the hand of fate guiding her, bringing her here for some reason.

Polly moved to the basin and began to wash the blood off her hands. "My aunt is a midwife. Your mother came to her to give birth to your brother. And then twice later, for you and your sister."

He's not my brother, she wanted to say. She looked at Katherine, sprawled out on the bed. *He's not my sister.*

"After your brother's birth, my aunt, she grew sick. Too sick to work. Laurie, he blamed your mother. Said she brought us bad luck. I was the one who helped midwife you and your sister."

Elizabeth stared at Polly's hands, calloused and red from work, as she dried them on one of the towels by the basin. *Those are the hands that birthed me?* She felt again as if her mother was close by, her skin prickling at being so close to her own beginning.

Once her hands were dry, Polly pulled back the covers of Katherine's bed. The sight shocked Elizabeth out of all thoughts of her mother.

She had expected to see a mess of blood and bandaging. Katherine had been shot at close range, then ridden with the wound for more than an hour.

Impossibly, it was half-healed. The unbandaged skin looked raw and red, but there was no wound. Elizabeth's eyes flew to Polly's face.

"You see?" said Polly. "I know how it feels to be drained. And what it means to keep a secret, mother and daughter. We have some of the old power in my family too."

A healing power, thought Elizabeth. A line of midwives, keeping what they could do secret, out here in the middle of nowhere.

"You're a descendant," said Elizabeth.

"A what?" said Polly.

Elizabeth opened her mouth to tell her, then shut it again. Polly was helping her, she was a nice lady who used her power to heal people who came to her village. She didn't know about the old world, or the Dark King. She shouldn't be dragged into it. Katherine had been dragged into it. Only bad things had happened after that.

"The danger you're running from," said Polly. "It's the same danger your mother was running from, isn't it."

Elizabeth nodded. Eleanor might have hidden here, but she hadn't told Polly what she was hiding from.

"There's a man chasing us," Elizabeth said carefully. "He killed one of my friends. Sarah. Redlan George told us to come here. He said to find Ellie Lange, that she'd know what to do."

Polly looked back at her. The blood on Polly's clothes didn't seem so frightening now that Elizabeth knew she was a healer.

"I can take you to her, but she's not what she was," said Polly.

"I just want to talk to her."

"Very well," said Polly, as if deciding something. "Tomorrow, we'll go together. Your sister will be awake by then."

She turned and tucked the blankets back in around Katherine. Then she left the room, closing but not bolting the door behind her.

Elizabeth was left alone with Katherine.

She dragged the heavy wooden chair closer to the bed and climbed back onto it. She looked down at Katherine's white face, her hair falling out of its curls, uncharacteristic smears of mud and dirt on her skin.

When Katherine had pretended to faint, Elizabeth had always stood lookout, saying, *It's all right, they've gone,* when the way was clear.

"It's all right, they've gone," she whispered now, but nothing happened.

Because it wasn't Katherine. But it looked like her, it looked so much like her, and maybe while Visander was asleep, she could pretend that her sister was still here.

"You're wearing earrings," she said, thinking of what would make her sister happy. "Aunt must have let you have them. Your dress has those sleeves you like. I'm sorry about the color."

There was no change in the face on the pillow, not even a flicker.

"You married Phillip. It was just like you wanted. I was going to stay with you, and there was going to be a big stables for Ladybird and Nell. I was going to make sure things were nice, I wasn't going to complain about you playing Schubert all the time, even that one with the loud part."

She had her hands clenched in her skirts, sitting on the wooden chair that was too big for her.

Please wake up, she didn't say. *I'm really frightened.*

"You're Lady Crenshaw. You can have parties. Phillip's not an old man."

No answer.

The reality in the small room seemed to press at her. Katherine looked like a body laid out before burial. As if her aunt and uncle would appear to pay their respects, before men came to get her and take her in a funeral procession.

Katherine was dead.

She was looking at her sister's dead body, which in the morning would get up and walk around, inhabited by her sister's killer.

She rubbed her forearm over her eyes and looked over at the purple orchis in the vase on the side table. Before they had come to London, Katherine had liked to pick flowers. Elizabeth took a sprig of the orchis and put it on Katherine's chest.

"I'm sorry it doesn't match your dress."

And that was when Katherine's eyes opened.

He saw the girl. She was hovering over him, all eyebrows and frown. The room stank of humanity. Wood smoke, sweat, and under that the thick smell of blood. A human house. A human village. *It's just humans as far as the eye can see.*

And yet, there was this girl. And he had seen. He had seen with his own eyes this girl summon light. He sat up, brushing a flower stalk off his chest.

"Where are we? How long have I been asleep? I tried to bring you to your village but I felt myself growing weak. That man's weapon, it was more powerful than I thought."

"Speak English," said the girl, frowning and rubbing her arm across her eyes.

Visander put his hand on the place in his side where he had just had a fresh wound, only to find it tender but scabbed as though it was days old, and healthy, free from infection. "Are you the one who healed me?"

"No. That was one of the *humans* in this house."

"You're not one of them."

"Yes I am. And so are you. So you can shut up about humans, because they're helping you even though you killed my sister."

"You are her heir. You have her power," said Visander. "Lightbringer."

He felt his eyes welling with tears. It was wonder and relief and rightness.

"It cannot be dark where there is light." The old words rose to his lips. "Where there is darkness, there will always be a Lightbringer."

He thought of Indeviel, in that miserable room, his light extinguished. And here in the human squalor of this house was the Lightbringer.

"Does Indeviel know that you live, Lightbringer?" His heart hurt, worse than the wound in his side, which was healing so fast he could almost feel it knitting together.

"I don't know those words," said Elizabeth. "I don't speak that language."

"Do you not know what you are?"

He pushed himself up in the bed, careful of his still-tender stomach. This human body was fragile, and had almost bled out. His shoulder twinged, and he pushed the cloth of his garment down to see a canine bite mark, also part healed. A second more, and the shadow hound would have torn him apart.

This girl had saved him. He looked at her. She had dull brown hair and overly dark eyebrows. She stood in front of him on short child's legs in a stained pinafore. She looked human. A child. And she didn't know. She didn't know what she was.

"I know about the Lady," she said.

The Queen. She's talking about the Queen. The girl undid three buttons at the neck of her dress and drew out a chunk of metal on a leather tie. She thrust the metal out at him.

Caught in his thoughts, it took him a moment to recognize what the girl was holding. When he did, he almost reeled back.

The hawthorn medallion.

So much time had passed that its bright surface was forever tarnished. It looked ancient, a forgotten relic. It was like a symbol of all that was lost.

He hadn't expected to return and find the whole world gone, and the only thing left this girl.

He stared at her. The feeling that came over him was almost like grief, a feeling of being utterly alone. The Dark was already here in this world, and the Lightbringer was a child.

Untrained, and too young. Yet here the medallion was, a sign, like the light that had burst out of her when the darkness had closed on his throat.

If she was all there was, then he would protect her. He would guard this single spark. All alone out here in the dark.

He was pushing out of the bed, this time ignoring his injuries, and going to his knee.

"My queen," he said. "I am your champion."

Instead of touching his head and telling him to rise, her frown deepened.

"If I'm your queen, or whatever, you have to do as I say, so get out of that body."

"Your sister is gone," said Visander. "I can no more leave this body than you can leave yours."

Perhaps she could feel the truth of it, for her eyes welled with tears. But they were tears of anger.

"Then let it die. Get out. Get out!"

"We have to find Ekthalion," he said, "and stop Indeviel from returning the Dark King."

"No, we don't," said Elizabeth. "I don't have to do anything with you. I'm going to meet Mrs. Lange like Redlan told me to do before you killed him."

"The hounds have my scent. We can't stay here long."

"Then go," said Elizabeth.

"I am sworn to protect you," said Visander.

"You can do that by going away." The girl's face was cast like the sky in a storm.

"You are my queen," said Visander. "And I am your champion."

Elizabeth stayed where she was, and Visander tried not to feel like he was planting a banner in the ground on a battlefield when he was just facing down a little girl.

"Then we're going to meet Mrs. Lange," said Elizabeth, "and she's going to help me find my friend Violet, and you're going to shut up and not kill anyone, and not say anything else in that weird language."

CHAPTER TWENTY-EIGHT

IT WAS KETTERING'S idea to enter the palace at night.

The locals won't go in at night. They're too afraid, he'd said. Will had agreed. Day or night, it would be just as dark under the mountain.

Leaving the dig reminded Will a little of his long-ago escape from the Hall with Violet and Cyprian. That day, Cyprian had simply lifted his chin and told the Stewards on watch, "My father has sent for the prisoners." Now it was Kettering who said, "on Sloane's orders," and got them past the guards.

The men on watch at the palace entrance looked nervous and unhappy to be on night duty. They did not challenge Kettering's arrival or his right to enter the palace at all, except to say, "*La morte bianca . . . non portarla qui.*" Don't bring the white death here.

Huge and black, the outer doors to the palace stood open. There was no sign of activity beyond the entryway. Since the deaths, no one had been inside. Will felt a sudden reluctance to pass out of the thin moonlight into the unknowable dark.

"We can't take the horses inside," said Kettering, dismounting near the doors.

"Why not?" said Will, frowning.

"Not a single animal has been willing to enter, not even the mules," said Kettering. "We go alone with packs, and make our way on foot."

He was right; the horses acted out even before they reached the doors, their heads tossing and bits chinking, breath frosty in the moonlight.

Nothing would go in at night, except them.

Darkness fore and aft; it felt like being swallowed. Holding aloft lamps on poles, they passed through the outer entrance, and it was not long before they saw the twisted inner doors standing warped and battered. Dwarfed, they walked through them.

Kettering took the lead. The outer chambers had been cleared of rockfall and debris, and there were torches installed along the walls, though they didn't light any of them. They moved through the dark with their two lamps swinging on their poles, keeping their progress and direction hidden. Once, Cyprian turned into a wide entrance, only to find Kettering holding him back. "No, that's the way to the barracks," said Kettering. "Follow the roped pegs." Like a thread through a maze, the roped line left by Sinclair's workers led them deeper into the palace.

They walked for perhaps a quarter of an hour, until they came to a pile of abandoned work tools and an overturned wheelbarrow. There Kettering stopped, lifting his lamp to show the scattered items.

"This is where the men died of the white death," said Kettering.

The chamber ahead had not been cleared. There were no more roped pegs. This was as far as Sinclair's men had come.

Will looked up. If this was where Sinclair's men had died, the locus of what they sought must be right in front of them.

"Will! Over here!" Cyprian was bent over a shape that lay in the recesses of the dark.

Bringing his lamp over, Will saw a white body with eyes staring up at the cavernous ceiling. Kettering was striding forward and going to one knee beside the body.

"Another of the workers . . . he must have been left behind." Kettering was anguished.

"What should we do?" said Cyprian. "Burn him? Bury him?"

"No!" said Kettering. "Cover the body. He should be taken to his family."

Will took a step; a crunch under his foot.

He looked down. He had stepped on a wrist bone; underfoot was a rib cage, a spine, a skull.

"He's not the first person to have died here," Will heard himself say.

Kettering was rising, holding up his lamp on the pole. What had looked at first glance like scattered rubble or uneven flooring were piles of bones. The pressing horror of it almost made Will gag. There were thousands of them.

"You said any bones would have decayed," Will said to Kettering.

"They ought to have," said Kettering. "These bones aren't from the ancient world; they're more recent . . . a few hundred years, maybe longer."

"Another group who tried to enter the throne room," said Cyprian.

Kettering was shaking his head as if he didn't understand. "But the outer doors were sealed up. . . ."

"You think these people died of the white death?" said Will.

"I pray they didn't." Kettering looked truly shaken.

"What *happened* here?" said James.

Grace held the other lamp, and she was using it to follow the train of destruction. "A lot of the bones are clustered here, near the doors," she said, by far the most disturbing observation.

"You mean they were trying to get out?" said Cyprian. "You think they were trapped in here with something?"

Will took one of the unlit torches left by Sinclair's workers. He touched it to the small flame from Kettering's lamp, and when it flared into life he held it up and took it to the mouth of the chamber.

Hundreds of people, hundreds of years ago. It was as if anyone who had ventured beyond this door had been struck down. He remembered the warning he'd read in Calais, in Gauthier's handwriting. *None may enter Undahar and live.*

"None of you should go any farther," said Will. "It's too dangerous." He began to step forward.

James's hand on his shoulder stopped him. "You're joking. You're not going in there by yourself." James said, "I'm coming with you."

To Will's surprise, Kettering also came forward. "I asked my men to enter this place. I ought to be prepared to enter myself."

Cyprian and Grace both nodded. "We're coming too," said Cyprian.

"I saw Katherine die of the white death," said Will, looking at each of them. "There was no warning, and it couldn't be stopped. That's what you're risking."

But he saw in their eyes that they each knew it, and had made the decision anyway.

"All right," said Will, seeing the determination on their faces. "But I go first. You all touch nothing, and stay behind me."

That won him reluctant nods. James's hand on his shoulder released.

Will walked forward with his torch aloft, the others in twos behind him. Alert to any sense of danger or of magic, the fear was constant that his friends would drop to the ground behind him, their skin turning white. Or was it his own presence here that protected them, the king returning with his retinue?

Don't think about that.

He passed through the entryway, whose twin doors lay like two giants of twisted metal on the ground. And he entered the palace throne room.

For a moment, it was as if the torch lit everything and revealed a chamber of blazing gold, the Sun King resplendent on his shining throne, the chamber filled with supplicants and joyous celebration, a golden disc on the flagstones, a sun emblem below to match the splendor of the fiery orb above.

Then Will blinked and saw the room was dark and empty, with black marble floors and a long, dark approach to black stairs. The only thing that remained from his vision was the disc of gold embedded into the floor, but it no longer blazed like the sun. It looked abandoned and cold.

Above it rose a pale throne; beautiful and terrible, appearing like bone out of the dark. Its power could be felt: the hum of force, a demand of subjugation. It rose in dominating horror over the room, promising a conqueror the gift of violence and destruction.

"One throne," said James. "Just as you said."

Will saw himself climbing the steps to sit on that pale throne, the ghosts of the past rising around him from these crushed ruins, a word from him returning the splendor of those distant days. It was in his bones, in his teeth, in his head. He would have said the throne was hungry for it, but the hunger wasn't in the throne; it was in him.

James strode past him, took the steps two at a time, and put his hand on the carved armrest, turning to face him.

"Let's try it out. How does it feel to be a king?"

"No!" Will grabbed James's arm as he began to sit, jerking him back. They stared at each other, Will's immediate and instinctive action not easy to explain.

"Want it for yourself?"

James's tone made a joke of it, but this close to the throne, he was breathing shallowly. And Will . . .

Will had come too close, and now the throne was just a step away, its pale height towering over him, and he knew the way it felt to sit, the black silks of his robes spread out around him, and to know he had power over all before him—

"No," said Will. "No one sits in it."

He expected James to resist. But after a tense moment, James shrugged, relaxing and moving back as if it was of no consequence.

"All right."

A little more light. Kettering was ascending the steps with his own torch, using the dais as a kind of lookout to survey the throne room. Grace and Cyprian were approaching, but their presence only seemed to highlight the emptiness of the chamber. Nothing else was visible.

"Is this what Sinclair was seeking? A throne?" Cyprian sounded scornful, a little confused.

"It's symbolic," said James.

"The locals believed a great evil would be released," said Will, shaking his head.

Grace spoke. "And the Elder Steward said what Sinclair sought was a greater threat than the return of the Dark King."

Kettering turned to James. "Can you think of what the Dark King might have hidden here? Or perhaps you know the location of a hiding place, a secret door?"

"Why would I know that?" said James.

"You've been here before," said Kettering, lifting his torch to show what lay on the dais.

A thick gold chain, coiled at the foot of the throne. A permanent fixture, it was bolted at one end to the black marble. It conjured to mind a magnificent beast chained to a king's feet, Sarcean reaching down absently to scratch his exotic pet. But it was not a dragon or a leopard that had been chained here. The other end of the chain had a clasp set with red rubies.

Humiliation in James's cheeks, the same color. He looked up, as if daring them all to comment. No one did, but the silence burned.

"He liked to show off his possessions," said Kettering, and it was Will's turn to feel his cheeks flame hot.

"We all knew that," said Will.

"It's a declaration. 'You see? I have tamed Light's champion.' I can't think of a greater show of his power."

Anharion on display for every visitor, every courtier, every vassal. Kneeling at his feet, dressed not in armor but in paint and silks to show off that at night he—

"Ignore it," said Will. "We're here for something else."

Kettering raised his torch, looking out again into the darkness of the throne room. "Aside from the throne and the chain, this room is empty."

"Spread out and search," said Will. "But be careful. If you feel or see anything out of the ordinary, don't approach it without me."

"We don't even know what we're looking for," said Cyprian.

"We'll know we're close when someone dies of the white death." James didn't even say it with his usual ironic humor, instead grimly matter-of-fact.

Kettering was right: walking its length revealed a vast but empty chamber, with black pillars reaching upward in an avenue to the dais. The floor itself was black marble covered in rubble.

The only other dominating feature was the immense gold circle embedded into the floor. Once the depiction of a gold sun, part of the white-and-gold shining glory of the Sun King, it now provided an uneasy contrast to the black marble that surrounded it.

Why had Sarcean kept it? Will wondered. The answer returned to him: *To tread on it.*

"We've missed something. It's here," Will said when they returned to the dais.

"We believe you, Will. It's just—" Grace said.

"It's here." Somehow. Somewhere.

"Have Sinclair's men already been here? Cleaned the room out?" said James.

"No, I told you, we abandoned work when the men died," said Kettering. "Besides, you saw it for yourself: this chamber was undisturbed."

"We split up," said Will, "and clear the rubble. We're going to find whatever's here."

Hours clearing rubble from the floor only revealed more black marble flagstones that did not move or turn over.

"If this place was once the Sun Palace, how did it fall to the Dark King?" Will asked Kettering as they searched.

"Sarcean warred with the Sun Kingdom for years before he conquered it," said Kettering, "attacking from the north, but unable to defeat the combined sorcery of the Lady and Light's Champion. No one knows how it fell."

So Sarcean had left the Sun Palace, Will thought. And then what? He'd grown his own empire in the north? Set his sights on the Sun realm? Years of open warfare, facing Anharion across the battlefield? Until he captured him and forced the Collar around his neck?

As Kettering and the others turned their sights toward the far end of the chamber, Will found himself in the dark recesses behind the throne. At all times, he could feel its presence, looming over him. Instinctively, they were all avoiding it. The footsteps surprised him.

James's hair gleamed in the torchlight, a golden crown of his own, slightly mussed by the fingers he'd pushed into it. Will found himself wondering how James would brush it into its fashionable style away from the conveniences of the dig. He felt, then extinguished, the desire to run his own fingers through it.

"If I was wearing the Collar," said James quietly, "he didn't need a chain."

"No," agreed Will.

"The chain was there because he liked me in it."

Will, who had realized this, was silent.

"There's something I have to show you." James glanced out at the chamber, as if making certain no one was watching.

When he saw that the others had moved away, and that he and Will were hidden by the throne, James drew a cloth-wrapped shape from his pack.

Will's stomach dropped, recognizing the shape. Before Will could stop him, James drew the cloth back.

Gleaming gold and red, it wanted to choke him, enclose him; it wanted to gild him, adorn him. A circle of sadistic opulence that begged for James's throat.

The Collar.

Will shoved himself back from it, staring at James with his heart pounding. "You *brought it here*?"

"What did you think I had done with it?"

"I don't know, I—" Will broke off, feeling the full force of it, sickly seductive. "Why would you have it with you!"

"*Because!*" James's answer snapped with emotion even as he kept his voice hushed. He cut himself off, looking toward the others again, only continuing when he saw they were too far away to hear. "*Because it wants to be around my neck*," James said, even more quietly, with even greater feeling.

"All the more reason to keep it at a distance." His own hissed reply as he pushed the cloth back up over it.

"I *can't*," said James. "I can't hide it. I can't lock it away." No matter where James hid it, it would be found. And the person who found it would be filled with the need to collar him. Will remembered Kettering saying, *These objects have their own agenda. Like blind things seeking in the dark*. "Knowing it was out there, I couldn't think, I couldn't sleep," said James. "It would be searching for me every day. No ocean is deep enough. No fire can melt it down."

James had been carrying it all this time. Will stared at him. "When you were weak from the gate—those soldiers who captured us—any one of them could have taken it and put it on you!"

He realized with horror as he said it that James had known that, and had drained himself for them anyway. James had drained himself knowing everything he risked, which had been far more than any of them had realized.

"You wouldn't," said James, and Will's skin seemed to tighten. "You had the chance to put it on me in London. And you didn't."

James chained to that kitchen range, turning under Will's hands to expose his neck. His flesh had trembled hot under his shirt, and Will had felt the shiver too, keeping his hands on James's body longer than he had to.

"I wanted to."

The admission just came out. He didn't have to remember how hard it had been to resist the Collar. He could feel it now, could almost see himself reaching out, sliding the warm gold around James's throat. Its unused chain lay by the throne, a siren song: the open Collar, the ready chain, the empty throne, each of them calling.

"You need to put it away. It's really," said Will, "not safe to—"

The cloth slid away like a negligee slipping to the ground. The naked gold and rubies hit both of them with its power. Will felt it in his teeth. James's eyes were swallowed with pupil.

"Someone is going to do it eventually."

"You don't know that," said Will.

"I do. I feel it. My past. My future—"

He took Will's hand and put it on the Collar. "Someone's going to do it." Searing, to touch the metal with his bare hand, to feel its heat and its need.

"If someone's going to do it," said James, "I want it to be you."

Will had him pushed against the back of the throne before he knew it. Hot gold in his hands, as James made a sound and went pliant as if that same hot gold ran like sweet need through his veins.

"Do it," said James. James's shirt was open, his golden hair mussed around his face, his eyes glazed and yielding. James looked like he was already surrendered, wanting to give himself over, willing the latch to close. "Put it on me."

Will gritted his teeth and called on every particle of willpower. He snatched up the cloth and wrapped it around the Collar. The instant it was covered, its power lessened. Under his hands, the dazed look slid out of James's eyes.

Breathing shallowly, Will realized he still had James pinioned to the throne. A glance showed the others still on the far side of the room. But anyone could have seen them. Will looked up at the pale throne, its shadow lying across them both. He realized how little James had been in control of his actions, how out of control he felt himself.

He pushed back, his cheeks burning.

"Anyone else would have done it." James wet his lips, looking over at

Will from where he remained sprawled against the throne. His pose was still surrendered, unresisting.

"You're testing me," said Will. "You shouldn't."

"Why not? You're the perfect hero, aren't you?"

"I'm not your salvation," said Will.

"Are you going to let someone else put it on me? Let someone else—"

"No," said Will, the vehemence of it taking both James and himself by surprise. And then: "There must be a way to destroy it. When this is over. We'll find a way." He let the words sink in, James's blue eyes wide. "If you still want me to order you around after that, I can."

James let out an astonished breath that was part laughter, as if he couldn't believe Will had said that.

"God, you're not like anyone else," said James.

"Neither are you," said Will. It came out low and soft. "Put the Collar away. Follow me because you want to."

"I am. I do. Shit."

He fumbled the Collar out of sight. Will felt instant relief, and forced down the simultaneous disappointment. He tried to forget that the Collar was there. He couldn't.

"Shit," said James again, throwing his arm over his face, as if only now realizing the edge he had brought them both to.

"It's going to get worse," said Will, "the longer we're down here."

It would likely get worse the longer James carried the Collar. He had to wonder how many of James's decisions and interactions had been powered by it, or what it had already driven James to do.

James putting hands on his waist and whispering in his ear to do magic—James challenging him to sleep beside him in their rooms—for all he knew, all of it was the invidious work of the Collar. Or if it wasn't the artifact, it was the seductive whisper of the past: time and time again, James had thrown himself back into the role of loyal general rather than striking out for freedom. What was James's decision to follow Will if not echoes of his former life?

If the Collar was eroding James's resolve, Will would have to be strong for both of them, and he would. For as long as he had to.

James said, "It makes me feel better to know that you feel it too."

"It really shouldn't," said Will.

James shifted to face him.

"I keep thinking . . . when I was a boy, and Simon told me about my power, about how strong I was going to be, I thought I could show my father. I thought I could take my power and do something big with it. Something so big and important that it would prove I was right to have it. Until I understood what it was for."

"What it was for?"

"Him," said James. *Him.* Sarcean. Pulling the strings behind everything. "But maybe it doesn't have to be. Maybe it could be for—"

James broke off.

"Good at making people talk, aren't you."

"Am I?"

"Yes. One look into those big dark eyes. Say something about yourself for once."

This was easier, just to gaze back at James, as if they were two friends sharing secrets.

"Like what?" said Will.

"I don't know. What was it like, growing up the savior of mankind?"

"There's not much to tell." Will gave a casual shrug, one shoulder. "My mother was strict; we didn't do much."

"Have to protect the chosen one," said James. "I'll bet you were a real mama's boy. Everyone doting on you."

"Something like that," said Will, with an easy smile.

"I can see it. Tucking you in at night. Pampering you when you were sick. No wonder you turned out the way you did."

Another smile. Lying was unlabored. "And how's that?"

He'd expected James to reply with another quip. But James gazed back at him and said, "Someone I believe could save this place." And then, so quietly Will almost didn't hear, "Someone I believe could save me."

CHAPTER TWENTY-NINE

ELLIE LANGE'S COTTAGE was on the edges of Stanton, a final outpost before the village gave way to dark hills. The landscape around the cottage was weird, with huge gouges, and places where things were bare and dead. Even the garden was weird, thought Elizabeth, parts of it overgrown, and others sloughed black rock and earth.

Walking up the path with Polly and Visander, Elizabeth was nervous, not a feeling she was used to, at least not this jittery, nauseous feeling. She had never met anyone who had known her mother. She didn't count Will, who lied about everything. She wished Katherine were here, so that she could hold her hand. She made her hands into two fists instead.

Polly knocked on the blue-painted door with its brass knocker, and a stern-faced housekeeper in black appeared, her graying hair pinned back in a severe bun.

"Mrs. Thomas." Polly greeted the housekeeper, and held up the basket she had brought, with its homespun cloth cover. "We're here to see Aunt. We've brought a hamper."

Mrs. Thomas gave no glance down at the basket with its offering of baked goods. "Mrs. Lange isn't well today."

"She might have one of her good spells." Polly wasn't deterred. "We can wait and see."

Mrs. Thomas didn't look like she agreed, but she stepped back from the doorway. "It's your time to waste."

"Thank you, Mrs. Thomas," said Polly, and Elizabeth followed her to the drawing room.

The room had a fireplace with a hob grate, green wallpaper, a cornice coving, and skirting boards. A scattering of chairs with footstools and a couch filled the space, heavy velvet curtains drawn over its large windows.

Visander stalked in first, and checked the door and windows, securing the room with the sort of economy of movement that Elizabeth associated with Cyprian. Then he stood as if on alert by the sofa, watching both exits.

Elizabeth sat gingerly on the sofa next to him. Polly gave her a smile. "It doesn't look so different from when your mother stayed here."

Elizabeth's eyes flew to her face. "She stayed here?"

"In that room across the hall," said Polly. "The last time was about ten years ago. She gave birth here, in this house."

Elizabeth didn't need to be a mathematical genius to do those figures. "And then she gave me away. Like my sister."

To her surprise, Polly nodded. "It was my brother who helped find you both a home. He worked in the household of a gentleman. Mr. Kent. He and his wife wanted children. Someone to raise. They were too old to pretend you were their own, so they agreed to say you were their niece."

She looked around at the room. She felt like she should remember this place, but she didn't. She thought of her aunt and uncle, and their cozy house in Hertfordshire. They had never taken the title of parent, staying at the more remote level of guardian. Her real family had been her sister.

Katherine had played at *mama* with dolls sometimes when they were little. Had Katherine remembered their mother? How old had she been when they had been parted? Old enough for some dim recollections? Would she have remembered this house? Elizabeth looked at the soldier from the old world, standing at alert in her sister's stolen body, and felt a bright burn of anger, because Katherine should be here with her.

"I'm going to check on Mrs. Lange," said Polly. "You two wait here."

Elizabeth sprang up from the threadbare sofa at once. She didn't want to sit alone here with Visander. Feeling almost repelled by his presence, she found herself in the hallway, outside the room where her mother had stayed.

The door was open.

Having grown up without, she had never really wanted a mother. Her early life in Hertfordshire had been spent clambering over sties and running about in the little woods, meeting frogs and crickets and rabbits and otters, which had kept her entirely busy.

Her aunt and uncle had told her no stories about her mother. They had said only that she was a gentlewoman who had died giving birth. The slight mystery had been cause for talk; the prettier Katherine had grown, the more persistently the talk had followed them. Defensively, Elizabeth had always insisted that her mother was a gentlewoman, thinking from whispers and gossip that maybe she wasn't.

Now she imagined her real mother. Running from Simon, she had come here to give birth, and then handed the child to someone else. To protect her, Will had said. It suddenly occurred to Elizabeth that she was that child. She had been here before, as a red-faced infant. She had been held in her mother's arms, then been handed into the arms of another.

This was her birthplace, this house half-hidden in the hills.

She walked in farther, looking for ghosts. The room wasn't a birthing room, or even a bedroom. It was a morning room, a rather bare one, with a single table and four chairs. It had a window with an unnerving view of one of those bare strips of land outside. There was nowhere that a bed had stood. Elizabeth looked for any signs of her mother. There were none.

"If you ask me, you're lucky she gave you up."

Elizabeth startled and turned to see Mrs. Thomas in the doorway, her hard, lined face inscrutable.

"What do you mean?"

At first it didn't seem as if Mrs. Thomas would answer. And then: "She had an abnormal relationship to that boy."

"Boy?" *Will.* Will had been here? Elizabeth felt the hairs on her arms prickle.

"Kept him locked up. Six or seven, he would have been," said Mrs. Thomas. "A well-behaved little lad. She treated him like a criminal. Tied him up to the bedpost. And the way she'd look at him, like . . ."

"Like?"

"He got free when she was sleeping. He came out to see the baby. It's natural for a child to be interested in a sister. She went wild when she woke and saw him with the infant. She . . . well, the less said about that the better."

It wasn't the story she'd hoped to hear about a mother she'd never met. It gave her that jangly feeling again. Elizabeth put her hand around the medallion. How had Will described her? She remembered Will saying, *She raised me as best she could.*

"I brought him a bit of kidney pie, and it was like I'd won a friend for life. He followed me around chatting away, helping me with the chores. Never once complained about his bruises, poor mite. And I'll tell you this.

"Around that time, a man of means was staying here with his wife. He was a terror to the staff, put his hands on the maids. Put his hands on me. Well, a lamp got knocked over in his rooms, set his clothes and his belongings on fire. He left the next day. The boy never said anything, but I knew it was him. He done it for me. A smart lad. And loyal." The housekeeper said, "She looked at him like she'd kill him, if she'd only had the courage."

A sound from the doorway made Elizabeth turn. Polly stood with a hand on the wooden jamb, expectantly.

"Mrs. Lange has come around," said Polly. "If you're going to speak with her, you had best come now."

The room was dark, with the stifled stillness of a sickroom. A heavy velvet curtain was drawn on the room's only window, swathing and muffling it.

"She doesn't like the light," said Polly, the words a murmur. She kept the small lamp she held half-covered by her hand, and rested it on the cabinet by the door, as far away from the bed as possible. The room was dim shadows.

"Mrs. Lange," said Polly. "It's Eleanor's girls, come to see you like we talked about."

"Who?" said Mrs. Lange.

"She forgets," said Polly. "Faces. People. You can't take it personal. She thinks it's Monday when it's Friday. She thinks it's seventeen years ago, sometimes." She motioned for Elizabeth and Visander to join her by the bed.

"Eleanor's girls. I told you," she said to the old woman.

Mrs. Lange was a woman of perhaps sixty-five, with rheumy eyes, a face full of wrinkles, and gray hair falling from a white cloth cap. She lay in the center of the bed, with her head on its single pillow. She looked up at Elizabeth and Visander.

"Eleanor," Mrs. Lange said to Visander. Elizabeth felt a ghostly sensation, as if her mother were in the room, when it was just Visander with the candlelight on his face.

On Katherine's face.

"It's a boy," said Mrs. Lange.

"What?" said Visander, frowning.

"Your child," said Mrs. Lange to Visander. "It's going to be a boy."

"I'm sorry," said Polly to Visander. "She gets confused. She lives mostly in the past. And you're the spitting image of Eleanor."

"He's strong, and healthy," said Mrs. Lange. "And you're so far along. Eight months."

Will, thought Elizabeth again. *She's talking about Will.* She looked at the old lady who was reliving the past.

"It will be hard to kill it," said Mrs. Lange. "But you've come to me just in time."

Elizabeth felt cold water run down her spine.

"Kill it?" she said.

Mrs. Lange started thrashing on the bed, her head whipping from side to side and her limbs moving strangely.

"Ar ventas. Ar ventas, fermaran!" said Mrs. Lange.

Beside her, Visander took a step back, his eyes wide. "How do you know that language?"

"Fermaran, katara thalion!" said Mrs. Lange.

"What's she saying?" said Elizabeth.

"Eleanor," said Mrs. Lange. "He's fighting me. He's fighting."

"Who's fighting?" said Elizabeth.

"The child! Oh God, Eleanor! What have you brought to me?" And then, "He's too strong. He's too strong, I can't—"

She broke out into old world language again.

"You said she was a midwife," said Visander.

"She is. She was," Polly said. "I told you, she has these turns. I don't know why." *After your brother's birth, my aunt, she grew sick,* Elizabeth remembered her saying.

"We shouldn't have come here," said Visander. "This woman cannot help you."

"I don't understand," said Elizabeth. "What's wrong?"

"She tried to kill the child. But his magic was too powerful. Nothing could stop him from being born, and the attempt broke her mind." Visander said, "Its effects are carved into the land. You can see it outside."

The great gouges on the landscape, sloughed rock like the ground had melted, and nothing growing there even after seventeen years.

"She can't help you. Her mind is fractured. Her natural healing staved some of it off, but she is caught between past and present, and she cannot speak truth."

"Polly?" said Mrs. Lange, looking up, her eyes clear. For a moment it was as if a fever had broken. She looked up as if she was herself.

"That's right, Mrs. Lange. It's me. I'm here with Eleanor's daughters."

"Eleanor's daughters," she said.

"Show her the medallion," said Polly.

After the thrashing fit, Elizabeth was nervous to show her anything that might set her off again. She came forward hesitantly. Fishing the medallion out of the front of her dress, she held it out, thinking as it swung on its tie that the room was almost too dim to see.

"Redlan George said to come to you," said Elizabeth. "After he saw this."

"The hawthorn medallion!" said Mrs. Lange. "The Lady's symbol!"

"He said you could help me," said Elizabeth. "That you'd know what to do."

Mrs. Lange's eyes opened full on hers. A second later, Mrs. Lange's clawed old hand reached out from the bedclothes and clasped her own urgently.

"You must go to the Stewards," said Mrs. Lange. "You are the only one who can stop him. . . . You must go to the Stewards before *he* finds you. Or darkness will come for us all."

Elizabeth thought of all the dead Stewards she had never met. She couldn't go to the Stewards when they didn't exist anymore. She supposed Grace and Cyprian were still alive, but they weren't Stewards exactly, and they talked all the time about how they didn't know what to do. Mrs. Lange's words were too late.

This whole journey was a dead end. Mrs. Lange didn't know the answers. She didn't even know what was happening outside her room.

Elizabeth looked down at her, patting the hand that gripped her arm hard. "Don't worry. You don't have to worry. We already stopped the Dark King coming."

Mrs. Lange let out a peal of crazy laughter too loud in the small room.

"Stop him coming?" said Mrs. Lange. "Weren't you listening? *He's already here!*"

The window shattered, and Elizabeth turned to a sudden view of a black muzzle opening on razor teeth in snarling jaws, and felt hot canine breath almost on her.

Polly screamed, as Elizabeth saw a whirl of darkness. *A shadow hound.* It had burst through the window, glass scattering everywhere. In the next moment, Visander yanked down the heavy curtains and threw them over the creature. Pushing up from the ground, Elizabeth saw him rolling with the writhing blanket, until he snatched up a glass shard, and stabbed it downward. There was a terrible wail, then stillness.

Polly and Mrs. Thomas were staring in shock at Visander. He stood and brushed off his dress in front of the howling open window, with the lumpen shape in front of him. To confirm the kill, he pulled back the curtain that wrapped it. The shadow hound lay dead, a hideous creature, part nightmare, part dog. From outside the window came the howling of other beasts, as though they were connected to their lost companion.

"They'll come for this house, unless we lead them away," Visander said.

Polly shook herself. "There's a cellar where your mother went out last time," she said. "The tunnel will take you out to the hill ridge."

"Take us there," Visander said.

CHAPTER THIRTY

SARCEAN WALKED INTO the garden like a shadow falling across the day.

It hadn't been difficult to find his way back into the palace, even after months of absence. He knew every secret of its paths.

She was waiting for him, beautiful as the dappling light.

He had imagined that meeting with her in secret would feel tawdry. But he was surprised all over again at the sharp, genuine intensity of his feelings. Proximity to her was painful, as much now as on their single cataclysmic night together.

She said, "I didn't think you'd come."

"You called for me," he said, and took her hand and only felt it tremble once.

It was she who led him, beneath flowering trees, along bowered paths, to the place where they had first met. He hadn't expected that, and was surprised at what it did to him. In the sweet-scented air, it was difficult to breathe.

He let her talk. She put her hand on his chest and told him that she missed him. She told him that she had no solace while he was gone. Was this what love felt like? The same torn-up, dizzy feeling he had when he looked at Anharion, as if he stood on one side of a depthless chasm.

He brushed his thumb over her cheek, looked down at her face, and said, "When are the king's men coming to arrest me?"

"What?"

Her upturned face looked just as beautiful as he'd remembered as he said, "This is a trap, isn't it?"

In her eyes the shock of acknowledgment, of being seen. She stepped back, slipping out of his grasp, leaving the space between them empty.

"If you knew it was a trap, why did you come?" She sounded like it hurt her, and maybe it did.

He said, "You called for me."

Her eyes went wide. The sound of armored footsteps broke the silence before she could speak. He thought he was ready for it. But turning to face his captors, he felt his stomach drop and his chest hollow. At the head of the Sun Guard, a shining golden comet of justice, was Anharion.

Sarcean felt it: to be braced for the blow, and instead to receive a knife to the heart, piercing and unexpected.

"You're under arrest for high treason," said Anharion. "For plots against the king, who you have attempted to ensorcell against his will."

Sarcean said, "Both of you."

The two of them standing side by side had a wrenching similarity, the chasm deepening. Anharion was beautiful, the sort of untouchable beauty that was painful to look at. Yet Sarcean had never been able to look away.

He couldn't look away now, hurting himself.

"Ensorcelling the king," said Sarcean. "Is that what he told you?"

He almost felt a flash of unexpected pride, finally enough of a threat that the king would move openly against him. Beneath that, the churn of his anger. Beneath that, the first turning of the machinery of his cold, careful planning.

"For your crimes, you will end your days in the oubliette," said Anharion.

He looked at that golden, beloved face. "And if I fight?"

"You know my power is the greater."

"And if I run?"

"I will find you," Anharion said. "I will always find you. Try to run."

Sarcean looked at the gold-armored Sun Guard arrayed behind their general. They were afraid, he could smell it on them. He let the silence stretch out, feeling their terror crest, their heartbeats pounding behind their carefully blank faces.

The obsidian manacles Anharion held were thick and heavy, every inch carved over with symbols, created to suppress magic, rendering him helpless.

Sarcean extended his wrists, a gesture of submission that shocked everyone, even Anharion, who stepped forward and closed the manacles around Sarcean's wrists. Even Sarcean was surprised as they snuffed his magic out, a stifled, dizzying feeling.

He was taken to the throne room.

A cathedral of light; radiant; breathtaking. It was built to dazzle and soar, to uplift and glorify. He saw the Sun Throne at the height of its splendor, a room of gold with glittering columns and high, sparkling ceilings.

Sarcean's anger burned like acid in his veins, though he didn't show it in his graceful limbs, or in his face. Resplendent and impersonal in ceremonial armor, the Sun King gazed down at him from the throne. Anharion and the queen took their places on the dais, arrayed against him like unreachable gold statues. Every courtier in the palace was gathered to watch. He could feel their pleasure in seeing him brought low, alongside a flicker of fear that he still might have some way to escape the manacles.

They were right to be afraid. He would not be merciful.

"No last words, Sarcean?" The Sun King's eyes looked amused. He thought it would be easy. It wouldn't be.

"You'll hear them when the sun sets," said Sarcean.

That only seemed to amuse the Sun King further. "Do you believe your allies will save you?" said the Sun King. "Your uprising has been rooted out. All are to be cast down with you into the oubliette. You and yours will end your lives in darkness, and never again see the sun."

He couldn't help the laugh that spilled out of him. A terrible punishment indeed for those of their kind.

"You think I fear the dark?" said Sarcean.

On his throne, the Sun King sat in a ceremonial posture. His jewels gleamed; the silks that accompanied his armor fell shining to the ground. He commanded the hall, its sun legion, its courtiers and creatures, a blaze of authority.

"You may not fear it now. But you will." The Sun King made another gesture. "*Aragas.*"

Like a slowly dilating eye, the oubliette opened.

Will gasped and came back to himself.

The pit was still opening; it was opening inside him, all his attention fixed on it. His heart was pounding, the dream a swirling part of him. Except it wasn't a dream, it was a memory. *Here,* he thought. *Here, here, here.*

He stood up from the rubble he was clearing and walked right up the dais steps to the throne.

Behind him, he heard Cyprian, turning in surprise as he passed him. "Will?" Will ignored him.

The throne was a pale, towering presence. He stood before it, looking at its marble surface like fine ancient bone. The others were approaching;

he could hear the murmurs behind him: "*Will?*" and "*What is it?*" and "*What's happening?*"

He sat down on the throne.

Immediately, he was assailed by a vision of being thrown downward, falling deep into the earth, the light disappearing above him.

Had Anharion watched as Sarcean had been cast into the pit? Had any regret flickered in those beautiful blue eyes? Will didn't remember. But he did remember the long fall, and light winking out above him, imprisoning him in the darkness under the throne forever.

Now he sat where the Sun King had given the order, looking out over that giant sun emblem in strident gold on the black marble floor.

Will commanded, "*Aragas.*"

The grinding sound of stone dragging against stone rent the air, and the huge sun in the center of the room began to move aside. Opening a widening black crescent, its immense disc slid back until where a sun had been there was only a black hole.

Undahar. The Eclipse.

Oh God, it was real. The pit inside him was real. He had been imprisoned down there.

Shaken, Will rose and came down the steps toward it. The vision in his mind hung like the cobwebs of a dream. He didn't want to go down there. Something terrible and unremembered lay at the bottom. It was an experience he couldn't relive. *Not ever again.* He could feel the others gathering around him at the lip. They were shocked and unnerved by his actions. He could feel that too.

What lay down there? What was it that exerted this terrible pull on him?

"How did you know how to do that?" said Grace.

He didn't answer as the others peered downward.

"Ugh, the air is stale," said James, pressing his forearm to his nose.

"What—what *is* it?" said Cyprian, peering down into the dark.

Kettering was the last to come forward, answering in fear-tinged awe, "It looks like an oubliette. A prison pit, where those cast are given a death of nightmare."

James's expression twisted. "Of course the Dark King kept a *prison pit* under his throne."

Will looked up at him. *No,* he didn't say. *It's the Light who punished with darkness.*

"Where does it lead?" said Cyprian.

Will said, "Down."

He took a torch from Cyprian and dropped it. A long fall, the light getting smaller. It lay on the ground. Around it was darkness.

"Give me another," he said.

Once there were five torches flaming in a circle below, they tied a rope to the nearest column and dropped it down into the pit as well. Will stepped forward and began to descend.

It was a long way, hanging in the dark.

He remembered—

Filth and stench; the dizzying weakness of thirst and hunger. The spiked pain of the helmet. Muffled booms and echoing voices from the throne room above. He didn't know how long he lay before his head was lifted and the helmet was drawn off.

He couldn't bear the light, as weak as he was. The figure cradling him blurred.

He came. Golden hair and gold armor, Sarcean saw him hazily, like a figure in a dream. He had always been like sunlight piercing the dark. Sarcean's feelings swelled in him, the hope he had never admitted, even to himself. "*Drink,*" he said, and Sarcean tasted the waters of Oridhes, tipped from a flask to his lips.

And then the figure resolved; and he did have golden hair, and he did wear the sun emblem on his chest.

But it wasn't only Anharion who bore the sun. He was looking at the young Sun Guard with whom he'd dallied. *Sandy*, he'd nicknamed the young guard that night, for his hair the pale gold color of sand.

"Sarcean." Sandy was kneeling beside him, his face earnest with desperate worry. "I came as soon as I could."

Sarcean heard his own breathless laughter; he hadn't thought he had breath left. His eyes were wet, streaming from the stinging light after so long in the dark.

"What is it?" Sandy's eyes were full of concern.

Sarcean smiled thinly. "I thought you were someone else." It was a whisper, the rustlings of dry paper.

"I could not come until the king and court left for Garayan." Those eyes, full of concern for him. "I feared the darkness would drive you mad."

"Perhaps, had I been born of the sun," said Sarcean. "But my power comes from darkness."

"Here, lean on my shoulder."

"Take me to my men," said Sarcean.

Weak and thin as he was, each step hurt, as if the bones of his feet scraped on cold stone. But he was determined. Light from above illuminated a circle on the ground, but they moved into the dark, where disturbing and unmoving shapes were lumped in shadow.

"This place is ancient," said Sarcean. "It was here before the palace was built, a natural formation in the rock. Traitors, killers, monsters have been thrown in here for centuries. They die of hunger, or madness, or violence to themselves or others. But they take out the bodies. They must, or the pit would have filled to the brim. And the throne room would reek from the stench. More than it does already. But blood remains, and the memory of blood, and in blood there is a great deal of power."

Sandy's eyes were wide. "How do you know all that?"

"I studied this place. Would you not study the prison where your enemies would confine you?"

"You almost talk like you meant to be captured," said Sandy nervously.

Another edged smile. "Do I?"

His allies were dead, all but one, a metalsmith named Idane. Hollowed eyes stared up at him. With a parched throat, Idane attempted to say Sarcean's name.

"It's all right," Sandy the young Sun Guard was trying to reassure Idane. "Your master's here, he'll get you out."

"Give me your knife," said Sarcean to Sandy beside him. Sandy hurriedly obliged him.

Holding the knife, Sarcean knelt beside Idane, cradling his head as he might a lover's. "*Help me,*" said Idane, looking up at him.

"A reward for your loyalty," said Sarcean.

And with a neat cut, he slit Idane's throat.

Sandy jerked back in horror. "You killed him!" He was staring at Sarcean in revolted shock. "Why? Why would you—"

Sarcean looked up at him and said, "To be reborn, you have to die."

Will's foot touched the bottom.

It jarred him out of the vision; he blinked, letting go of the rope and stumbling. He felt like he had slit that man's throat himself.

Sarcean's first experiments in death. Sarcean had left the bodies of his loyalists behind in the pit. Later, while the Sun King raged that Sarcean was missing, they would be brought out and interred. But Sarcean had known what the others hadn't: his followers would rise again. Buried inside the palace's magical defenses, waiting sightless and soundless until the moment Sarcean needed them most. Then, like blind seeds, they would sprout.

A macabre Trojan horse, to help him take the palace. Like Simon, it seemed Sarcean needed blood to bring people back. He had chosen the pit because it was soaked in it. And that meant . . .

The torches they had dropped flamed around him in a circle, illuminating a few feet of empty space beneath the pit. There were piles of dust underfoot near the torches. Will looked beyond the light.

A figure looked back at him. He jerked backward. A moment later he realized he was looking at a body, a husk in armor as though it had been mummified. He whirled away, only to see another face staring at him from the dark. They weren't statues, they were bodies, grotesquely frozen in place.

Lifting his torch, he saw rows and rows of them, extending endlessly into the dark.

The others were descending behind him. *"I don't like it,"* Cyprian said. *"It's so dark."* Grace said, *"The darkness is its own danger. Don't venture beyond the light."*

And he understood, a greater horror coming over him, as he realized what he was looking at.

"Don't touch it," said Will. "Don't touch anything."

"Why? What is it?" said Cyprian.

"It's an army," said Will. "An army of the dead."

He was backing up toward the dangling rope ladder. "We need to get out." The others didn't understand. "We need to close this place up so that no one finds it again."

"Dear God," said Kettering, lifting his torch to the nearest of the figures. A black helm flickered in front of him, its eye sockets empty. "This is it, it's really here, just like in the legends—"

The dead crowded out every part of the cavern. Not just dead men, but dead creatures. They were ringed by them. The space beneath the pit was the only empty space, a small circle piled with dust, like a single island of light where they could stand.

"The Dark King's army," said Will. "Ready to return."

Idane's death in his vision had just been the first. Decades later, Sarcean had commanded his entire army to die when he did, in order that they could return with him—and here they stood.

"Will's right. We can't stay here." James was moving his own torch, not toward the figures but toward the floors. Black obsidian gleamed beneath the dust piles, scrawled over in script identical to the walls in the prison under the Hall of the Stewards. "This place, it's designed to block magic." James sounded more unnerved than Will had ever heard him, as if he'd been thrown into hell and told that he would have no strength while he was there. "We need to go."

"This one killed himself." Kettering's torch showed the dagger lodged in the husk's throat, its armored gauntlet still wrapped around it. He cast his torch around at the others, all of them with daggers protruding from their necks. "They all . . . killed themselves. . . . The stories say Sarcean ordered them to their deaths, and they did it by their own hands. . . ."

Cyprian turned to James. "Your contemporaries. Do you recognize any of them?"

"No!" said James, stepping back, utterly revolted.

Will stared out at the endless rows of faces. He couldn't imagine killing that many people. A force like this could roll out over Europe, and nothing could stop it. The freakish bodies stood upright as if ready to march into battle, despite their rotted forms.

He suddenly felt like anything could awaken them. A sound, a movement . . .

"Sinclair can never find this chamber," said Will. "He can't be allowed to find this army, or have a chance to raise it."

"Too late for that," said Howell from above them, a figure in torchlight at the top of the rope ladder.

CHAPTER THIRTY-ONE

ELIZABETH PUSHED OUT of the long tunnel into a goat pen, whose inhabitants bleated nervously. She could see the Lange cottage in the distance and hear the baying of hounds.

The shadow hounds hadn't yet re-caught their scent. Emerging after her, Visander was tearing his bandage into strips of bloody cloth, and preparing to tie them to the trees as he had done before. Elizabeth looked around the goat pen. She remembered chasing Mr. Billy around with Katherine for hours after he got out and not catching him.

"If you tie them to the goats, it will give us more time."

Visander looked at her in surprise. But he nodded, tying strips around the necks of the goats, then hauling the wooden gate open, freeing them to run in all directions. Strange how quickly even a broken heart adjusted: she barely blinked at the sight of Katherine wading through mud, bodily heaving wood logs open, chasing out goats, then grasping a pitchfork as a rudimentary weapon.

"We can't escape on foot. We need horses," Visander spoke, hefting the pitchfork. "They're back at Polly's house."

Polly's home wasn't close to Mrs. Lange's, and required them to skirt the village, until they reached the horses and were away. They cantered out onto the rolling green slopes, Elizabeth urging Nell forward, and Visander riding a newly stolen bay horse, carrying the pitchfork like a knight's lance. At first they heard the howls of the dogs echoing over the hills, but then even they faded.

They only stopped when they were hours away, in a different valley, dismounting at a stream to water the horses.

Leading Nell to the water's edge, Elizabeth found her teeth were chattering, her mind still ringing with Mrs. Lange's words. That the Dark King was already here. Elizabeth knew what that meant. That the Dark King had been born in her cottage. That the Dark King was Eleanor's son.

Will.

It made her feel shivery sick. She thought of all the times he'd given a casual smile. All the times he'd given the others advice and they'd taken it. He'd been lying to everyone.

He's a liar. She'd tried to tell everyone. He'd lied to her sister. He'd lied to his friends. Lying wasn't right. She'd told them.

"That midwife believed that the Dark King was birthed in her house," said Visander, echoing her thoughts. "Born from one of the Queen's descendants. An obscene violation, even for Sarcean."

She said, thickly, "His name is Will Kempen."

"You know him? You have met with the Dark King?" Visander stuck one end of the pitchfork in the ground as he knelt, grasping her shoulder urgently. "Lightbringer, has he tried to hurt you?"

Strict honesty forced her to say, "No."

She thought of him high up on the battlements, sitting beside her with the wide-open marsh stretching out before them. He could have killed her then. A single hand in the middle of her back. A single push. Or the night she'd confronted him in the stables. They'd been alone together.

He could have done anything to her.

He'd sat beside her and given her the medallion that had helped her, and talked to her quietly about her mother.

Lying.

She burst out, "He's a sneak. He's always sneaking around. He made my sister fall in love with him. And then she d-died."

"He seduced this body?"

She scowled. "Not exactly."

It was hard to say exactly what he had done, except turn up, after which Katherine had spent hours gazing dreamily out the window, waiting every day for his return. She'd ridden out of the Hall after him, her whole attention fixed on him, while his had been fixed on Simon. Katherine had looked at him like he was her world, and he'd looked back at her like his world was full of secrets and concerns.

But to her surprise, Visander nodded.

"Yes, that is his way. He grows his power in the dark. Every action looks innocent on the surface, and has dark tendrils growing beneath."

Visander drew in a breath and appeared to look around at the countryside.

"Tell me everything you know of him."

Elizabeth opened her mouth to answer and then stopped. What did she really know about Will? Dark hair and pale skin and intense eyes, but no history to speak of.

She frowned and thought. "He does things in secret. He acts different around different people." She thought more deeply. "He's good at thinking. Everyone does what he says, even though he's not in charge." Visander's face was growing grim as she spoke. "He makes everyone think he's their friend."

"And his powers?"

"He doesn't have any."

"Then we may be in time." Visander stood, a decisive movement. "It is as she planned. I have arrived while his powers are still locked away. We must stop him before he gains them. Once he does, it will be too late."

She looked up at him, at the different cast that he gave Katherine's features. He had told her he was the Lady's champion. But as he stood, she understood perhaps for the first time that it was true. Visander was the Light's champion, and he was here on the Lady's orders to stop the Dark King.

Elizabeth thought of Violet, Cyprian, and Grace. They were helping Will without knowing what he was. He was tricking them. Tricking all of them.

They thought they were fighting for the Light, when they were fighting for the Dark. They were standing beside the Dark King, thinking he was their friend. A terrible pit opened up in her stomach.

"The others, they don't know!"

"What do you mean?"

"My friends. We have to warn them."

"Where are they?"

"They went somewhere." She remembered the gate and the gash in the world. "They went somewhere with him. The Sun Palace." She tried to remember what the others had said about it. "It's a place in Italy."

"I do not know where to find this 'Italy,' but I know the location of the Sun Palace, if you will only show me a map."

They were in the middle of nowhere, a rocky hill summit on one side, a forested slope on the other. You never knew when geography would come in handy.

Elizabeth reached into her pinafore and pulled out her homework.

It was dirty and stained, but she unfolded it and took out a pencil. On it was the half-completed map of the world that she had been copying with her tutor. She put her tongue between her teeth, and drew the last half from memory with the pencil. She thought she had it pretty well. Perhaps she had Switzerland and Lombardy in the wrong place, but that didn't matter, did it? Underneath Switzerland, she painstakingly drew the boot outline, then shaded a bit in the middle.

"What is this?"

"That's the Papal States." She knew Umbria was somewhere in the Papal States. "That's where my friends are." She drew a circle around Umbria. Probably.

"This isn't what the world looks like. There is no ocean here, or here." Visander pointed.

"Yes, there is. You must not be very good at geography."

It was something Visander and Katherine had in common. Instead of arguing, Visander just looked troubled, with another glance around the hillside, as though all of it was foreign to him.

"And where are we now?"

She stared at him. "England."

"Where's that?"

She stared at him. "You don't know?"

"I do not know the names of minor human outposts."

Elizabeth frowned, and pointed. "Well, it's here." Even on her small map, it still looked quite far away from Italy. The Channel was in the way, and so was France. She tried not to let that dishearten her. "We'll need a ship. And some money to pay for our passage. I just don't know where to get those things. Or how."

There was a long silence.

Visander didn't sound at all happy when he said, "I do."

"What do you mean?"

"I mean," said Visander, "I know how we travel to your friends."

"I can't wear this," said Visander.

He stared at his reflection, a wave of disorientation swelling, ready to crash and drown him.

The girl in the mirror was dressed in a white-and-lilac confection, with bows and ribbons woven through a gauzy fabric. Her satin shoes had the same lilac ribbons as her hair.

"If madam could explain what was wrong?"

He stared at the shop lady, thinking that the problems were self-evident. The clothes were tight and constricting. Simultaneously, they puffed out and slowed movement. The shoes had soles with no grip. As a final indignity, he had a small hat perched on his head.

"How do I fight in it?"

He raised his arms partway to demonstrate. Any higher would split the dress.

After a few aborted slashing motions, the shop lady disappeared, and returned to hand him a frilly lilac stick.

He frowned at it, then turned to Elizabeth, only to find her speaking to the shop lady. "We'll buy it," said Elizabeth. "And a dress for dinner. And a—a—"

"Perhaps a dinner dress, three day dresses, nightclothes, and some undergarments?" said the shop lady, who had seen the state of their clothes when they came in.

"Yes, that's right," said Elizabeth, with relief.

The shop lady left to organize the purchase.

"What weapon is this?" Visander held the frilly stick out to Elizabeth.

"It's called a parasol. You carry it about."

"Does it work like the 'pistol'?" He turned it over, then looked at Elizabeth for confirmation, only to find her staring at him with a strange look on her face. "What's wrong?"

Elizabeth said, "My sister liked clothes."

"Why?"

"I don't know. She just did. She liked dressing up in them."

Visander looked back at himself in the mirror. It was impossible, with countless generations between them, but he looked like his Queen. The same eyes, and the face so similar it might have been twinned. It was an unsettling feeling, to look like her, to be her. . . . Except that his Queen had worn armor, and had carried a weapon, not a lilac stick.

And she hadn't had this youthful innocence. Her eyes had been hard. As if everything in her had been razed, and all that was left was a hatred of the Dark King, and a determination to save what was left of her people.

"Thank you, ladies, visit again soon," said the shop lady.

They emerged from the Little Dover Dress Shop onto the street, Visander in one of the day dresses, and Elizabeth in a new blue pinafore. The town was a small human enclave nestled on a harbor ringed by white cliffs. Visander had wanted to go to the ship right away, but Elizabeth had convinced him that they must blend in. That had meant these clothes, bought with money traded for Katherine's pearls. And a hired carriage that was waiting for them. Visander turned toward it.

"You can't walk like that," said Elizabeth.

"Like what?"

"You have to walk more like this." She demonstrated a more gliding step, with her two hands clasped in front of her.

"You don't walk like that," said Visander.

"I'm not a lady," said Elizabeth. "And you can't talk how you talked in the shop. You have to say things like, 'I hope your family is in good health,' and, 'You are most kind.'"

"Who is most kind?" said Visander.

"Everyone," said Elizabeth. "If you meet someone, you say good day or good evening, and you hope their family is in good health, and if you *have* to say something else, you say it's remarkable weather we're having. And you should nod your head like this."

Elizabeth did an awkward half head bob, half curtsy. It was a ludicrous greeting. Elizabeth looked at him expectantly. He copied her without much enthusiasm, only to find himself completing the motion gracefully and with the kind of ease and muscle memory that he had not found while fighting. He rose unnerved, with his hands full of dress ruffles.

"Like that," said Elizabeth, "and don't kill anyone."

They took a carriage down to the docks. The town was a harbor scooped out of chalk, with white sails clustered on its waters, those white cliffs rearing up on either side. The dark ship was striking against that backdrop, flying its three black hounds.

"He flies the *vara kishtar* as his flag."

The shadow hounds were disturbing. He felt an aversion to the ship. But what did an emblem matter when the Dark King himself was already in this world? *Sarcean. Here.* And he was young enough to be defeated. That thought made Visander's heart quicken. This world had a chance if Sarcean was not at his full power, was not yet fully himself.

There was another part of him that thought, *This time I know you, Sarcean. This time you are the youth, and I am the man. This time you can be stopped, and I am going to stop you.*

As he made his way forward, a human he had never seen before was striding down the ship's plank toward him.

"Lady Crenshaw," the man said with a bow. And then when Visander stared back at him blankly: "I'm Captain Maxwell. We were introduced in London."

"Good day, Captain," Visander said, evenly. "I hope your family is in good health."

"They are in excellent health, thank you," Maxwell said, looking pleased. "What a pleasant surprise to see you and your sister."

"You are most kind," said Visander.

"It shouldn't be a surprise, because we're coming on the ship," said Elizabeth.

Maxwell blinked. "Did I hear correctly that you—"

At that moment, a second carriage pulled up, one that Visander knew well, with its shiny black patina, and its four black horses polished to a high gleam.

Phillip stepped out, and Visander took him in anew, his youthful looks and his tumble of black hair. He was dressed in long pale breeches and a black coat, with shiny boots and a tall hat that sat perfectly on his head.

Phillip's eyes met his.

"You!" Phillip did a double take, then turned white. Looking for a way out, he found none on the pier. He looked like he wanted to clamber back into the carriage but couldn't, having already been spotted by the captain.

"Lord Crenshaw," said Captain Maxwell. "You didn't tell me that your lady wife and her sister would be joining us on this voyage."

Before Phillip could open his mouth, Elizabeth ran over to clasp his hand and said loudly, "Uncle Phillip, you're here!"

"'Uncle Phillip'!" said Phillip, utterly outraged.

Elizabeth didn't let go of his hand. "You said you would show us the cabins, and that I'd get first pick."

"Now see here—"

Visander stepped up and took Phillip's arm that Elizabeth wasn't holding. The apple knife, still in his possession, dug its point into Phillip's rib cage.

He felt Phillip go very still.

"Remarkable weather we're having," said Visander.

There was a moment when he felt Phillip hesitate, and he pressed the knife in harder.

"Well, uh, we couldn't bear to be parted," said Phillip, smiling weakly at Maxwell.

"Young love," said Maxwell, shaking his head ruefully.

Inside the cabin, Phillip immediately spun on his heel and said, "What the deuce are you doing here? You were supposed to have run off, and good riddance!"

"Your ship will take us to Italy," Visander said. "The girl and I have business there. If you stay out of our way, you will come to no harm."

"Oh, you speak English now, do you?" Phillip said. "Well, you might've spoken it before!"

"Believe me," said Visander, "if I could have stayed away from you, I would have. We simply need your vessel."

"I'm just supposed to play along? What's to stop me from tying you up and sending you right back to my father?"

In two strides, Visander was across the cabin, his hand around Phillip's throat.

"Foul creature. You are lucky I do not kill you where you stand." Visander said, "You serve the Dark King. It would satisfy me to slay his liegeman. Since he slaughtered so many of my kind."

"I see you only speak English to make threats. How perfectly typical of you." Phillip's hauteur didn't seem at all affected by Visander's hand around his throat. "Is everyone from the old world a scoundrel, or just you?"

"A scoundrel!" said Visander. "You tied me to you in a human ceremony against my will!"

"D'you think I *wanted* to marry a soldier from a dead world? I didn't!"

"You can't tie us up, Captain Maxwell is expecting us for dinner," said Elizabeth.

Visander turned to look at her. After an interval of Elizabeth staring back at him from under her frown, he let go of Phillip reluctantly.

He watched as Phillip straightened his shirt points, then ran a finger around the inside of his collar. "Well, we're stuck here," said Phillip. "And you can't have first pick of rooms, because this is all there is, you little brat."

"Do not speak to her that way, or my hand on your neck will seem like a kindness." Visander was stepping forward, only to find Elizabeth and her frown in his way.

"You said you wouldn't kill anyone."

"I said no such thing, and I will certainly kill him if he endangers our mission."

"Better that than ruin another of my cravats," said Phillip, lifting a hand to wave him off. "I'll take you to Italy. It doesn't seem that I have much of a choice. But it won't do you any good."

"What is that supposed to mean?" Visander glared at him in suspicion.

"My father has opened the palace," said Phillip. "By the time we arrive, there won't be an Italy."

CHAPTER THIRTY-TWO

HOWELL LANDED IN the dust, coming off the ropes with Rosati and his other men landing around him.

A deep drive to protect his own: as Howell's men pointed pistols and held up torches, Will stepped out in front of the others.

"You traitor, I knew you'd lead us right to it." Howell brushed the dust from his forehead with an arm as he addressed James. "*Simon's Prize.* I had you pegged from the start." He ordered the two locals with him: "Tie them up."

"Captain, you are mistaken." Unexpectedly, it was Kettering who stepped forward. "They're here with me—on Sloane's orders." Kettering was shaking his head.

It was the story that had gotten them past the men outside. Howell simply didn't believe it. His dislike of James was too great. "Kettering. I'd have thought you were too smart to take up with a doxy. What did he offer you? A cut of the treasure?"

"But there's nothing of any great value down here," said Kettering. "Just dust and mummified corpses. The kind of thing we've seen many times before."

"He's lying. The chamber's full of riches. The helms are pure gold," said Will. "You can see it under the dust."

It almost worked. Howell reached out for the nearest helm, but stopped with his fingers an inch away. "No. I don't think I'm going to touch it." He turned back to Will. "Clever, aren't you?" Will just stared back at him.

A soldier called down from above. "Captain! What do you see down there?"

Howell said, "It's just as Sinclair described." He looked out at the figures beyond the ring of light that could not be seen by his men above. "An ancient army. Send men back to the camp. Tell Sloane they've found it." And then, "It goes on for miles."

They heard the faint shouts and sounds of action from above, orders given and men sent back to report to Sloane what they'd found. Will's tension spiked. Sinclair's men couldn't be allowed to return here, couldn't be allowed to wake these figures, releasing the armies of the dead to swarm across the countryside—

"We're going to explore this chamber," said Howell. "And you lot are going to go in there first." He gestured at Will and the others with his pistol. "Call it a test."

"No." James stepped forward, flexing his fingers as he often did before using his power. "If any one of you takes a step, I'll crush you."

The locals looked at one another nervously. But Howell just smirked.

"I think if you could do that, you'd have done it already," said Howell. "But let's test it out."

"No!" Will cried out, pushing himself forward as Howell lifted his pistol and shot James right in the chest.

The shot was horrifyingly loud, echoing in the immense chamber. James fell with a cry, landing in the dirt by one of the torches that still flamed on the ground.

"James!" said Will, going to one knee beside him, pressing down on the bloody wound in James's chest. There was so much blood, there was—

"I'll heal," said James through gritted teeth.

But he didn't look like he would heal; he looked white-faced and in agony. Will looked up at Howell, James's warm, sticky blood under his hands.

If you knew what I was, Will thought, feeling an echo of Sarcean's anger, *you would never dare challenge me, beneath my very throne.*

Howell had a brand. Will could control him. Will could make him pay for what he had done. He felt the desire surge in him, and he turned his head to one side desperately, squeezing his eyes closed in case they were turning black, even as his hands gripped hard into the front of James's soaking shirt.

"You see? St. Clair isn't a danger," Howell was saying to the locals. Now he was waving his pistol at them. "I'll take them into the cavern. You collect a few of these figures and take them back to camp."

Will's eyes flew open and his head whipped back around as one of the locals took a step forward. "No, don't touch any of them!"

Whatever vengeance he wished down on Howell, he couldn't let the innocent workers on the dig die right here in front of him. He called it out again in Italian, *"Don't touch! Don't touch the dead!"*

The local man hesitated, but stepped forward to stand in front of the nearest figure. It was the one Will had first illuminated, wearing the helm and armor of a Dark Guard. The local man looked up at the helm for a moment.

"Well? Hurry up," said Howell. And nervously, the man brushed his fingertips to the statue's armored shoulder.

"No!" Will cried, lifting his hands from James's healing wound, too late.

Nothing happened for a moment, but it had been that way with her too, her arm raising the sword up triumphant, and that moment of stupid hope that everything would be all right.

Will wrenched the man backward, and for a single second they stared at each other, and then the man looked down at his own hands, where black tendrils were traveling up his skin over his body to his face. "*No, no, non posso morire così.*" As the armored statue in front of him dissolved, crumbling to dust, the man fell to his knees, keeling over, his face dead white.

Will had thought at Bowhill that it was Ekthalion, that she'd been killed by a drop of his blood. But it wasn't Ekthalion. It was something else.

And whatever it was, it was here, crowding around them. The piles of dust under their feet were remnants of other Dark creatures from the old world, dissolved like the statue in front of them.

"*The white death!*" He could hear the exclamations from the locals around him as they backed nervously away from the figures. "*La morte bianca! The white death!*" They had returned to the tight circle under the opening of the pit, standing back-to-back as though to ward off the dark of the chamber around them.

Howell looked just as afraid. "Why is the white death here?" he demanded from Kettering in a tight voice, backing up. "Is the chamber cursed? Did these figures die of a plague?"

"I don't know," said Kettering, red faced.

"*Burn him,*" Will heard the locals saying. "*Burn him. Quickly.*" They looked scared of the white body. They looked scared of the figures. They looked scared of the dark.

Will looked down at his feet and saw there were several piles of dust just like the one newly formed by the crumbling figure. Had there been other figures here, the white death somehow spread from them to the men who had died on the dig?

"*This place, it's the origin. The source,*" said Will quickly, in Italian. "*The white death lives here. If you go farther in, you'll die. All of you."*

"The source! This chamber must run the whole length of the mountain." Howell's voice was louder, edged with panic. "Is this how it's been seeping up? Infecting us?"

"Anyone he sends in there will die," Will continued saying in Italian, speaking not to Howell but to the locals. *"You all need to get out."*

But Howell just rounded on him. "You." He gestured at Will. "Get in there. Find out what else is there. How far the statues go."

"No," said James, pushed up on an elbow, still clutching his chest. "Will, you can't."

"Or we shoot him again." Howell pointed his pistol at James.

Will stepped in front of James at once.

"I'll do it." He faced down Howell's pistol. And then to James, "It's all right."

"The white death will kill you," James pushed out.

"It won't," said Will. Then, looking up, "I'll go. Just don't hurt him." And then again to James, "I'll be all right."

It wouldn't kill him. It hadn't before. Nor had any Dark object. And besides, this was his chamber. These were his plans.

He stepped forward. He didn't know what would cause these figures to come back to life. It was possible that his simply walking nearby would wake them.

"Hurry up," said Howell, and Will took a second step.

"There's nothing here," Will said. "Can't you see? Whatever you're looking for, this chamber's just full of the dead."

"Put your hand on that statue," said Howell.

Oh God, would it wake him? That was his greatest fear as the figures loomed ahead. *Howell's panicked need for control is going to get us all killed.*

Will had reached the figure nearest him, still in sight of Howell and the others. It too wore the armor of the Dark Guard, but it was winged, with huge feathered pinions, fifteen feet in span. Will reached out and put his hand on the statue's chest.

Unnervingly, he felt something flicker beneath the surface, as if somewhere in it there was life. Instinctively, he spread his fingers out over the statue's chest and closed his eyes.

He felt a flash of wings unfurling, felt the strain in his shoulder blades as if he flew himself, pulling hard to rise up into the air. He smelled the thick, acrid smell of fires on the battlefield. The figures on the ground looked small, but his eyesight was different; he could see each one of them clearly. When he found the one he sought, he would plummet and strike.

He snatched his hand away and opened his eyes, only to see the others staring at him. His heart was pounding, caught up in what he had sensed from the statue. *I felt his life, I felt him fly.* Still half caught up in avian sense, he didn't understand the way the others were staring at him at first. Had he given away any part of what he had seen?

But as the seconds passed, he realized they were waiting for him to show signs of the white death. When he didn't, their looks became exultant and amazed. Grace and Cyprian had an almost holy reverence in their eyes. James's eyes were wide with something shining and victorious.

They saw the Lady in him, he realized. A hero with enough light to overcome the darkness.

There was a reaction among the locals as well, a rippling awe of their own.

"*The white death,*" he heard one of the locals say behind him. "*He's immune to the white death.*"

"It didn't affect you," Howell said, the edge of panic still there but now twined with disbelief.

"Maybe this figure's safe," said Will. "Why don't you touch it?"

"Why doesn't your little lover touch it?" said Howell, gesturing at James.

Will stepped instinctively between James and the figures, moving without thinking. Howell smiled.

"So it's just you who can touch them. Why?"

No one answered. Howell pointed his pistol at Will.

"Why?"

James gave a little shake of his head, as if saying, *Don't let them know you're Blood of the Lady.*

He felt the terrible rasp of a laugh in his throat, and had to stifle it. He knew better than anyone that he couldn't answer. No one could know what he was. Not when he was here, surrounded by the army that he had killed to return with him, that seemed right on the cusp of awakening.

"Go farther in," said Howell.

He walked in, one step after another, the figures looming around him.

"What do you see?" said Howell.

"This one is blindfolded," said Will. His own torch revealed new figures as he went deeper into the dark—the one to his left had metal across its eyes. He put his hand on its shoulder and had a vision of flesh melting; it could melt things with its eyes.

"Stop this," said James. "Will, get out of there."

"Keep walking," said Howell.

Will looked at the next figure. "This one has scales. They're not part of its armor, they're part of its skin." With each step he was careful, wary of awakening the forest of statues around him.

"Will, don't go any farther," said Grace.

"Keep walking," said Howell.

Another step. "This one carries a flail. It has marks on the handle. I think each one is a kill."

"Will," said Grace. "You don't know what will happen."

"Go farther," said Howell. "Go beyond the light."

Will looked forward into the vast black cavern that he knew wasn't empty. He could feel the darkness ahead of him, the source of the pressure in his head. There was something in the darkness that called to him. The heart of corruption. A terrible impression of ghosts, or crowding presences trying to get at him, as if the world bulged with the past trying to get through.

"What are you looking for?" said Will. "These creatures died a long time ago. There's nothing here. Whatever Sinclair's after, it's somewhere else." He stared into the dark without entering it.

"Shut up," said Howell, a flunky throwing his weight around, but with an edge of desperation to his voice. "Keep walking."

James said, "Howell, you fool, if the army in this cavern is awakened, we're all going to die—"

"Rosati," said Howell. "Shoot him."

The two locals on either side of Howell shared a look as Rosati took out his pistol.

Then, calmly, Rosati shot. But not at James.

He shot Howell.

Howell fell to the ground with a startled sound, the echoing of the shot terrifying in this vault, as though it would awaken the dead.

It snapped Will out of his reverie. He turned and found that he was breathing quickly, as if after heavy exertion. He moved dizzily back from the figures toward the others. It felt as if a great danger had been averted; the whirling invisible press of whatever waited out there in the dark was frightening.

By the time he backed up the few steps toward them, Howell was dead, staring up with blank eyes at the mouth of the oubliette. The man called Rosati was beckoning him forward.

"*You helped us*," said Will in Italian. "*Why?*"

"You," said Rosati. "You are immune to the white death."

"I don't understand."

"When the great evil comes, it will be fought by one who cannot die to the white death," said Rosati. "A champion. Or so say our legends."

Will felt that horrible dry laugh in his throat again, and held it back. At the edge of the torchlight, Cyprian was helping steer a rattled Kettering back toward the hanging ropes. On the ground a few steps away, James had healed enough to be levering himself up.

I'm not a champion. The champion died at Bowhill when she picked up the sword.

"You are here to stop the evil under the mountain," said Rosati. "You must go. Before reinforcements arrive." There was a rapid burst of Italian, and then Rosati said, "If you follow me, I will get you out."

"You'll be blamed," said Will. "We can't leave you."

Rosati pointed at James. "We'll say the witch killed him. That you escaped. But you must go now."

With a last look at the dark expanse of the cavern, Will nodded, and they went.

CHAPTER THIRTY-THREE

VIOLET PICKED UP the giant axe, then looked at the room of artifacts stretching out unnervingly around her.

As she looked around at the cabinets full of horns and the tables heaped with jewels, she was struck by the sense that a collection like this was gathered not simply to own the items, but to exercise control over the world itself. She wondered if its confinement here was part of its charm, assembled to be gazed at in secret. She remembered the India room in her father's house, into which he had allowed select guests, explaining this or that about the artifacts that he had assembled, all of which lay passive beneath his words. She wondered if that had been part of the charm too. Objects couldn't talk back. Her father's control over India in that room had been total.

Strapping the axe to her back, she felt her own temptation to stay here and gather up everything she could, take as much of it with her as she could carry, in case—in case what?

She would never know who these objects had been made for, but they hadn't been made for her.

She was turning away when her eyes fell on the table full of parchments that had absorbed Leclerc.

The words were all in French, some written in new ink, some in writing so faded the parchment almost looked blank. Generations of Gauthiers had taken notes on their collection. Perhaps because she couldn't understand the French, it was a sketch that caught her eye.

The sun was inked out in black, as if there was a hole in the sky. Her eyes moved helplessly on to see an eruption of black ink from a mountain, like a volcano retching out shadows, then a terrible horde.

And then she saw a single figure, drawn in an old-fashioned style, slightly out of proportion, which only made it more frightening.

She was looking at the Dark King.

Someone's idea of the Dark King, drawn centuries after his death, with dark horns—or was it a dark halo?—holding aloft a stick or a staff that was too small to see clearly.

Black lines were drawn from the object like unholy sunbeams, connecting it to the horde as though it controlled them.

In English, in modern handwriting:

> *Sinclair believes he has located the Dark Palace. He sends shipments south by sea to Calais, then over the mountains through the pass of Mont Cenis into Italy, where his men dig ceaselessly. He seeks to release the Dark King's army. He believes he has the means to control it.*
>
> *We were right to follow those leads in Southampton. A force must be dispatched immediately from the Hall. We must send Stewards to Italy, to stop Sinclair.*

She stopped, her eyes fixing on the words. They were written in what looked like a journal. She reached out, almost as if compelled, and turned the pages to the beginning.

Justice, if I am too far gone when you arrive, you must take the words I write here to the Elder Steward. We do not have much time.

They know. They know about the Cup. They are waiting for me to turn.

But Sinclair has greater plans than any of us knew, and what I have learned is of vital consequence to the Stewards.

No. Oh no. It couldn't be, could it? Her shaking hand turned the page before she could stop herself.

I have been here for perhaps a week. My captors are James, who has taken the name James St. Clair, a woman named Duval, and her brother Leclerc.

Leclerc visits each mealtime, making continual notes, as if I am a specimen to be observed. He notes my movements. How much I drink. How much I eat. He notes down my words, though I speak little. He writes all he observes in his leather journal, that I yearn to yank from his hand.

At first I thought Leclerc and Duval studied Stewards, but I have come to understand that they study shadows. It is as if Sinclair's plans with shadows extend beyond my turning. There is a great darkness in their actions, a terrible pattern that I can glimpse but not yet see.

James visits rarely, and always at night.

He has grown into a vicious servant of the Dark. He has embraced all of the worst parts of his nature. He likes to see me in chains, yet he fears that I may escape him. He talks about his new position and boasts about his destiny. He taunts me with what I will become.

My father was right about him. He wants nothing more than to sit beside the Dark King on his throne. He is not redeemable. He will kill us all if we do not kill him.

The worst of it is, his taunts cut deep. For he is right.

I am turning.

I need to die before my shadow claims me, but my chains are too short, nor have they left any kindly weapon for me to use. I stole this journal from Leclerc with no thought to write in it. I thought the pen would puncture an artery. I held the tip over the vein in my arm.

I couldn't do it.

The shadow is too strong. It wants to live. That is what they do not tell us. We must kill each other because a point comes when we cannot kill ourselves.

I know now my only chance is to hold on. Justice, if I can tr—

I must stop writing. I can feel the first tremors. It is worse in the mornings. I will meditate to hold steady.

Her heart was racing. The words were written amid scrawled drawings, that upraised staff, and a mountain, drawn over and over again. It was too much, pages and pages of it, and she knew she had to take the journal and run, but she couldn't tear her eyes away.

I kept looking at you as we tied up our horses. You seemed newly alive to me, or perhaps it was the simple joy of being alone with you outside the Hall.

The last thing that I remember before my capture is you smiling, your hand on my cheek, offering me a night together with no duty.

I think I was turning then. I wouldn't have agreed if I had been myself.

She couldn't bear it. It was too personal. She skipped forward.

I begin to fear that all we have done has been not of the Light but in service of the shadow. Why did we isolate ourselves behind our walls? Why did we keep the knowledge of the old world hidden? Why did we not forge alliances, or enlist others of the old world in this fight?

Were our decisions our own, or did they come from that dark seed that we carry inside us, the shadows planted by the Dark King?

I think of the day I drank, years of training leading me to the Cup. All I wanted as a novitiate was to be worthy to be your shieldmate.

I think about that moment now. Not the test or the celebration, but the moment when they brought forth the Cup.

I think of Cyprian. I do not want him to drink. I do not want him to feel this inside him. To lose himself. To be trapped in the shadow. As I feel. As I am. I am lost in the dark. But he has a way out. It is too late for me. It is not too late for him.

It's harder to hold the pen. My hands aren't steady. I have to concentrate to stay myself. I fear sleep. If I close my eyes, I will become a shadow completely.

I will hold. I will not falter.

In the darkness I will be the light.

I will walk the path and defy the shadow.

I am myself and I will hold.

Flipping forward again she saw that the handwriting had changed. Deteriorating over the course of the journal, it was now a wild scrawl, barely legible. Even the words felt unstable.

They talk freely in front of me now.

They believe that I am too far gone. They think I no longer have the will to work against my shadow master. They talk of the staff. They believe they can command what lies beneath the mountain. They think no one can stop them.

They say they will find the vessel. The vessel will birth the King.

They think us old-fashioned in our ways. Ill-matched with the modern world. They say the Final Flame is waning, and the time of the Stewards is done.

They do not know my mind is clear.

The Stewards cannot do this alone.
We must gather the old allies.
We must Call for the King
We must find the Lady of Light
We must find the Champion who can wield Ekthalion
And reforge the Shield of Rassalon

The Dark grew strong when the old alliances were broken. For we will surely fall if we are sundered. Is not that the way of the Dark, to let us turn on each other, and not the greater threat?

Let us put aside old grudges and differences. Let the shadows find us united. Let us stand against the Dark as one.

The shadow fears these thoughts. It fights my pen. It wants us to splinter, as the shield splintered. At times it becomes me, and I want us to splinter. I want us to break apart.

It's very dark here. I can't see the stars. Justice, were you a dream? I think if you were not real I would have had to dream you. I'd hold on for such a dream, that I would hear your footsteps, and look up and see your smile.

I am not a shadow. I am Marcus. I am Marcus.

This cage will open. I will see your face. And you will draw your sword. I know that you will be the last thing I will see. I know it. Justice.

It's just so dark.

He is coming.

He is coming.

He is coming.

He is coming.

He is coming.

He is coming.

He is coming.

He is coming.

He is coming.

He is coming.

He is coming.

He is coming.

He is coming.

He is coming.

He is coming.

He is coming.

He is coming.

He is coming.

There was a sound behind her.

She snatched up the papers and shoved them into her jacket, jerking around to see what had caused the sound.

It was Mrs. Duval.

"You see now what we face," said Mrs. Duval, "and why you need to learn to fight."

Violet's heart was pounding. "Why is that?"

"Because more than the Dark King is going to come back."

Suddenly, the statues and the figures with their staring faces were sinister. Violet said, tightly, "What do you mean?"

Mrs. Duval was a dark silhouette on the stairs, the light from above limning her, making it hard to see her face or expression.

"When Sinclair releases the army under the mountain, they will lay waste to our world. Italy will fall first, but after that they will spread across the map until every human is under their control."

"Italy," said Violet, "is where my friends are. I have to warn them!"

"I told you before," said Mrs. Duval. "You're not going anywhere."

And when she tried to move, Mr. Duval's power stopped her. She tried to throw her whole body at the power that held her in place like shackles. She tried to spit at Mrs. Duval in frustration.

She couldn't do any of that. She had to just stay in place as Mrs. Duval descended the stairs.

"Italy will fall," said Mrs. Duval. "It's too late for your friends. But it's not too late for this world. You need to stay here and complete your training. You need to be ready to fight your brother, and to beat him. When the past comes pouring back into the present, the world will need a true Lion. Only a true Lion can defeat what lies beneath Undahar."

Movement on the periphery of her vision. Violet couldn't move her limbs, but she could move the direction of her eyes.

Deliberately looking at a spot over Mrs. Duval's shoulder, she said, "Behind you."

"I'm not going to fall for that," said Mrs. Duval scornfully, as if irritated by the juvenile trick.

Leclerc chose that moment to push himself up, groaning.

Mrs. Duval turned. It was enough. Violet sprang forward instantly. She had seconds, perhaps less, before Mrs. Duval's eyes were back on her. But it was enough time to leap and bring Mrs. Duval down. *Go for the kill,* she'd been told, in dozens of lessons. *The weak point.* She put her thumbs over Mrs. Duval's eyes and pressed down.

She heard Mrs. Duval shout in French. She could feel the round orbs under their delicate covering of eyelid. "Strike where they're most vulnerable, and do it without mercy," she said, readying herself to grind her thumbs down. She'd have to blind Mrs. Duval to get out of here.

"Wait!" said Leclerc. On all fours on the ground, Leclerc was pleading desperately. "Wait, don't, I beg you, I'll tell you anything. Just spare my sister."

"*Don't tell her,*" Mrs. Duval was saying. "*She will leave, she will run right to Italy, and she's not ready, let her take my eyes, she must stay, she is not yet a true Lion, when the army awakens, she'll be killed there—*"

"No. You saved me from a lion once," said Leclerc. "Now I'll do the same."

"What's really happening at that dig?" Violet said. "What's Sinclair's plan? What did Marcus come here looking for?"

Leclerc began to talk, and Violet went cold at his words.

She had to get back to her friends.

CHAPTER THIRTY-FOUR

THE TRUE WET unpleasantness of the voyage did not make itself known until the ship left the harbor.

This vessel did not cut the waves, or glide over the beauty and spume, exalting in its fizz and spray. It was swamped by the sea, as if it would be drowned at any moment. And the sea was choppy and unmagic, a wet surface that lurched them about in a rising up and slapping down of the boat.

The faint nausea stayed with Visander, for whom it became part of the backdrop of this mission, traveling toward the Dark King. *Here. He's here.* His stomach felt like the ocean, rising and falling.

Would Sarcean know him? Would he know, as Visander killed him? That thought brought its own sick excitement that mingled with the nausea. To look into Sarcean's eyes as he drove the blade in—for that, he would endure these humans on their human vessel. He would endure anything. Lifting the skirts of his dress, he stepped out onto the deck.

Phillip was horrified. "You can't wear that to dinner!"

Visander looked down at himself. "Why not?"

"It's not a dinner dress."

"My dress," said Visander through gritted teeth, "isn't—"

But Phillip took him by the arm and dragged him back toward the cabin with more emphatic force than he'd shown since Visander had known him. "You may be a dead man from a defunct world, but you are my wife, and you can't appear at dinner without dressing!"

Phillip threw open the chest that contained Visander's clothing, and pulled out the white silk gown with the high waist and narrow silhouette, pink rosebuds embroidered on the hem. Phillip pinched the bridge of his nose.

"It's three seasons old, at least," said Phillip, in a pained voice. "What sort of provincial backwater did you buy it in?"

"The Little Dover Dress Shop." Visander bit out each word, fuming that he knew the answer.

"It still has an empire waist," said Phillip, a kind of agony on his face. "You know, *here* we have *fashion,* we don't just go about wearing *robes* for ten thousand years."

"I care nothing for your human fashions, worm," spat Visander.

"You know I can't understand you when you speak that language." Phillip spread the gown out on the bed, frowning. "Well, at least the captain won't notice, he's worn the same waistcoat for fifteen years."

When Phillip left, Visander put on the gown, a series of short, annoyed motions. The stays pressed into his skin, and the dress's short sleeves and low rectangular neckline chilled him in the cold sea air. He looked down at himself, feeling irritation.

He strode out of his quarters, ignoring the seamen who stopped in their duties, staring at him. The thin dress was a poor match for the wind and spray on the deck, but at least they were not in rough seas.

Entering the captain's dining cabin, he found Elizabeth and Phillip already seated. Captain Maxwell was also present, along with two of the ship's officers. The cabin itself was a narrow, domed room of dark lacquered wood, with long vertical paned windows and a long table, lavishly set.

It was Visander's first time socializing with humans, and he approached with some trepidation, noticing that there were eight chairs but only six party members, which implied two guests yet to arrive. The room would be crowded. He didn't like spending time in small wooden rooms with the doors closed. Already he wanted to go back outside.

"Lady Crenshaw, you are truly a beauty without equal," said Captain Maxwell. "You light up my humble cabin."

"You are most kind," said Visander.

Elizabeth gave him an encouraging nod for his use of this phrase, and Captain Maxwell seemed delighted all over again. Taking a seat opposite Phillip put him next to the captain's chair, and he saw Captain Maxwell beaming over at him.

"We were surprised to see you arriving at the docks on your own, Lady Crenshaw," said Maxwell. "What happened to your escort from London?"

"I killed them," said Visander.

There was a short, spectacular silence, into which one of the officers laughed uncertainly.

"Is that some sort of new expression?" said Maxwell.

"No, I killed—"

"Ah, here come our other passengers!" said Phillip, quickly.

Visander looked up, and everything stopped.

Devon stood in the doorway with his hand on the arm of a Lion.

Visander rose up hard, his chair screeching against the wood of the ship's flooring. Reaching for his sword, he realized to his horror that he didn't have one. Even the parasol was back in his cabin, he thought absurdly.

"Take your hands off him, Lion."

The Lion looked back at him quizzically, not understanding.

"Your wife is very accomplished," Maxwell remarked to Phillip. "What language is that?"

"Latin," said Phillip. "Or French."

"I can never tell the difference," said Maxwell.

"Yes, that's just what I said!" Phillip looked vindicated.

The Lion was a boy of about nineteen, with auburn hair and a handsome face scattered with freckles. He wore the same clothes as Phillip, the jacket with its cinched waist and high collar. Beside him Devon was a slender, pale boy, his white face and white hair part hidden by the cap on his head. Visander felt the wrongness of it drive into him, Lion and unicorn.

"How could you," said Visander to Devon. "How could you so betray your kind."

"I like him," said Devon, stepping in closer to the Lion, the familiarity implying—that they were—

"You wouldn't," said Visander. "Not with a Lion."

Phillip said determinedly, "Mr. Ballard, may I introduce my wife, Lady Crenshaw. Katherine, this is Mr. Tom Ballard."

"Lady Crenshaw," said Tom.

He couldn't fight a Lion, not in this body and without a weapon. He couldn't say, *Take your hands off Indeviel*. He couldn't say, *I will cut you down as your kind cut down mine*. He would be killed, and his queen would be killed.

Everyone was staring at him. He wasn't behaving as he should. He was aware of that, even as anger burned in his veins. He was in a human body. This was a social gathering. He was supposed to sit down and become an acquaintance to this Lion.

He felt the long slow awfulness of seconds passing, with everyone's eyes on him.

"I hope your family is in good health," he forced out.

"My mother and father are in excellent health, thank you." Tom's eyes clouded a little. "I hope, that is—I hope we will soon hear news of my sister."

A mother, a father, and a sister. *Four Lions.* Visander made himself sit, unable to take his own eyes off Devon, who sat beside the Lion as though they sat often together. Men in livery brought in the dinner.

To his horror, they lifted silver trays to reveal cooked meat, carving it up right in front of Indeviel. He felt sick. Grotesque slices of flesh: certain Indeviel would object, he watched as Indeviel instead served it onto his plate. When Indeviel lifted a fork and put the flesh into his mouth, it was too much. Visander stood up and thrust himself out, dizzy with nausea.

A stumbling push outside, everything too tight, constricted, his breathing difficult. He had to get out but there was nowhere to go, the ship its own kind of confinement. He hit the ship's railing, felt its constant rocking motion. In a sudden rush he vomited, retching up the repast of bread and fruits they had eaten at luncheon.

Indeviel and a Lion . . . He remembered the first time he'd encountered Indeviel, a shy creature of quicksilver, barely glimpsed through the trees. He remembered riding him, the pure exhilaration of racing over fields faster than any other creature alive. And then as the war commenced, the proud battle unicorn with neck arched and mane and tail flying, horn a strident spear on his forehead.

He remembered years later, the pale bodies of slain unicorns, torn apart by lion claws, rotting slowly on the field. Indeviel had sworn vengeance against the Lions then. Had he forgotten that too, along with everything he was? Had this world ruined him forever?

Wiping his mouth off with the back of his hand, Visander became aware that Phillip had followed him out—was standing at the railing beside him.

"One's first time at sea is always difficult," Phillip said. "When my father first started to drag me about with him, I'd get sick all the time." An odd smile. "Or perhaps it was just me. Simon never got seasick."

"I'm not seasick," said Visander.

"No, of course not," said Phillip.

"Your world makes me sick. The way it's so full of ugliness. Of rot. You eat the flesh of a sheep. It's repulsive."

"It's all very well caring about a sheep when you killed six of my men," said Phillip.

"This isn't my *first time at sea*." Visander was breathing a little shallowly, from the exertion of retching. "I'm not a young girl on her first voyage, whatever I look like."

"Atlantic? Pacific?"

"The Veredun," said Visander.

He looked out at the night expanse of black water. This did not feel like the Veredun, or like any sea he had known. Above them the stars were a white spray like foam, but beyond the swinging lamps of the ship there was very little light.

"What was it like?" said Phillip.

"What was what like?"

"The old world."

He wanted to say that it was wondrous, a world of shining towers, great forests, marvelous creatures.

But all he could bring to mind was the stench of death, the dark shadows in the sky, the Final Flame guttering, the only light left.

"Gone," said Visander.

"Well, obviously."

Visander didn't try to explain, didn't say that it was gone long before he had left it, destroyed by a man who would break the world rather than allow someone else to rule it.

But something must have shown on his face, because when he looked up, Phillip was watching him.

"You knew him. You knew the Dark King."

"Yes. I knew him." Brief. Cut off.

"What was he like?"

That magnetic presence that drew every eye in the room. The mind that planned for every outcome. The charisma that brought allies of unwavering loyalty to his side. And the sadistic force of absolute dominion.

Visander set his teeth.

"The Dark King sent his general to destroy the kingdom of Garayan. He ordered it razed to the ground, no inhabitant left alive, no trace of it remaining. When his general returned with a single stone that was all that was left of those once-great lands, what do you think the Dark King did?"

"Displayed the trophy?" said Phillip, uneasily.

"He flayed his general alive for not pulverizing that last stone to dust," said Visander. "You humans crave power, but you don't understand the cost. You do not know the man you are trying to bring back."

Phillip shook his head. "I'm not trying to bring back anything. That's my father's dream. Not mine."

"Then why do you do this? Why aid the Dark King's return?"

"I'm his descendant," said Phillip.

Said in Phillip's affable, easy voice, he didn't comprehend it right away. As the words started to penetrate, he was stumbling back and away, staring at Phillip across the deck planking.

Nauseated and horrified, Visander looked at Phillip anew. Dark hair, pale skin. Handsome, for a human. Aside from his coloring, there was no obvious resemblance. He wasn't looking at Sarcean. Phillip looked human; Phillip *was* human. At least insofar as Visander could tell. But the Lightbringer had seemed human too, and the light she had summoned . . .

Or was there a resemblance in that coloring, in those dark eyes? *Watered down*, he thought, as though he was looking at Sarcean's features diluted over the centuries.

His gorge turned over as he realized that he had been conjoined against his will to Sarcean's descendant. Worse that it had happened in this body descended from his Queen, which so greatly resembled her. It was a revolting travesty, the Queen's descendants married into Sarcean's line.

Had Sarcean planned this? Was he playing out one of Sarcean's twisted amusements? Sarcean would laugh at it, that beautiful, terrible laugh that made Visander's blood boil.

Devon knew. Devon had sat across from him at that table, knowing. He understood suddenly that there was some terrible larger scope to Devon's plans. Visander stared at Phillip's human face, feeling sickened and entrapped.

"That's why my father wants to bring him back," Phillip was saying. "We're the Dark King's heirs, and when the Dark King returns, we'll rule alongside him."

Visander let out a humorless laugh, a high, girlish sound, and found once he started that he couldn't stop. His laugh spilled out like blood from a cut that hurt, an endless flow that couldn't heal.

"Why do you laugh?"

"Rule alongside him?" said Visander. "The Dark King does not like competitors. I promise you. When he returns, he will kill your whole family."

CHAPTER THIRTY-FIVE

"WE CAN'T LET Sinclair get his hands on that army," said Will.

They had stopped at a clearing some miles from the palace, smuggled out of the mountain by Rosati and a handful of local men. The locals had stayed back to keep up pretenses with Sloane's English soldiers, while Rosati had mounted and directed them downslope. He rode double with Kettering, who still looked half-stunned by the army. It was midday, the sun disorientingly bright after the darkness of the oubliette.

Will looked down at the ground under Valdithar's hooves. How big was that chamber? Did the army extend this far beneath them?

"We could cave in the entrance," said Grace.

"It wouldn't work," said Kettering. "The mountain opened of its own accord. It works for Him. For its King."

"It might buy us a day or two," said James.

Will shook his head. "We can't risk trapping any workers still inside."

"How else are we meant to stop it?" Grace said.

Cyprian, on the other white Steward horse, had turned back to face the shape of the mountain.

"Stewards. That army . . . it's what the Stewards were supposed to fight, isn't it? Before we were wiped out."

Will didn't answer him. But the Stewards could not have defeated that army. The Stewards had been obliterated by a single shadow. This was an endless force of monstrous soldiers, vast and terrifying. Will had felt the flickers of their spirits . . . their minds. There were great generals there. They hungered for power. Yet the terrible thought came to him: That was his army, asleep beneath the mountain. His forces, that he had wielded to take over every part of the world. *Would they take orders from me?*

"The Elder Steward told us to find Ettore," said Will, pushing those thoughts away. "She said only with him could we stop what was to come."

"He must have known," said James, "how to stop that army."

"Or how to control it," said Will.

"But he's dead." James said it succinctly.

Will turned to Cyprian.

"Those bandits, they were the last ones to see Ettore alive," said Will. "You met with their leader."

Realizing what Will was about to suggest, Cyprian was already shaking his head. "No. He hates us."

"You speak of il Diavolo," said Rosati.

Will turned to him. "Cyprian says he stays at the osteria in the village. Would he help us?"

"They say the Devil will do anything for the right price," Rosati mused.

"He's a murderer. He killed Ettore. He has no qualms about killing us," Cyprian said.

"This is too important," said Will.

If that army was released, it would overrun everything. He remembered the vision that the Shadow Kings had given him, himself standing atop piles of the dead, all killed by a force that nothing in this world could withstand.

"The owner of the osteria is my brother. He can send word to il

Diavolo, if you wish a meeting," said Rosati. Will gave him the nod.

"A deal with the devil," said Cyprian. He didn't look happy.

"We need to find out what Ettore knew," said Will. "Now more than ever."

The approach to the village of Scheggino was a tree-canopied road, then a bridge over clear water and the multicolored pebbles of a trout stream. The village itself rose above them, growing up out of the hill surmounted by its single stark tower.

So far, they were not followed. But it was only a matter of time before Howell's death was discovered, and Sloane sent soldiers out to find them, searching through the hills. They all knew it, and the sense of haste drove them to ride hard.

As the first of the terra-cotta roofs came into view, Rosati urged his horse forward. "Excuse me. To arrange your meeting, I must speak urgently with my brother—"

Reaching a stone house on the outskirts of the village, Rosati dismounted, greeting a white-haired woman dressed all in black. She sat on a stool outside the house, peeling vegetables while watching the world pass, as seemed to be the custom here. Rosati addressed her as *nonna,* speaking rapidly in the language of the region. She ignored him, her eyes fixed on James, still mounted on his horse.

"You . . . you're one of them," she said. Will went cold.

"One of 'them'?" said James politely.

"The old blood." She spat. "It returns, like a weed in the garden it must be pulled out, killed before it can flourish. You bring this here? You bring this into my house?"

"Nonna, they're friends, here to help," said Rosati. "There is a great danger under the mountain—"

"Help, they cannot help, they can only destroy, they force themselves into our world, they look like us, but they are not, they are a plague that we must wipe out—"

Will said, "We need to wait elsewhere."

They tied up their horses out of sight. Looking around, Will could see many of the houses had second floors with covered walkways criss-crossing the streets, in a manner that wasn't familiar from London. They needed to stay hidden. The last thing they needed was word of their presence to spread, drawing the attention of Sinclair.

"How did she know what I was?" said James.

Kettering said, "I ought to have warned you. The people here kill anyone with power."

"What?" said Will.

The picturesque village suddenly took on a sinister quality, as though something evil might lie behind those stone walls, or in the silence of these trees.

"Scheggino is built at the foot of the Dark Palace. You think there aren't descendants born here? No one wants those powers back. The locals have a saying, '*Non lasciarlo tornare.*'"

"'Don't let it return,'" quoted Will.

He imagined Dark forces fleeing the palace into the surrounding hills after the war. They would have done so by the dozen, by the hundred . . . there might be thousands of descendants out here. This place, it was like the source of a river from which all tributaries ran.

"They live in the shadow of the mountain," said Grace. "We cannot know what they have experienced here, over the centuries. Their beliefs may have merit we do not understand."

"Barbaric local practices," said Kettering. "Primitive, superstitious beliefs—"

"You won't find a sympathetic ear with these two," James told Kettering. "Stewards do their own killing."

The Blood of Stewards, the Blood of Lions . . . for the first time, it occurred to Will to wonder what other magical bloodlines might have survived out here in secret, hiding their powers from others. To have identified James at a glance, the old lady must have some latent abilities of her own.

"You're all in danger if the locals find out what you are," said Will. "Not just James. We need to be careful."

"What do you mean, we're all in danger?" said Cyprian.

"All three of you are descended from the old world," said Will. "I don't think these people discriminate between the Blood of Stewards and the blood of everyone else."

The shock on Grace's and Cyprian's faces said plainly that they had not considered themselves the same as James.

Will kept imagining that old white-haired woman who looked too much like the Elder Steward in black clothes, pointing a finger at him and saying, *He's here.*

They waited in a taut huddle for what felt like ten slow minutes, though there were no clocks out here on the mountain.

"I'm sorry," Rosati apologized in a low voice when he returned. "She believes in the old ways more than most. The white death took her son."

"Your father died of the white death?" said Will.

Rosati shook his head. "No, not my father. My uncle. My father's brother. It happened when he was young. Eleven, helping shepherd up in the hills. He went out with the flock and didn't come back. It took almost three days to find him. The body was like stone when it was brought back, and the face white. My father was older. He burned the body."

"I'm sorry. That must have been awful." Will had seen it himself now, more than once. The bizarre wrongness of it, life transformed into white stone.

"Her words . . . It is the way here. *Non lasciarlo tornare.* We do not let those with power grow into adults. They are killed before they can become a threat."

Beside him, James's face was carefully blank. Rosati didn't seem to notice, clapping his hand on Will's shoulder.

"My brother has arranged your meeting with the bandit," said Rosati. "You must go quickly, before word of your presence spreads in the village."

CHAPTER THIRTY-SIX

"THE DEVIL," SAID the Hand, "will only deal with one person." Cyprian knew before she pointed the stump at him. "Him."

They had entered the osteria quickly through the back, only to find her waiting for them, sitting with her knee up and the point of her knife sticking out of a table. She looked just as Cyprian remembered: dressed in the torn waistcoat and kerchief that these bandits favored, in clear command of the men sitting around her. He saw at least one musket resting on the thighs of one of the bandits, who stared at him with hostile eyes.

"He's not going anywhere alone," Will began, but Cyprian was already speaking.

"I'll do it." Cyprian lifted his chin. "Where is he?"

Behind him, James snorted. Cyprian kept his focus on the Hand.

"No," Will said, stepping up beside him. "We all go. That's reasonable."

Will didn't back down. His insistence had the adamantine quality it had had when he had brought James into the Hall. The Hand looked at him for a moment without much interest. Then she looked back at

Cyprian. "You go alone, or any deal is off."

"Take me to him." Cyprian stepped forward before Will could speak again.

The Hand stood, pulled her knife out of the table, and said simply, "This way."

The osteria had a set of narrow stairs leading up to a poorly lit mezzanine and a few rooms where patrons could sleep off their wine. The Hand led him up, taking the stairs with a purposeful stride. She had sheathed her knife in her belt, on her right hip. Cyprian only glanced briefly.

"Ask me," she said.

Cyprian flushed to have been caught looking.

"Or are you too much of a *poltrone*?"

Very well. "What happened to your hand?"

"The Devil," she said, "cut it off."

"And you *follow* him?" Cyprian jerked back, revolted.

"It's why I follow him," she said.

Sickened, he just stared at her, his stomach churning. She looked back at him with a dry, amused look, as though at a child with no understanding of the world.

"In there." The Hand rapped on the door with her leather-bound stump, then simply left. Cyprian forced his eyes ahead to what awaited him. Seconds passed.

There was no answer to her knock, so Cyprian pushed the door open. It was a low wooden door that he had to bend to enter. Straightening inside, Cyprian saw that there was a single lamp on a rough-hewn stool providing the only light in the dim interior of a room with curtains drawn over its small window.

The Devil lay heavy-limbed on the room's bed, his muscled torso an expanse of olive skin scattered with black hair. He was watching Cyprian's entrance with satisfaction. As Cyprian's eyes adjusted, he saw that there was a figure in the bed with the Devil. A woman, sloe-eyed and satiated.

And then he saw what she was wearing.

The last tatters of Ettore's Steward tunic. It was deliberate. He was being provoked, and a part of his mind knew it. But the disrespect was too great.

"How dare you—"

"Now, now, Twinkles," said the Devil. "I thought you were here to make a deal."

A deal, when the Stewards were dead and this bandit was dressing his bedmate up in their clothes, like wearing the skin of an animal you have killed, like dancing in it. Anger rose in him, thickly.

Steward, hold to your training. Cyprian forced his eyes away from the tunic.

"We are here to make a deal. We want to know everything you can tell us about Ettore," said Cyprian. "Who was he, where did you find him, what was his mission."

"He's dead," said the Devil. "What does it matter?"

He gritted out: "We're looking for something."

"Something valuable?" said the Devil.

The venal quality of the man was repellant. But these scraps of tunic were not all that was left of the Stewards. What was left was the mission, the task that the Elder Steward had entrusted to him, and the way he stayed true to their memory.

He made the plea in the only way he knew how. Honestly.

"There's an army under that mountain," said Cyprian. "An army of the dead that for thousands of years has slumbered. If it wakes, it will overrun this village, this province, this country. Ettore knew how to stop it."

"He did? How?"

"He was part of an order sworn to protect this world."

Saying it in this stained and soiled room, he felt the Stewards already passing out of life and into story, one that he was unprepared to tell.

"Not much of a protector if a few of my men could take him out."

The Devil said it with a mixture of pride and amusement. Cyprian felt fury and disgust overwhelm him.

"Ettore gave his life in service, he was noble and self-sacrificing. That's something a mercenary like you wouldn't understand."

"You're right, I'm too busy doing other things." The Devil pulled his bedmate in toward himself. "You can stay and watch if you like."

He didn't. The Devil's laughter followed him downstairs as he turned and stalked out of the room.

His friends were waiting, along with the Hand and a few tables full of bandits, who were not quite trapping them inside, but were certainly in an uneasy standoff with James, hands on muskets, muttering in Italian.

"What happened? Did you speak with him?" Will rose immediately Cyprian returned.

"He won't help us," said Cyprian. "It's pointless talking to him." He had told Will as much on the mountain. Now here they were in a village in the middle of nowhere, having wasted a day on this fruitless journey. "I told you—" Cyprian began, stopped.

The Devil had emerged from upstairs, ostentatiously tucking in his shirt.

Cyprian flushed. Instead of greeting them, the Devil took a flask of spirits from one of his men, then chugged it, then went to the seat in front of the osteria's hearth fire and threw himself down on it, a grimy king sprawled on a grubby throne.

Will stepped forward, youthful in the light from the hearth fire. His build was boyish, and he didn't carry any weapons. Cyprian was conscious of the rough men here with their muskets and long knives, utterly outmatching him.

"If we find what we're after, you can take everything in the palace," said Will.

And suddenly he had il Diavolo's full attention.

"Will, what are you doing?" said Cyprian.

"You know what's inside," said Will. "Or you think you know. You've been trying to get in since we arrived here. Gold armor encrusted with jewels, gold chains as thick as your arm, gold cups and plates and mirrors. You'll have it all to yourself."

The Devil didn't say anything. After a long moment, he took another swig of the spirits, wiped his mouth with his sleeve, then gestured at Cyprian with his chin.

"Make that one ask nicely."

Cyprian didn't have to turn to know Will's eyes were on him.

"Please," said Cyprian, flatly.

The Devil let out a snort of breath through his nose. He looked at Cyprian in the firelight, a long look overbrimming with sadistic satisfaction.

"On your knees."

Humiliation heated his cheeks, hotter than the flame from the hearth fire. He could feel the eyes of the banditti on him, hungry with amusement and mockery. The point was to see a Steward besmirched. He knew that.

But what made him a Steward was his duty, and he knew that any Steward would give his life to stop the army that lay under the mountain.

Deliberately, he dropped to his knees, ignoring the hot spill of shame in his stomach. He ignored everything, keeping his eyes on the floorboards, notched and sticky with years of spilled wine.

"Please," he said, "help us. You are the only one who can."

The shocked silence made it clear that the Devil hadn't expected him to kneel. Cyprian braced for a round of laughter and mockery, expecting to have his request demeaningly refused. But when the seconds passed, he looked up, only to find the Devil staring back at him with a strange, helpless look in his eyes.

"There was a place . . . on the white peak . . . your friend Ettore was searching for something. I'll take you there in the morning," said the Devil, the expression shuttering as he acceded to their request. "Tonight, I get drunk."

Everyone got drunk.

Cyprian left the osteria as tin mugs clanked together, sloshing red wine over the rims. Behind him, one of the bandits played a pipe and others danced. Others spilled out into the small town square, laughter and whoops and shouts ringing out over the valley at the thought of the palace spoils that lay ahead of them.

He was in no mood to join them, or to think about how differently the Stewards would have prepared for a morning mission. Instead, he found a place to himself outside the village, near the river, where he could keep watch, in case Sloane's men came.

Hearing footsteps behind him in the cold outside air, he expected Grace, seeking her own calm over the debauched chaos of the osteria.

But when the figure came to stand beside him, it was James.

Cyprian braced himself again for ridicule, the kind he had expected in the osteria. He looked over, only to find James watching him with a complicated expression on his face.

"I made Marcus kneel," said James. "On the ship."

"Good for you," said Cyprian.

For once, James didn't answer right away. Cyprian looked at him and wished him gone. Wished he had never existed. Wished that he could exchange James for the world of the Hall, which James had destroyed forever.

"I kept him in chains," said James. "We sailed the Channel. He fought the whole time. When we docked in Calais, he—"

"Why are you telling me this?"

His words stopped James in his tracks. A look of surprise flickered on his face, as if he didn't know himself why he had spoken.

"I don't know," James said, after a long moment. "I didn't like watching you kneel for that bandit." As if he was pushing the words out. "I don't like being reminded that Stewards can be—"

"What?"

James didn't want to answer. Cyprian could see that in his eyes. "Selfless."

That was too much. "I wish Father had killed you. Marcus would still be alive."

"And if he'd never tried, I'd be a Steward," said James.

"What?" said Cyprian.

"You think I didn't have all the same dreams as you, little brother? Take the whites and defend this world from the Dark?"

"It's not the same," said Cyprian.

"Why not?" said James. "Because I'm a Reborn and you're a Steward?"

Anger, fueled by pain. The Stewards were gone, and James was still here. The unfairness of it gripped him. He drew in a breath of cold mountain air.

"Because you *killed them*," said Cyprian. "You killed all of them. You probably dreamed about it, about the day you'd kill us, you probably—"

"The Stewards," said James, "spent my whole life trying to kill me."

"Marcus didn't," said Cyprian. "Marcus spent all his time trying to talk Father around. Even when you started killing for Sinclair, he thought there was a way to bring you back into the fold."

James just stared at him.

"And I—" *I thought for years there was some mistake. I spent years in your shadow after.* He wouldn't tell James that.

"You what?" said James.

He didn't answer. He didn't want to bleed like this in front of James. He didn't want to give him the satisfaction.

"I'm your unfinished business," Cyprian said. "I was meant to have died that day with the others, and I didn't." The promise was calm and steady. "I'm going to make you regret that."

"You really are just like Father," said James. "You can't believe I'm on your side."

"Until Sinclair collars you. Or until the Dark King returns. Then you'll go running back." Cyprian stared him down. "You're the Betrayer. I'm just waiting for you to turn."

"Like a shieldmate?" said James.

The gall of that left him breathless. "Is there nothing you won't mock or tear down?"

"Go do your exercises," said James. "Go take up your sword and practice the empty forms and the chants and the ceremonies, perfecting them endlessly for no one."

CHAPTER THIRTY-SEVEN

"RIDE," THE DEVIL told Cyprian, "with your right eye closed."

They had set out at dawn, mounting up with a small cavalcade of hungover bandits. Cyprian had consulted briefly with Will, then swung up onto his horse, avoiding James. He would have been happy to avoid James for the rest of his life. The same went for the Devil. But when they started to ascend the mountain, he found himself riding between them.

It wasn't long before the Devil's words made sense: their path through the mountains had a sharp drop to the right, and as they rode, it narrowed until it was no more than the whisper of a thin shelf. Stones kicked by horses rattled downward. Even the grass tufts and shrubs barely seemed to cling to the slopes. Looking down into the beetling crevasse to his right, Cyprian saw with a little shock the remains of other travelers at its base.

"Let me guess, they didn't take your advice," said James.

"You could say that," the Devil called back over his shoulder cheerfully. "We ambushed them."

Cyprian felt a rush of disgust. "So you just kill people for money."

"That's right," said the Devil. "What's the matter, Twinkles? Don't like money?"

"'Twinkles,'" said James, considering the word dryly.

Cyprian said nothing. Of course James had befriended the Devil, two Steward killers getting on splendidly together. He kept his own eyes fixed ahead of him. *There,* the Devil had said, pointing to the top of a nearby mountain this morning. *That's where your friend Ettore was mooning about. Not that it will do you any good. The place is empty.*

They were riding to the place where Ettore had died. Cyprian had braced himself to look over the edge of a drop and see a rusted armor set, a collection of bones. That would be a manageable pain, after witnessing the deaths in the Hall. But the Devil was wrong that the place would be empty. A Steward wouldn't have come all the way out here without a mission.

They rode single file, with bandits fore and aft. The Steward horses sprang lightly upward with the grace of ibex on impossible rock. The bandits all had scrappy mountain ponies slung with packs that seemed to have endless stamina. Will's heavier horse, Valdithar, did not like trudging up the thin, rocky paths, and was struggling.

"You said Ettore was supposed to be the one to help stop a war or something?" the Devil called back to him. Cyprian kept his breathing calm.

"He was."

"If he's so important," said the Devil, with a snort, "why'd your people send a kid to find him?"

I'm not a kid, Cyprian didn't say. *I was five weeks away from my test.* He didn't say, *By now, I'd be a Steward.*

"Because they're dead," said Cyprian. "They're all dead."

The Devil was casual in his seat on the horse. "Oh? How'd they die?"

"I killed them," said James. "So don't get fancy."

More ridge than peak, the mountain had stomach-swooping views of the surrounding rises and valleys. At its crest, a clearing opened up, long dry grass and a beech tree growing at a strange angle, as if it was grabbing on to the hillside with its roots.

"Here," said the Devil with little enthusiasm as they summited. "This is what your friend found. An empty mountaintop."

He was right; there was nothing but height and sky. Near the descending slope, Cyprian saw a few strewn stones. But when he dismounted and stood among them, they were no more than parts of the mountain. Trying to make the best of it, Grace said, "They might have been a cairn, or—"

It should have been him or Grace who thought of it, but Will was the one who said, "Could there be something here hidden by Steward wards?"

"What do you mean, 'Steward wards'?" said the Devil. He was looking at the scattered stones with a frown.

"The Stewards use wards to hide their strongholds," said Will. "What looks like an old archway or a broken piece of stone could hide an entrance to a whole citadel—"

Cyprian was calling out, "Clean it out! Clear out everything here!"

The Hand gestured, and her men hurried to do the work, ripping up grasses and scraping thick dirt. Under a layer of soil and moss were two smooth stone slabs, spaced like the pillars on each side of a door.

Cyprian drew in a breath, and stepped through them.

Nothing happened.

In vain he waited for an effect, waited for a hidden space to show itself just as the Hall of the Stewards had always done. He turned back helplessly to the others.

"Grace, why don't you try?" said Will.

Grace rose and came forward to stand beside him. Nothing appeared to them on the hillside.

Cyprian was opening his mouth to say that Will was mistaken when he saw the carving on the slab.

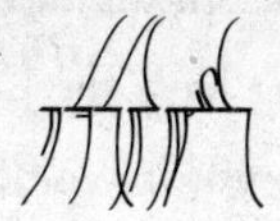

"'Only a Steward may enter,'" read Will, his fingers passing over it.

Grace had moved forward to examine the script more closely. "That word is older than the word *Steward*. It's more like *guardian*."

"Then why won't it open?" said Cyprian.

Grace was looking back at him with a strange, sad look in her eyes, as if she knew the answer—and as if he did too, if only he would see it. Denial rose in him sharply.

"No," said Cyprian.

"I'm a janissary," said Grace, "and you're a novitiate."

"No," said Cyprian.

"The Hall opened for anyone of Steward blood. This needs a Steward. One who has completed the tests and made the vows."

"No," said Cyprian.

"Ettore," said Will.

Cyprian stared at the bare rock, still dark with wet soil. He thought of that scrap of white fabric he had taken from the bandits, the remains of a man who might have helped them. The Stewards were gone, and without them there was no one to open this door, which would now remain closed forever.

A wave of feeling rose up in him, from an ocean of despair. The end of his Order, not just his family and friends, but of sacred places and traditions. He had known that he and Grace could not carry on the Steward ways alone. Now he saw Steward workings already lost to them, nothing here but an empty mountainside.

He heard the scuff of footsteps behind him.

The Devil coming to stand beside him, an odd, wry expression on his face. Furious at the intrusion, Cyprian moved to stop him, unable to bear this final sacrilege. He wouldn't have the Devil trample this site, or speak whatever sarcastic, dismissive words would spill out of his lips.

But the Devil ignored him. "You need a Steward, don't you?"

He stepped between the stones, and the ancient pillars began to glow with light.

A pavilion swam into view between the pillars, held aloft by four high columns, with steps leading to an altar carved into the rock. It was like watching the entrance to the Hall open on the marsh, the same magic. It was here, and it wasn't, a structure high on the mountain, hidden by Steward wards.

Cyprian stared in wonder at what must once have appeared as a soaring lookout, a beacon to the valleys below, a white star atop the mountain.

There was only one man who could have opened those wards: the man they had searched for and had believed murdered. Cyprian turned to the Devil.

"You're Ettore," Cyprian said, in utter shock and disbelief.

The Devil stood in front of it, the light reflecting on his unshaven cheeks, his dirt-streaked, greasy clothing, his poorly kept sword.

How? How could this man be the last Steward? It had to be a mistake, didn't it? It had to be some kind of cruel joke.

"I've opened your room for you," the Devil said with a cursory look around the pavilion. "Take what you need, then my men clear the place out."

"Wait." Cyprian stepped hurriedly forward and took his arm. "You—you're a Steward—you—"

The cold eyes of a bandit stared down at him. The words dried up in Cyprian's mouth.

The Devil had said he had killed Ettore. Was this what he had meant? That he had forsaken his vows? Forsaken his shieldmate? Forsaken the Hall? Become a mercenary, venal bandit with nothing of a Steward left in him?

"Cyprian!" called Grace.

It jerked him out of his thoughts, though he still felt hollow with shock as he turned toward her, and it took him a moment to see what she was seeing. Grace was staring down at a long-dead figure. A skull, and a skeleton, and rotting robes, it seemed oddly intact, as if nothing had broken the stillness of the years. It was posed in front of the pavilion's altar, kneeling. Its robes resembled Steward robes, but were long to the ground like a janissary's, not cut off like a Steward's tunic at mid-thigh. They were rotted and blotched, but it was still possible in patches to see the color, not white or blue, but the dark red of spilled, rotting wine.

"Looks like you missed your rendezvous with him," said the Devil with a snort. "By a few hundred years."

"Longer than that," said Grace. "These remains are thousands of years old . . . preserved . . . . perhaps because this place was closed up."

"Then how can he tell us how to stop the army?" said Cyprian.

Will had walked past all of them. He seemed once again to have made the deductive leap that Cyprian ought to have made himself.

"The altar. It's white quartz. Just like—"

"The Elder Stone," said Grace.

The altar did have the same white, milky consistency as the Elder Stone. His heart began to beat faster at the idea that the stone might talk to them from the past—might contain a message from the Stewards.

"It can't be a coincidence." Will turned to the Devil. "Touch it."

The Devil's brows rose skeptically. "The Elder what?"

"Touch the altar," said Will.

"You touch it," said the Devil mulishly.

Will put his hand on the altar, as if to say, *It's safe*. And then lifted his brows at the Devil.

The little air of challenge worked where a request didn't. With a returning arch of his brow, the Devil—Ettore—put his hand on the altar.

Cyprian gasped in wonder as the scene in front of him suddenly shimmered and changed.

The pavilion was restored to its former glory of high marble columns sparking with gold and silver and a high domed roof upflung to the stars. He'd always thought the Hall beautiful, but as he looked at this pavilion, he realized that the Hall was a ruin, and that he'd never seen Steward architecture at its height.

The figure in red was restored as well, his robes rich velvet and his dark hair loose and flowing down to his waist. He was rising from where he knelt, and as he came forward to greet them, Cyprian was shocked to find that it was a young man not much older than he was himself.

"I am Nathaniel, Steward guardian of Undahar, and I speak to you now at our darkest hour."

The figure—Nathaniel—had a gold star on his chest, and his robes were not white or blue, they were a deep crimson red.

"Our order is overrun. Of twelve hundred woman and men, I am all that is left. Let my words be both call and warning, for what has happened to us must never be allowed to happen again."

He seemed to look right at Cyprian as he spoke, though that was surely impossible. Nathaniel was not really here, Cyprian had to remind himself, just as the Elder Steward hadn't really been in the Hall when she had returned in her ghostly form. He was only a vision held in the stone.

"It began only six days ago. The throne room has always been sealed and off-limits, but one of our number opened the doors. Immediately after, he fell victim to a strange affliction. His skin turned white, and his blood hardened until it was like black stone. We had never seen an illness like it. By the evening the affliction had befallen six others."

"The white death," said Cyprian, turning to the others behind him, his pulse racing. "It's struck here before." It was a sign they really had come to the right place. Even if Ettore himself—the Devil—was standing with his arms crossed, frowning.

"The High Steward feared a plague," said Nathaniel, his face pinched with remembered anxiety, "or worse, some unnatural magic of the old world. We drew back to hold vigil over our fallen brethren, and to discuss ways to cleanse and restore the throne room, where the first of the deaths had occurred."

It reminded Cyprian of the hushed conversations of the Stewards as they gathered in groups and whispered uneasily about Marcus. Worried, yet unaware of the sheer calamity about to befall them.

At the same time, his mind raced with questions. Who were these Stewards who had once guarded the Dark Palace? Why had he never heard of them, or of the white death?

"There was nothing like this plague in any of our texts," Nathaniel continued. "Falling back to the outer chambers, we set our guards to stand watch.

"They saw nothing. But in the morning we woke to find white bodies among the sleeping that did not arise. Fear began to spread. Some said that we should leave the palace, though that would mean forsaking our sacred duty as guardians of Undahar. Others said that we must stay and that we might ourselves be a danger, if we carried the plague out with us.

"We ought not to have gathered. In the midst of a plague, we were vulnerable. As we argued, I saw a terrible sight. My brothers and sisters of the order collapsed, each of them turning white before they fell as if a white ocean rolled over the hall. We fled that white wave amid panicked screams, barring the doors behind us. Yet from behind the door we heard a dreadful sound, shrieks and cries that curdled my blood.

"'We cannot hold,' said the High Steward. 'What lies in Undahar is waking up. It will unleash a terror on this land worse than any plague. Our only hope is to seal it in, and to bury this place so deep it will never be found.'

"'How can that be done!' one of our number cried.

"'It can be done,' she said. 'But it will take our lives.'

"'Very well.' I stepped forward, knowing she meant us to bury ourselves inside the palace. I was ready to do it.

"But the High Steward held me back. 'One Steward must survive. You must get word to the Hall of the Stewards. And if we fail to hold back the darkness of Undahar, you must Call for the King.'

"'Ouxanas,' I said to her, calling the High Steward by her name. 'Do not make me leave you.'

"'It is as it must be, Nathaniel. You know what lies under the palace.'

"As the High Steward spoke, the doors burst open.

"Through the doors I saw the white fallen bodies of my brethren, and above them something else that seemed to whirl and rail at the burst of light that came from the ward stone on the High Steward's staff, as the very palace began shaking.

"I ran. From the eastern pavilion, I watched as Undahar sank beneath the earth, and in its place rose the displaced earth and stone, creating a mountain and valley where there had once been a bountiful plain. The sacrifice of the Stewards had stemmed the eruption from the depths of the palace, and buried Undahar where it would not be found.

"Perhaps the tale should have ended there. I wish it had.

"I stayed in that lonely place for two days and two nights, sending word by messenger bird to the Hall of the Stewards, and waiting for their reply, recovering my strength, with the new mountain looming over me.

"On the third day, as I woke and looked out for the rock dove to return with word from the Hall, I saw the High Steward emerging alive from the valley.

"'Ouxanas!' I called. But she did not seem to recognize her name. 'Ouxanas—you're alive! I thought you had fallen to the white death!'

"She was bewildered, confused, but she showed no sign of the white plague that had befallen the others. Yet I saw when she came closer that her arms and fingers were scraped and scratched and smeared with dirt, as if she had dug herself out from the mountain with her bare hands.

"Hurriedly, I took a flask from my pack, thinking to offer her the healing waters of Oridhes. But when I turned back she was standing with a broken tree branch raised behind me. Before I could stop her she struck me on the head with it. I stumbled back, almost falling. She lunged with both her hands for my throat. I cried her name but she did not hear me. She was shouting at me to release the army beneath the mountain. She said that she would force me to do it.

"We grappled on the cliff. I was weak and wounded from her blow to my head. She was changed, different from the Ouxanas who I knew. On the edge, we wavered, but it was she who fell.

"I was left on the new mountain, alone.

"Some evil inside Undahar had infected Ouxanas. I knew it, yet it felt as though I had killed my kindly mentor. I wept, knowing I had killed the last of my brethren with my own hands.

"It was in that moment that a rock dove landed near my feet. I stared at it, and only after long moments understood that it bore the reply I had been awaiting from the Stewards in the Hall.

"The message I received shocked me. They said that the palace must remain buried. That the army and the plague it brought with it must stay lost. The Sun Gate would be closed forever. Even the knowledge of this place must be forgotten. Only the Elder Steward would remember Undahar, and even the Elder Steward would take an oath never to speak to any but their successor of what lay beneath the mountain.

"As for me, I might be infected with the white death. I must shut myself into the watchtower and let the wards close and hide me forever.

"And so I did. And so you find me . . . or so I hope you find me . . . I hope I keep to my vow and do not leave, though the temptation when I run out of food or drink will be very strong. But I will use my will to stay in place.

"To the Steward who hears this message, heed my warning. Do not seek what lies beneath the mountain. Do not enter Undahar, or break the sealed doors. We thought we could stop what was coming. We were wrong. When evil came, we did not defeat it. We only buried it. And told ourselves to forget.

"But what is buried is never gone. It lies beneath, waiting to return."

The figure began to fade as it spoke the final words, until it was gone completely, and Cyprian was left staring at the skeletal remains and the disintegrated red robes of a forgotten sect of the Stewards. He had knelt to the very end, through hunger and thirst, devoting himself to his duty.

"All right, let's start cleaning this place out," said the Devil, stepping toward the robed skeleton as if he intended to strip it for parts.

Cyprian blocked him. "You can't. You can't just rob his grave."

"That's exactly what I'm here to do."

"He was a person," said Cyprian.

"That was the deal, Twinkles. You get the information, we get the loot. I'd say you got the best of it. There's not much here but the dregs . . . even his robe's likely rotted. But his belt and adornments might be worth something."

Cyprian felt the frustration crest. "Stop it! Can't you respect the dead!"

"What's to respect?" The Devil's face darkened. "These fools messed around with forces they didn't understand, and it went badly. Typical Stewards."

The unfairness of it rose in him, brittle edged and painful. Cyprian looked at the kneeling figure and remembered kneeling himself, morning after morning. He remembered hours spent in meditations, perfecting the forms, strong in the belief that what he was doing mattered.

"He saved you! If it wasn't for his sacrifice, the world would be overrun!" said Cyprian. "We don't leave him here to be picked over. We burn his body. Send him into the flame."

"There isn't time," said Will. Cyprian rounded on him, only to find Will with an implacable look on his face. "Didn't you hear his warning? The throne room is open, Sinclair's on his way, and we don't have a way to stop that army."

Cyprian felt the urgency of it. But he couldn't turn his back on the figure kneeling before the altar. Not knowing that he was the last, and that he'd kept his lonely vigil here with only his Steward rituals to accompany him.

"We make time," said Cyprian.

It wasn't like the great blaze at the Hall of the Stewards. He and Grace gathered sticks and dried grasses from farther down the slope, taking a tinderbox from one of the bandits. When the kindling was ready, Cyprian placed Nathaniel's bones at the center, knelt, and struck steel to stone. He thought—it should be a giant pyre burning atop the peak like a beacon. But there was only coldness on the mountain, and the fire was small.

"Nathaniel." It felt important to say his name. He thought—true death is to pass out of memory. It doesn't come when you die. It comes when your name is spoken for the last time.

"I have heard your message, and I will take up your mission. I will stop the army from issuing forth from Undahar."

The day would come when Nathaniel's name would be forgotten, as everyone's name must be forgotten, but Cyprian wanted to say, *Not yet.*

"Let this place be Nathaniel's Rest. For your work at last is done."

He looked up to see the Devil—Ettore—staring at him, something wide and open in his dark eyes, as if he glimpsed just for a moment something he had believed was lost.

Cyprian rose from where he knelt.

"Take what you like," he said, walking past Ettore back down the rock.

CHAPTER THIRTY-EIGHT

"YOU WILL TEACH me how to use this," Visander said to Phillip, who threw himself sideways across the deck, flattening himself against the ship's wooden railing.

"Don't point that thing at me, devil it! Put it down! Put it down!"

"You fear the weapon?" said Visander. He turned it in his hand.

The weapon was made of wood, with a metal tube at one end, and engraved metal detailing on what looked like the handle. Phillip stared back at him.

"Are you mad? You could kill someone. Where in devil's name did you get this thing, anyway?"

The instant Visander shifted his grip on the weapon, Phillip was moving to take it and point it away, down at the floor.

"I took it from one of your men, who injured me with it," said Visander. "And now I wish you to teach me so that I may injure others if there is need."

"Oh thank God, it's not loaded," Phillip was saying. "Well, look, it's not difficult, you point and shoot. Honestly, aiming isn't even all that useful, the blasted things pull to the right or the left half the time."

I don't understand you when you speak that language. The words everyone said to Visander rose to his lips now. "Show me."

"Shooting isn't exactly my forte," said Phillip. "I don't suppose you want to learn a waltz or a quadrille? Disarm them rather than shoot at them? Dance is terribly useful."

"Not where we're going," said Visander.

"I don't know, Italy's rather a romantic destination," said Phillip.

Visander said again, "*Show me.*"

"You must first promise that you're not going to shoot me with it."

"I promise nothing. If you try to aid the Dark King, I will do all that is in my power to stop you," said Visander.

"Touché," said Phillip. And then: "That's French."

He looked again at Phillip's features. He supposed, if he was looking for it, the same coloring, dark hair and pale skin. *Sarcean's heir.* Phillip didn't have that riveting vibrancy, that beauty that was impossible to look away from, or that consuming power that Visander remembered before the Sun Palace fell.

But he was handsome, and he drew the eye, with an effortless charisma that he seemed to squander on frivolous interests like carriages and clothes.

It was ridiculous to think that Sarcean's looks could have passed themselves down across eons of time. But his Queen's had: he was standing here with her face. And he could not underestimate Sarcean's virility, stamping himself on all his descendants.

Phillip held out the weapon.

"This is a Queen Anne, quite old but effective. It's meant for firing at close range." Phillip stood close beside him. "Like this, you see?" In the next moment he was behind Visander, pressing the weapon into his gloved hand. "You hold it out like so. You want the muzzle pointing at your target."

"Like this?"

Phillip's arms were around him, one hand on his waist, the other guiding his hand. The height difference between their bodies was unnerving. Visander hadn't been this much smaller than another man since he was a boy. He felt surrounded, engulfed. It unbalanced him, made it hard to think.

"That's right. First you cock it, like this." Phillip flipped a small metal mechanism on top of the pistol, then drew Visander's attention to a metal loop that hung down beneath it. "This is the trigger. You slide your finger in there. And then you pull it back to fire. No, harder, the trigger pull is heavy. Here, you'll need to—uh—"

"What?" said Visander.

Phillip had stopped. His body against Visander's was warm. His voice was breath above Visander's ear.

"Nothing. It's just. This is a little . . . You're Simon's fiancée."

"I'm not Simon's fiancée. I am your wife," said Visander, and something very strange happened inside him when he said that.

"I," said Phillip, carefully not moving his hand on Visander's small waist, "suppose that's true."

Visander pulled the trigger.

Nothing happened, just a little *click*.

He felt as if he was waiting for something, on the edge. "It didn't work," he said, a catch in his breath.

"I," said Phillip. And then, "You have to load it."

"Load it?"

"Powder and ball. Maybe for our next lesson."

Phillip had stepped back determinedly.

There was now a gap between their bodies. "Very well," said Visander. *Go and fetch the powder and ball,* he should have said, *and we will practice now.* But it was oddly hard to think.

"I will leave you to the deck," Phillip was bowing and saying.

When Visander drew in a breath and turned, he saw Devon standing and staring at him, like a pale ship's figurehead. Long stretches of deck separated them, active with sailors pulling ropes. Visander felt the painful distance between them; a memory, galloping through the snow on his back, fingers curled in his flying silver mane.

Devon was coming toward him, and he tucked the pistol in the waistband of his skirts, realizing grimly what Devon had seen: the Queen's Champion standing in the arms of Sarcean's descendant.

"Making your own alliances," said Devon.

"You lie with Lions," said Visander.

"Lions are loyal."

I was loyal, Visander wanted to say. *I was loyal to you.* "You knew Phillip was Sarcean's descendant."

Visander felt sick when Devon didn't deny it, just gazed back at Visander with an even look on his too-pale face. It got worse not better with every meeting: seeing the human boy in front of him dressed in human garments, cloth dyed with woad and indigo, dead animal skins on his feet.

"I didn't know they'd marry him to you." Devon said it after a moment.

"Well, they did," said Visander. "While I was barely conscious, still adjusting to this body. Was that part of your plan too?"

Devon was looking at him the way he had at the inn, as if he gazed at Visander from a great distance, and couldn't fully comprehend that he was there.

"I didn't think you'd come back," said Devon. "I'd stopped believing that you could. I'd stopped thinking about you at all."

That hurt, a sharp pain in his chest. "I see."

"There was a time when I thought of you every day," said Devon, in that distant voice, "but that was thousands of years ago."

Visander turned away to the ship's railing, feeling cold air damp with ocean against his face. He could at all times smell the sea brine, even now, when breathing was difficult.

"The Lion." He sounded sullenly jealous, and he couldn't help it. "Do you let him ride you?"

"You are my only rider, Visander." Devon had something hard and awful in his voice. "I can't transform."

Visander turned back to him. He wasn't sure what he was expecting to see. Devon's white face wiped of all expression.

A horrified sympathy welled up inside him, to know Devon was trapped in that body forever. *This distance can never be crossed,* he thought.

"I know why you're here," said Devon. "Sarcean, your obsession. He's the one you returned for. Him," said Devon, "not me."

"You're the one who's choosing Sarcean. Without him none of this would have happened. Without him you and I would be—"

"Rider and steed?"

The mocking way he said it twisted something pure into something painful, that made anger twist its own way inside him.

"Does it please him to see a unicorn serve him? Are you his new prize, taking the place of Anharion?"

Visander flung the words at Devon's indifference, hoping for some impact, a crack, a flare in Devon's eyes.

"You know I cannot lie, so hear this," said Devon. "You cannot stop what's coming. Your Lady has no power here. She's dead. The Dark King has risen. You died for nothing."

He returned to his cabin and found Elizabeth.

She was doing her homework. At ten years of age, she appeared to need to concentrate ferociously while writing, her dark eyebrows pinned together. It was inconceivable to him that this child could kill the Dark King.

He thought, *I am a champion without a lady, and a rider without a steed. I am lost in this place.*

And yet there was this child.

He wouldn't let it all be for nothing, his own death and the death of his world.

Surrounded by the dark vastness of the ocean, he was sailing toward Sarcean, to kill him at their fated meeting. But Devon was wrong. He was not alone.

He said, "I am not *aladharet.*"

She didn't look up. "I don't understand that language."

Those words were almost a ritual between them when he spoke without thinking. It took effort to use the language of this body.

"I cannot do magic," he said. "I have never trained with the"—there was no other word for it—"*adharet.*"

"So?" She had finally stopped doing her homework. Human writing looked like spiders dead on paper, he thought.

"At your age, the Queen had been in training for five years, and could already lightweave and summon. I do not know those skills. I only know what I have seen, watching the *adharet* cast spells as I fought to protect them."

"You're saying . . . that you're a fighter, you can't use magic?"

He looked down at her child's face. She had no one to show her the path. The immensity of the task stretched out before him.

"I'm saying that you are no student, and I am no teacher," said Visander. "But I will train you if I can."

CHAPTER THIRTY-NINE

ELIZABETH PUT A candle on the table and sat down in front of it, ready.

Visander frowned down at it. "What is that?"

"For the magic," said Elizabeth.

"A block of animal fat."

"Will said he started by trying to light a candle."

They were alone in the cabin, Phillip off with Captain Maxell talking about ship things. The unlit candle with its black wick seemed as if it was waiting for something that hadn't come, the same way she felt. Around them, the nighttime cabin was lit with hanging lamps that swayed with the motion of the ship.

"That is foolish. Fire is not your power." Visander picked up the candle, and moved it to one side. "You do not light a candle. You are the sun."

"Light," said Elizabeth, glumly.

"That's right," said Visander. "You are the Lightbringer."

"Light doesn't do anything," said Elizabeth.

"Light defeats shadows," said Visander. "Light is the only power that can stand against the Darkbinder."

"How?"

Visander stood, unhooked a lamp from its chain, and picked it up, carrying it around the room as she watched the shadows move away from it. The shadows shortened when the lamp came near, as if falling back.

"You see how they flee from it? When shadows attacked in great numbers, our mages held them off with barriers, but only for so long. As each mage fell to exhaustion, their barriers collapsed and the shadows claimed them. Only the Queen's light could strike terror in a shadow, drive it back, even vanquish it forever. As long as her light shone, the war could be won."

Then he took the lamp outside. Outside, in the dark, the small light was just enough to see the planking under her feet. It didn't penetrate the black night that shrouded the ship. Elizabeth heard the calls of the ship's men echoing from out of the dark.

"Indeviel and I once rode across the shadow plains of Garayan," he said. "They called it the Long Ride. Six days and nights we galloped in pitch darkness, our only light the sphere she cast around us, protecting us from the shadows that would have swallowed us whole."

Visander looked across at her. "Darkness surrounds us now," he said. "And you are the one who brings light."

She looked out at the dark sea. *You are the sun,* he had said, but it seemed more like she was the lamp. That didn't sound very grand, but maybe there were times when you needed a lamp. She remembered when Violet had fought the Shadow King, and how helpless she had felt, running away to the stables. She liked the idea that she could have fought by Violet's side, protecting Nell. A bubble around a pony wouldn't need to be very big.

She said, "What do I do?"

He took her to the ship's main mast. "You summoned light when we were in the forest. Was that the first time?"

She shook her head. "I lit a tree before that."

As far as she knew, it was still lit, shining all the way down in the bowels of the Hall. She hadn't been trying to light it, her memories of that moment a confusing jumble, a sharp shove to her back, tripping and flailing with her hands, and then a burst of light.

Visander put his hand on the mast. "This was a tree. Light it."

She didn't light it, just looked up at the mast.

"Put your hands on it if you need to."

"We can't sail with a tree," said Elizabeth, remembering the Tree Stone bursting into flower, imagining the mast sending bright roots down into the planking.

"Then take this splinter."

Visander prized a little spike of wood from the mast with his apple knife. Elizabeth took it, held it out in her fist, and thought at it, *Light up.* Nothing happened.

"I have heard mages use words or commands to focus the mind," said Visander. "Think of the light and speak your command to the wood."

"Light up," said Elizabeth.

Nothing happened.

"Shine," said Elizabeth.

Nothing happened.

"Glow," said Elizabeth.

Nothing happened.

"When you summoned light in the forest, it was at a moment of great importance," said Visander. "You were protecting us from the *vara kishtar.* Maybe if you think of that now . . . think of something greatly important, of this world, of its people, of saving all you know from the Dark King."

"Saving everyone," said Elizabeth, staring at the splinter.

Nothing happened.

"Perhaps we will wait until daylight," Visander said, frowning at the night's darkness around them. "It may not be so difficult then."

"Giddyup!" was what the coachman used to get the horses moving, so she tried that. And, "Go on with you!" And, "Hya!" None of them worked. She tried to think about what Visander had said. The thing of greatest importance, the thing she most wanted to do. "Stopping Will." The splinter did not burst into light.

"What are you doing, talking to that bit of wood?" said Phillip absently. He had several jackets spread out on the bed, and most of his attention stayed on them.

Elizabeth thought about trying to explain, but there weren't really any parts of it that she ought to tell Phillip, who was technically their adversary. "I'm trying to think of something important," she said instead, which was not a lie exactly.

"Jackets are important." Phillip held one up in front of him. "I think blue looks well on me, but is it as handsome as the burgundy? What do you think?" He turned to her.

It was so similar to something that Katherine would have said that Elizabeth stopped, feeling a terrible pang.

"What?" Phillip raised his brows.

"I think you would have liked my sister." It was easy to imagine the two of them trying on clothes and attending balls together. "My real sister. If you weren't following your stupid father's stupid plans."

"Believe me, all my lady wife talks about are the dangers of the old world."

She said, "I've seen things from the old world. They're a lot worse than Visander."

"Really? What have you seen?" Phillip flung himself down on the bed, and put his head in his hands, looking at her.

"A Shadow King," said Elizabeth. And then, with scrupulous honesty, "Well, I didn't see it. I heard it. The sound was awful and Sarah started crying. It turned the sky black. It turned everything black. And cold, like it was night during the day. You couldn't see anything, not even your hand in front of your face, and it felt like it would never be warm, like all the light in the world was gone forever."

"I don't know if that is worse than Visander. You haven't seen him on a bad day," said Phillip.

Elizabeth opened her mouth, then closed it. Phillip was teasing, but she wasn't good at teasing, so she just said, "I have seen him on a bad day, I think those are the only kind he has."

Phillip started laughing as if she'd made a joke, when she'd just been honest, which also reminded her of Katherine. She'd always liked that, Katherine's warm laughter, her spontaneous hugs, as if she was charmed by whatever Elizabeth had to say, when other people just seemed to get cross with her.

"Well, let's try to give him a better day, then." Phillip said it with an easy smile that was genuine, and that reminded her of Katherine too, that boundless, good-natured generosity.

"I like you better than Simon," she decided, suddenly.

He let out a strange breath. "Not many people say that."

"Well, I do," she told him.

She couldn't interpret the look on his face, but he sat up and ran a hand through his hair, before giving her an odd smile.

"Thanks, kiddo," said Phillip. "Good luck talking to that piece of wood."

She nodded and went over to her cot, sitting down on it. Out in the dark, she could hear the occasional call of the ship's helmsman.

"Phillip's jacket," she said to the splinter, experimentally.

Nothing.

She went back out after dinner. She had found two places she liked to sit: the rigging out of the way of the boom because it was exciting, and the round, high bow because she could see the view. The bow wasn't much use at night, but it was somewhere she could be alone. She sat down and concentrated on the splinter.

This time, she tried to remember the feeling she had had when the shadow hounds attacked. The moment the light had burst out of her was blurry. She remembered throwing herself in front of Visander, remembered turning and seeing the hound—

"My sister used to sit by the bow too," said a voice.

She turned. Standing in front of her was the young man with the freckles and red hair called Mr. Ballard. He had sat opposite her at dinner and talked about other expeditions he had joined. His role on the ship was not easy to understand. He was not a passenger, but he also did no work. He just seemed to tell Captain Maxwell things. His friend, the white-haired boy named Devon, also didn't seem to do anything, except trail around after Mr. Ballard and have occasional intense conversations with Visander.

"You work for Sinclair, don't you," she said.

"That's right."

He sat down next to her. She wished he wouldn't. She thought anyone who worked for Sinclair was terrible. She wanted to say, *Did you know he kills women? Did you know he's trying to return the Dark King?* The trouble was, he likely did know.

He tucked his legs up under him and crossed them, looking out at the view with her.

"It must be nice traveling with your sister."

"Sort of," said Elizabeth.

He leaned back on his hands. He didn't seem to notice that they couldn't see the view.

"My sister always wanted to sail with me. She was never allowed to."

"Why not?"

"Our father's strict."

"So your sister's stuck at home?"

"No, she's—" He broke off. "You don't need to hear my problems." He gave her a smile. He seemed to have a nice nature, but Will had seemed like that. "I just wanted to make sure you and Lady Crenshaw have everything you need. You can ask me any questions. You must have some."

She did have, lots. Most people didn't encourage her to ask questions. She looked at him skeptically.

"What do you do? You don't seem like you have a job, but you're always talking to the captain."

He laughed. "I'm leading the expedition. When we reach Umbria, I'll be in charge of the dig."

"I thought Phillip was in charge," said Elizabeth.

"He is, of course," said Tom. "But I'll do the day-to-day running of things."

That didn't sound like Phillip would be in charge. Her skepticism grew.

"My sister says your friend Devon is a unicorn," said Elizabeth. She was careful to refer to Visander as her sister. "But I don't see how that can be, since he doesn't look like one at all."

After a blink of surprise at her, Tom said, carefully, "He's a boy who used to be a unicorn."

"I didn't know a unicorn was something you could stop being."

"Unicorns were being hunted. Humans killed them all, then tried to kill Devon. They cut off his horn and tail. If he wanted to survive, he had to become a boy."

That sounded awful. "Somebody should have tried to stop them."

"Somebody will," said Tom.

Elizabeth frowned, thinking it over. "And then he'll turn back?"

"No," said Tom. "He won't ever turn back."

"Is a unicorn more like a goat or more like a horse?"

"I don't know," said Tom, stifling a laugh, "and I'm not going to ask him."

They sat in the dark and she asked questions until she ran out. Then he said, "It was nice talking. I missed talking to my sister."

She just nodded. He might miss his sister, but he didn't know what it was like to miss someone who was right there. Who you saw and thought was with you, until they turned to you with someone else's expression on their face, and you realized that even if they were smiling, you were never going to see their smile again.

He rose to leave her in her viewing spot in the dark. She thought of another question when he was a few steps away, and called out to him.

"What do you think's most important?"

Tom said, "Family."

She looked down at the splinter.

The night Katherine had died, Elizabeth had been in the Hall of the Stewards. But she would have done anything to have been at Bowhill. To have been able to help Katherine. She couldn't imagine Katherine alone in the dark at night. Katherine had never liked the dark. She would have been afraid. When Katherine had been afraid, Elizabeth had used to sit with her and hold her hand.

It had gone both ways. Katherine had sat with her and coaxed out a smile when Elizabeth had been sad or glowering. She felt like Katherine was her light, and now it had gone out.

"Katherine," she said.

It would have been nice if the splinter had started to glow. If it had dissolved into many small particles that had risen like stars and drifted away into the night.

But it didn't. Elizabeth wiped her eyes and looked up to see that Devon had come out onto the deck, a pale smudge against the dark. He always followed Tom, she thought. He was watching her with a cynical smile. For a moment they stared at each other.

I'm sorry about your horn, she didn't say, because she knew by now words didn't help, and that when things were broken they never really got mended. You just went on. You just went on as best as you knew how.

CHAPTER FORTY

"WE HAVE TO stop Sinclair before he gets here," Will said.

It was the one thing he knew for certain. He looked at the others. He could see that Cyprian and Grace were still emotionally half caught on the mountain, and maybe Ettore was too, though the bandit was harder to read.

They were sitting at tables in the osteria. Will and the others had been rejoined by Kettering. Ettore was offering his opinions from a long-legged lean against the cracked plaster wall in a pose that reminded Will of James. James himself was sitting on a barrel near the door, one knee cocked. A scattering of bandits sat around him, including the Hand.

"He knows how to raise that army," said Will. "And how to control it, even if we don't."

He knew Sinclair well enough to know that. Sinclair was ahead of all of them. Sinclair was sailing right now to the dig, where he would wake Sarcean's army from the dead.

He knows how to raise it, and we led him right to the chamber. He didn't speak that part of it aloud. He was the one who had opened the chamber under the throne. Not Sinclair. Not the others. Him.

He felt like he was playing a game against himself, the Dark King in the past making moves that Will could barely see, let alone counter. He'd planted that army and was waiting for them to awaken. And he had some plan for them, just as Sinclair had some plan for them. Will just couldn't see yet what it was.

Cyprian frowned, his eyes troubled. "The Stewards were supposed to stop that army."

"But they didn't," said Will. "They died of the white death instead."

Sinclair wouldn't care that he was unleashing the white death. Probably, like Will, he was immune. Sinclair could simply walk through a palace full of white corpses to the throne.

James spoke from the barrel, an edge in his voice. "Sinclair's ship arrives in three days. That doesn't give us long."

"We cut him off before he reaches the mountain," said Will. "But I think—"

"You think?"

"I think we have to be prepared that we may have to fight that army."

James's eyes went wide with shock. "You mean—"

"I mean if the Dark army is released, the locals here deserve a chance to fight. We need to tell them. Prepare them for what's coming."

He watched that sink in. His friends and Kettering had seen the vast cavern under the throne room that could hold hundreds of thousands of soldiers. And Ettore and the bandits had heard Nathaniel tell of whatever lay beneath the mountain killing thousands of Stewards.

"You really want us to prepare these people to fight the Dark King's army." Cyprian said it as though he couldn't believe it. Or was only starting to believe it.

"How will you feel if they're released, and we haven't warned the villagers or given them a chance to fight?"

Cyprian was nodding slowly, the Steward lieutenant finding a role for his gifts outside the Hall.

"We can arm them," said Cyprian. "Give them some basic training. How to fight. When to fall back. There are legends throughout the villages of the evil rising from under the mountain. They at least will have a reason to believe us, and to fight."

"We split our forces," said Will. "One group attacks Sinclair's convoy, while the other stays behind to ready the towns and villages for what might come."

He saw nods from his friends, but the greatest surprise came from the banditti. The Hand sitting with her legs spread put down her tin mug and stood, the action like a promise.

"I'll fight Sinclair with you," said the Hand. "It's what I've wanted to do this whole time."

"Hand," said Ettore.

Their eyes met, and something passed between them, an understanding that Will didn't recognize. But all Ettore said was, "If she will, I will." *Anch'io* came the agreeing call from the other bandits. *Combatterò anch'io.*

"As will I," said James. "If your men don't mind fighting with a witch."

"I'd rather fight with you than against you," said Ettore, ever pragmatic.

A murmur of agreement from his men. Even with their ancient muskets, their torn clothes, their unwashed faces, Ettore's bandits were a small but significant militia, ready to fight. Ettore had renounced the Stewards only to gather a new fraternity of fighters around him, Will reflected, reenacting his past even as he turned his back on it. Just as well: they might soon need every fighter they could get, even this tarnished, scornful re-creation of the Stewards.

"What can we expect?" the Hand asked James, frankly.

James straightened on the barrel, surprised. James was perfectly capable of ordering others around, but he didn't seem to expect people to look to him for any sort of serious leadership. Anharion had commanded armies, but James had been trained by Sinclair as a singular weapon who answered to only one man.

"He'll dock at Civitavecchia." James was thinking it through as he spoke. "A ship's worth of men, that's two to three hundred soldiers. And he'll likely bring his inner circle to protect him. His son Phillip can wield dark objects. The unicorn is an enigma. Almost certainly he'll bring his Lion, who will be very hard to fight."

"Tom Ballard," said Will. "I've seen him fight before, on the *Sealgair*. He killed a dozen Stewards without breaking a sweat."

"You can fight a Lion with magic," said Cyprian.

"Yes, but—" James broke off.

"But?" said Cyprian.

"But Sinclair knows I'm here," said James.

It wasn't the first time he had said it. He didn't like speaking the words out loud; his lips drew back from his teeth. He didn't like admitting that he might be outmatched in a fight. Underneath that was a deeper reluctance. James feared a confrontation with Sinclair, who'd been a father to him after he'd escaped from the Stewards.

"You can't just ride three hundred men into the Papal States," said Kettering. "Not without local objections. How is he bringing them here?"

"Protection for his convoy, 'workers' for the dig—no one will ask questions," said Ettore. "A lot of money changes hands in this region."

"He's been planning this for a long time," said Will. "Years. Decades, maybe. We need to be prepared for what's coming."

"What *is* coming?" said Grace. When the others just looked at her, she said, "The army, what form will it take?"

Cyprian said, "What do you mean?"

"They won't be Reborn, like James. They won't be infants. Will those frozen figures under the throne room reanimate? How is it done?"

"Nathaniel never described the armies," said Cyprian. "Just the white death that came before them."

Will had seen in his own vision an army that stretched out to the horizon, and a roiling black cloud that blotted out the sky.

There were too many questions left unanswered. But the mission was unchanged. What lay under that mountain could not be allowed to wake up.

"It doesn't matter what form they take. We know what they'll do," said Will.

"What's that?" Cyprian frowned.

He could feel it, waiting under the mountain. It seemed to resonate deep in his bones.

"Conquer," said Will.

CHAPTER FORTY-ONE

THOSE WILLING TO fight took up pitchforks and sickles alongside cutlasses and old pistols. They had no concept of strategy. In living memory they had never fought off an attack on their town. So Cyprian taught them how to dig ditches, how to make use of the stream as a line of defense, how to barricade streets and retreat through the town up the motte.

Even if it was no longer used as a fort in these modern times, the bones of the town's old purpose were still there. Set high on a hill with a tower at its summit, it was easy to imagine the signal flames going up as they would have centuries ago. The beacon defiant in the night.

Climbing to the town's tower himself with Rosati and the Hand, Cyprian looked down at the stone houses and rolling slopes of the nearby hills, and thought of the armies of the Dark swarming across the land and reaching the outskirts. He realized with a chill how much of the training he'd received from the Stewards had been about defending a small outpost from an impossibly large force. This was what the Stewards of old had known, the onslaught of the Dark, while they fell back and tried to hold out.

"And if they attack with magic?" said Rosati.

"Then you're f—" the Hand began, and Cyprian said, shocked, "Hand!" He said quickly to Rosati, "If they attack with magic, we find a way to fight it. And if we can't, we fall back as we planned."

It was Will who had planned all the contingencies, insisting on a path of escape if overrun, as well as the need to warn neighboring towns. Cyprian didn't like planning for failure, but he recognized that his Steward instincts to dig in and fight to the death would not help if this town did fall to the Dark. He imagined Sarcean's army planting its first flag here, then marching on the unsuspecting neighboring townships, and then to the larger cities, Terni, then Rome.

"It's funny to think how many descendants with magic may have been born here," said the Hand. "They could have helped fight if they hadn't been killed." It was too much like James's words, spoken to him nights ago at the river.

"You think they would have?" Cyprian said, unnerved.

"Why not? It would've been their town too," said the Hand.

That thought stayed with him.

Returning to the main square, Cyprian saw Ettore sitting outside the osteria on an overturned crate, eating meat cuts and bread and drinking from a glass of red wine.

His stubble was dirty, his grimy jacket and waistcoat hung open. He was not working or preparing, his glass of red wine looked to be his fourth or fifth, and he had that slightly glazed look of one who had drunk too much in the midafternoon sun.

How could this man be a Steward? Cyprian thought of the training, the willpower, and the discipline it took to earn the whites. He saw nothing of it in the slovenly man on the wooden crate, munching on salami.

Cyprian felt his frustration in his teeth. "Why are you here, if you're just going to drink?"

Ettore squinted, chewing. "There's a palace to loot, remember?"

"Money," said Cyprian in disgust.

"We've risked our lives for less," said Ettore.

"Of course."

"Besides, it's personal for Mano."

"Just not for you."

Every other person in the town was working on fortifications, transforming this place of narrow cobbled streets, crooked rooftops, and uneven stone steps into a last stand, because they cared about it.

"You're no help to us. You're a liability. I think you should leave."

Ettore gave an amused snort and kept eating. He didn't seem perturbed, just spoke around the bread.

"You need pistols and muskets. That's your best chance. If that army rises, it won't have seen modern weapons. Even then, you're better off using bandit tactics in the hills. Smaller sorties, traps, raids . . . You're not going to win at siege warfare against an army that took every citadel in the old world. And with untrained villagers?" Another piece of bread popped into his mouth. "If you really want a land war, you ought to go north and find some of the Piedmontese who fought Napoleon."

Cyprian stepped forward. Ettore's words made sense—even sounded a little like Will's words of this morning—but his casual attitude made Cyprian furious.

"Do the others know? What you are? What you'll do?"

"Excuse me?"

"You drank from the Cup." Anger burned in him, hot and bright. "You might act like a bandit king, but you're not. You're a shadow. You'll kill everyone around you. It's only a matter of time."

He felt a flash of satisfaction as Ettore put down the wineglass after stopping mid-swig. But all Ettore did was lean back and look at Cyprian, a long, assessing look with another snort at the end of it.

"Like Marcus, you mean?" said Ettore, spreading his arms over the jutting stone behind him. "Your brother told me what happened."

My brother? But how could Marcus tell Ettore anything? He stared at Ettore blankly, wrong-footed. And then sudden understanding. "He's not my brother." He said, "He killed my brother."

To his surprise, Ettore laughed, a loud, hearty laugh.

"High and mighty, aren't you? You're like every kid before they drink from the Cup. A fool. They put you in a room, and they tell you to drink, and you think you know how bad it'll be, but you don't. You have no idea what that darkness is. No idea what you're about to take inside you. What you'll be for the rest of your short life. You should thank your brother for saving you from that fate. He killed the Stewards? Good riddance. If you were smart, you'd spit on their graves."

Anger rose in him. Because Ettore was wrong. He was wrong about the Stewards. "A star is light in the dark."

Ettore didn't say anything, just shrugged, as if arguing with fanatics wasn't worth his time. As Cyprian watched, he picked up the salami and tore off another chunk with his teeth, chewing. It infuriated Cyprian in a way that he didn't understand. He wanted to get something out of Ettore. An admission. A reaction. Anything.

"Are you turning?" He flung the accusation at him.

For the first time, he saw something hard and genuine in Ettore's dark eyes. A moment later, Ettore wiped his mouth, then stood and wordlessly picked up the wooden rake by its little pile of stones against the wall. He swung it.

A beautiful, familiar arc. The first triten; the pain in Cyprian's chest swelled. He'd never thought he'd see the Steward forms again. He knew the movements as if they were carved in his bones: the memory of performing them as part of a group of novitiates in the Hall; the ache of how it felt to do them each morning alone. Ettore's rake cleaved the air, then stopped, perfectly still in the final position. Not a single tremor.

"Looks like I'm steady."

The pain became anger again, at the debasement of the last vestiges of all he held sacred, the triten done with an old rake by a man who spat in the face of the Order.

"You're an oathbreaker! You deserted when you swore to defend the Hall! You ran," said Cyprian, "when the Stewards needed you most."

"Sounds like if I'd stayed, I'd be dead." Ettore sat again on the wooden crate. Cyprian stared at him. He was refilling his glass of wine. "So that worked out well for me."

"You traded your sworn duty for drink and prostitutes," said Cyprian.

"Don't judge them until you've tried them." Ettore tilted the glass at him in a little salute.

"You—" Cyprian broke off.

Around them, the hewn stone houses that faced onto the town square threw out afternoon shadows that would lengthen as the night approached and they drew another day closer to Sinclair's arrival. This messy life in the village might be nothing to the forces of the old world, this simple humanness that was forged out of the rocky earth. But it meant something to these villagers; it was what they were fighting for.

"Why don't you say what you really want to say to me?" said Ettore, and Cyprian felt the words burst out.

"How can it be you! How can my brother and father be dead and you're still alive? How can you be the last Steward!"

Ettore just sat there in the afternoon sun, his arms spread in a careless gesture, as if the army under the mountain affected him not at all.

"Because life isn't fair, kid," said Ettore. "That's why you take what you can."

"Why do you follow him?"

He couldn't hold the question back any longer, planting his shovel in the dirt. The Hand paused alongside him, the two of them digging a trench with six men from the village. They were doing the work that Ettore was shirking. Ettore, as far as Cyprian was aware, was still drinking at the osteria.

"He cut off your hand, didn't he? He doesn't care about you. He doesn't care about anyone. Why follow a man like that?"

It was not a childish demand. It was a need to understand; a need for there to be some reason to it all. And maybe the Hand realized that. She looked at him in silence, as if she was weighing something.

"I worked for Sinclair."

She said the words in English, a language she rarely used. Her accent wasn't Italian, lacking the lilting emphasis and rich vowels. She sounded like a Londoner.

"*What?*"

"I worked for Sinclair."

Shock; looking at her, her clothes bandit-style, her face dirt-smudged where she had rubbed the back of her hand across her forehead, she seemed a thousand miles away from Sinclair's empire in England.

"And what? Bandits were an improvement?"

She just stared at him, a steady stare with her dark eyes.

"My parents owned a malt house on the London docks, but died of cholera when I was eleven. I had no money to support myself. I tried my luck on the docks. . . . I was lucky, in truth. The man who approached me wasn't looking for what dock girls were selling. He was an overseer, he managed Sinclair's stevedores, and he was looking for a runner."

None of this made sense. Her story didn't connect to this remote Umbrian town. Somewhere deep inside Cyprian a voice whispered, *James was eleven when Sinclair found him.* The same age as the Hand, he thought.

"At first, the work was good. I rose up the ranks, from runner to assistant. I knew the work from my parents, and I was good at it: warehousing, inventories, distribution. I could read and write, and Sinclair gave me every opportunity. I was sixteen when I was asked to be overseer of his London warehouse. But there was a catch. I had to take the brand."

"Did you know?" said Cyprian. "Did you know it was the mark of the Dark King?"

The Hand shook her head. "The truth is, I was proud. Excited too. Everyone said the brand opened doors, offered chances for advancement . . . man or woman, African, Irish, Egyptian, French, if you were loyal, Sinclair didn't care. I drank a lot and celebrated and ignored the pain in my arm. I thought I was lucky. Then."

"What changed?" said Cyprian.

"It started small. The first time, I woke late, but I wasn't rested. When I arrived at the warehouse, I learned that I had slept through four whole days. That's what everyone told me, slapping me on the back and joking with me for being gone. That I'd slept.

"I put it down to drink. I went about my work, and I might have forgotten it. But it happened again a week later. And then again six days after that. I began to wake up in strange places, not knowing how I got there. Hours of my days and nights were missing. Once I woke with blood on my dress that wasn't mine. Later I learned that a woman had been killed nearby. As I washed the blood out, I started to think that maybe I wasn't just sleeping.

"I talked to my landlady. She said she'd seen me. She said, *You weren't yourself*. Mr. Anders the publican had seen me too. And so had the street sweep. And every time I woke, the *S* on my wrist was burning."

"Sinclair," said Cyprian. The thought made him shiver.

"I tied myself to my bed at night. I told others to watch me. To no avail. It didn't always happen at night, but at times and places I couldn't anticipate. I didn't know what was happening.

"And then I saw Captain Maxwell of the *Sealgair* talking to one of the stevedores in the warehouse one night as I was working late. Except that it wasn't Captain Maxwell. His posture. His manners. His voice . . . He was talking with Sinclair's voice.

"And I knew. I knew that as Sinclair was puppeting him, so too had he puppeted me. He had used my body as though he had it on a string, to do his bidding.

"Maxwell turned and our eyes met. I saw Sinclair in him. And he saw me. He *saw* me, and he knew I saw him. He knew that I knew everything.

"I ran. I ran as fast and far as I could. I booked passage on a ship to Calais. I traveled south through France. Then I found a carriage to take me through the mountains into Italy. I hoped that if I just ran far enough, I could escape him.

"It's a terrible feeling, knowing someone else has been in control of your body. Knowing they could take you over at any moment. I thought maybe . . . if he didn't know where I was . . . if the mountains were between us . . . if no one knew my name and I kept running . . .

"But then he came. Into me.

"I blacked out, as I always did, but this time I fought it, and because I fought it, I felt it. It was as if I was falling into a dark pit. I couldn't see. I couldn't speak. I screamed and no one heard me. I was trapped in darkness, choked, paralyzed, and muted. It was like being drowned, for hours, in cold thick water with no way to get to the surface of myself.

"And then I woke up.

"I was tied to a tree in front of a campfire. And Ettore was there, eating stew.

"He said, 'Oh, you're back.'

"'Who are you!' I demanded. 'Let go of me!'

"He didn't let me go. He just kept eating. I called him every name under the sun. 'You'll run out of names before I run out of stew,' he said. I did run out of names, but not until he went for his second helping.

"'What do you mean, "You're back"?' I asked him finally.

"He said, 'You were someone else for a while.'

"My heart jammed into my throat. 'You kidnapped me! You tied me up!' I tried not to show how much his words disturbed me.

"'Because he's going to come back,' he said.

"I went cold. He knelt down in front of me and pushed up the sleeve of my jacket to show the S. It was burning, red and raised as it always was after one of my turns. Ettore said, 'You lose time. You wake up in strange places. People say you've done things. Things you don't remember. Don't you?'

"I wanted to curl in on myself, away from him. 'How do you know that?'

"'Because I know Sinclair.'

"I was really afraid now, and struggled in my bonds.

"'Who are you?' I said. 'What do you want with me?'

"All he did was shrug. 'Around here, they call me the Devil.'

"'A devil who knows the Earl of Sinclair.'

"'You must have really done something to piss him off,' he agreed, sitting back down opposite and starting in on the new bowl of stew.

"'Why do you say that?' He didn't answer, and an awful premonition passed over me. 'What did I do?' I said. 'While I was— While I was—'

"'You tried to kill yourself,' he said.

"I leaned over and was sick. Still roped to the tree, my stomach heaved. I was repelled by my own vomit on the ground next to me, but the waves of nausea wouldn't stop.

"I thought, *There is no way out.* I could run, but there was nowhere to run. Wherever I went, Sinclair would take over my body. And he would end my disobedience by making me die by my own hand. *He will push me back down into that dark pit, and I will never reach the surface again.*

"Ettore just watched me from the other side of the fire.

"'No stew until you stop throwing up,' he said.

"I laughed weakly. With my hands tied, I couldn't wipe my mouth. 'It's the brand, isn't it? That's how he does it,' I said. 'That's how he takes control of me.' Ettore nodded.

"'And there is no way to stop him.' I said it aloud.

"'There is one way,' Ettore said."

She stopped, staring at him again.

Cyprian realized he was supposed to glean something from her story. But he didn't. "I don't understand."

"Ettore said there was a way to stop him, and there was," said the Hand.

She held up the stump.

It was as if the mountain rearranged itself around him. He looked at the stump and felt sickly naive. He looked over at Ettore, drinking in the sun.

"Why are you telling me this? To prove he's a good man?"

"He's not a good man," she said. "But he helped me." She shrugged, pushing herself away. "And we're helping you, though the Stewards never did anything for any of us."

CHAPTER FORTY-TWO

THE SLOPE WAS thickly forested, with rich, fertile earth, a place where pigs nosed for truffles by the roots of high trees. The canopy overhead blotted most of the sunlight, and the trees around him shielded him from view. The deep forest silence was broken only by birdsong and the sound of his footsteps crackling twigs and leaves underfoot. Will stopped far enough away from the village that he could hear nothing of the clatter of preparations—far enough that he didn't think the others would find him, even if they went looking.

Kneeling, Will brushed the leaves away from the damp earth. Then, with the blunt end of a fallen branch, he drew an S into the black soil.

Instinct; or memory. He just knew what to do. Other things were difficult, but this was easy. He remembered the Elder Steward's words. *Close your eyes. Concentrate. Look for a place deep inside.* He didn't need to. He didn't need concentration or chants or even to be touching the scarred skin of Howell's wrist. He just needed the symbol, and to reach out.

He remembered how easy it had been, remembered it as it had been in the ancient past, flinging himself out across a different world. This time, he was looking for Sinclair's men. A cluster of bright points close by. *There.* He found the nearest to him, opened his eyes, and saw the inside of Sloane's office. *I'm in John Sloane.* That was not where he needed to be. He drew in another breath and reached out further.

A second cluster beyond the dig, five or six points, moving slowly through the dark. In a rush, he was inside the one with the strongest pull.

Expecting to find Sinclair's men at sea, he opened his eyes and took a breath, anticipating the smell of salt and the sounds of wet wood. But instead he smelled fresh mountain air with its hint of beech and cypress, identical to the woods he stood in. And the view he saw when he looked ahead turned him cold.

He knew that road, near the mountain, one day's ride.

Close. Frighteningly close. They must have made landfall at Civitavecchia days ago. *It can't be them, not this close.* They were already past Terni. A day's ride—had he made a mistake? Was he inside the body of one of John Sloane's men from the dig, who had wandered out into the hills? Will turned—

Behind him was a shiny black carriage, a banner of three black dogs, one of a train of carriages and covered wagons stopped in a camp made at a roadside clearing.

His stomach dropped.

Sinclair's camp. Sinclair's men, a day from the palace.

Could he stop them? Will looked down at himself. He saw soft, aged fingers and the dark cuff of an expensive jacket. Not the hands of a servant or a laborer. This was an older gentleman, who wore a stifling jacket even in the hot Italian weather. Who was he? Will took a step and wobbled, but less than he had as Leclerc. This man was closer to his height. His body held itself differently, upright with his shoulders back, his arms loose by his sides with his thumbs facing forward. No limp.

Will kept a hand on the carriage for the first few steps, to make certain that he didn't fall.

The easiest way to slow Sinclair down would be to sabotage one or more of the carriages. He ought to immediately begin his disruptions. But he couldn't stop the thought that Sinclair himself was here.

He had to see him. He had to know . . . what he looked like, how he moved and spoke. His fantasies of confronting Sinclair rose in him. *I killed your son. I destroyed your business. I've taken over your men with brands.* He had to see him, at least. He had to—

Will scouted the camp first, moving slowly. James had been right: there were at least two hundred and fifty men camped here, including those at ease around scattered campfires. They were clearly soldiers, armed and still wearing pistols even at rest. But the real threat would be any men or women with old world power that Sinclair had brought with him. Will let his eyes pass across the camp, taking a meticulous inventory.

"Prescott?" said a voice. "What the devil are you doing lurking about down here?"

Will turned. *Simon,* he thought with a shock, almost taking a step back. The young man approaching looked so much like Simon, it was like staring into the face of the dead.

"My apologies," said Will, and then, "I was looking for the Earl of Sinclair."

"You're looking for Father?" He was given an odd look. "Are you doing all right in this heat, Prescott? You look a little unsteady."

Sinclair's son, thought Will, experiencing it like another shock in his brain. Younger than Simon, but more ostentatiously dressed, with a dandyish air, though he had the same pale skin and dark curling hair.

Not Simon. The younger son. Phillip.

God, he looked just like Simon, a youthful version, slimmer, with a higher brow. He had to assume that both sons looked like their father, the imperfect stamp of Sinclair on their features.

His mind raced in multiple directions. From Phillip's reaction, Sinclair wasn't here. But why? Why would Sinclair have sent his son, but stayed in London himself? Did he know something Will didn't? Will felt the sharp flicker of new danger, the sense of Sinclair's plans always larger than he had thought.

At the same time, he couldn't help staring at Phillip, as if he could see Sinclair in him, glean some critical piece of information from the planes of his face or the cut of his hair.

Will raised his hand to his temple, and offered a wry smile. "Yes, I think it's the heat."

"I told you this blasted country was too blasted hot," said Phillip. "I don't know why people come here, better off leaping into a furnace."

"I'll find somewhere cool to recover." Will made what he hoped was the fanning motion an old man made with his hand.

"Good luck," said Phillip, without much optimism.

Will made for the grandest carriage. It was the one vehicle that the whole convoy would stop for: it therefore became the target of his sabotage. He had to slow their progress toward the mountain. He likely couldn't cause a breakdown of more than a few hours, not if the repairmen were industrious. But once he was done with the carriage, he moved to the supply wagons and began what further disruptions he knew would be effective.

He was rounding the second of the supply wagons when a voice speared him, sharp and keen.

"I don't see why I have to stay with the carriage," Elizabeth was saying. "If you're going into the palace, oughtn't I to come too?"

"You are not safe in the Dark Palace," replied a second voice, one that made Will stop, and turn, and stare, for what he was seeing couldn't be real.

Elizabeth was sitting on the grass embankment, a white muslin dress spread out around her. She was holding a stick of wood and frowning at it ferociously.

The girl sitting opposite her was—

"*Katherine?*" Will whispered, shocked.

It couldn't be her. It couldn't. She was dead. He'd sat by her body for hours, white and cold and stone still. Her lifeless form had never once drawn breath. Yet that golden hair and extraordinary profile were unmistakable.

He just stared at them, watching the surreal, pastoral scene of two sisters in the sunshine. It was as if some unspoken wish had been granted and time had been wound back to a moment when the girls were safe, and none of his darkness had touched them.

Alive. After the first moment of shock and confusion, a strange, painful hope pushed up in him. Maybe—maybe it was all right, had been all right all along. He hadn't killed her. He'd been mistaken at Bowhill, and Katherine had survived the sword. He stood fixed in place, staring.

He felt like a voyeur watching them now, an orphan standing outside a window looking at a family. He wasn't their brother, and whatever miracle had happened at Bowhill, they wouldn't want him. But the yearning was there, acutely. The thought came that if he greeted them as Prescott they wouldn't recognize him, and maybe he could sit and even talk with them. Katherine had liked him, before she had known what he was.

Across the grassy slope, Katherine looked up and saw him.

It seemed to happen all at once: their eyes met, and hers went wide; she was rising and coming toward him with a large, uncharacteristic stride; she was closing the gap between them, and drawing a sword from a strap on her back.

A cold, primal fear. Will stepped back as soon as he saw the blade. But he wasn't a swordsman. He couldn't even control Prescott's body particularly well. He stumbled, as he did in nightmares when a different hand held a knife. *Mother, no. Mother, it's me. Mother.* In another stride, she was on him.

"*You,*" Katherine said.

And she ran the sword through his body.

Pain exploded sickly in his stomach, a rush of wet and blood as it drove him to the ground, knocking the air out of him. His hands tried to clutch at his wound and cut themselves on the sword that was in his guts.

He was barely aware of the screams of Elizabeth. "What are you doing? That's Prescott! That's Prescott!"

Katherine was bending over him, her knee hard in his abdomen, her face splattered with his blood and twisted in hate.

"This is what I'm going to do to you," said Katherine in the old language. "Over and over, until every underling you inhabit is dead." Her voice was hard with a new cadence; her eyes blazed coldly down at him. "I'm going to be the one to kill you. I want you to know that." Her hands tightened on the hilt.

"I want you to know it's me, Visander, the Queen's Champion. And this is how your death feels at my hand."

And she twisted the sword in his guts.

He choked on blood. He was a boy in the body of an old man. With horror and slicing agony together, he looked up.

He saw a man staring back at him out of Katherine's eyes, full of hate. A man in Katherine's body. This wasn't Katherine. Someone else was inhabiting her. A warrior, sent from the old world to kill him.

Will woke on the hillside, gasping. He rolled and clutched his stomach, a gaping hole in his guts that wasn't there. His body was intact, the wet, horrible wound gone. Yet his whole torso curled around it, feeling it like it was still happening. He was dead, he was dead, he was—

Alone on the hillside, he looked up and saw the symbol he had carved into the dirt, the S, now burned into place as though he had branded the earth.

"I know what the white death is," said Will.

Will still felt like he had been stabbed, unsteady in his own body. It took everything he had not to press his hands to his abdomen, where he'd been run through.

He had to force himself to focus on where he was, and on what he had learned, the one piece of knowledge he had seized on as he lay gasping and disoriented on the forest floor.

The others were gathered around one of the long wooden tables in the osteria. James sat with his back against the wall in a sprawl, while Grace and Cyprian stood like two sentinels. He had summoned them first, unwilling to face Kettering or Ettore, at least not yet.

"Will, are you all right?"

It was hours later. Hours wasted, pushing himself up unsteadily in the forest, leaning his weight on a tree trunk. Moving from one tree to another, he'd made his way back to the village.

Grace was looking at him with more concern than she had the night the Hall had been attacked. He could only imagine what he looked like. *Death*, the word entered his mind, along with the repeated sensation of being stabbed.

He forced it from his thoughts. This was too important.

"We need to evacuate. We need to get everyone out of the village. We can't stay and fight them. We can't let anyone be near the dig. We have to get them as far away as possible."

"What are you talking about?" Cyprian's eyes were wide.

He couldn't stop seeing Katherine. Katherine's face with someone else looking out of her eyes. He had wanted so badly for her to be alive. He wanted so badly for her to still be in that body somewhere. But he couldn't help thinking of the inscription on Ekthalion. *Who wields the sword becomes the Champion.*

"The army of the dead . . . it's not just an army of fighters," said Will. "This is an army that possesses people."

Katherine . . . her face had been the same, but her movements, even her posture, had been different. And her expression . . . it had been full of hate, a fresh hate, a fighter who had closed his eyes in the old world and opened them in this one. *I am Visander, the Queen's Champion. And this is how your death feels at my hands.*

"You asked what form the army would take. This is it: people from the old world aren't just Reborn. There's another way to come back. You can return into the body of someone else."

He saw the shocked looks of the others as they absorbed what he was saying.

"Not a Reborn," he said. "A Returner."

"You're talking about true possession," said James.

Will nodded. "The white death. It's the first sign. . . . Someone who died in the past is returning into the body of someone in the present."

He'd stayed with Katherine for hours and seen no signs of life. She hadn't sat upright as if awaking from a dream. She'd just been dead; marbled like white stone. He remembered Nathaniel's tale of Ouxanas the High Steward, who had been missing for three days and thought dead. Until she came back, changed.

"The Returner must be dormant for a short time," Will said. "Perhaps they're adjusting to the body. And then they wake up."

The white death appeared to be a kind of magical hibernation, the skin turning to stone a form of protection, like an eggshell or a chrysalis, until the Returner was ready to emerge.

"Not here," said Grace. "The locals cremate the bodies."

As did the Stewards. It gave sudden weight to the old ways, a cultural practice born of a terrible knowledge: the dead could return. But not without a vessel. Burn the body and kill the Returner. How many Returners had died that way? How many had opened their eyes in the new world only to find themselves burning alive?

But Katherine hadn't been cremated. She had been buried in a coffin. He imagined her opening her eyes underground. Trapped in a small, dark space. He had to remind himself forcefully that it wasn't Katherine. God, he'd left her behind, and that thing had woken up in her body.

"If that army is released, there will be a wave of death, hundreds of thousands of people, they'll fall to the white death and when they arise, they'll be Returners. They'll be his army. The past will be here to take over the present."

It explained why Sinclair himself wasn't here. Why he had sent his son instead, with so much power for the taking, but also so much risk.

It felt like the old world was coming back, just like the Returner in Katherine had come back: for him.

Cyprian's face was white. "Are you sure?"

It was James who answered. "It makes sense, doesn't it? It's risky to be Reborn. You're birthed. You're a child. You don't remember who you were. And you're vulnerable. You're alone. Look what happened to the children in this village," James said. He didn't say, *Look what happened to me.* "This way they come back into an adult body, knowing who they are."

Unspoken was the thought of what else they would come back knowing. Had the Dark King given them instructions? Would they be carrying out his plans? Will shivered at the thought of facing his predecessor's orders so directly, when fighting him at a distance of centuries had already cost so much.

"Then what do we do?" Cyprian spoke for the others. "We can't fight an army that can take us over."

A familiar voice from the doorway said, "Wanna bet?"

CHAPTER FORTY-THREE

IN THREE QUICK strides, Will had his arms around her in a tight hug, and Violet closed her eyes and felt him warm and real against her, alive as she had feared he wouldn't be.

"You found us," said Will, and she only hugged him tighter.

It was so good to see him. It was so good to see everyone. Violet finally drew back, wiped her eyes, and punched Will in the shoulder. His smile broke out; she'd missed it so much.

He had grown taller in the weeks they had been apart, and his tumble of dark hair was a little longer—just enough so as to be too long for its cut. But there was another change she couldn't name, a difference in the way he was holding himself. It reminded her of the way he had looked taking charge after the slaughter in the Hall: as if he had the instincts of a leader, and wasn't hiding them.

When she looked around, she saw Grace and Cyprian, and to her surprise, Cyprian also looked different. He was still handsome as carved marble, but the statue stiffness was gone, as if he was a little more of the world. Then he did something that she had never expected. He stepped in, following Will's lead, and hugged her, so fiercely she felt oddly breathless.

"Cyprian," she said in surprise, and she found herself hugging him back, and that surprised her too, as if they'd both changed without her realizing it. She hadn't ever thought he would put his arms around her willingly.

"I did not doubt your strength," said Cyprian, with his usual straightforward honesty, "but you were in my thoughts often, and I am glad you are here."

His cheeks were a little flushed. Violet tried not to think that Will and the others were looking at them. "As am I," Grace said, with a warm nod of greeting.

"I can take you or leave you," drawled a voice, and she drew back to see James St. Clair.

The differences in James made her more uneasy, still a young aristocrat in fancy clothes, but if you looked closer, he was a little rumpled, as if he'd been in the same jacket for more than a single luncheon. And was she mistaken, or did he look a little less guarded? No, not less guarded, but more . . . comfortable. His insouciant lean against the wall was exactly as she remembered, but he no longer looked like an outsider. His time with the others had made him one of them, and that disturbed her.

For a moment, all she could think of was Marcus's words: *He is not redeemable. He will kill us all if we do not kill him.*

"What happened?" Will was saying. "Is it true you were held prisoner in Calais?"

Violet shook off her thoughts and slung her pack down onto a nearby chair. "There is something you all need to see."

With James present, she kept Marcus's journal back, and pulled out the sheaf of loose papers from her pack, illustrations and notations in French and Latin. The others recoiled in shock from what they saw.

He had a terrifying presence, even in effigy, as if he might step out of the picture into the world. He surmounted the darkness spewing from the mountain, unmistakably commanding it, a staff held aloft in his hands. Black shadow horns curled from his helm, and in it . . . Violet's eyes fixed on the dark space where his eyes would be in the black helm. The artist had drawn only a black void. If he took the helm off, what would be the obliterating sight of his face?

"It's him," said James, sickly.

"It's not original," said Grace. "It's been copied. Likely hundreds of times, since it was first drawn. We don't know what errors may have been introduced into the image."

"It's him," James said again.

That was even more frightening, for the Dark King to retain his power over James, even in a faded copy. She thought of Sinclair, the many-times-diluted version. Marcus's words pushed back into her mind. *James wants nothing more than to sit beside the Dark King on his throne.* Was it Sinclair's ancestry that had called to James? she wondered. Was he drawn by the Dark? Was that why he had sought Sinclair out after leaving the Hall?

"I found out what Sinclair's after." Violet spread out the papers further and told them what she had learned from them and from Leclerc. "I was held in Gauthier's old family chateau, outside Calais. Gauthier's family—they weren't just obsessed with the Collar. There was something else they were searching for . . . the Dark King's staff; they called it *potestas tenebris.*"

Grace said, "The power of the dark." And then, passing her finger over the illustration, "Or here, it's *potestas imperium,* the power to command." She looked up at Violet. "The staff?" In the drawing, dark lines connected the staff to the horde below.

Violet nodded. "The staff," said Violet. "It commands the armies, and it's inside the palace. Under the throne. In a place called—"

"The oubliette," said Will.

She looked up at him in surprise. The name had disturbed her, but it was even more disturbing seeing the others echoing Will's expression of grim acknowledgment. "You've been there," she realized.

"It used to be a prison," said Will. "Now it houses the Dark King's army, ready to wake up."

The few images of the army she had seen in Gauthier's collection had been terrifying. She took a breath. "Well, the Gauthier family believed that this staff was held in the same place."

"And Sinclair knows this?" said James.

Violet nodded.

"Of course he knows," said Will. "He's going to use the staff to raise the army. And command them, as though he were the Dark King."

"We can't let him do that," said Violet. "They'll possess the bodies of everyone in this country."

"We get to it before he does," said Will. "And we use it to stop the armies once and for all."

"You mean go back in there?" said James. And then, "No one can use magic in the pit. We'd be on equal footing with Sinclair."

"All the more reason to get to it before he does."

Will spoke with certainty, as if the matter was settled. He didn't know what she knew. The terrible conundrum that the Gauthier family had wrestled with. The reason they'd never dug for the staff themselves.

The reason Sinclair had captured Marcus, and waited for him to turn.

Violet shook her head. "Only a creature of the Dark can go near it. Anyone else will be killed. It's why the forces of Light didn't destroy it when they killed the Dark King. They couldn't get close."

She knew Will remembered the corrosive power of a single drop of the Dark King's blood, which had torn the *Sealgair* apart and rotted its sailors from the inside out. How much worse would be the source of his power?

"The Stewards were forced to guard it," said Cyprian slowly. "They couldn't get close enough to destroy it, so all they could do was watch it for generations. It was too dangerous to leave alone."

"Like the Cup," said Grace.

"Like the Collar," said James, frowning.

"And when the army woke, all they could do was sink the palace under the mountain, and hope that it would never be found. It's what Nathaniel told us." Cyprian was frowning.

"You can't bury the past," said Will.

He was right. The past always seeped out into the present. She felt her own past press at her: a country she never let herself think about, a series of early memories that she didn't want to face.

Violet said, "So . . . we need a Dark creature of our own."

"James," said Cyprian.

"Oh, thanks ever so," said James.

"No." Will stepped forward protectively. "He could die, I won't risk it. He was of the Light before he served the Dark King." Violet recalled Will hovering solicitously over James back in the Hall. She opened her mouth to remark on it when Will said, "Besides, we need James to open the gate."

"What?" James's head whipped around.

"The *gate*?" said Violet.

"We need to get the locals out of here. That hasn't changed. We can't let that army roll over these towns and take over their people. We have to evacuate the village. Not just the village. The dig as well. The surrounding countryside. The soldiers in that army will possess the first people they find."

Evacuate the region? It didn't seem possible. It would be a huge mobilization, if they could even convince people that the dangers they warned about were real.

And beneath that lurked the other, darker thought. *That includes us. The army could possess us as well.*

"Ettore," said Grace.

"What?" Violet turned to her.

"He is a creature of the Dark," said Grace. "Or he hosts one. He has a shadow. He can get to the Dark King's staff without it costing him his life."

She said it with the calm of a janissarial pronouncement. She spoke not to Violet but to Will, as if they'd shared many such conversations in the weeks since they'd been here.

"'Only with Ettore can you stop what is to come,'" quoted Will.

"I would theorize that his shadow makes him immune to the white death as well," Grace said.

"Why is that?" said Violet.

It was Will who answered. "Because a shadow possesses him already." Violet shivered at Will's words. "At the very least, a Returner would have to fight his shadow to take him over." The image of a Returner battling a shadow for possession of a Steward was unnerving. Two parasites battling over a host.

"We are not giving *Ettore* the power to command the Dark armies," said Cyprian, and for a moment Violet thought she saw a flash of distaste for the idea on Will's face too. "He's a mercenary and a drunk. He can't be trusted."

"Didn't the Elder Steward send us here to find him? Shouldn't we trust her to lead us in our mission?" said Grace.

When Violet looked back at Will, his expression was no longer readable. He'd adopted that easy, agreeable manner he sometimes had as he went along with others.

As if to say, *You're right,* he said, "We talk to Ettore."

"No way," said Ettore. He put his feet up on the table.

Dark haired, with an amused, cynical gleam in his eyes, Ettore sat outside on a barrel, swilling alcohol. He had enough stubble that it was almost a beard, and his hair looked like it hadn't been cut in a year. He was dressed like one of the many bandits Violet had avoided along the mountain roads, in stained leathers and a grimy shirt, half-open on the heavy muscle of his torso, now relaxed in a sprawl. And when they told him what they knew, he just snorted.

Grace frowned, as if this wasn't part of her plan. "What do you mean, 'No way'?"

"I mean no way am I going into that place to get you some Dark object that might kill me. Won't happen."

Learning that Ettore was the last surviving Steward, Violet had pictured him like an Italian version of Justice, but Ettore was nothing like that. As she watched, he lifted his flask again, swilled the drink around his mouth, then deliberately swallowed. The smell of spirits was strong enough to reach her six steps away. It said clearly: we're done.

"The Elder Steward sent us to you," said Cyprian. "She told us you'd have a part to play."

"The Elder Steward never did anything for me, kid." Ettore shrugged.

"You have a shadow inside you," said Cyprian. "A dark force that will shorten your life. You made that sacrifice when you took your whites. Don't you want it to mean something?"

Ettore looked at him, his mouth twisting. "Mean something? You think it means something? I drank from the Cup, you know what that means? It means I got screwed just like the rest of them. It means one day I'll be a shadow, a hollow killer, a mindless servant of the Dark for eternity. Until then, I live my life. What little of it I have left."

"Then do it for your men," said Cyprian.

"My men and I are going with pretty boy to get out by the gate." Ettore indicated James with his thumb.

"The Leap of Faith," said Cyprian.

Violet wasn't familiar with that name. Her attention stayed on Ettore. He was looking back at Cyprian, a strange, half-mocking look on his face. The two could not have been more different. She wondered if Ettore saw in Cyprian a past version of himself. At one time, he had to have believed, or he would never have drunk from the Cup.

"Better faith in a gate than faith in the Stewards," said Ettore as Cyprian frowned.

"We can't force you to help us," said Will.

"That's right, you can't," said Ettore, raising his flask in a little toast.

They left him drinking in the square, returning to the shade of the awning to try to find a way forward without him. "It is not like the Elder Steward to be mistaken," said Grace, as if she couldn't understand it. "Perhaps Ettore has another role to play, one we don't yet know."

"Or maybe he's just a louse," Violet said.

"You have grasped him at a glance," said Cyprian.

She looked over at Will. He had the same easy manner he'd had when he'd suggested speaking to Ettore—he did not look at all worried or dismayed by Ettore's refusal to help them. He'd expected it, or something like it.

"Nothing's changed," said Will. "Our first task is to evacuate the mountain, and to stop Sinclair from reaching the palace. James, you'll open the gate for those who are leaving, while we intercept Sinclair and stop him before he gets here."

The cavern-like stone osteria was not unlike the cellar where she'd been kept under Gauthier's mansion. It had the same arching ceiling, and even its own scattering of barrels. The trellis tables where locals sat and ate were empty, which felt like an oddly ominous portent. Soon the village would be empty. The region would be empty. One way or another.

"I'm sorry," said Will. "I should have been there."

"I made it out," she told him, shaking her head. "I'm here."

"You came for me; I should've come for you." He had always been like that, she thought. As though he'd move heaven and earth to help her.

She said, "No need; escaping was easy." And threw him a grin.

Will answered her with a smile of his own, but there was something else briefly in his eyes.

Truthfully, she wanted to tell him how frightened she had been that she wouldn't make it back in time. She wanted to tell him about Mrs. Duval's warning that she should stay and complete her training. She wanted to tell him about Marcus's journal. She wanted to tell him what she had learned about her mother.

She missed their nights in the Steward Hall, sprawled on one another's beds, swapping stories about their day.

He killed my family too. It wasn't the right time, here on the eve of battle. She wasn't even sure how much of it was true. There were parts of what Mrs. Duval had told her—the parts about Tom, about her destiny—that she still didn't want to believe. As for the rest, as for—

—her mother—

Her life before she had come to England had always been a space she'd kept carefully blank. Whenever anyone in her family had talked about India, she had scowled and stared down at her feet, or left the room. Now that blank space was coming alive with shifting flickers of unremembered memory and thick feelings that she didn't know how to name.

Instead, she drew out Ekthalion.

Will's eyes fixed on it. Forged to kill the Dark King, the sword had a disturbing presence. It had been cleansed of the Dark King's blood, but it still radiated a deadly purpose. Violet felt the weight of it in her hands.

"There's more to Rassalon's story than I've been told," she said. "Mrs. Duval said he was a true Lion. The last true Lion. She said a true Lion could fight what's under the mountain." Violet looked up at Will. "We know Rassalon's shield can fight shadows. I think there's a way for us to fight what's under the mountain together, Lion and Lady. Me with the shield and you with this." She held the sword out to him.

Will's eyes were very dark and wide, and just for a moment seemed to beg for mercy, a haunted expression she'd never seen on him before. But the expression shuttered. She saw him breathe in and out, a shaky breath, as if he was deciding something. Then he approached and drew his hand along Ekthalion's silver length. He looked up at her.

"You should keep the sword," he said.

"I'm not the champion," she said.

"Are you sure about that?" he asked her with a wry smile.

"There's someone this is meant for," she said. "And that person's not me."

He just kept his gaze steady on her.

"You're the one I trust with it," said Will. "The one I know will do what's right."

She lifted Ekthalion and angled it in the light. It gleamed all the way along its silver length. "I just hope I never have to use it."

"Me too," said Will.

CHAPTER FORTY-FOUR

WILL MADE HIS final rounds as the sun began to set.

The preparations now were not for fighting but for evacuation. Goods were bundled and packed up on donkeys, and makeshift sleds were roped together for the elderly who would move too slowly otherwise. Will tried not to think about holdouts, stubbornly determined to stay in their houses, foolhardy or unable to believe what was coming. There was only one way forward now. The evacuees would head for the gate, while a smaller force launched an attack on Sinclair's convoy to stop it before it could get to the palace.

"You know the old ways," he told Rosati, who was directing a small group, instructing them on who to follow up the mountain. "Burn any bodies you find that have died of the white death. But if you see men near you starting to fall from it—"

"If we see them fall?"

"Run," said Will.

Rosati nodded. Will moved on to a cluster of barrels outside the osteria, where a group of bandits were sitting around throwing back a last drink.

"We'll have loot to last until we're too old to spend it," he heard one say.

"I'll buy a home with a cellar full of wine," said another.

"I'll buy a new suit for my father," said a third.

A painful feeling lodged in him. "When the gate opens, any garrison still guarding the Hall will be taken by surprise." The bandits stopped and looked around at him. "Take them out fast, and you'll have that loot you want. A Hall full of it."

"May you not outlive your money." The first bandit raised a glass to him.

He found Cyprian sending out the last of twelve riders to warn the neighboring towns and villages. They needed as much of the region clear as possible. It was Will who had done the job of finding emissaries, men and women who had relatives or friends in nearby towns, and who had at least a chance of being believed when they gave their warnings.

There was so much he wanted to say to Cyprian, who had followed his orders since he had returned to the Hall. He had watched Cyprian transform from a sheltered, bristling novitiate to a loyal lieutenant who was doing his best to adapt to the outside world. Cyprian held to his duty, to the promise of a greater mission, and Will admired him for that. But when Cyprian turned and saw him, Will spoke only of practical things.

"Getting close to Sinclair's carriages will be too dangerous. We don't know who or what he has protecting him. Our attack will have to be at range."

"We have pistols, muskets, and bows," said Cyprian. "And I'm a good shot."

"Let me guess," said Will. "The best archer among the novitiates."

"Yes."

Not a boast. Simply a statement of fact, without any self-awareness of how arrogant it might sound. It was very like Cyprian, who still performed the Steward exercises every morning, a graceful, solitary figure.

With that painful feeling again inside him, Will said, "Don't change."

Grace was overseeing the transport of supplies: sleds, donkeys, packs, and stacks of worldly possessions. Tomorrow, while the bandits accompanied James and the villagers to the gate, she would ride with Cyprian and the others to join the fight against Sinclair.

"If something happens to me, you need to take charge," Will said to her. "You need to lead them, and if they can't win the fight against Sinclair, you need to get them out."

"Me," said Grace.

"That's right."

She gave him a long look, as if she was trying to make him out. He just looked back at her steadily.

But, "All right," was all she said.

And then, when that was done, he walked the narrow cobbled lane with its gray stone buildings clustered on either side until it petered out into a dirt path, up the steep hill to the crumbling tower that looked out over the town.

James was watching him, blond hair bright in the last light of sunset. James's only role was to conserve energy so that tomorrow he could open the gate. He leaned against an outcrop of stone, the town fanned out in front of him. The tangled bonds that tied them together tightened like bright wire.

There was something impossible about his beauty. He suited the sunset, as if he was part of the light that was slipping from the world. Will thought, *The land would be cold and dark if you were gone.* Seeing him now, Will felt lost forever to the knowledge that James was all he had wanted in his past life, and could never possess in this one. James leaned back and regarded him with the same warmth with which Anharion had first regarded Sarcean.

"Take me," said James. "Take me with you to fight Sinclair."

Will realized that from this vantage, James had been watching him as he spoke to each of the groups in the village below. But even James did not understand.

Will kept his voice casual. "We need you at the gate."

"I can't protect you at the gate."

Warmth. Like drowning in hot sunlight. He felt selfish for wanting it this badly, for taking it under false pretenses, even as he said with a little wellspring of that golden light, "You're worried about me."

James frowned and didn't deny it. "I—"

"You don't need to be," said Will. "I'm going to stop all of it."

"You're always so certain."

"That's right."

Looking out, he saw that, as well as the town, you could see a view of the mountain, and somewhere on that mountain was the gate. Tomorrow, James would climb the mountain, while Will would descend alone.

"If that army wakes up," said James, "they'll know me." When Will didn't answer, James turned to face him. "If they remember the old world, they'll *know me*."

"Like Devon knew you."

"That stupid gelding. Yes."

The army would know him too, just as Devon had known him. Devon had recognized him the moment he had walked into Robert Drake's ivory shop. And if his army knew him, his friends would learn who he was all too quickly. James would learn who he was.

"I know you," said Will, as James's eyes widened. "Those people you'll be taking to the gates, I know you won't let them down. I know you'll do everything you can to protect them. That's what you are, you know. A protector."

James's eyes widened further, as if he had never received that kind of praise before, and didn't know what to do with it.

"I see that in you," Will said, "even if your father didn't. I've seen what you've given to fight on this side."

James turned away as if his feelings had crested, and this was what Will wanted to protect in turn, this part of James that was so rarely seen.

"I didn't—with Simon. That wasn't a lie." James said it with his back to Will.

Will flushed as he grasped James's meaning. "I know that."

"He wanted it, as a sign of status. But he was too scared to touch me. They all were. I belong to one person. And they're terrified of my owner." The full meaning of what James was saying spread through him.

"You mean you've never—"

James didn't answer, but he turned back to Will and the truth was there on his face.

Will couldn't help the acquisitive sound in his voice. "You stayed faithful to him."

To me. The idea of James staying pure for him was illicit. Raised in a culture of abstinence by the Stewards, and then keeping himself chaste while he thought of his owner. It was sickly pleasing, even as at the same time he was jealous: a violent jealousy of his former self. He wanted to be the one James had made his vows to. He wanted to be the one to make James break his vows, even as he knew those vows were to himself.

"If he came back," said James, "and I felt something for anyone, it would be a death sentence." *A death sentence for them,* thought Will. *The Dark King would kill anyone who touched his property.* "I told myself that I was protecting them. . . . But I'd be lying if I said that I'm not—that I wasn't a little in love with him. With the idea of him. The dark conqueror, who could have had anyone, and chose me. I was young."

"And did you? Feel something for anyone?"

"How could I, when he was there? No one was him," James said. "I thought he really was going to come back. The idea that I was for him was exciting. It was a way out of the Stewards. A way to feel that I was special. Chosen by the most powerful man on earth. But the more I learned, the more it was frightening. He was all-consuming. I thought—"

"What? What did you think?"

"That he was my end. And I was rushing toward it. I couldn't see past him. Until I met you."

"James—" said Will.

James's blue eyes were on his, the openness in them uncharacteristic, and clearly difficult for him, breathing shallowly as he offered what he had never offered to anyone.

"Take what was his. Prove you're not afraid. And that nor am I. We have the night," said James. "One night, before the end of the world."

Like a man at the edge of a cliff yearning to throw himself over, James wanted an act that was irrevocable. He wanted to sever himself from the Dark King forever. And Will wanted it too, ached to step in and take what James was offering him, ached to touch where others hadn't, to bring him to true surrender, to know how it felt to give himself to another.

He dragged himself away.

"We can't," said Will. He was breathing unevenly.

"Why not?" said James. "Because I'm—"

"No. That isn't why. I— After," said Will. "When this is all done. Come to me after."

He saw James realize that it wasn't rejection: it was an offer, a desperate hope for the future—a future in which they might be just themselves, if that was even possible.

James's lips curled, his lashes lowering. "Is that an order?"

The question flashed through Will hotly, and his own words came out in a voice he barely recognized. "Would you like that? An order?"

"I—" James didn't answer, just said, "I want to be yours, not his."

They were moving toward one another again, that cliff edge drawing closer. "I want that too."

"Kiss me," said James.

He stepped forward, and it was Will's turn to use his hands, cup James's face and slide fingers into his hair. It was more tempting than the Collar, Anharion's lips against his, but never like this, sweetly willing. And that thought held him back, even as the kiss seemed to throb between them. He brought their foreheads together instead, holding James tight in his arms.

"Will—" said James, helplessly.

"After," said Will. "I promise."

Will waited until everyone else was asleep, and then went alone to the edge of the village.

Slipping out of the osteria meant walking past James, asleep on one of the cots by the embers of the hearth fire. Cyprian was not far off, also sleeping, the unlikely brothers for once at peace.

Turning James away had torn him asunder. He could still feel their almost-kiss, the teetering possibility of it, his own desire to close his eyes and fall. He wanted selfishly to have him, to know what it was like to have James to himself.

But he could never have James while Sarcean lay between them. Will didn't even really know if James wanted him, or if he was just drawn to the echo of Sarcean. He could see the fingerprints that Sarcean had left all over James. It would have been so easy to put his own fingers on all those places. James felt like Sarcean's most personal message, sent across time, a knowing enticement, as if to say, *You see? We are the same.*

He turned and looked back one last time at the village. His Reborn general, his Lion, and his army were all ready to fight. There was a part of him that wanted to reply to Sarcean, *They're mine, and I did not need to force them.*

No, you just tricked them, the amused reply seemed to come back to him. He ignored it.

Maybe they were the same. But this time, it was going to be different. He was going to make it different.

He was going to prove to that mocking voice that he wasn't a Dark King. He would consign Sarcean to the past, end his plans, end his influence on the world. And then he'd be free to make a new future.

He walked out past the outskirts of the village, into the sloping hills clustered with trees. No one stopped him. No one suspected him, but then again, no one ever had.

He stopped when he reached a small lookout from which he could see the road.

And he waited for what he knew was coming.

CHAPTER FORTY-FIVE

WHEN THE SHADOWED figure crept out of the village, Will was ready.

Good at hiding and staying out of sight, Will slipped silently from the nighttime cover of the trees out onto the path in front of him.

"Will!" said Kettering. "I was just—"

Will looked at Kettering's well-brushed hair and his neat sideburns, his glasses and his mismatched professorial clothes.

"You're one of them," said Will. "A Returner."

Kettering pushed his glasses up the bridge of his nose, an agitated habit. "What? My dear boy—we're all on edge, we're all—but this is—"

"The barracks," said Will.

"What?" said Kettering.

"In the palace, you knew the way to the barracks. But you'd never been there. Not in this life. No one had. No one knew the layout of the palace. But you led your men to the throne room directly. And you were the only one who didn't die of the white death when you got there."

Kettering was staring at him.

"At the dig, you were trying to stop them from burning the bodies," said Will. "I didn't understand why, until I learned what the white death was. To you, it wasn't just burning bodies. It was—"

"Killing my countrymen," said Kettering.

His face had changed while Will spoke. Will's heart was pounding. It was one thing to guess, but another to have it confirmed. Will spoke steadily.

"You're one of them," said Will. "And you're going to the palace to wake them up."

To his surprise, Kettering gave a sharp laugh. "Them! I don't care about them," said Kettering. "I only care about her."

Her?

Before his eyes, Kettering was shaking off the identity of the harmless historian. He wasn't denying it, as Will had expected. Maybe there was a part of him, alone with his secret, that wanted to be seen. Will knew what that felt like.

"I woke up on a pyre," said Kettering. "In the body of a seven-year-old. They burn Returners here, but you know that. They burn anyone who dies of the white death. They wanted to burn me. But they waited too long. I woke up, and a woman started screaming at them to stop. She was this body's mother. In the confusion, I got free and ran. I didn't know then that I was lucky . . . the only one of my kind to have survived. How many dozens of us have opened our eyes in flame? How many hundreds? Awakened into the screaming pain of an inferno?"

The heat of it, Will thought, the blast of it like a furnace. The binding of rope, sweating in the heat, then burning. He'd seen bodies char and crisp in the Hall of the Stewards, when they'd burned the dead.

"What was the boy's name?" said Will.

"The boy?"

"The boy whose body you took over."

"How should I know?" said Kettering.

"Maybe his mother was screaming it," said Will.

"That was thirty years ago," said Kettering, dismissively. "I left this place, this backwater. I went to England to study history, only to learn my people were forgotten. Forgotten! The whole world was a backwater. These people think they know what death is. They haven't the first idea. They only imagine their own death. . . . They don't imagine everyone they know dead, everyone in their city dead, everyone in their era dead, millions of lives swallowed by a black hole of forgetting. Until it was as if none of it had ever happened at all."

"Who is 'her'?" said Will.

Kettering's expression flickered. "She was my . . . she was important to me. I made her a promise. We swore we would return together. And she's still down there, in the dark."

He's still caught in the past. As every Returner would be, thought Will. Every grudge, every passion, they would open their eyes in their new bodies feeling it all. And being fully of the old world, they would care nothing about this one.

Just as Kettering cared nothing for the boy whose body he had stolen—whose life he had overwritten with his own.

There was a darker thought. Kettering clearly had not recognized Sarcean or Anharion. Perhaps he'd been a mere soldier, too low ranked to have laid eyes on the King and his consort. But the generals in that Dark army would, like Devon, know them both on sight. The moment they were released . . .

"I'm going to wake her, and I'm not going to let you stop me," said Kettering. Will drew in a breath.

"I'm not here to stop you. I'm here to go with you," said Will. "The

Dark King's staff . . . you know where it is, what it looks like. I want us to go there together."

He'd surprised Kettering. He saw it in his eyes. Just as he saw himself in Kettering's estimation: a boy, a mere youth, a single life just begun in this new world, like a sapling with no knowledge of the extent of the great forest.

"You want it for yourself," said Kettering, figuring it slowly. "The power to control his army." And then he laughed. "You can't reach it. Only a creature of the Dark can even get close. A boy like you won't stand a chance."

"We'll see," said Will.

"You really want to accompany me to the palace?"

Kettering's expression had turned sly, assessing. Will could see Kettering's calculation: he would need at least one body for this lady of his to inhabit. He could use Will, he was thinking. Perhaps noting especially Will's youth, which would give his lady as long a life as possible.

"By the time we reach the pit, the village will be evacuated," said Will, who had planned it carefully. "You can release your lady, and I'll take up the Dark King's staff."

With the mountain empty of people, he could use the staff to stop the army before it found its way into living hosts.

"All right," said Kettering, with the new lightness of one who thought he had found a dupe.

"Sneaking off?" said Violet.

His stomach dropped as she stepped into the middle of the path. *That word again,* part of him thought distantly, as panic hit and he had to force it down. It was too much like the night he'd set out for Bowhill, only to find Elizabeth blocking the stable door.

Violet wasn't alone; Cyprian and Grace were with her.

Violet said, "You're going after the Dark King's staff by yourself, aren't you?"

His body locked with tension. His heart was pounding. "And if I am?"

"Last time you fought alone," she said. "This time we fight together." She hefted the shield on her arm. "We're coming with you."

"You can't," he said, a blurt that sounded panicked, even to his own ears.

He had to get rid of them. He couldn't stop the army while his friends were watching. He imagined how it would be—the swirl of black across his eyes as he took up the staff, his friends realizing what he was and falling back from him as Katherine had done.

He was so close. So close to the edge, his plans in danger of tipping.

"Violet, you can't. You're not immune to possession. If the armies get out, they'll go right for you."

"I can handle a few shadows," said Violet. "Besides, you might not be immune from possession either. You need a Lion to protect you."

The steadfast, unwavering goodness of her made everything worse.

"Only a Lion can stand against what lies beneath Undahar. And I'm your Lion." She was prepared to stand against shadows to help him. Even as he drew in a breath to speak, she said, "There's nothing you can say that will stop me coming with you."

She smiled, Cyprian and Grace flanking her on either side. The three of them stood arrayed in front of him in awful solidarity.

There wasn't time to make another plan, not with Sinclair's men closing in on the mountain. He felt the impossible difficulty of it: no way to dissuade Violet, no time to turn back himself . . . a handicap, to do this with his friends present, but he didn't have a choice.

"Follow me," Will said.

It was disconcerting to reach the palace and to find it unguarded. Sloane's soldiers were missing. The entrance was utterly deserted.

Violet, who had never seen the palace before, was wide-eyed at the sheer scale of it as they entered the crevasse, then passed through the huge doors.

Within a few steps, they discovered why there were no soldiers: dozens of white bodies lay on the marble just beyond the entrance. Sloane's guards had all fallen to the white death, and now lay in that disturbing rictus. It confirmed Will's theory that the process was accelerating, the Returners continuing to leak out of their chamber.

"More deaths," said Grace.

"Do you think they'll wake up?" said Violet uneasily.

It was her first time seeing the white death. It was his first time to see it knowing what it was. Knowledge gave him new eyes, the marbled flesh a disquieting cocoon from which a new creature would arise.

"They will awaken," said Grace. "But the process takes several days."

"Let's hope they haven't been dead for that long," said Violet.

He imagined Returners beginning to stand up throughout the palace. *Burn them,* no one said—but everyone was thinking it. Will glanced at Kettering, who showed nothing on his face.

The double doors opened onto the throne room, its pale throne gleaming in the dark. Its majesty beckoned, and its sinister promise. He had sat here and brought realms of the world one by one under his control. But the throne wasn't his destination.

The oubliette was still open, a gaping pit of black. The ropes and rope ladders they had thrown over its edge were still in place. Had no one been here in their absence? Will looked down into the lightless hole and wondered if Howell's corpse would still be there.

He took Kettering by the wrist, holding him at the edge of the pit.

That was where he had to go—deep into the earth under the throne. Then past those rows of figures ready to awaken, until he reached the staff. And he had to do it quickly.

"You three guard the entrance," Will told his friends. "I go down with Kettering and retrieve the Dark King's staff."

"You're going to go down there just the two of you?" said Violet, looking at the gaping mouth of the pit.

She looked skeptical, but she didn't try to stop him. He nodded, readying himself.

"I have to," Will said. "I have to be the one to do it."

"You can try," said a voice that made the hair on his body stand on end. "But I'm going to stop you."

His stomach dropped. Cold, he turned to face her. Because he knew that voice, even if it wasn't her. It wasn't the girl who had stood on the Dark Peak and picked up Ekthalion to kill him.

It was a soldier who had run him through with a sword.

A soldier whose presence meant the end of everything. *You,* he'd said as he drove his sword into Will's gut only a day earlier.

But the face was so identically hers, standing there as she had stood on the Dark Peak, like a ghost from a past he couldn't escape.

Here to stop him; here to stop Sarcean.

"*Katherine?*" said Violet.

"That's not Katherine," said Will.

He took a step toward the pit. The others reacted with the same shock as Violet. But understanding slowly began to dawn on each of their faces.

"It's one of them," said Cyprian shakily. He drew his sword. "A Returner."

"I am Visander, the Queen's Champion," said the soldier in Katherine's body. "And I am here to kill the Dark King."

Will took another step toward the pit. He had to stop the army. He had to reach the staff. Yet he wasn't here. He was back in Bowhill: with Katherine drawing a sword; with his mother's hands around his neck.

Violet was frowning. "The Dark King—what are you talking about?"

"Has he lied? That's what he does." Visander drew a sword, just as Katherine had done. "He's here to take command of his army." Visander's eyes were cold, determined, an expression he had never seen on Katherine's face. "And I am here to kill him."

"Violet, take care of it," Will heard himself say as his hand opened, releasing Kettering from his grip.

"I don't know who you are, but if you're here to stop the Dark King, we're on the same side." Violet stepped forward, bracing her shield on her right arm.

"Lion!" Visander reacted to the Shield of Rassalon with fury. "I kill your kind where I find them."

Violet drew her sword.

If seeing the shield had made Visander furious, the sight of her sword seemed to hit him like a blow, staggering him before he focused on her with complete attention. "You—*dare*—to wield Ekthalion? You foul creature of the Dark, I will strike it from your hands and run it through your heart!"

They clashed, as Kettering dashed for the pit.

Violet was Lion-strong, and she had been trained by Justice. She had skill born of hard work and dedication alongside the kind of dominating strength that had held back wave after wave of Sinclair's men. It was an impossible combination of gifts that had allowed her to kill a Shadow King.

Visander inhabited a body that was not his own, that was untrained and weak, and that before Bowhill had never even held a sword. He looked like he ought to be dancing a quadrille with a dainty hand atop that of his dance partner. Not fighting to the death with a two-handed sword.

It didn't matter. Within a handful of seconds, Violet was bleeding from the arm, where he'd flicked a knife at her, and then from the leg, looking shocked that any blow had landed on her at all. Cyprian leapt toward him with a cry, only to be disarmed and sent sprawling. Visander kept his attention on Violet.

"Did you think I hadn't fought Lions before?" Visander said, with a strike so hard it knocked Violet on her back and sent the Shield of Rassalon clanging from her hand to the ground. "You're not even a true Lion." He lifted his sword.

It was too fast for Violet to dodge, Visander's sword swinging toward Violet's unprotected neck—

A small whirlwind flew out of the shadows and threw itself in front of the sword.

"Stop it! Don't hurt her, don't hurt Violet! Stop!"

Elizabeth stood right in Visander's way, her hair mussed and her dress dirty and torn, panting with effort and urgency.

His blade had stopped. He was staring at the young girl in front of him. Elizabeth stood with both feet planted wide, staring back at him.

But it was Will who stood rooted in shock. Of course she was here. Of course Visander had told her not to come, and she had ignored him, and followed him doggedly over the mountain on her pony.

There was a rumbling from the direction of the pit.

"Elizabeth!" said Violet. She closed her hand on her shield and pushed herself back up onto her feet as Visander said, "My Queen. Get out of my way."

"No. Violet's my friend!"

"Your friend is a Lion. She serves the Dark."

"If I'm your queen, you have to do as I say," said Elizabeth, "and I say leave her alone!"

With a brief, bitten-off snarl, Visander lowered his blade, the ten-year-old prevailing over the Champion.

Violet, quick to use any advantage, no matter how strangely it was created, was instantly holding the sharp edge of Ekthalion to Visander's throat.

"It's over, Returner," said Violet.

Only to find Elizabeth dragging at her arm with her full weight. "No, let him go!"

"He tried to kill Will!" said Violet.

Elizabeth said, "*Will is the Dark King.*"

Everything stopped; a twisting, terrible sensation as his friends turned to look at him, to look at him and *see* him. He needed to speak, to open his mouth and deny it, and he couldn't. It was like a sensation of falling. Or maybe he'd been falling since Bowhill, and it was the moment when everything hit.

"Will?" said Violet.

The pit exploded as a violent pressure from the depths was released, sending them all flying. Huge chunks of marble plunged like meteors, slamming down around them as the ground itself split. Half crack, half eruption, it collapsed the chamber in a burst of dust and rubble.

Will couldn't see anything at first, coughing out the dust, his arm over his mouth. Wide-eyed, he looked around in the haze, needing to see from which direction the attack would come. From Visander. From Elizabeth. From Cyprian. From Violet . . . please not from Violet.

As the brutal shaking of the earthquake stopped, the dust began to clear.

The throne room was in ruins, chunks of ceiling collapsed between shattered columns. The pit had widened, part of a new crack that ran all the way through the floor. Slices of the ground had reared and tilted. Like icebergs grinding against one another, the sound of their occasional movement was an ominous groan.

He saw the others. Visander had thrown himself over Elizabeth, protecting her. Violet was pushing a fallen stone column aside with strength that didn't seem real. Behind it, Cyprian and Grace were emerging from where they'd been trapped.

Grace said, "Where's Kettering?"

"The pit," said Cyprian, staring past Will, who turned to face the oubliette.

Like a nightmare, the first Returner came rising from the crack. It didn't have a stable form, but seemed to flicker, a face appearing and disappearing in its amorphous darkness.

The army that had seemed like an endless chamber of horrifying statues was rising, not as figures but as spirits—no, as shadows—ready to possess the first body they touched.

Violet immediately thrust herself in front of the others, swinging her shield.

"Get behind me!" cried Violet. A second Returner was rising from the crack. This one turned its sightless eyes on the others and shrieked, a sound that turned the blood cold.

Shadows, thought Will, that could possess people. No one alive could fight them. Except Violet. She had killed shadows before. She killed this one, decapitating it with her shield, then swung at the second, pushing it back.

Will didn't get behind her.

"Will," she said urgently.

He walked forward toward the pit, where another Returner was rising, a monstrous shadow. He saw the fear in Violet's eyes at where he was going, now that there was no choice left at all.

Will said, "I'm sorry. It's the only way to stop this." He took the rope.

And dropped down into the pit, where the shadows whirled. "Will!" he heard her scream behind him, and then he was too deep inside to hear anything.

CHAPTER FORTY-SIX

IT WAS HER worst nightmare come to life. Not just one shadow but hundreds, a spewing mass of writhing shapes, rising up out of the pit in the floor.

Violet pushed in front of the others, and without thinking drew her shield.

"Get behind me!" she shouted to Cyprian and Grace, knowing that if a shadow so much as touched them—

If a shadow so much as touched any of them—

Will. Her mind was whirling. *Will, Will, Will.* He had jumped into the pit, running toward the danger as he always did, to save people. Will was a hero. He was Blood of the Lady. He wasn't—

She swung the shield and hit the first shadow, which exploded, shrieking. The next had a clear shape, torso and long arms, and the flickering impression of a head that she decapitated with a hard swing. Behind it, a knot of shadows screamed and rushed at her. She killed one. Two. Three. "Fall back!" said Cyprian.

"Will's in there," she said. "We have to get to him!"

Cyprian said, "You can't fight a whole army!"

Violet said, "I will if I have to!"

The shield was heavy on her arm. She swung it over and over, her body aching. She fought as they backed out of the throne room, into a corridor: a bottleneck where the shadows couldn't swirl around her and take her friends. If even a single one got past her, it would take Grace or Cyprian or Elizabeth. Her friends would fall to the white death, and rise with someone else in their body.

She kept killing. Could you kill the dead? How many swings did she have left before she could no longer lift the shield? She remembered her lessons with Justice. He had forced her into utter exhaustion, and then said, "*Again,*" as if he had known that she would have to fight like this, kill like this, again, and again, and again.

We train for the opponent that we will face, Justice had said, *when the day comes that we are called on to fight.*

It was how Justice had fought at the end, holding off the shadow as long as he could, fighting to buy the Elder Steward time. That was what she must do. Hold them off until . . . hold them off until . . . what?

Until Will stopped them? Until a hundred thousand shadows had swarmed out of the pit, infecting everyone on the mountain? She fought harder, panting, and when she thought she could fight no more, she drew on some last reserve and clanged Ekthalion and her shield together as she let out a roar, challenging the shadows like a defiant gladiator in the arena. For a moment, the swirling shadows hesitated, as if no single shadow wished to challenge her.

In that pause, she was panting, sweat dripping from her, and she'd told Will she could do it, that she could hold back the horde, but as she looked at the torrent of darkness that faced her, she realized that it was impossible.

There were too many shadows, and she could not fight forever; they were going to overwhelm her.

She felt a presence beside her and expected it to be Cyprian, come to stand with her at the end. But it wasn't.

It was a girl with golden curls and the face of a porcelain doll.

"Lion," Visander said. "Give me Ekthalion."

She looked over at Katherine, changed and strange. There was a fierceness in her expression that Violet had never seen before. And a soldier's assessing of the odds that she remembered from Justice's face. *Not Katherine,* she reminded herself. *Visander. The Queen's Champion.*

He said, "I know we are on opposite sides, but I will protect the girl." He looked at Elizabeth, whose face looked pale but stubborn in the flickering torchlight.

"You can't fight a shadow. No one can." Violet shook her head. It wasn't a matter of skill. You couldn't fight what you couldn't touch. She remembered how it had felt to face the Shadow King: her sword had passed through his shadowy form as though it were made of air. Nothing but the Shield of Rassalon could stop a shadow.

Visander only looked more determined, unafraid of the shadows before them, even defiant as he faced them.

"That sword was forged by Than Rema to cut down the dark. Put Ekthalion into my hands, and I will show you the power of the champion."

A moment of hesitation; fate turning. She tightened her grip on the sword, then tossed it to Visander.

He caught it, sweeping Ekthalion around in an arc as the dark whirl of shadow forms screamed and seethed, almost boiling at that blade of shining silver that seemed to be made of light. In the next moment, the shadows burst forward toward them.

Visander was, she realized, the best fighter she had ever seen. Better than Cyprian. Better than Justice. Better than any Steward. He was hampered by a body weaker than his own, but his knowledge and skill were such that it overrode this limitation. Marcus's words came back to her. *We cannot do this alone. We must gather the old allies.*

We must find the Champion who can wield Ekthalion

And reforge the Shield of Rassalon

Ekthalion sliced the first shadow in half, and as Violet swung her shield, Visander was already moving to kill the second, showing none of the fear or hesitation that she might have expected.

This was the power of the champion. Visander had fought shadows before. Perhaps he had even fought hundreds of shadows, his sword cutting through the dark in the same way as her shield.

A Lion and a Champion fighting side by side.

She felt the significance of it, creating a wall of strength, even as she knew that she was not a true Lion, and could not hold out forever.

She buckled first, for she had been fighting longer. Visander was not fast enough to fill the gap. A shadow was through; she whipped her head, frantic to stop it reaching Cyprian or Grace. Shouting to warn them, for a single moment she broke her concentration.

Rushing black filled her vision; there was a Returner forcing its cold, horrifying way into her mouth, into her nose, another trying to get into her eyes, darkness filling her. She thrashed and tried to hit out at what was already inside, feeling shadows stream over her, like the breaking of a dam, to burst over the others.

A small girl's body threw itself over hers, and the last words that Violet might ever hear were Elizabeth, screaming desperately—

"Phillip's jacket!"

Light exploded outward; a shattering ball of a thousand suns.

The shadow was blasted away from Violet's eyes, the sudden light so bright that she couldn't see. Blinded, she threw her shield up in front of her eyes to cover them, but the retina-searing light burned even through her hot, aching eyelids. Her single glimpse of the others—crying out and covering their own eyes—was etched into her mind before everything went white.

She could feel Elizabeth, still curled to cover her, breathing shallowly.

Brightness faded, and after long minutes of silence, she dared to lower her shield.

Slowly, she opened her eyes.

She expected—she wasn't sure what she expected. To be dead. To be blind. Through burning, tear-filled eyes, she saw a swimming vision of the others sprawled on the ground around her, as though a blast had thrown them there. And around them all was a gentle, cocooning light.

Violet began levering herself up, blinking sore eyes and looking around in shaky wonder.

A bubble of light enclosed them. It was keeping the shadows back, though they swooped and screamed impotently at its boundary, shrieking in frustration when they couldn't reach them, powerless.

For darkness cannot bear the light.

At the center of the glowing sphere was Elizabeth, who stood with her short legs planted, her eyebrows drawn down fiercely.

We must gather the old allies. Marcus's words rang in her mind.

We must Call for the King

We must find the Lady of Light

We must find the Champion who can wield Ekthalion

And reforge the Shield of Rassalon

Her eyes were still streaming, Violet realized as she raised the back of her hand to wipe them.

"Will this hold?" said Violet.

"Yes," said Elizabeth, but the word seemed born of stubbornness rather than knowledge.

Violet recalled just how quickly holding open the gate had drained

James of his power. If Elizabeth was creating the light, it would not last long.

Violet looked back toward the pit, still shrouded in darkness. Will was down there. Will had walked into those shadows as though they were nothing.

He just left us here. He just left us.

Doubt put its cold fingers on her, a chilling touch. The light protecting them had been conjured by the Blood of the Lady—by Elizabeth. They stood together, allies in the light. Will had walked alone into the dark.

"The Dark King seeks to take control of his army," said Visander, hefting Ekthalion onto his shoulder. "We must stop him."

"Will is not the Dark King," said Violet.

The others were staring at her. They stood together, Cyprian and Grace alongside Visander and Elizabeth, the silence thick.

"He couldn't light the Tree," said Cyprian slowly, as though he didn't want to believe it.

Even slower: "But he could touch the Corrupted Blade," said Grace. "He was immune to its corruption. He was immune to the white death."

The light around them was as warm and beautiful as the Tree of Light. Will hadn't conjured it, she thought. Will had never been able to conjure light. But she had seen him walk into shadows. In the Hall, she had seen him touch the Shadow Stone.

"He's my friend," said Violet.

"He lies. He is the King of Lies," said Visander. "He will say and do anything to achieve his ends."

"You don't know him," said Violet. "You don't know him like I do."

"Don't know him!" Visander's eyes blazed. "I know him far better than any of you. I have seen the dawn bring no day, I have ridden a valley of death, sailed a black ocean where nothing stirs, fallen back to a once-great outpost where the last flickering light illuminated only despair. It is you who knows nothing. Noting but his lies. You have no idea what he can do."

"Are you certain?" said Cyprian.

"Look around you. He has returned to his palace," said Visander. "He has unleashed his armies. And he is about to take up his throne."

Violet looked toward the pit, streaming with darkness, an endless vomiting belch like black smoke pouring from a chimney column.

"We can't get inside," she said. "Only a creature of the Dark can get close to the Dark King's staff. There's no way to follow him."

She heard herself say it. She knew it only proved everything Visander claimed. How else could Will have walked through the shadows? How else could he withstand the power of the Dark?

But the thought that Will was the Dark King was too huge to take hold of; it was a gash in her mind, a hole where thoughts just dropped away.

She looked back at the others. The light starkly lit each of their faces. . . . Was it dimming? Was it going to wink out? What could be done if the light was failing? If they couldn't enter the pit, and Will was—Will was—

She saw Cyprian and Grace turn to one another as they sometimes did, in silent communion.

And then Cyprian lifted his chin in that characteristic way he had.

"There is a way."

He looked determined, spine straight and shoulders squared, a novitiate reporting for duty.

She looked at him, not understanding what he could mean. Behind him, Grace's face was set with calm knowledge.

"I drink from the Cup," said Cyprian.

She was shaking her head before she realized it.

"No. You can't."

"I have to." He looked resolute. "Someone has to go down there. Someone has to stop this." His eyes turned to the pit, to the swirling darkness spewing from it endlessly. "All these shadows, they were people. All this darkness, it's because of the Dark King." She could hear his unspoken words. *We can't let Will command the Dark King's army.*

It was happening too fast. She wasn't ready for it.

"You're the last star; you can't do this."

She ignored the others. She just looked at him. *Don't let Cyprian drink,* Marcus seemed to plead from the past. *Don't condemn him to my fate, to lose himself in shadow forever.*

Marcus wouldn't want you to do this. She didn't say those words. She just stared at him with a terrible ache in her chest.

"I have to," said Cyprian. "This may be the very reason why the Stewards kept the Cup."

"But I just got you back," she said in a small voice, and he gave her a sad half smile.

"I know. I wish—"

From her pack, Grace drew out the Cup.

Violet had seen it in the Hall, gleaming like a dark jewel, the color of polished onyx. It was carved with four crowns. Four crowns for the four kings. *Callax Reigor* read the inscription. The Cup of Kings.

When she had first come to the Hall, Violet had watched with Will as the young hopeful Carver had earned his whites and become a Steward. Everyone in the Hall had gathered to see him test himself against the Dark, and everyone had cheered his success when he proved himself worthy.

But no one had seen him drink from the Cup. That part of the rite was shrouded in mystery. He'd simply emerged in his new whites once it was done, to a jubilant crowd

It was oddly poignant that Cyprian didn't know either. "How—how is it done?" He turned to Grace.

"There is a ceremony," she said, "but that is just for show. You simply drink."

His handsome face looked different, his green eyes serious, his expression unswerving. She couldn't see in him the boy full of righteousness who had taunted her in the Hall. That boy had had too much of his world broken to retain any of his youthful illusions. And yet he still believed enough to do this.

He took the Cup in his hand. Grace poured water from her flask.

It was just water. It looked innocent enough.

"I used to dream of the test," said Cyprian. "All I ever wanted was to become a Steward."

There was no ceremony. He just drank, one smooth movement.

Watching with tense apprehension, Violet didn't know what to expect. Would the change be fast or slow? Would it show? Or would there be no sign at all? For the first few moments, nothing happened, and Violet thought, *Is it done?*

Cyprian's face contorted. Behind gritted teeth, he let out a sound, and went down to one knee, clutching his stomach. And then she saw the shadow, clawing its way to the surface, distorting his skin as he made another sound, this one ripped out in agony.

"Cyprian!" she said, as he collapsed onto all fours. Grace held her back.

"No. You cannot fight his shadow for him. He must fight it himself, now and for every day that follows, until he can fight no longer."

Braced on the floor, Cyprian made an awful retching sound. She half thought he would vomit the Cup's water back up—vomit the shadow out. But he didn't.

He wasn't trying to vomit it out. He was trying to keep it in. To keep it back.

She was shaking just watching it, her own body clenched in horrific impotence as pain and spasms wracked him. Had every Steward done this—had Justice? When he'd been taken away after his test, had the cheers of the crowd hidden his screams?

It seemed to go on and on, Cyprian convulsed and barely conscious of anything but pain, the shadow glimpsed once or twice horrifically, stretching at the limits of his body.

Eventually the spasms lessened, until they were just helpless shivers that came at longer and longer intervals. And then even they were done.

Cyprian pushed up onto his hands and knees, raw and panting, and he looked up, his eyes wet.

He was himself. Slowly, he rose to his feet.

Then he held his hand out. Steady.

He looked at it as if he needed the proof. They all looked at it, a shadow more terrifying now that they had seen it fight for control. She hated that she looked too.

We are all turning, Justice had said to her. *But I've shown no symptoms yet.*

"When you enter the pit, he will say things to make you doubt your purpose," said Visander. "You can't trust him. All he wants is power. That is what you must remember. He is not your friend. He is the Dark King. He will end your world."

"I understand," said Cyprian.

Violet drew in a breath as he approached her. He looked different. The process had changed him, imbued him with that otherworldly quality that the Stewards had possessed—she couldn't help thinking of Justice. She couldn't help thinking of Marcus, who once had been a young man full of hopes for his future, and whose final wish had been that his brother never drink from the Cup.

"Cyprian—" she said.

"Kill me," said Cyprian. "As soon as I come out. I don't want to be like my brother."

"Cyprian—"

"Promise me."

"I won't promise that."

"You must. I won't live under threat of the shadow. Let me do this, and then set me free of it."

Justice had asked her to watch for him too. He had died soon after. She had never had the chance to fight beside him. She had fought beside Cyprian briefly in the Hall, a single wildly exhilarating engagement. She couldn't help wonder what it would feel like to fight beside him now that his strength matched her own.

He didn't want that future. He wanted to kill his shadow before it could hurt others. And he was right: Justice, hesitating to kill Marcus, had condemned every Steward in the Hall.

But the pain of it was too much, it seemed to push at the limits of her body, and she could feel herself in Justice's place, looking into Marcus's eyes, unable to lift the knife.

She said, "Is this what it is to be a shieldmate?"

"You're more to me than a shieldmate," said Cyprian.

As the pain crested, he lifted his hand to her cheek, and as her eyes closed, he kissed her, a long, aching kiss that she hadn't known how much she wanted because it was her first. She hadn't known it would feel like this, so right, with Cyprian's warmth against her.

"You see? I do know what a kiss is," said Cyprian.

Stepping back from her, he turned briefly to the others. His eyes passed over Grace, Elizabeth, and Visander.

"If she won't kill you," said Visander, "I will, Steward."

Cyprian nodded. And he went.

CHAPTER FORTY-SEVEN

JAMES LOOKED UP at the gate.

A stark outline against a sheer drop, it was an opening to nowhere. Stepping through it was something you would do only if you were a lunatic or terrified. When they had first crossed from the Hall, the pain of opening it, then holding it open, had been agonizing. The gate had reached down into his core, then ripped his power out of him, guzzling it as it hemorrhaged out of his body in a way he hadn't been able to control.

"I can only hold it open for so long," he told Ettore, who had dismounted beside him. "After that I'm—"

Useless. Vulnerable. He didn't say it. Didn't want to think it. He jerked when Ettore put a hand on his shoulder. The gesture was unnerving; he had to tell himself he was not being attacked or apprehended. It was the first time a Steward had touched him without anger since he was eleven.

"We'll protect you," Ettore said.

People surprised him. Ettore, with his slovenly clothes and his rough beard, resembled neither a Steward nor a protector. Yet here he was. Here they both were. James had never thought he'd fight for the Light. He'd never thought the Light would fight for him. But Will had asked this of him, with the unquestioning belief he would do it. *Protector.* Will had used that same word. *That's what you are, you know.*

Since he had left the Stewards behind, no one had believed that he could be a protector. He hadn't believed it of himself.

The road leading to the gate was thronged with women and men from the surrounding towns and villages with their packs and donkeys and chickens and children. James looked out at them, nameless, faceless. Any one of them would have killed him if he had been born into their village. The old resentment flickered, the old bitterness. He looked back at Ettore, nodded once, and faced the gate.

Push magic into it. He drew in a breath. He remembered Will shouting the word to him in the Hall, and then speaking it again in the palace, powerful and commanding while seated on that pale throne.

"Aragas."

Open.

The gate flared into life.

It hurt, but it was not the tearing pain of last time, when he had opened it while already exhausted. It was a familiar pain that would increase steadily as the gate took more of his power. *Hold,* he thought to himself.

It took all his focus: he was barely aware of the cries of shock from the villagers as the Hall of the Stewards burst into view. Already, the gate was draining him, and this time he would have to hold it for longer, far longer than he had before. Long enough for all these hundreds of people to get from one side to the other.

Hold. The old word, the old training. On the other side of the gate, he could see Sinclair's men shouting and exclaiming as the ancient structure they were guarding blazed into life.

"Can you hold it?" said Ettore, hand again on his shoulder.

"Get them across," he gritted out to him.

Ettore's bandits were already galloping through the gate into the Hall of the Stewards. Pistols fired, blades flashed; in the days and weeks of guarding a tedious courtyard where nothing happened, the handful of Sinclair's men left guarding the Hall had grown lax. They hadn't expected the gate to open at all, let alone on a mountain militia, and they were swiftly dispatched by Ettore's men.

The gathered villagers weren't as easy, stalled in fear of the gate that cast its light over their terrified faces. None of them had seen anything like it in their lives. "*Andiamo! Andiamo!*" the Hand was saying, trying to urge them through. Many of them were crossing themselves, crying out, or trying to get back.

They had called it the Leap of Faith.

They had to have faith in him. That he would not let them fall. That thought made James sick, and even more determined to get them through. Their lives were in his hands; Will had placed them there.

Will had made that leap of faith, in him.

He could hear their shouts. "It's the devil's work! It's unnatural!" They were scared of what he could do. He was used to that. He was used to the fear and the hatred and the violence that came when people saw his magic. Before Will, he would have been bitter, reveling in his power and the reaction. "*I'll show you unnatural.*"

But there was one person who looked at him and saw something more—more than a possession that was useful or pleasing. *Will.*

He wouldn't fail him. He could hold. He would hold. The stream of evacuees went all the way down the mountain. An hour for them all to pass through, maybe longer. James planted his heels in the dirt and gave himself to the gate.

He could feel them starting to cross. First a few, hesitantly, then a few more, exclaiming in wonder at the Hall and calling back to their neighbors that it was safe. With Ettore's men ushering them across, the trickle became a stream, and the stream became a flood.

God, it hurt. He had forgotten how much it hurt, to have the gate tear everything out of him, take it all and demand more. The pain felt right. Doing good should hurt, shouldn't it? After all, it was both penance and amends, one that he didn't deserve.

Hold. A stream of people who would live, if he could only face that it had to hurt, that he might even lose everything of himself.

He thought of all the times he'd used magic to serve Sinclair. Killing his enemies. Killing Stewards. He saw Marcus's face in front of his own. *How many of us have you killed? How many Stewards will die because of you?*

Every Steward he had ever known. Carver. Beatrix. Emery. Leda . . . Justice . . . the Elder Steward . . . Marcus . . .

His father.

Pain; like nothing he had ever felt. Worse than being branded. Worse than broken bone. Worse than being beaten, punched, shot in the chest. Worse than being forced to hold a hot coal. Worse than the Horn of Truth twisting in his shoulder.

Really, was this enough? How many people did he have to save to make up for those he had killed?

It didn't work like that. He dug deep, reaching right into himself to pull up the last of his power. *Hold.* The old words were there. *Steward, hold to your training.*

He thought of countless mornings waking at the bell, performing the exercises, his father's critical eyes on him looking for any error, and himself making certain there were none. His father . . . if he saw this, would he have been proud? He almost laughed. It came out as a choked gasp. He lifted his head and with a cry he found a last reserve. A new wave of power that he sent into the gate. He had been the best in the Hall. He could hold. He would hold.

That was when he felt the earth tremble.

Those lining the path were thrown this way and that, bandits and villagers alike sent sprawling. Gripping the stone, James half expected the gate to split and his magic to go spewing up out into the air. But the gate stayed open, greedily glutting on power from him even as stones at the cliff's edge went tumbling down into the chasm below. He could still see the Hall of the Stewards beneath the arch, the bandits and villagers who had passed through staring in confusion: on stable ground in the Hall courtyard, they did not understand what was happening on the mountain.

As suddenly as it had begun, the shaking stopped. As the villagers on the path began to stand and right themselves, Ettore and the Hand began once more to try to usher them through the gate. But, dusting themselves off, checking their belongings, none of the locals were now keen to rush through. James gritted his teeth as the gate dragged more power from him. "*Go!*" he said, or thought he did. There had been an earthquake the day they had arrived, he thought. It was fitting that there should be an earthquake the day they left.

And then the screams began.

Faint at first but growing louder, they came from the base of the mountain, then got closer. James couldn't see, but the villagers on the path went from looking to murmuring to shouting, then started pushing their way desperately through the gate. Behind them, a frightening plume, spewing out of the mountain below.

Oh God, was the army awakening? It couldn't be, could it? Not with Will down there, and him here tethered to the gate?

The screams were louder—closer. He saw people on the mountain path visibly change color, whitening in the moonlight, then falling to the ground. They didn't cry out or struggle, they just toppled. A terrible white wave, spreading up the mountain.

"*The white death!*" came the call, people screaming and pushing for the gate. Animals and belongings were abandoned. The rush became a stampede, spreading white coming toward the gate exactly as the ancient Steward Nathaniel had described.

The army of the dead, released from Undahar.

Spirits searching for hosts, they swarmed up over the fallen white dead, a ravening horde possessing bodies as soon as they touched them.

Beside him Ettore drew his sword, and so did the Hand.

James gritted out, "You idiot, you can't fight them."

Ettore said, "Close the gate."

"There's still people—"

"If you let the Dark army get through that gate, they will infect all of London. That's tens of thousands of people. Here it's mountains, the countryside, there's a chance they won't find a body in time, and if they do, they'll be scattered—"

"Then go through," said James. "Go through the gate, get as many people through it as you can—"

"James, it's coming, close the goddamned gate!"

Every moment saved a life. He held on as the men and women around him started to fall. He held on as long as he could. He saw a face right in front of him turn marble white. Then he slammed the gate shut. The men and women around him, not having anywhere to go, were pushed from the cliffs. He saw one or two of them throw themselves off in a desperate attempt to get away from the white death. Then he saw a shadow rear up in front of him.

He tried to hold it back.

That was what the mages had done in the old world, wasn't it? They had shielded the people in their care. They had held the shadows off, pushed them back.

He couldn't do it, too weak to hold against the battering pressure of thousands of spirits, the sheer weight of them. They burst through his attempt at a barrier. Half-collapsed, his limbs cold, his throat and nose full of blood, James saw the Hand whiten and fall. Through a haze, he saw Ettore run to her side. "*Hand!*" he shouted. He was bent over her, crying.

James tried to throw himself bodily in front of them, tried to find some last spark of magic. But he had neither strength nor power left. The last thing he saw was a dark torrent blotting out the sky—blotting out everything as he lost his hold on consciousness and fell.

His eyes opened sometime later.

He was alone among a sea of white bodies. He couldn't see an end to them, as if a mad sculptor had strewn the mountainside with marble statues, then dressed them in peasant clothes. There was no one else alive: every man, woman, and child on the mountain had fallen to the white death.

Oh God. This was the army in larval form, waiting to wake up.

Will. He had to get to Will.

The roil of shadows was gone, had swirled away looking for other targets, like a locust swarm that has stripped a field clean, and moved on. Scanning the stillness of the mountain, he saw a flicker of movement. A single upright figure was kneeling on the ground six steps from the gate.

It was Ettore, bent over the Hand.

Her face was white. Her limbs were white. Her face had a frightening, frozen look, as though she had been cast in white marble in a moment of final terror.

But Ettore—Ettore was alive, breathing, weeping, clutching her stone-white hand.

How? James wanted to ask. *How are we both alive?* But of course no shadow had been able to possess Ettore, James realized with a strange sensation, because Ettore had a shadow inside him already.

"We have to get away from here before they wake up," said James. His lips felt blurred. His vision swam.

"Can you help her?" said Ettore, looking up, his face wrecked with grief.

"I don't know, I'm not—"

He tried to stand and get to them, and collapsed. How had he made it off this mountain last time? He remembered dizzily that Will had carried him. Will had put him on a horse, then put him to bed and lain down next to him. He remembered looking up into Will's eyes, remembered how it had felt to have all that attention focused on him, dark eyes looking down into his own, a warm hand brushing hair from his face.

God, he hated when he was weak.

He put a hand on the stone of the gate beside him to try to drag himself up. He made it to his feet, the stone behind him taking all his weight, when another flash of movement on the mountain caught his attention.

A second figure was weaving its way past the bodies toward them, like a crow picking over carrion. It wasn't a villager, or a bandit, or an ancient warrior.

It was John Sloane.

Had he survived as well? How was that possible? What was he even doing here? James stared at him, not understanding.

Sloane had something in his hand. James didn't see that it was a pistol until Sloane was raising it toward Ettore. He saw it hazily, too weak to stop it, and Ettore himself, cradling the Hand, was too trapped in grief to notice or care as Sloane fired right at him.

"Ettore!" James shouted, too late, as Ettore toppled sideways.

Sloane tossed the pistol casually to one side, then brushed off his palms. He stepped over Ettore as if over a fallen branch. But he did pause to regard the Hand's stone-white body.

"She shouldn't have cut off her hand." Sloane spoke in a cultured, familiar voice, and James's stomach dropped. "Her brand would have saved her. The Dark King protects his own." He lifted his own branded wrist, as if to demonstrate. Then he looked over at James. "You should know that better than anyone, Jamie."

James was shivering—the voice, the pet name, the eyes meeting his with heavy paternal authority. His breathing was shallow in his chest.

"Sinclair," he said.

He could almost see the man, the ghost of him overlaying the body of John Sloane. Somewhere in London, the Earl of Sinclair was sitting in one of his wingback armchairs or standing with a hand on the mantel, sending his mind out to possess this body.

"You were special, Jamie," said Sinclair. "A special boy. Your potential was limitless. With your powers, you could have ruled at the Dark King's side. That's what I always tried to teach you. But it seems you didn't listen." A long perusing look, of the kind he used to give when he'd sit on the wingback and James, returned from a mission, would give his reports. Now instead of praise and the offer for James to come sit at his feet, he said, "Bad boy."

James was so cold, his teeth were chattering uncontrollably. He told himself it was because of the gate, not his reaction to being chastised by Sinclair.

"Are you here to k-kill me?" said James.

He made himself look up, look Sinclair right in the eyes, and found an expression he wasn't expecting: amusement and pleasure.

"My dear Jamie, why would I kill you when I know you have it with you?" said Sinclair.

"It?"

Foolishly, he thought of the artifact Will and the others were seeking: the Dark King's staff. Weak from the gate, he didn't understand.

"You spent so long tracking it down. You'd be terrified to let it out of your hands. Terrified to let anyone else have it. You know just where it wants to be," said Sinclair. "Around your neck."

The Collar, thought James in dizzy horror.

He was too weak to stop it. He was too weak to fight. He tried, pushing at Sinclair ineffectually with his mind. But even if he had been able to fight Sinclair, he couldn't fight the Collar.

A dog returning to its master: the Collar exerted itself now as it had in the throne room, slipping from its wrappings and dropping from James's jacket. Rolling, it came to rest at Sinclair's feet.

Sinclair picked it up and stood over James with the Collar in his hand.

"No," said James. *No no no no no no.* Blind panic. He was crawling away desperately. He couldn't run. He had no way to hide. But he could make it to the edge and get over. The Leap of Faith. The long drop into the dark. Perhaps six seconds of freedom before he hit, which would be the end.

Better that than the Collar around his neck.

He didn't make it. Sinclair took him by the hair. James used the last of his magic to try to push him away, but had so little strength left that it was as if Sinclair was buffeted by no more than a weak breeze.

"You were like a son to me, Jamie," said Sinclair. "You could have followed me willingly. But you chose this path . . . you chose the Collar. How could you not? To serve is your destiny. This Collar was made for you, and whoever closes it around your throat becomes your master. Forever." He said that word with satisfaction. "I think deep down you want it that way. To belong to me. To never have to think. To be owned completely."

"*No.*" He fought as he had never fought, the Collar's compulsion growing the closer it came to his throat. His limbs felt like lead. He couldn't prize Sinclair's hands away. He felt the Collar touch his neck, felt his mouth flood with terror, too weak physically to get Sinclair's fist out of his hair, to push the Collar away. He made a desperate sound of negation.

"Please, I'll do whatever you want, whatever you want, I won't question you, I'll do whatever you say, just please don't—"

The Collar clicked closed.

Try to run.

He saw a man with piercing eyes of black flame and long black hair. A man he'd fought, and hated, even as he'd given himself in aching surrender. *Sarcean.* He remembered the feeling of being taken, melting heat and the fall of hair around him like black silk. *I will always find you.*

No end and no escape. He hated how good it felt, a flood of power filling him. It wasn't his own; it came from the Collar. It connected him to a power so immense it seemed endless, a vast dark reservoir that was shudderingly familiar. *You,* he thought. *You, you, you.*

"You've made things very troublesome for me, Jamie. But you're going to be a good boy now and do as you're told. Get on your knees."

He heard the command, and he almost moved, for he was mastered now. But he felt no compulsion. That realization broke over him. He felt no compulsion. He felt nothing at all.

James started to laugh, an uncontrolled, breathless laugh. He couldn't stop; didn't, until his eyes were wet.

Then he looked up at Sinclair.

And said a single word.

"No."

He stood up. Slowly, pushing his limbs up from the ground, so that there was no doubt what he was doing.

"I said get on your knees."

He was the same height as Sinclair's borrowed body, and he looked right into Sinclair's eyes. He saw the doubt flicker there. Sinclair glanced down at the Collar, then back up.

He knew what Sinclair was thinking. *It should be working.* And it was. It was working. Just not in the way Sinclair thought.

"I don't understand." Sinclair looked like a man about to shake his watch to find out why it wasn't keeping time. "The Collar controls the Betrayer."

James heard another awful, breathless laugh escape him. He bent down and picked up Ettore's sword. He could feel the truth of the answer, in his teeth, in his blood, in his bones.

"It does," said James.

He could feel the craving he had to serve, to give himself over. But the stories were lies. Or else they were the grubby dreams of those who wished to enslave him. It didn't matter who put the Collar around his neck. The Collar had only ever had one master. A jealous master, who would never allow his possession to belong to another. Why had he thought it would be any different? Always and forever, he was bound to one person.

"But the Dark King is its master," said James. "And I serve Him, not you."

And with a single slash of his sword, he severed John Sloane's head from its body.

CHAPTER FORTY-EIGHT

WILL LANDED IN the heart of the maelstrom. Blind in the surging dark, his foot hit Howell's body, and he almost fell. He moved his torch and it lit nothing. Shadows surrounded him, blotting out all light.

The swirling thickness of the air made him gag. He forced himself to keep his lips sealed shut, instinctively afraid to let this moving miasma in, even as it ignored him, rushing past him like a stream past a rock.

He staggered forward into it, into thick sludge churning with the unknown shapes of the dead. He had to guess at a direction, unable to see. And he had to move fast, before the dead overran Violet and possessed his friends. But he had barely gone three steps when the cavern suddenly cleared, the swarm of Returners vanishing upward, as if they had realized en masse that they did not have to follow the tunnels and could simply rise up through the rock.

He raised his torch. The chamber it revealed was empty. The statue-like frozen figures that had stretched out in rows throughout the cavern had disappeared, transforming into the shadows that had swarmed around him. All that remained of their corporeal form was dust, a gray powder under his feet that made the floor feel like walking on an expanse of sand, as if the cavern were a midnight beach.

And then what lay under his feet changed. In the dust he saw a Roman helmet with its hanging cheek plates, its bronze gray with age, and any decoration rotted away. Another step and he saw the chain mail of a crusader. The heavy greaves of a knight. The flared crest of a conquistador . . . the star emblem of the Steward, as though even they had been tempted, for these were the remains of those who had come here seeking power.

He walked past the first of them, but soon had to wade through them, the detritus piled up as though some had made it farther than others, perhaps more resistant to whatever deadly force emanated from this place. The closer he got, the more the armor was only that of the old world, ancients who had known what lay inside the palace. After a time the bodies started to thin out again, as though few had made it this far.

And then he reached a clearing, beyond which no one had come. And in the center he saw a single figure lying lifeless on the ground.

Kettering.

As Will got closer, he saw the blood pooled beneath Kettering, saw his slack, unmoving face, and when he knelt down beside the body, he saw that his skin was scoured, his flesh not strong enough to withstand the power that had coursed through it.

Kettering had made it into the pit, he had crawled here over the bodies, and with his last breath he had taken up the staff and unleashed the army. And he had died for it, clutching the staff in his hand.

Will looked down at him, silent in death. This man had been given a second life, and instead of living it, he had spent his every waking hour studying, seeking, searching for the means to awaken his beloved. He had turned his back on the world, existing in the shadow realm of memory.

He had found the staff, he had awakened the Returners, but he had died before he could be reunited with his lover.

He looked so alone, the shadows of his countrymen having flooded out of the chamber, the one he searched for gone. With his mismatched professorial clothes, he had the appearance of a scholar who might have spoken at some royal institution, but he had never had that life, and neither had the boy whose body he had stolen.

Who knew if the woman he had died for was out there even now, possessing a host, taking them over? Kettering would never know. His quest had killed him.

Will knelt to slide the staff from Kettering's hand. Kettering's fingers were still warm—it startled Will; the coldness of death had not yet crept over Kettering.

But the real shock came when he drew out the staff.

Will had imagined it would be an ornate scepter, made for ceremonies, perhaps inset with a magical stone. It wasn't.

It wasn't ornately made. It wasn't a scepter.

It was a brand.

The *S* brand, blackened with time and countless plunges into fire. It emanated dark power, a stronger call than the Collar. The first brand, Will thought. The first time Sarcean had put his mark on people. He would have made it, then held it in his hand and pressed it into his followers' flesh, binding them to him forever.

Holding the plain iron handle, Will reached out and touched the *S*.

The vision hit him like a punch in the teeth.

The throne room was piled with the dead, their bodies burst open, their armor crumpled. Magic had gouged holes in the white marble and burned black seared marks across it like tendrils of rot. The slaughter pleased him, as did his unimpeded walk to the throne with his own Dark Guard behind him. A conceit, to take the iconography of the sun and twist it. The flamboyant irony of it pleased him as well, a Dark Guard to replace the Sun Guard, a Dark King to replace—

"The Sun King is gone," said Sarcean to the Queen. "Fled. With his stewards and his inner guard, and his Champion, the Sun General."

The Queen faced him, with only a single Sun Guard alive with her.

And when Sarcean saw who the Sun Guard was, he let out a laugh that echoed through the throne room.

The young guard was older now, for a great deal of time had passed since Sarcean had been cast out of the palace. In that interval, he had grown into a spear, handsome and honed for fighting, his hair a shade or two lighter than his Queen's, his eyes pale.

"It's been a long time," said Sarcean, "since we dallied in the sun, Visander."

For the Queen's last defender was the same Sun Guard who had freed him from the oubliette.

Sandy, Sarcean had nicknamed him then, amusing himself. A trifling, easy to fool.

"You killed them!" Visander was saying. He was shuddering. "I believed in you, and you—you—"

"Shall I kill him too?" asked the Dark Guard.

Sarcean answered, "No. He helped me once."

"Very well."

"You see? I keep my promises, Visander."

The hate in Visander's eyes burned pure. *I see why she chose you*, Sarcean might have said. Visander would pursue him like no one else, because he had once believed in him. The Queen's choice of Visander as her champion, both brilliant and shocking, was his first glimpse of the opponent she would become.

But Visander was a lesser concern to Sarcean, whose eyes had turned to the Queen.

She stood straight before him in her white-and-gold ceremonial robes, her long blond hair hanging in a plait behind her, tipped like a lion's tail.

He hadn't expected his feelings of their one night together to catch him so unawares, to recall how painfully and how beautifully they had found themselves matched. Whatever might have been between them was broken now, of course. It might have been broken from the moment that he went to her door.

"You will never be the true king," she said. "Those who serve you will only ever be unwilling slaves. No one would ever join you by choice. Not if they knew what you were."

"And what is that?"

"Dead," said the Queen. "I am going to kill you. I won't stop until I do it. There is nowhere you will be able to rest. I will hunt you down, kill you as many times as I have to. It's going to be me. My sword in you, Sarcean. The Light will always stand against you."

"The Light?" said Sarcean. "Today I have put out the sun."

"Light is not something you can extinguish," she said. "Even in the darkest night, there is a star."

Will gasped and came back to himself.

Cyprian stood in front of him, holding a sword.

CHAPTER FORTY-NINE

CYPRIAN LOOKED LIKE vengeance, all in silver. He'd crested the bodies and stood atop them, staring down at Will. How could Cyprian be here? How could he be alive when everyone else who had tried to take this power had died?

Will could feel his own guilty exposure, clasping the brand, Kettering dead, and himself revealed by Visander as the Dark King.

"I know how it looks," Will said. "But—"

"Give that to me," said Cyprian.

"I can't." Will instinctively took a step back, clutching the brand. "Cyprian. I can stop what's happening. I can stop Sinclair once and for all."

Cyprian just kept coming, sword in hand.

"You lied to us. We let you into our Hall, thinking you were there to save us. We'd survived for thousands of years," Cyprian said. "Until you."

Cyprian had pulled Will from his horse that first day he'd arrived in the Hall, tearing his shirt half from his body, looking for a brand. Cyprian hadn't wanted to let him inside the walls. He'd said Will was lying to them. He'd been right. He'd been right, the whole time.

"That's not who I am." Waves of denial and fear were making his stomach cramp. He needed to get away, to get out. But there was no way out of this dark pit. "I helped you against Simon. I helped you against the Shadow Kings!"

"And Katherine. She died chasing you. Did you kill her too?" Cyprian's green eyes flashed.

"The sword killed her." There was nowhere to step back. "That warrior out there whose words you believe killed her!"

"God, you brought James into the Hall," said Cyprian. "Does he know? Were the two of you laughing at us the whole time?"

"No," said Will, rejecting it violently. "He doesn't know. He's innocent. Cyprian—"

"Visander said you'd say anything to take power," Cyprian said bitterly.

Visander, who wore Katherine's body like a pelt. Visander, who Sarcean had seduced and tricked, and who had borne the grudge across centuries, a hatred greater because it was humiliatingly personal. The Lady had known when she sent him that Visander would not stop until the Dark King was dead in whatever form Visander found him.

As she had known when she returned Visander into a body so like her own that it would feel to Will like she was killing him, just as she had promised.

Her eyes, staring at him across time.

Mother, stop. Mother, it's me, Mother—

"He's a soldier from a war I never fought in." Will was shivering. It was hard to breathe, as though there were hands around his throat. "He remembers a person that I never was."

"But you were. You were." Cyprian spoke with awful certainty. "Everything's turned out the way you planned." Cyprian's eyes were like green poison, looking at him the way his mother had looked at him: as if he was something so terrible it could not be allowed to live. "But not this time."

Even with his teeth chattering, he couldn't stop the strange laugh that bubbled up. "You think I planned this?"

Cyprian said, "Didn't you?"

He was clenching his upper arms to stop himself shaking. His mind cataloged desperately. He'd lost Cyprian, of course. He'd lost Elizabeth. He'd lost Grace. James he'd lose as soon as he found out. Had he lost Violet?

"If I don't take control, that army will kill everyone above ground." Will was surprised he could get the words out. His teeth chattering had worsened.

"You make it sound so reasonable," said Cyprian. "Just let the Dark King have his army. . . . This is how you do it, isn't it? Take away all our choices, so that the only choice left is yours." Cyprian's hands tightened on his sword. "But it isn't. We have the Lady—the real Blood of the Lady, and she's up there right now. Maybe we have to fight a war. But at least we have a chance, if you're not the one in control."

He'd known. He'd known how it would be. It was why he hadn't told them—why he'd never told anybody. To be seen was to invite the violence of destruction.

But now that it was here, he found he couldn't swallow it, a deeply buried kernel within him rebelling.

"You'd rather let that army loose than trust me," said Will.

"The Stewards exist to stop you," said Cyprian. "That's what I'm going to do."

Cyprian took another step forward, and in that moment the ground plunged, then bucked upward as if the very palace was trying to throw him back. The earth tore, a black crack forking across the ground between them. Cyprian threw out his hand for balance, and Will stumbled, the brand tumbling from his hand as the widening gap between them became a chasm.

Regaining his footing, Will saw that he was now on one side of an open crevasse, with Cyprian standing on the other—ironically, it was Cyprian who had kept his feet with extraordinary balance. But Cyprian now had no way to reach him. Vertiginously deep, the black rift seemed to plunge into the heart of the earth. It was easily twelve feet across, separating him from Cyprian by a great distance.

Miraculously, there had been no cave-in. The structure of the cavern was intact. Will looked around for—

The brand was there, only a few paces away. It was on his side of the chasm.

"This place . . ." Cyprian saw the brand too, and looked at Will across the gap. "It's trying to protect you. But it won't work."

"Why not?"

In an impossible leap, Cyprian jumped the crack, landing in front of Will and rising to look right at him.

"Because I'm strong now."

With a terrible wrench, Will understood. There was only one way that Cyprian could have made it through the shadows, only one way that he could approach the brand. The one thing he had sworn never to do.

"You drank from the Cup," said Will.

He stared at Cyprian, seeing the dark pain of acknowledgment in his eyes, and remembering the boy who had vowed to remain pure. *That's how badly he wants to stop me.* Anharion. Visander. The Lady . . . Sarcean had twisted them all, re-formed them into distorted shapes. And Will was doing the same: first to Katherine, and now to Cyprian—

They both looked at the brand at the same time. Cyprian was closer, and stronger. He was going to take the brand and smash it, and there would be no way to stop the Returners from taking thousands of bodies, then marching their way across the land.

Will had to stop him. He knew how. It was the one thing Cyprian would never forgive.

The circle of people Will had spent time with in his life was small. His mother, who had kept from him a horrifying secret. The men he'd worked with on the docks, those relationships made while always conscious of his status as an infiltrator. He'd been playacting with them, as he had been with Katherine, until she'd spilled out into real when she'd kissed him, and he'd realized, jerking away, who she was.

But in the Hall of the Stewards, he had let himself become friends with others for the first time. Tentatively, knowing he could never tell them what he was, knowing he built on rotten foundations, but hoping he could be what he pretended. For them.

Cyprian, he knew, had come to trust him. First, as a lieutenant begins to trust a new leader proving himself slowly in the field. Then, perhaps, as a friend. That might have been their future, though Will's idea of that kind of friendship was vague, not having had it before.

But that future was shattered. And it would never be repaired. Not now.

As Cyprian began to move toward the brand, Will said, "*No.*"

Cyprian froze. The shocked confusion on his face when he found he couldn't move turned furious with betrayal as he realized that the shadow inside him was following Will's command.

It obeyed Will just as the Shadow Kings had obeyed him at Bowhill: because it was sworn to him, in the same unholy bargain that the three Kings had once made. Power, at a price.

For a moment they stared at each other, Cyprian panting with impotent effort, desperately fighting his shadow. His body was trembling with exertion, but held in place by his shadow's unrelenting grip.

"I'm sorry," said Will. "I didn't want to do this. I just—I can't let you stop me. This is the only way to save the others."

To save everyone. To stop the unfolding plans of his former self. To stop Sinclair.

Cyprian looked at him as if he would kill him. "You are him. You really are him."

His own trapped body seemed to nauseate Cyprian. It was awful, watching him throwing everything he had at the shadow and failing, a tortured statue unable to move.

"I'm sorry," said Will again. "I have to do this."

Cyprian's face changed. Instead of struggling again like a man throwing himself uselessly against chains, Cyprian stopped fighting. He closed his eyes, almost seeming to center himself. Then he drew in a breath, as though calling on something deep inside him. "I will hold. I will not falter. In darkness—"

"Cyprian—" said Will.

"—I will be the light," said Cyprian, and Will's skin prickled as he recognized the words he'd chanted with the Elder Steward, the words Carver had used in his ceremony. "I will walk the path, and defy the shadow. I am myself and I will hold."

His words were firm, his breathing was steady.

With a look full of calm victory, Cyprian's eyes opened.

And he began to move.

He had beaten his shadow. Will tried to exert his own will again, only to feel the shadow inside Cyprian shrieking in frustration, banished to a small space deep inside. In two steps, Cyprian was on Will, thrusting Will sideways and snatching up the brand.

Will hit the ground just as Cyprian drew the Executioner's axe from a strap on his back. Cyprian lifted the axe and brought it down hard, shattering the brand into a thousand pieces.

"*No!*"

The explosion rocked the chamber, throwing them both backward and sending them sprawling. Will had the breath knocked out of him, his skin scraping away from the base of his palms as he thrust out his hands to break his fall.

He barely registered the pain, instantly pushing himself up, scrabbling desperately for the brand. Oh God, was there anything left? Any part of it they could reassemble?

"It's gone," said Cyprian, watching this and letting out a breathless laugh. "You can't use it." He was laughing. He was *laughing.*

Searing anger and disbelief churned in Will, even as he stared up at Cyprian. *"Don't you understand what you've done?"*

"I've stopped you," said Cyprian, triumph in his voice. "I've stopped the Dark King from taking up his army."

The threat unleashed was a horror beyond description, a world remade in darkness, and fear spiked in Will at what might now happen to Violet and the others. Beneath that, his anger was hardening into something like cold fury, stony and unyielding.

"So you can take a shadow," said Will, "you can pledge yourself to darkness, but I can't be trusted with my own power, even when I want to use it to do what's right?"

Cyprian didn't answer, taking Will in an iron grip by his arm. Will tried to resist but was yanked up, Cyprian dragging him forward. Stumbling over Kettering's body, Will only realized after a few seconds that Cyprian wasn't killing him. Cyprian was tying his hands and pulling him back through the bones and armor to the others.

That was worse. That was—

"The others are going to see you for what you are," said Cyprian.

Will could see the circle of light shining down in the distance, like a far-off sun. He was struggling, and it had no effect on the hard, corded muscle of Cyprian's body at all. The newly ripped-open chasm was no obstacle either, Cyprian leaping it again, gracefully.

"Visander will kill me," said Will, but that wasn't what was making his mind almost white out. It was the thought of Violet looking at him with betrayal in her eyes.

His mother, Katherine, Elizabeth, Cyprian, Grace—

Not Violet, not Violet, not Violet.

Cyprian ignored him, strong enough to climb the rope ladder while lashed to a prisoner. Half-rigid with panic, Will was thrown over the lip of the pit to sprawl onto the flagstones of the throne room above.

The torrent of shadows had gone, leaving the chamber shockingly quiet. Violet and the others were clustered together in a slowly fading sphere of light.

It was Violet he looked at first, Violet whose eyes locked with his, widening at the bonds he wore, and that he was obviously Cyprian's prisoner. She was standing with the others, and all Will could do was stare back at her and think, *She knows.*

She knows, she knows, she knows—

He felt sick, to be exposed, to be seen, Violet's eyes on him like the cutting off of air, the crushing of his throat. Primal panic, that he couldn't be known like this. *Not you,* he wanted to say. *Not you.*

He was so focused on Violet that it took him a moment to see what was happening behind her.

Armed with pistols and knives, Sinclair's men were appearing out of the darkness, their leader an auburn-haired boy who Will had last seen on the *Sealgair,* fighting and killing Stewards like it was nothing.

"We'll take it from here," said Violet's brother, Tom.

CHAPTER FIFTY

"*STEWARDS*," SAID TOM, the same way Cyprian had once spat, *Lions*. "You're like cockroaches: just when we think we've stamped you out, you crawl back out of the cracks."

Violet jerked around and saw him. He was staring right at Cyprian.

"Tom?" said Violet, her eyes wide with shock.

It was her brother, stepping over the rubble, Sinclair's men holding torches behind him, creating an island of light.

"Violet?" Stopping the moment he saw her, as shocked as she was. "What are you doing here?"

All she could do was stare. It couldn't be real, could it? He couldn't be here.

He looked just like he had when she'd last seen him at home in London, the same auburn hair cut to reach his collar, the same scattering of freckles on his nose. He was so out of place in this monstrous underground palace—it was like opening the door to the throne room and seeing instead the parlor of her London home.

As her shock receded, it was replaced by rising tension and the speeding up of her pulse. She'd missed him so much, and for so long.

Now all she could think about were Mrs. Duval's words. That she and Tom were fated to fight.

"I escaped from Sinclair," she said. *Mrs. Duval trained me to kill you.* She didn't say it. Tom wasn't her enemy. She hated that Mrs. Duval had put these thoughts in her head. Though somewhere a voice whispered that the one who had first insinuated the thought was not Mrs. Duval. It was her father.

Tom can't come into his true power without killing another like him, her father had said.

"I was a prisoner." *Did you know that?* she wanted to ask him. *Do you know what Father plans to do with me?*

"These people are dangerous, Violet. Step away from them." Tom was looking at her friends as though they were a threat. But she found a new and unsettling question rushing into her head.

"How are you alive?" She was staring at Tom and the armed men with him. It didn't make sense. "How did you survive the white death? The army must have passed right through you."

It was Visander who answered. "He bears the Dark King's brand. It marks him as the Dark King's servant, and protects him from possession."

The smell of burning flesh, and Tom refusing to bite down on leather. She wanted to be sick—she knew Tom had the Dark King's brand. Her stomach turned at the idea that it had saved him. That he was safe from the shadows because he was already the Dark King's creature.

She looked at the men around Tom with their torches and pistols. They must all have the brand. The army of the dead had been released, and she was looking at their modern-day equivalent: the army of the living, sworn to the Dark King, and led here by her brother.

She knew her family worked for Sinclair, but she hadn't ever truly thought of Tom as the Dark King's soldier. *The Dark King's Lion.*

She stepped back in front of her friends instinctively.

"You don't understand what's happening," Tom said. "You've been away too long. But I can keep you safe until there's time to tell you."

"You're too late, Lion," said Cyprian to Tom. "Sinclair will never control that army. I've destroyed the brand."

"Steward," said Tom. "Get out of my way."

Tom had killed Stewards with a crowbar on the *Sealgair.* She'd seen him do it. Only Justice had been strong and skilled enough to fight Tom to a standstill.

And here was Cyprian, the most talented novitiate in a generation, Justice's natural successor, challenging her brother.

There came the slow, horrifying realization that if they fought, she'd have to stop them.

Tom will come to kill you eventually, Mrs. Duval had said. *Either you're trained to fight him or you're not.*

"He's let that army loose," said Will to Tom. "If you want to stop them, we'll need to work together."

"The Dark King commands his Lion," said Visander.

Violet swung back to look at Will. With his hands tied behind his back and his face smudged with dust, Will still somehow managed to command attention. Will had always been able to make people listen to him, and Tom was no different, turning on Will.

"You," said Tom.

"That's right. The boy you chained up on the ship," said Will.

They recognized each other. Will had been a prisoner on the *Sealgair.* But Will had never talked about his time in captivity. Now she realized—of course Tom must have been in charge of it. Tom had ordered Will chained in the ship's hold. Did Will know a side of Tom that she didn't?

In the ship's hold, Will had been bloody and bruised, having endured at least one severe beating, likely on Tom's orders, maybe even at Tom's hands. What else had passed between them? Will had never talked to her about any of it . . . had never even told her he knew her brother. Why?

What else had Will never told her? It wasn't the first time that she had felt like Will was a stranger, or noticed that for all their closeness, Will shared very little. *How well do you really know him?* a voice whispered.

"You killed Simon," said Tom.

"Among other people," said Will.

Tom immediately gestured protectively for her to come to his side, a motion that she knew so well it hurt. "Violet, that boy—these people are dangerous. Come with me, and we can talk after."

"Come with you?" She said it in disbelief.

"You'll be safe. Just come over to our side."

"Safe! Don't you know what your father wants to do with her?" Will said.

No, she thought, her stomach cramping. She couldn't bear to hear the answer. She'd never asked Tom herself, because as long as she didn't ask, she didn't have to know.

Tom's face showed no sign that he understood. "Do with her? He wants her home."

"He wants her dead." Will's words felt like they were splitting her brain, the truth out in the open. "Don't you understand anything that's happening? While we talk, that army is killing everyone for miles. They'll fall down in the white death, and when they wake up, they'll take over our world. We don't have time. We need to stop them."

"What are you talking about?" said Tom. "My father has been searching for Violet for months. And if the army's a danger, it's because your Steward set them loose. Sinclair was meant to have wiped the Stewards out."

He didn't see, she realized. He'd been taught all the wrong things. By Sinclair, by Father . . .

She'd wanted to be like him for so long that it was disconcerting to see his limitations. He'd been her whole world, but for the first time she saw him as a small cog in the larger machinery of Sinclair's plans. *Father killed my mother,* she wanted to say. *Father wants you to kill me.*

"You're the one who doesn't understand," she said. "Sinclair isn't what you think. None of this is what you think. Tom—"

He was shaking his head. "Violet, step out of the way. I'll deal with the Steward." It was all happening too fast.

Cyprian, with a shadow newly in him. Cyprian, with the Executioner's axe in his hand. She heard herself say, "I'm not going to let you hurt my friends."

"We don't have time to fight," said Will. "There's only a handful of days when a Returner is dormant inside the body they're possessing. . . . We only have until they wake up to stop them. You need to stand down."

Later, she'd remember that Will had been the only one talking about stopping the army, while the rest of them were caught up in old feuds. But at that moment, she barely heard him. All she could see was Tom. "Tom, please, you don't have to—"

Tom wasn't listening. "Take the boy. Shoot the Steward. Leave the girls alive."

She flung up her shield to take what bullets she could, running toward Cyprian even before Tom finished speaking. But she was too far away. She braced, knowing she wouldn't be in time.

The sound of shots never came.

As the seconds passed, she lowered her shield, expecting at every moment the *crack* of a shot. What she saw instead was so horrifyingly unnatural it chilled her to the core.

The man closest to her was frozen, his eyes glazed over and his pistol arm outstretched. Statue-still, he wasn't moving. None of Sinclair's men were moving, each halted in the middle of an action, one of them even arrested mid-step.

And Tom . . .

Tom was frozen in the same rictus, his mouth half-open, about to speak. His arm, upraised in an unfinished gesture, revealed his brand, glowing on his wrist. *Burning.* She could smell the burning flesh, the memory of his branding on the ship choking her nostrils.

"I said, we don't have time," said Will, and every man in the chamber said it with him in deadened uniformity.

Violet turned slowly. Having believed the horror to be in front of her, she saw it was behind her.

Will's eyes were black, the entire surface of each eye showing neither iris nor white, like windows into an endless dark. His hair and clothing streamed back from him, as if wind whipped around him. He crackled with dark power, a young god crowned in dark glory.

Magic. Will's magic—and it was not a warmly lit candle, not a tree bursting into flower, or a life-giving explosion of light. It was a cold, dark exercise in raw strength, as Will overrode the humanity of those around him and took their bodies in absolute control.

There were so many of Sinclair's men now frozen in the chamber. And Tom—Tom was no ordinary man—Tom was a Lion, or had been a Lion, his blank, slack face now echoing those of the men around him. Once individuals, they were now puppets of flesh, subservient in every way to the twisted oath they had made to their master.

To Will.

"You *are* the Dark King," said Violet, in horror.

Will didn't deny it. He couldn't, controlling Sinclair's men with the dark brand. He hadn't denied it before, she realized. He had just disappeared into the pit, seeking the means to control the Dark King's army.

His army. It was like the pit was opening under her feet. Like she was the one falling into it.

"I swore I'd never follow you," she said, feeling sick. "I swore I'd be different from Rassalon."

Will said, "Violet, I'm Will."

Except that they all said it, every man in the chamber, parroting Will's words in that awful monotone, as though Will was all of them, a malevolent insect with a thousand eyes.

"Let him go," said Violet. "Let my brother go!"

"They see you for what you are," said Visander.

He was closing on Will with Ekthalion in his hands. She saw Will fixate on the blade, and as if that switch in attention broke his control, Sinclair's men each instantly collapsed down into a dead faint.

"Tom!" she cried out, running to where he'd fallen, on her knees beside him, checking desperately for a pulse. His skin was cold. "Tom!" Her fingers pressed into his neck and felt the slightest pulse—alive. He was alive. She clutched him to herself, as if she could protect him from possession with her body. She looked up blindly to see Will, half swaying, half staggering. Had controlling so many men left him weak? Will collapsed down onto one knee as Visander came to stand over him.

His eyes had returned to their normal color when he looked up at Visander, and it made him look like the boy she knew.

But he wasn't. She hadn't known him. Hadn't known who he was or what he could do.

"How fitting that I should strike you down in the place where you once took everything from me," said Visander.

"You gave him Ekthalion?" Will said to her.

He sounded utterly betrayed, and as he looked at her, his eyes began to turn black again. He fixed them back on Visander. To her horror, she felt Tom's body begin to twitch under her hands. A moment later, several of the men on the ground lurched up onto their feet. Visander ignored them, even when they stumbled toward him.

"You're the same age now as I was when you killed my family," Visander was saying. "But I'm not you. I'm not going to kill your friends. I'm not going to kill the people you care about. I'm just going to kill you."

Visander lifted Ekthalion, but the mountain was responding to Will, the ground shaking as Will's black eyes flashed with anger, a huge rock crashing from the ceiling to smash down inches from Visander. He was going to destroy this place, Violet thought desperately, destroy Visander, destroy them.

"Starting without me?" said a familiar, drawling voice.

James strolled into the torchlight.

His arrogance had always been galling. He'd arrived like an idle dilettante to the final act of a play, utterly uncaring of anything that had come before his entrance. With the entitlement of its prince, he walked the length of the throne room. It was as if he believed courtiers bowed and scraped to him as he passed, and perhaps they had, once, long ago.

He stepped mincingly over a sprawled, unconscious body—one of Sinclair's men. His eyes were fixed on Will.

It wasn't until James stood side by side with Visander that Violet realized how similar they looked, both in coloring and in otherworldliness, beautiful and terrible, angelic and unearthly. Instruments of vengeance on the one who had hurt them the most, it was as if Anharion and the Lady stood together against Will.

On his knees in the rubble, Will said in a strange, terrible voice, "Both of you."

But neither of them attacked. Visander was frozen. And it was not Will holding him in invisible bonds. It was James.

James said to Will, "Darling, I'm not here to kill you."

James only had to gesture once, and Visander went flying backward, hitting a pillar and then the floor, his body slumped and slack. Cyprian took a step forward, and James merely glanced at him, and sent Cyprian careening across the floor.

Will was staring at James in shock. James looked down at Will and held out his hand. "Well?"

"*He's the Dark King*," said Violet.

"And I'm his lieutenant," said James, "here to fight by his side."

CHAPTER FIFTY-ONE

WILL LOOKED UP at James as at a mirage in the desert.

The men Will had possessed were still unconscious, littering the floor like the dead. Violet was kneeling beside Tom with horror on her face. Cyprian and Visander were both sprawled in the dust, Elizabeth running to Visander's side.

James ignored all of them, slashing open the restraints binding Will's hands. "Can you move? We need to go." Blue eyes full of concern.

Will couldn't make sense of it. James had heard Violet call him the Dark King. But if he knew, how could he—

"Tell me that you know," said Will, "what I am, what I—"

"I know," said James.

"Tell me you don't care," said Will.

"I don't care," said James.

Will went hot, a shiver right to the core of him. He met James's eyes with the jolt of a connection locking in place. "Tell me again." He needed to hear it.

"I don't care." Another shiver, this one deeper.

"Anharion." Visander spat it.

He was trying to get up, and was too hurt to do it. Cyprian was the first to move, shaking his head to try to clear it, his gaze fixed right on James. "I knew you'd turn." Cyprian's words had a hard edge of pain.

Will looked over at him. His friends—arrayed against him, staring at him in varying states of shock, fear, and revulsion. But that was expected. That was . . . he had seen that look before in his mother's eyes.

He hadn't expected James at his side.

Part of Will was still waiting for the knife, for the hands around his throat. Each moment that didn't happen felt like hope. Each moment a spark inside him grew.

Maybe—this wasn't Bowhill, where both his mother and his sister had tried to kill him. Maybe it wasn't even the old world, where both lovers had turned on him.

Maybe he wasn't alone, fighting to prove he wasn't the monster his mother saw, when he wasn't sure he believed it himself.

James believed—in him, in *Will*.

"What would you have me do?" said James.

Will said, "Get us out of here."

James pulled him into his arms. Will put his arms around James's waist in turn. A second later, he felt James's power push into him, just as he had at the dig. This time, he closed his eyes and let it happen. A circle completing itself: the seeking tendril of James's magic connected to the vast reservoir of his own.

Will made a sound as raw power burst from him, and he glimpsed the night sky above him scattered with stars, barely aware of the screams around him. James said, "*Hold on to me,*" and Will was only just starting to realize his power had blown a hole in the mountain when they were rising in it, a rushing of air as James's gift swept them up and out of the palace.

Flight. They were flying, or something like it. Beneath them the palace was growing distant, as power and air rushed past them. Clutching tight to James, all Will could do was hold on while the wind whipped at him. He hadn't known that James could use their combined power to fly. He'd never seen Anharion fly in any of his dreams or visions. Maybe Sarcean had never lent him the power. How could he have ever forgone something so exhilarating?

"I thought you'd hate me." The words were all breath. Will could feel the warmth of James's body against him. His fingers gripped at James's waist. "Tell me you don't hate me."

"I don't hate you."

Another shudder. His fingers gripped tighter. "I should have told you." The words were tumbling out. "I should have—I was afraid; I thought if I told you that you'd kill me, or try to. I thought that you'd—tell me again."

"I don't hate you."

The words touched something deep inside him, a place that had never known acceptance. That had been braced, waiting for the blow not just since Bowhill. All these years. Even as a child . . . his mother had . . . because she had been afraid.

He hadn't meant to make her afraid. He hadn't meant to make any of them afraid.

James wasn't afraid. Against all odds, James trusted him.

Will's gratitude was incandescent. He felt it spilling out of him. He felt bursting with loyalty of his own that he had always wanted to give to someone. He wanted to give James power, the world, everything.

His feet touched the earth. They had landed in a small forest clearing, where the dark trunks of ancient beech trees stretched upward all around them. The ground was leaf-covered, and the few fallen logs were soft with moss. Hushed green privacy shrouded them.

"We said after. If you came to me after." Will could feel James warm and real against him, as he said, "You came to me."

James said, "You asked me to."

Because maybe it was enough to have one person, one person who believed, one person who had faith in him.

Sarcean had lost everyone, but Will hadn't. Will had carved this one point of difference—this one thing of his own. It meant he could be different. He and James, they could both be different. They could cast off the past, and make a new future together.

James had given him this chance to be—himself.

"Tell me you know—me," he said, gazing into blue eyes full of loyalty, and he wanted to hear James saying the words forever. "Tell me you know who I am, and you're mine."

"I'm yours. I know who you are. Will—"

Will kissed him. It was good, it was so good, to feel James give himself, as eager as Will. James felt like he would give him everything, gasping, "I'm yours," as Will kissed him and kissed him. "I'm yours," as Will's hands pushed inside his jacket, up over his warm shirt. "I'm yours," as Will touched his shivery hot skin, then pulled his cravat from his throat. "My King."

It was like the whole world shifted around him. His mind splintering, Will staggered back from what he saw.

The Collar encircled James's neck in opulent red and gold.

It glistered, a strident slash, revealed by James's half-open shirt. James's cravat lay on the forest floor, leaving him half-undressed, disheveled. Will stared at him in horror.

James's hair was mussed, his cheeks flushed, his lips parted in surrender that was almost unbearably erotic, except that the gleaming rubies of the Collar looked like a slit throat.

"My King?" said James.

Nausea rose in Will violently. He flung his hand out and clasped on to the trunk of the nearest tree. His stomach clenched, then heaved, spasming as he vomited onto the earth. Dizziness threatened to overwhelm him. He closed his eyes on it, only to see an image of Anharion lying dead on the ground as the executioner sawed at his throat. He vomited again, bent in half, then pressed the back of his hand to his open mouth.

James's voice behind him. "What is it? What's wrong?"

"What's *wrong?*"

Everything was wrong. Everything was broken. Will looked up at James despairingly. The gleaming rubies of the Collar seemed to mock him.

"I'm yours," said James. "I know who you are. I don't hate you." A rapt prayer from a supplicant handpicked for his beauty. James looked achingly genuine.

They were his own words echoed back to him. His orders, he thought sickly. James looked like himself, but he wasn't James. He was no more than a mirror of Will's desires, and it was terrible to see them so starkly reflected. *No one would ever join you by choice, not if they knew what you were.* The Lady had said that to him in Undahar.

"Are you telling me what I want to hear?"

"Yes," said James.

Will tried not to flinch at the answer. "And what's that?"

"Your dream is within your grasp. You can take this world. Your army is ready. I will rule with you, by your side."

And that wasn't right. He wanted—

He wanted what he'd had, just moments ago. What James had given him. What he'd never had after all, alone here on the mountain. He clung to the moment when he'd thought himself different.

"That's his dream. Not mine."

"You are him."

James said it with confidence, as if he knew it beyond doubt. He faced Will as if he saw in him a figure from long ago. A figure he served. A figure he knew.

"You remember," said Will.

James looked back at him with the past in his eyes.

"Sarcean. I remember everything."

ACKNOWLEDGMENTS

MY FAMILY COMES from Scheggino, a small medieval town in that part of Umbria known as the Valnerina. The first time I traveled there alone, I climbed the mountain to the neighboring town of Caso, glimpsed the remains of giant Roman architecture slumbering in the hills, walked the stream where my family had poached trout from their window, and looked out at the view that would become the Leap of Faith. I knew I wanted to set part of *Dark Heir* in those hills, and I had planned to return and rewalk the Valnerina as I had walked the Dark Peak in Derbyshire.

By the time I came to write *Dark Heir,* the pandemic had closed down the world; the airports and the streets were empty, and travel everywhere had stopped. I had to reconstruct Scheggino from memory, poring over my old journal entries and unearthing my old photos taken before the age of digital cameras that seemed to be fading before my eyes. But perhaps, in the end, that was fitting.

Writing alone through the isolation of pandemic lockdown made each friend who stepped into the world of *Dark Heir* with me all the more precious: thank you to Vanessa Len, Anna Cowan, Sarah Fairhall, Jay Kristoff, Beatrix Bae, and Tom Taylor, who read countless drafts, workshopped ideas, and offered feedback. This book would not be the same without you.

Vanessa, our hotel lobby nights became blurry evening FaceTimes that I treasured as we sat on our respective couches with our headphones cutting in and out. Jay and Tom, our weekly writing day accompanied by toasties and chips are a creative joy. I will never forget the shellshock as we learned one afternoon while writing together that we would have to suspend our sessions because we were entering a third pandemic lockdown. To my geographically far-flung friends Anna, Sarah, and Bea, our online writing sessions, calls, and virtual company were lifelines.

Thank you also to Ellie Marney, Amanda C. Ryan, Amie Kaufman, and Sarah Rees Brennan for your friendship and thoughtful insights, and to the gang of the Melbourne Writers Retreat, for invaluable friendship, support, and advice.

I also have to thank those who were with me during the most intense times, Rita Maiuto and Luke Haag. Thank you for celebrating the highs and supporting the lows, and accompanying both with great wit, great taste, and great food. Thank you also and especially to Jan Tonkin, who has enlarged my life beyond counting since our first meeting, and to whom I owe an enormous debt of gratitude.

Thank you to my wonderful agent, Tracey Adams, and to Josh Adams for your enthusiasm and support. Thank you to the team at HarperCollins, in particular Rosemary Brosnan and my editor, Alexandra Cooper. In Australia, I have been so lucky to work with the incredible Kate Whitfield and Jodie Webster at Allen & Unwin; thank you both for your fantastic editorial work and all your help shaping the book.

Finally, thank you to Magdalena Pągowska for her stunning cover art, and to Sveta Dorosheva for a beautiful map of the Valnerina in 1821, as well as to the design team at HarperCollins, who brought all the visual elements together.

Researching *Dark Heir* meant reading many Italian travel journals from the 1820s, including those of Mariana Starke, Charlotte Anne Eaton, Galignani, and even Lord Byron, who traveled and lived in Italy, and who wrote in response to another mountain's terrible eruption about a darkness that covered the world. In the strange timeless time of the pandemic, those long-ago journeyers gave me a way to travel when I could not, and for that I owe them a great many thanks.